The Laird of Stonehaven

*Also by Connie Mason
in Large Print:*

The Dragon Lord
To Love a Stranger
To Tame a Renegade
To Tempt a Rogue
The Outlaws: Jess
The Outlaws: Rafe
The Outlaws: Sam
The Rogue and the Hellion
The Black Knight
Lionheart
Seduced by a Rogue
Sheik

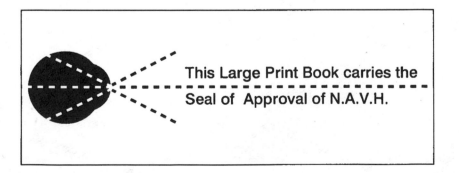

This Large Print Book carries the
Seal of Approval of N.A.V.H.

The Laird of Stonehaven

Connie Mason

WHEELER
PUBLISHING

Published in 2003 by arrangement with Leisure Books,
a division of Dorchester Publishing Co., Inc.

Wheeler Large Print Romance.

The text of this Large Print edition is unabridged.
Other aspects of the book may vary from the original edition.

Set in 16 pt. Plantin by Al Chase.

Printed in the United States on permanent paper.

Library of Congress Cataloging-in-Publication Data

Mason, Connie.
    The laird of Stonehaven / Connie Mason.
      p. cm.
    ISBN 1-58724-575-2 (lg. print : hc : alk. paper)
    1. Highlands (Scotland) — Fiction. 2. Women healers —
Fiction. 3. Large type books. I. Title.
PS3563.A78786L35 2003
813′.54—dc22   2003065759

The Laird of
Stonehaven

National Association for Visually Handicapped
-------------------------- *serving the partially seeing*

As the Founder/CEO of NAVH, the only national health agency solely devoted to those who, although not totally blind, have an eye disease which could lead to serious visual impairment, I am pleased to recognize Thorndike Press★ as one of the leading publishers in the large print field.

Founded in 1954 in San Francisco to prepare large print textbooks for partially seeing children, NAVH became the pioneer and standard setting agency in the preparation of large type.

Today, those publishers who meet our standards carry the prestigious "Seal of Approval" indicating high quality large print. We are delighted that Thorndike Press is one of the publishers whose titles meet these standards. We are also pleased to recognize the significant contribution Thorndike Press is making in this important and growing field.

Lorraine H. Marchi, L.H.D.
Founder/CEO
NAVH

★ Thorndike Press encompasses the following imprints: Thorndike, Wheeler, Walker and Large Print Press.

The MacArthur Prophecy

According to legend, a Faery Woman with extraordinary powers will be born from time to time into the MacArthur clan. She will be a healer with the knowledge and ability to help others, but her strength and endurance must be tested by obstacles. If she survives ordeals by fire, water and stone, she will be forever blessed by God.

The Faery Woman must be wary of falling in love, for if her love is not returned, she could lose her powers. But the Faery Woman fortunate enough to find her true love and be loved in return shall survive the ordeals and live happily ever after.

So sayeth the legend.

Prologue

Gairloch, Scottish Highlands, 1432

He was naked. Magnificently, blatantly naked. His body was sheer perfection, with wide shoulders, a deep chest and corded ribs. She couldn't look away. Her gaze wandered over his muscular arms, slim hips, flat belly and taut buttocks, finally moving down to his groin. He was fully erect, his sex jutting boldly upward amidst a swirl of dense raven curls.

Her gaze shot up to his face. The shadows parted, and for the first time his features were revealed to her. His was a handsome visage, hardened now by lust. His obvious desire terrified her, but she refused to show fear.

Despite her wariness, she found his masculine beauty thrilling. Naught about him was ordinary. Neither his piercing blue eyes, generous lips nor dark hair tinged with fiery highlights.

He approached the bed; she cringed away from him. She knew what he wanted.

"Nay, you mustna."

"Aye, I must." Though he had come to her

many times in the past, he had never spoken before, and the deep thunder of his voice startled her.

Who was he?

"I canna love you," she whispered.

"I dinna ask for love."

He lowered himself to the bed, melding their bodies. Immediately a burning sensation consumed her. She cried out; the intense heat was unbearable. He spread her legs with his knees and flexed his hips. She flinched away, but he was relentless in his pursuit of her.

Splaying her hands against his massive chest, she attempted to shove him away. But her fingers touched . . . naught. He was gone. Naught remained but his masculine scent and the memory of him imprinted upon her body and in her mind . . . and smoke.

A scream rose from her throat as flames shot up around her, singeing her flesh and setting her hair on fire. Disembodied faces danced just beyond the ring of fire. Leering faces, threatening faces, frightened faces. Men, women, children, all chanting:

"Burn, witch, burn.
Burn, witch, burn."

"Blair, wake up! Ye're dreaming again."

Blair MacArthur was more than happy to awaken from the recurring nightmare. Though

10

the same frightening dream had invaded her sleep many times since she had become aware of her powers, this time was different.

She had seen his face and heard his voice.

"I am awake, Alyce."

"Was it the same dream?"

"Aye, but this time I saw his face."

"Did ye recognize him?"

" 'Twas no one I knew." She grasped Alyce's gnarled hands. "Something is about to happen. I can sense it. Quickly, get the candles and the bag of herbs."

"Oh, nay, Blair, yer father has forbidden ye to summon the spirits."

"My spells hurt no one," Blair argued. "My powers are God given. I am as faithful to the church's teachings as you are. To deny the powers I have been given is a sin. Please, Alyce, I must know the role the man in my dreams will play in my life."

Worry darkened Alyce's brow as she fetched four candles from the cupboard. When she returned, Blair had rolled up a rug near the hearth, revealing a chalk circle drawn upon the flagstone floor. Taking a deep breath, Blair stepped into the circle.

Alyce handed Blair the sack of fragrant herbs. Then she placed the candles at intervals along the perimeter of the circle and lit them with a faggot from the fire. Immediately one candle flame turned red, another blue, the third burned with a silver hue, and the fourth blazed a vivid purple. Blair aligned herself with the full moon, visible through the open window, sprinkled the herbs at her feet and chanted:

"Spirits, come to me.
Open my eyes and let me see
What the future holds for me."

Then Blair invited the spirits into her heart and mind, bidding them to reveal the unknown, to interpret her dreams and make known her enemies.

Closing her eyes, Blair inhaled deeply until she became one with the forces of nature and the universe. She cried out and stiffened as a surge of energy entered her body. The curtains at the open window blew inward and the skirt of her fine linen shift fluttered about her slim legs, and then everything went still as a vision formed behind her eyes.

She saw *him*. The man in her dreams stood large and virile before her. He wore the blue, green and black plaid of Clan Campbell. An aura of red, the color of war and bloodshed, hovered over him. Was the man a warrior? Abruptly the aura changed from blood red to blue, the color of love and peace.

"Who are you?" she whispered.

No answer was forthcoming.

"Are you my future?"

He merely smiled.

"I canna love you. 'Tis forbidden."

His smile taunted her, his voice challenged her. "Is it?"

Before she could question him further, the vision faded, replaced by that of her half-brother Niall, the man destined to become Chieftain of Clan MacArthur when her dying father breathed his last. His evil grin lacked warmth and sincerity. He reached out to her in a menacing manner. She screamed, breaking the spell.

"Are ye all right, lass?" Alyce asked. The candles were extinguished as Blair stumbled from the circle. "What did ye see?"

"The man in my dreams is a Campbell."

"A MacArthur ally," Alyce said with a sigh of relief. "Did ye see anything else?"

"My brother Niall. He means me harm."

"Aye." Alyce nodded knowingly. "Yer brother is up to nae good."

"We must be on our guard, Alyce. Once he is chief —"

"Hark!" Alyce hissed. "I hear angry voices at the gate. Do ye ken what they are saying?"

Both women flew to the window overlooking the gate. The moon had disappeared, replaced by a blood-red sunrise, and the voices that rose up were chanting the words from Blair's dream.

"Burn, witch, burn.
Burn, witch, burn."

Chapter One

Stonehaven at Torridon, Scottish Highlands, 1432

"Ye're mad, Graeme!" Heath Campbell chided the laird of Stonehaven. "You canna wed the MacArthur lass. Have ye not heard? I know ye've been away fighting in France with Joan, the Maid of Orleans, but surely you recall the MacArthur Prophecy. The MacArthur lass is said to be a Faery Woman." He lowered his voice until he could barely be heard over the jingle of their horses' harnesses. "Some say she's a witch."

Graeme's dark brows rose in obstinate objection. "I dinna believe in witches, Cousin."

"Mayhap ye should," Heath grumbled.

Graeme urged his horse onward toward Gairloch and Douglas MacArthur, chief of Clan MacArthur and a Campbell ally.

"Douglas MacArthur is dying," Graeme stated flatly, "and he fears for his daughter's life. I canna ignore his summons. The least I can do is speak with him. Mayhap I can suggest another to wed his lass."

Heath shook his shaggy head. "I canna believe ye would even consider wedding a Faery Woman."

"You place too much store in rumors," Graeme scoffed. "Blair MacArthur is known for her healing skill. There is talk of other powers, but I dinna believe what I canna see."

"What about Joan the Maid? Did she not possess unnatural powers? She claimed that her mandate to fight came from God."

Graeme gazed into the distance where the sun was rising to shed a crimson glow over the land. He was recalling the horrible fate of the young woman whom he had fought to protect but had been unable to save from a fiery death. His blue eyes turned murky and his handsome features hardened.

"Joan was a true saint. That much I know. She truly believed that God directed her actions. She died a martyr to her faith, but her fate was not easy for me to accept. In my eyes, no woman can ever live up to her. But Joan is no more, and I fully intend to obey MacArthur's summons. He saved my father's life once, and I owe him."

Heath blinked in dismay. "Then ye *do* intend to wed the witch."

"I didna say that," Graeme hedged. "I merely intend to hear MacArthur out."

"'Tis said the lass has stringy black hair and a wart on the end of her nose."

"Leave off, Cousin," Graeme warned. "I

can make my own decisions."

"Aye," Heath said glumly. " 'Twas yer decision to go fight on foreign ground."

"Better the English focus their army on France than Scotland. I did what I thought was right."

"And neglected yer holdings in the bargain. Not to mention the wound ye suffered at the hands of the English."

"Uncle Stuart proved more than capable in my absence. As for the wound, 'tis long healed."

"I see ye're set on this folly," Heath sighed. "But dinna let the witch cast a spell on ye."

Graeme shook his head at his cousin's superstition. He was too world-weary and too cynical to believe in evil spells or witchcraft. At eight and twenty he had seen and done things in France that had shattered his innocence. He had bedded accomplished courtesans, dockside whores and lonely widows. He had killed and maimed in battles fought on foreign soil, and found something so holy, pure and innocent in Joan the Maid that her violent death by fire had devastated him.

After her passing, he had returned to Scotland to heal, but the raw wound of her violent death still festered inside him. Trust in humanity no longer existed for him. Only Scotland was real, and Stonehaven. Though he had obeyed MacArthur's urgent summons, he would not wed his daughter if he could help it. There was no passion left inside him for a wife. He had given his all to Joan's cause and intended to dedicate the rest of his life to protecting the Highlands against English aggression.

When the keep came into view, Graeme paused, surprised to see a boisterous rabble clustered outside the gate. He drew his sword, advising his six kinsmen who accompanied him to do the same.

"Who are those people? Can ye hear what they're saying?" Heath asked.

Graeme moved cautiously forward. "I dinna like it. Be on your guard."

"They're not MacArthurs," Heath noted. "Some are wearing MacKay plaids. What do ye think they're up to?"

"I dinna know, but I intend to find out," Graeme said, spurring his horse.

When Graeme was close enough to hear what they were saying, the blood froze in his veins.

"Burn, witch, burn."

A curse on his lips, he plunged into the rabble-rousers, scattering them in all directions.

"What is the meaning of this?" he thundered.

" 'Tis the witch Blair," a man boldly taunted. "Her evil spells are causing havoc."

"Aye," a hard-faced woman agreed. "My bairn fell ill when she looked at him. 'Tis witchcraft, I tell ye."

"When she passed by my fields, my crops withered and died," observed a poorly dressed man.

"My cows no longer give milk," another contended. "The witch doesna belong here, living among good, decent people."

"Who among you are MacArthurs?" Graeme asked.

The shuffling of feet and evasive glances answered his question. There was not a Mac-Arthur among Blair's accusers. Who were they? Who had put them up to this? For what reason?

"There is no such thing as witchcraft," Graeme bellowed. "Go back to your homes."

"Not as long as the witch still lives to cast her evil spells," a man shouted. "Death to the witch!"

Graeme had seen and heard enough. Some evil was afoot here. The MacArthur chieftain had been right. Danger permeated the charged air around him. From all indications, Blair MacArthur was in deep trouble. The question was whether or not the charges against her were justified.

His face composed in harsh lines, Graeme waved his sword above his head and shouted, "Begone, I say! If you return, I'll set my men on you."

18

The threat was enough to send Blair's accusers fleeing.

"Think ye we've seen the last of them?"
Heath asked.

"I dinna know. Someone put them up to
this, and I intend to find out who."

Graeme pounded on the gate with the hilt
of his sword.

"Who be ye?" the gatekeeper asked.

"Graeme Campbell. Your laird sent for
me."

The gate swung open, admitting Graeme
and his guardsmen. "Are the others gone?"
the gatekeeper asked, peeking through the
open gate.

"Aye, I chased them off. Where are the
laird's guardsmen?"

The elderly man gave a contemptuous
snort. "Niall took them with him to Edinburgh, leaving behind naught but a handful
of aging servants to serve the old laird and
his daughter."

He closed and barred the gate. "Go on up
to the keep. The laird is expecting ye. His
business with ye is all that's keeping him
alive."

Graeme shook off his feeling of foreboding
as he approached the keep. A lad ran up to
take his horse as he dismounted, and he
quickly climbed the stairs while his men followed the boy to the stables. An old man
wearing the MacArthur plaid opened the

door; his face lit up when he recognized the Campbell plaid Graeme wore.

"Be ye Graeme Campbell?"

"Aye," Graeme said, stepping over the threshold. "Your laird is expecting me."

"I be Gavin. Sit and refresh yerself while I tell the laird ye're here."

Graeme crossed the spacious hall and sprawled into a chair near the hearth. A serving maid appeared, thrusting a leather cup filled with foaming ale into his hand.

"Would ye like a wee drop of uisge breatha?" she asked timidly.

"Nay, lass," Graeme said. In truth a wee drop of strong Scottish whiskey would sit well on his stomach after his long ride, but he wanted a clear head when he spoke with Douglas MacArthur.

Graeme was just finishing his ale when his men entered the hall. Mugs of ale and glasses of uisge breatha were passed around as the men took their ease. All but Graeme, who remained tense and on edge. The situation here was more serious than he had suspected. Cautiously he glanced over his shoulder, as if expecting to find a hook-nosed witch hovering over him. Cursing himself for a fool, he drained the last of his ale.

The Scots were a superstitious lot. Graeme recalled stories of a man named Jubertus who was supposed to have murdered children and made them into powder. From the powder, imitation children were made for demons to inhabit. According to the church, witchcraft was heresy — and the punishment was burning.

Unfortunately, King James had done nothing to ease the hysteria surrounding witchcraft. Indeed, he seemed to have a sick fascination with witches and felt no remorse over burning those unfortunate souls convicted of witchcraft. Graeme thought of Blair MacArthur, and a chill of apprehension raced down his spine.

"Laird MacArthur is eager to see ye," Gavin said from behind Graeme. "Follow me. I will take ye to him."

Jerked from his reverie, Graeme surged to his feet. "No more anxious than I am to see him. How fares MacArthur?"

"He is weak but lucid. I fear he is not long for this world. Mark my words — things will change around here once Niall becomes laird. And not for the better."

The last was spoken with such bitterness that Graeme was immediately put on guard. What little he knew about Niall MacArthur had come from rumors, and none of what he'd heard was good.

"Douglas tires quickly," Gavin warned as he led the way up the staircase to the master's bedchamber.

"I'll try not to tax him," Graeme said as Gavin opened the door and stood aside.

"I'll be just outside the door should ye have need of me," Gavin said.

Graeme stepped into the chamber.

"Shut the door and come closer," demanded a weak voice.

Graeme closed the door and approached the bed. "I am here as you requested, Laird MacArthur."

"Thank ye for that, Graeme. I heard ye were wounded in France."

Graeme scarcely recognized the emaciated man lying in the bed. The once robust MacArthur had wasted away to a mere shadow of himself. His sunken eyes and cheeks already had the look of death about them.

" 'Twas naught," Graeme said. "A lance wound to the thigh — long since healed." He pulled a bench up to the bed.

"Did ye read my letter?" Douglas asked.

"Aye."

"Is that all ye can say? Is yer answer yea or nay? I havena much longer in this world, and I would see my lass safe. Ye are the only man strong enough to protect her."

Graeme considered mentioning his confrontation at the gate but decided it would be best for Douglas's failing health if the danger to his daughter was kept from him.

Graeme's silent contemplation seemed to agitate Douglas. "Dinna dither, mon! 'Tis little enough I ask of ye. Did I not save yer father's life when he was arrested in 1425 on charges that he supported the Duke of Albany during the years King James was a prisoner of the English? Did I not put my life on the line when I swore that Ian Campbell was a loyal supporter of the king?"

"Aye," Graeme acknowledged, "and grateful I am for it. But what you ask is —"

"I suppose ye heard the ruckus at the gate when ye arrived," Douglas interrupted. "'Tisna true. None of it. My lass isna a witch, she's a healer. She is a Faery Woman and well loved by her clansmen for her healing skills."

He rose on his elbow and clutched Graeme's arm with a bony hand. "I love my daughter, Graeme. I wouldna see her harmed."

Graeme eased him back down on the bed. "Who would harm her if she is so well loved?"

"Listen carefully, Graeme, for time grows short. Ye must wed Blair and take her away before Niall returns. I've settled a generous dowry on her, and it will all be yours, including rich lands on the Isle of Skye."

Graeme frowned. "Are you saying Niall wishes Blair harm?"

"Aye. He is jealous of his sister and fears her powers. He will give her to MacKay once I am dead and he becomes clan chief. Much as it grieves me to say so, Niall isna a good man."

Confusion darkened Graeme's brow. "How could Niall give Blair to MacKay against your wishes?"

"I have been ill a long time, and Niall has been slowly usurping my authority. He earned the loyalty of my guardsmen when they realized I was on my deathbed and Niall would succeed me as laird."

"How does MacKay fit into all this?"

"Niall has formed an alliance with MacKay. I'm not sure why, but I think MacKay wants Blair for her powers. With Blair's help, he intends to become the most powerful chieftain in the Highlands. He covets her for selfish reasons and not for the sweetness that dwells within her. I want a better fate for my lass. MacKay isna the mon for her."

"I am sorry, Douglas, but I have no wish to wed."

"Dinna say me nay, Graeme," Douglas pleaded. "Ye're my only hope of saving Blair."

Douglas's breathing was so labored, Graeme feared he was in imminent danger of expiring. Color drained from the old man's face, and his emaciated frame began to shake uncontrollably.

"Very well, Douglas, I will wed your daughter," Graeme said, respecting MacArthur too much to deny his dying request. "Announce our betrothal, and in a few years we will wed."

Douglas's distress was palpable. "Nay! Ye must wed her now! Today. Before Niall returns. Ye must be properly wed and the marriage consummated immediately. If Blair is to be protected from Niall's machinations, there must be no doubt about the legality of the marriage. Once Blair is wedded and bedded, ye can carry her back to Stonehaven with ye."

"Does Blair want this? Is she prepared to wed a stranger?"

Douglas's eyelids drooped. Graeme thought he had fallen asleep until he stirred restively and opened his eyes. "Blair is a stubborn lass, but she will obey me. Ye are aware of the Prophecy, are ye not?"

"Aye, I've heard of it, but I dinna believe in Faery Women or witches."

"There is one more thing ye must know about Blair. She is afraid of falling in love. According to the legend, a Faery Woman will lose her powers if she loves in vain, so she will resist ye."

Graeme let that news sink in and was relieved that Blair expected no more from him than his protection. He had lost his heart to Joan the Maid and still grieved for the innocent girl who believed that God spoke to her. He doubted he would ever love again.

"What say ye, Graeme Campbell? Will ye wed my lass and keep her safe?"

"Mayhap I should meet your daughter

first," Graeme hedged.

"Aye," Douglas said with a pained gasp, "but I warn ye, ye havena time to dither."

As if on cue, Gavin appeared in the doorway. "Shall I fetch the wee lass for ye, Douglas?"

"Aye, Gavin, ask Blair to attend me."

Douglas fell back against the pillow, his face ashen.

"Why does your daughter not heal you?" Graeme asked. "You claim she is a healer, yet you are gravely ill."

Douglas gave Graeme a sad smile. "I am an old mon and have earned eternal rest. Blair is a healer, nae a miracle worker. I've seen her heal a wound by merely touching it, but there is nae cure for the cancer inside my gut." He sighed and closed his eyes. "My one regret is leaving Blair at the mercy of those who wish her harm. 'Tis why I summoned ye to my bedside, Graeme. Will ye have my lass on those terms?"

The door opened. "You wished to see me, Father? Are you in pain? Shall I fetch something to ease your suffering?"

Steeling himself for his first look at the Faery Woman, Graeme turned to confront Blair MacArthur. He prayed she wasn't as ugly as Stuart had described. Could he bed a woman with no beauty and naught to commend her but her reputation as a witch?

Graeme blinked, blinked again, then stared

rudely at the vision poised in the doorway. The girl was slim and delicate, with an ethereal quality about her. A cloak of silver blond hair wrapped her slender form in mystery. Graeme watched as she approached the bed. She did not walk like a mere mortal; she floated. Her face bore not one blemish, not one mark of witchcraft. Her eyes were the same violet as the heather that graced the Scottish moors. Graeme realized he would have to look far and wide to find a woman as lovely as Blair MacArthur.

Her nose was straight and small. His appreciative gaze lingered on her high cheekbones, generous lips and stubborn little chin before moving on to her other attributes. The deep purple gown that covered her lithe form from head to toe did little to conceal her womanly curves. Blair MacArthur was no scrawny witch.

"Come closer, lass," Douglas said, crooking a bony finger at her.

Only a sidelong glance acknowledged Graeme's presence as Blair approached the bed. "How can I help you, Father? Are you in pain?"

"No more than usual, lass. There is someone here I would like ye to meet."

Blair turned to greet Graeme and froze. *It was he!* The man in her dreams, possessing the same vitality and raw male strength as the lover in her vision. His brows appeared as dark wings set above eyes as blue as the sea, and the black hair visible beneath his bonnet had a reddish sheen. Taller than the MacArthurs she had grown up with, he radiated power and agility. He was surrounded by an aura of maleness and danger and shivery desire, something she knew little about.

His hands were large, and the legs beneath the Campbell plaid were well shaped and athletic. Overall, his unrelenting masculinity was intimidating, but still she could not look away.

"This is Blair?" Graeme asked.

Pride temporarily banished the weakness from Douglas's voice. "Aye, this is my lass. Blair, greet Graeme Campbell, yer intended husband."

Blair's smile dissolved into a look of astonishment. "Father, what have you done?"

"What any caring father would do," Douglas said. "Graeme will keep ye safe after I am gone. I canna trust Niall to look after ye."

Blair's heart sank to her toes as she cast a sidelong glance at Graeme Campbell. What would he expect of her as a wife? She could only give so much of herself to any man. The Prophecy was clear. She dared not love, for to love in vain spelled doom for a Faery Woman. Healing was her life; she had no room in it for a husband.

She whirled on Graeme. "You agreed to this?"

Graeme shifted uncomfortably. "I owe your father a great debt. 'Tis the least I can do for him."

"Why are you not wed? You are of an age."

"I could ask the same of you," Graeme shot back.

"Enough!" Douglas growled. "Will ye wed my lass, Graeme Campbell?"

Blair's stubborn chin tilted upward. "I willna wed Graeme Campbell . . . or any man."

His strength fading fast, Douglas gasped, "Would ye prefer Donal MacKay? I didna want to tell ye, but Niall has promised ye to the MacKay laird."

A shudder of revulsion passed through Blair. She knew why MacKay wanted her. He coveted her powers and would force her to use them for evil purposes. "I dinna want MacKay. I want no man."

And especially not a man like Graeme Campbell. Too much about him attracted her. He was a man without equal, a man any woman could love. But the voice inside her warned that his heart belonged to another.

Could she wed Graeme Campbell and not grow to love him? she wondered. Her alliance with the Campbell laird was her father's dying wish. Could she deny his request and have any peace of mind afterward?

She could not.

Fortunately, she didn't have to love Graeme Campbell. And she would not.

"I would like to speak to Blair in private before she decides," Graeme said, interrupting her thoughts.

"Aye, but 'twill change naught," Douglas said. "Blair will have ye if she values her life."

Graeme sent Blair a speaking look and strode out the door, apparently expecting her to follow. Deploring his arrogance, Blair decided to follow and get this over with once and for all.

"Where can we talk?" Graeme asked.

"In here," Blair said, pushing past him into a curtained alcove. Graeme followed close on her heels. She turned to confront him. "What is it you wish to say to me that couldna be said in front of my father?"

"Only this. Your father is dying and he fears that harm will come to you after his death. He has asked me to wed you, and I am willing to fulfill his dying request." He sent her a challenging look. "Are you?"

"I canna be what you want me to be," Blair whispered. "The Prophecy —"

"— is but a legend. I believe not in legends, spirits or faeries. Nor did I ask for your love, if that is what you fear. I am a man of wide experience and have no difficulty satisfying my needs. If you do not wish an intimate relationship, then so be it. I dinna need an heir. I have relatives aplenty to take my place after I am gone."

She shuddered. "You make an alliance between us sound so cold."

"I am being practical."

"Do you love another?"

Graeme stared off into space, a cloud of sadness dimming his eyes. "Aye, but not in the way you think. My love is pure and true, on a higher plane than earthly love, but 'tis enough to sustain me."

Briefly Blair wondered what paragon held Graeme's heart, then quickly dismissed her question. She did not want to know. If she must wed Graeme Campbell, the less she knew about his emotional state, the better. Yet she could not forget her dreams, for they had seemed so very real.

So real that when she looked at him, her gaze penetrated his clothing to his warrior's body. She closed her eyes and saw him towering over her with his man part full, erect and ready. In her dream she had opened to welcome him. Heat engulfed her, and a cry escaped her lips.

Graeme's gruff voice pulled her from her vision. "Are you all right, lass?"

Her lids flew open and she saw him staring at her, his eyes narrowed in suspicion. "Aye, I am fine."

Graeme studied Blair's face with penetrating intensity. "Your father said you had

31

healing powers. Do you also have 'the sight'? Were you having a vision?" His expression grew stern. "Before you answer, know that I willna allow any dabbling in witchcraft. If we wed, I willna have you frightening my kinsmen with spells and such nonsense. You can heal their ills, but there will be no magic involved."

Blair turned away. "Mayhap I should take my chances with MacKay. Though I dinna fully understand them, I canna deny my powers, and there are times when I am visited by spirits."

Graeme sent her a quelling look. "Such talk is dangerous in these times."

Blair drew herself up to her meager height. "I didna say I was a witch, and my powers are not used for evil purposes."

"Evil or nay, there will be no casting of spells at Stonehaven. Shall we return to your father?"

Blair balked. She did not know Graeme Campbell. His outer beauty belied his harsh nature. What kind of husband would he make? He had promised to protect her, but that seemed to be as far as he was prepared to go. He had another love; his heart could never belong to her. But that was a good thing, was it not? Knowing where she stood with Graeme Campbell would keep her from losing her heart to him. She must heed the Prophecy's warning.

"Verra well, Graeme Campbell. I will wed you so that my father can die in peace, but there will be no intimacy between us."

Graeme appeared amused rather than disappointed. "As you wish, lass. I have no problem with taking a mistress or two."

The thought of Graeme bedding another woman caused Blair an unwelcome pang. Why did she even care? She knew little about the Campbell laird. What she did know had been gleaned only from her recurring dreams. And they had been more erotic than informative. However much she tried to deny it, the spirits had proclaimed him her future.

"So be it," Blair said. "I will wed you on my terms, Graeme Campbell."

"And I will wed you to repay a debt to your father," Graeme answered. He offered his arm. "Shall we tell him our good news?"

They returned together to the bedchamber, where Douglas anxiously awaited them.

"Did ye settle it between ye?" Douglas asked.

"We have," Graeme announced.

"I knew ye would not let me down," Douglas said, "so I sent Gavin for the priest. Ye must take Blair with ye to Stonehaven immediately after the consummation."

"Consummation?" squeaked Blair.

"Is that necessary?" Graeme asked.

"Aye. There must be no grounds to dissolve yer marriage. Naught must be left undone. Ye will consummate your vows immediately following the ceremony."

"Nay!" Blair cried.

"Ye will obey me in this, Daughter," Douglas insisted. He fixed his gaze on Graeme. "I will have yer vow, Graeme Campbell. Will ye wed Blair?"

Graeme glanced at Blair, moved by her beauty, yet uncomfortable with what and who she was. Neither he nor Blair wanted the marriage, but he did not have the heart to deny the dying laird.

"I will honor your request, Douglas," Graeme agreed. "I will wed your daughter and take her to Stonehaven with me when I leave. And I swear to protect her with my life."

Chapter Two

A discreet knock on the door announced the priest. Graeme watched with little enthusiasm and a great deal of astonishment as a raw-boned Scotsman wearing the MacArthur plaid over his black cassock strode into the chamber. Graeme stared at the priest's flame-colored hair and beard; he looked like one of the wild Vikings who had invaded their lands long ago.

"Gavin said ye were ready for me," the priest said in a booming voice.

"Thank ye for coming, Lachlan. Graeme Campbell has agreed to the marriage," Douglas said. "Ye can begin."

Lachlan searched Graeme's face, then thrust out his hand. "I'm Father Lachlan MacArthur. Is my kinsman correct? Have ye agreed to wed Blair?"

"Aye," Graeme answered.

"And ye, Blair? Will ye have Graeme Campbell?"

"Of course she will," Douglas snapped.

Blair nodded jerkily. Graeme thought she looked like a trapped doe looking for a way to escape. "Aye, I will have Graeme Campbell."

As if on cue, Gavin and an older woman Graeme had never seen before entered the chamber. Father Lachlan acknowledged their presence with a curt nod and began the ritual that would bind Graeme and Blair forever.

The ceremony was blessedly brief. In a matter of minutes it was over, leaving Graeme with a queer feeling in the pit of his stomach. Blair was not the wife of his dreams. Nevertheless, she was his to protect until death parted them.

"The bedding," Douglas gasped. "Get on with the bedding."

Blair sent Father Lachlan a pleading look, but he shrugged off her mute appeal. "Yer father has the right of it, lass. 'Tis for yer own protection. The Campbell is yer husband now, there is nae shame in it."

"Now I can die in peace," Douglas said, shooing them off. "Lachlan will comfort me in my final hours."

"I wouldna leave you, Father," Blair sobbed. "Let me stay with you."

"Nay, Daughter. My soul is at peace now that I know ye will be safe from Niall's machinations. If I am still alive on the morrow, come bid me good-bye. If I have already passed, dinna mourn me overlong, for I have lived a full life. Know that my last wishes are for yer happiness, so do as I say, lass, and go along with yer husband. As for ye, Graeme Campbell, dinna let a dying mon down. I will arrange for Blair's dowry to be transferred to ye."

Sensing that Douglas was at the end of his endurance, Graeme grasped Blair's elbow and ushered her from the chamber. "Where is your chamber?" he asked gruffly.

"Surely you dinna mean to . . . to . . . 'Tis full day, and my father lies dying."

Graeme stiffened. " 'Tis what your father wants, Blair. We've no time to delay. There *will* be a bedding."

While not fully resigned to the fate her father had chosen for her, Blair realized there was no escaping the fact that she was now Graeme Campbell's wife. Though they had privately agreed to an unconsummated marriage, her father had thwarted their intentions by imposing his will upon them.

"I will do this for Father's sake, but just this one time," Blair insisted.

"Agreed," Graeme replied. "I prefer my women willing and eager."

Ignoring his cutting remark, Blair proceeded along the gallery and turned down a long corridor. Pausing before a closed door, she hesitated but a moment before flinging it open.

"Allow me time to . . . prepare myself," Blair said.

The soft tread of footsteps in the dark corridor alerted Graeme, and he whirled in the direction of the sound. "Who goes there?"

Glancing over Graeme's shoulder, Blair saw Alyce approaching. " 'Tis only Alyce, my tiring woman."

"I've come to help prepare Blair for the bedding. Leave us, Laird Campbell. I will fetch ye when Blair is ready for ye."

"Have you a bathing room?" Graeme asked.

"Aye, beyond the kitchen. Ask Gavin — he will show ye the way."

"Aye, then. I will avail myself of a bath while waiting for my bride." Turning on his heel, he strode off.

" 'Tis not so bad," Alyce clucked when she noted Blair's stricken expression. "Yer husband is a fine, braw lad. He will please ye well and give ye strong bairns."

"Think you I care about that?" Blair cried. "Have you forgotten the Prophecy? As fine as Graeme Campbell is, I canna let him into my heart. Graeme Campbell loves another and will never return my love should I grow to care for him. 'Tis best I harden my heart, for to love in vain will bring the end of my powers."

"Och," Alyce scoffed. "That doesna mean ye canna enjoy the marriage bed. Yer husband is a virile man. Ye canna expect him to live like a monk."

"I know. I gave him permission to take a mistress, and he agreed. Tonight is for Father, because he demanded a consummation, but this night will be the first and last time I will be a true wife to Graeme Campbell."

"Foolish lass," Alyce muttered. "Come along. Let me prepare ye lest yer husband become impatient and arrive before ye are ready."

Refreshed from his bath, Graeme returned to the hall and sprawled in a chair before the hearth. When a serving girl approached, he requested uisge breatha. He felt in need of something stronger than ale before bedding an unwilling virgin.

Graeme was staring into the flames, brooding about his fate, when his cousin Heath joined him. "Will ye wed the lass?" Heath asked as he pulled a bench up beside Graeme.

"Aye," Graeme replied, reluctant to say more.

Heath groaned. "Och, mon, 'tis a bloody shame. Have ye seen her? Is she as ugly as they claim?"

Graeme sighed and took another sip of whiskey, savoring its smoothness as it slid down his throat. "She looks more like an angel than a witch."

" 'Tis just as I feared," Heath sighed. "She has bewitched ye. 'Tis what witches do. Let us leave now, before ye get in deeper."

"Yer bride is waiting for ye, laird," Alyce said as she approached the two men.

"Bride!" Heath gasped. "Never say ye wed the witch."

Graeme rose and stretched, his expression grim. "Your advice comes too late, Heath. My bride awaits me in our bridal bed."

Shocked beyond words, Heath froze with mouth agape as Graeme slowly made his way from the hall.

Graeme's feelings were mixed. He had taken a wife against his better judgment to please a dying man, and he didn't look forward to the bedding. Blair had made clear her objection to intimacy between them, and he knew he wouldn't enjoy bedding an unwilling woman.

Not that Graeme found Blair undesirable. Any man in his right mind would want Blair in his bed. It was the damn witch thing that put him off. Blair herself confessed to possessing powers, and while he wasn't a superstitious man, he was a cautious one.

Graeme reached the bedchamber and paused with his hand on the door latch. Calling himself foolish for hesitating, he opened the door and stepped inside. The day had turned stormy, and the room was deep in shadow, an eerie reminder of just whom he had wed. At first he didn't see her. When his eyes adjusted to the dim lighting, he spied her standing near the window, her arms raised as if embracing someone he could not see. A chill ran down his spine.

She must have heard him, for she spun around, and the ability to speak left him. She was dressed in something white, flowing and nearly transparent. Her arms were bare; the blond hair trailing over her shoulders seemed like a gleaming halo about her head. She was wraithlike and fragile, poised as if ready for flight. As his appreciative gaze roamed freely over her figure, he felt a definite stirring in his groin.

Blair MacArthur was womanly and feminine and had the curves to prove it. Witch or nay, he would have no trouble making love to her. A buzzing began in his head as he felt himself grow rigid with need. Slowly he advanced toward her, flinching when he saw her cringe away from him.

"Dinna fear me, Blair MacArthur. I willna hurt you." Blair's chin went up. "I fear no man. The Prophecy —"

"Forget the Prophecy. We are wed. Your father's dying wish must be fulfilled." He held out his hand. "Come to bed, lass."

Avoiding his hand, Blair carefully skirted him as she scooted toward the bed. Touching Graeme Campbell was not a good idea. Her dreams of him were still too vivid, too real. She knew from her visions how strong and virile his body was beneath his clothing, how he would feel inside her and the way her body would respond to his touch. She swallowed hard. This was reality. Far more potent than her dreams.

Blair had encountered Graeme in her dreams and visions so many times that she felt she knew him intimately, every hard-muscled plane and sculpted inch of him. And therein lay the danger.

It would be so easy to love Graeme Campbell.

Graeme watched Blair climb into bed with a great deal of anticipation, more than he would have thought. Eagerly he removed his vest and began unbuttoning his shirt, tossing both garments onto a nearby bench. Then he began unwinding his plaid. Like most Scotsmen, he wore nothing underneath, and when he whipped it off he heard her gasp.

He knew he was going too fast for an innocent maiden whom he had met mere hours ago, but he couldn't seem to help himself. She averted her gaze as he climbed onto the bed.

"Blair, look at me."

When she refused, he grasped her chin and turned her toward him. "Dinna be shy, lass. If this is to be our only time, I want to make it pleasurable for you." He stretched out beside her. "Relax."

Before she realized what she was saying, the words she had spoken in her dream escaped her lips. "I canna love you."

"I dinna ask for love."

Blair knew that. He loved another. "I am sorry for you, Graeme MacArthur. You were trapped into marriage by my father and had little choice in the matter."

"Nevertheless, we will make the best of this marriage once we get the bedding out of the way. You do understand why this is necessary, do you not?"

She nodded jerkily, understanding but still unwilling. She knew well enough what would happen to her once Niall became clan chief, but marriage to Graeme seemed a drastic step to take. Her visions, however, had clearly pointed to a future with the Campbell chieftain.

Her thoughts skidded to a halt when Graeme gently began to remove her shift.

"What are you doing?"

His hands stilled. "I want to see all of you."

"Is that necessary?"

"You're only delaying the inevitable, lass. Do you know naught of mating?"

She knew how it felt to mate with *him*. "I know enough."

He touched her breast, squeezing gently. She was so distracted, she was scarcely aware that he had bared her breasts and was pushing her shift down her hips with his free hand. She made a desperate grab at the material, but it slipped through her fingers. He lifted the shift off and tossed it onto the pile of discarded clothing.

Graeme's hands moved with slow deliberation over Blair's body, savoring the satiny feel of her skin, his own body reacting strongly to the soft female beneath him. She made a small, inarticulate sound and shifted restlessly. He smiled, aware that she wasn't totally immune to him. Her mind might be unwilling, but her body's need was unmistakable. He had known enough women in his lifetime to recognize desire, unproven though hers might be.

His own need was quickly escalating. It was as if he were touching someone familiar, someone he had known intimately in the past. But how could that be? Her flesh beneath his fingertips quivered, yet he sensed no fear in her. He gazed into the mesmerizing violet of her eyes and felt a jolt of something he could only describe as recognition.

When she shifted beneath his questing hands, rational thought ceased. Driven now by raw lust, he lowered his head and captured a pink nipple that seemed to be begging for his attention. He suckled gently, his tongue lapping at the puckered bud until she cried out and pushed herself deeper into his mouth.

Then the urge to kiss her, to commit her

taste to his memory, overcame every other need. His mouth left her breast to settle over her full red lips. He groaned his pleasure into her mouth, deepening the kiss as he probed the inner sweetness with his tongue.

Naught in his life had prepared him for Blair MacArthur. What he'd felt for Joan the Maid was innocent adoration, while this witch-woman writhing beneath him tasted of mystery and dark, forbidden secrets. Abruptly his mouth left hers and he reared up, staring into her eyes.

"What are you?" he asked in a strangled voice. "*Who* are you?"

Her expression dazed, Blair gazed up at him. "You know who I am."

"Mayhap I do and mayhap I dinna. If you plan to cast a spell on me, lass, forget it. It willna work."

Blair wanted Graeme to get on with it. The longer he lingered over the consummation, the more involved she became in the process. Something she had vowed to avoid. She didn't want to feel pleasure. She wanted to feel naught, but Graeme Campbell was making it difficult. Hot blood surged through her, and her body thrummed with the need to experience the pleasure she had found with Graeme Campbell in her dreams.

But somewhere deep inside her, voices whispered of danger, of lost powers and pain. However, heeding those voices while Graeme was kissing her was virtually impossible. Why could he not be selfish like other men? Why didn't he just spread her legs and take his pleasure? She didn't want her body to thrill to his touch.

Graeme's words about spells brought her abruptly back to reality. He believed she was a witch and would always feel that way, no matter how vehemently she denied it.

"I canna cast spells," she explained defensively. "I am a healer. People who do not know me call me a witch, but I am not. What I do harms no one."

He muttered something she didn't understand, then took her lips again in a soul-destroying kiss that sent her senses reeling. Willing her mind elsewhere, she wasn't prepared when he slid his hand between her legs and touched her intimately. She felt her body swell, felt moisture gathering, and shrieked when he inserted a finger inside her.

Her legs shook and her body literally exploded with feeling as his finger moved deep inside her tight passage, preparing her for his entry.

"Open for me, Blair. 'Tis time."

Blair resisted for a moment, then realized the futility of it and let her knees fall open. He moved over her, his demanding shaft prodding against her. He felt hard and swollen against her tender flesh . . . and hot. She stiffened slightly, preparing herself for his entry.

She heard the commotion at the door before Graeme did. She pushed at his chest, but he was so intent on consummation that it took several desperate attempts to alert him before he became aware of their unwelcome visitor.

"Who is it?" he roared loud enough to be heard through the closed door.

" 'Tis Gavin, Laird Graeme. I must speak with ye."

"Now? God's nightgown, I am with my bride."

"Sorry, mon, but 'tis important," Gavin persisted.

Blair was already scooting from bed and reaching for her chamber robe. "Father needs me. I must go to him."

Graeme wrapped his plaid around his waist and stomped to the door. "What is it?" he growled, none too pleased at the interruption.

"The laird is dead," Gavin said. "He died peacefully. Father Lachlan was with him."

"Father," Blair choked out on a sob. She pushed past Graeme before he could stop her. Graeme followed close behind.

Father Lachlan was performing last rites when they arrived at MacArthur's bedchamber. Blair knelt beside the bed while the priest anointed Douglas with holy oil and placed coins on his eyes. When he was done, he stepped back and placed a comforting hand on Blair's shoulder.

"Douglas's last words were for ye and yer husband, lass," he said. "He insisted that ye and Graeme should leave Gairloch immediately."

"Now?" Graeme questioned.

"Just before Douglas passed," Gavin explained, "a messenger arrived from Niall. The new laird will be home tomorrow, and Douglas wants ye both gone before he arrives."

"I canna leave before Father is laid to rest," Blair cried. " 'Tisna right."

" 'Tis yer dying father's wish," Lachlan reminded her. "Douglas was a canny mon. If he sensed danger to ye, then ye had best heed his warning. Alyce has already been alerted and awaits ye in the hall with yer trunks. She wishes to travel with ye to Stonehaven, if Laird Campbell has no objections."

"I'm sure Alyce will be of great comfort to Blair," Graeme allowed.

"Aye," Blair agreed. "I will be glad for Alyce's company. I canna recall when she hasna been with me. Nevertheless, I canna leave until after Father's funeral Mass."

"You can and you will," Graeme said firmly. "You must heed your father's last wishes, lass."

She shook her head, sending a cascade of golden curls tumbling into her eyes. "Nay, I canna! Dinna ask it of me."

"I will give you time to bid your father a final good-bye before we leave."

He withdrew, taking Father Lachlan with him.

"Dinna let the lass change yer mind, Graeme Campbell," Lachlan warned once they were alone.

"I willna," Graeme replied. "I made a promise to Douglas MacArthur and I intend to keep it."

By the time he had dressed and was ready to leave, the afternoon was already waning. Plagued by impatience, he opened the chamber door and stepped inside. Blair was kneeling at her father's bedside, her head bowed, her lips moving in silent prayer.

" 'Tis time to leave, lass," Graeme said. If she heard, she gave no sign of it.

Taking a firm grip on her shoulders, Graeme lifted her to her feet and turned her toward the door. "Dress as quickly as you can and meet me in the hall."

Blair moved woodenly toward the door, pausing once to glance over her shoulder for a final look at her father. Then Graeme hurried her out and down the gallery to her own chamber.

"I'll send Alyce up to help you," he said in parting.

Blair sat on the edge of her bed, unable to move or think beyond the fact that her father was dead and she was being forced to leave the only home she had ever known to live with a man she knew only from her dreams and visions. Blair had known from a very young age that she was the Faery Woman from the Prophecy, for even then she'd sensed her powers and spoken with the spirits, but it wasn't until the past few months that she had sensed any real danger to her.

No matter what people thought, she wasn't a witch. Though she admitted to summoning spirits, it was only for good purposes. And there were times she used her powers to heal wounds that could not be healed by other means. How could anyone accuse her of witchcraft when she believed in God's power and goodness and wanted only to help people?

"Yer husband is waiting for ye, lass," Alyce said, bustling into the chamber. "Why are ye nae dressed?"

"I know Father wanted me to leave before Niall arrives, but is it really necessary, Alyce?"

"Ye know it is. Up with ye now, yer husband awaits ye. I packed yer belongings while ye were praying over yer father so as not to delay the Campbell when 'twas time for the leave-taking. With any luck, ye'll reach Stonehaven before Niall realizes ye're gone."

Graeme sent Blair's trunks ahead on the pony cart and had horses prepared for Blair and Alyce along with his own. By the time the women arrived in the hall, a hasty meal had been set out on tables for them.

"I'm not hungry," Blair said, eyeing the food with distaste.

"None of that, lass," Graeme said sternly. "You'll eat even if I have to feed you. We'll be riding hard and fast, with few stops."

"Laird Campbell is right," Alyce said. "Eat up, lass."

Blair ate, but Graeme could tell her heart wasn't in it. He couldn't blame her. It couldn't be easy for her to leave before old Douglas was properly laid to rest. But a promise was a promise, and if Douglas feared for his daughter's life, then Graeme knew the danger to her was very real.

Graeme's men had eaten and left to see to their mounts when Graeme rose and signaled to Blair and Alyce that it was time to depart. Father Lachlan came forth to bid them goodbye.

"Godspeed," he said. "Unfortunately, Douglas died before he could make arrangements for Blair's dowry, so ye must speak to Niall about it when he returns."

"Verra well. There is something I would ask of you, Father," Graeme said.

"Name it. If 'tis within my power, I will see it done."

"Keep me informed of any mischief Niall might plan against Stonehaven."

"Aye. Many here remain faithful to the old laird and his daughter. If Niall plans mischief, ye'll know of it." He pulled Graeme aside, out of Blair's hearing. "Treat the lass well, Campbell, else ye'll answer to me."

"I dinna abuse women," Graeme said, "but I willna allow the lass to cast spells or summon spirits."

Just then Heath hailed Graeme, forestalling Lachlan's reply. 'Twas time to go.

"Good-bye, Father Lachlan," Graeme called as he mounted his horse and led the small party away from Gairloch.

Blair's back hurt and her legs were chafed, but somehow she managed to keep up with Graeme. She knew how to ride, of course, but had never ridden any great distance before. When night fell they made a rough camp, but they were up again and in the saddle soon after dawn.

Had Blair not been so distraught, she would have appreciated the majestic mountain peaks rising above them and the carpet of purple heather blooming on the moors. She couldn't recall ever traveling so far from Gairloch. Because of her powers, her father had been unwilling to let her venture beyond the village.

"We're nearly home," Graeme said, riding back to join her. "Keep looking toward the west and you'll see Stonehaven's towers.

Stonehaven isna as grand as your father's keep, but you should find it comfortable."

Blair spotted the square towers situated on a spit of land that jutted out into Loch Torridon a few minutes later. Stonehaven might not be as grand as Gairloch, but it was nevertheless impressive with its thick walls and iron portcullis guarding the keep. As they rode through the village of neat cottages clustered outside the gate, the cotters came from their houses to stare at her.

Their expressions, ranging from sullen to frightened to downright hostile, did not bode well for her. Blair was not immune to the whispers trailing in their wake, but if Graeme heard them he gave no hint of it. It appeared her undeserved reputation had preceded her, for the word "witch" struck her over and over like physical blows.

"Pay them no heed, lass," Alyce advised as she rode up beside her. "They'll soon change their minds."

"Graeme must know what his people think of me," Blair lamented. "Why did Father do this to me?"

"Ye know why," Alyce maintained. "Give it time, Blair. Things will change."

They passed through the raised portcullis and rode across the bailey to the front steps of the keep. Graeme dismounted and lifted Blair from her horse while Heath assisted Alyce.

"Welcome to your new home, Blair," Graeme said.

The sturdy oaken door opened as they started up the stairs. Graeme's uncle, Stuart Campbell, stepped out to greet them.

"That didna take long, Nephew. I'm glad ye managed to avoid wedding the witch." His appreciative glance found Blair and lingered. "Who is this lass? Did one of MacArthur's kinswomen catch yer eye? She's a comely wench. Glenda will be a wee bit jealous, but she had ye to herself too long."

Graeme sent Stuart a warning look and cleared his throat, hoping to stop his uncle's prattle. Unfortunately, Stuart seemed oblivious to Graeme's admonition.

"Are ye going to introduce me to the lass, lad?"

"Cease your blathering, Uncle," Graeme said. "If you let me get a word in edgewise, I'll introduce you to my wife. Blair, this is my uncle, Stuart Campbell — a more talkative mon you'll never meet. Uncle, this is Blair, Douglas MacArthur's daughter and my wife. We were wed yesterday."

Stuart lurched backward as if struck. "Ye wed the witch? What is she, a changeling? What happened to her hooked nose and straggly black hair? Where is the wart?"

"The stories about Blair were wildly exaggerated. My wife is a healer, not a witch. And as you can see, she is beautiful."

"A changeling," Stuart muttered.

Hands on hips, Alyce stepped forward, shielding Blair from Stuart's view. "Keep yer opinions to yerself, old mon. My lassie is sweet and good, better than the likes of ye. Hurt her and ye'll have me to answer to."

"Who are you?" Stuart asked, keeping a wary distance from the irate woman.

"Alyce. I raised Blair from the time she was a wee bairn. I know her better than anyone in this world, and I am telling ye she isna a witch."

Graeme moved to intervene before Blair's pugnacious defender attacked Stuart. "Do me a favor and find Maeve, Uncle. Chambers need to be prepared for Blair and Alyce, and I want to introduce Maeve to her new mistress. I'll explain everything to you later. We're all tired from the long ride and in need of food and baths.

"Maeve is the housekeeper," he said in an aside to Blair. "She and her husband Jamie have run the fortress since my father's time."

"Are ye looking for me, laird?"

An elderly woman with iron-gray hair, full figure and eyes as blue as Graeme's bustled over to join them.

"Aye, Maeve," Graeme said. "I want to introduce you to your new mistress." He pulled Blair forward. "Greet my wife, Blair Mac-Arthur."

Maeve stared at Blair, then hastily crossed

herself, her lips moving in silent prayer. "Ye've gone and done it now, Graeme Campbell. Have ye taken leave of yer senses? Ye have wedded yerself to a witch."

Once again Alyce flew to Blair's defense. "Mind yer tongue, woman! My lass isna a witch. If ye know what's good for ye, ye'll spread the word to yer kinsmen. My lass is the mistress here and —"

"Leave off, Alyce," Blair said gently. "I can fight my own battles." She smiled at Maeve. "I'm sure Maeve and I will get along just fine. I am a healer, Maeve, and I hope my skills will prove useful to my husband's kinsmen. I can prepare infusions, herbals, salves and simples for their ills and injuries."

Maeve didn't look convinced, though she put on a brave face. "Aye, mistress, if ye say so. If ye'll excuse me, I'll see to yer food and bath." She scooted off as fast as her plump legs could carry her.

"Wait for me," Alyce said, hurrying after Maeve. "I will help prepare Blair's food."

"Your people fear me," Blair said.

" 'Tis unfortunate," Graeme agreed, "but their opinion can be changed. 'Tis up to you to show them you are naught more than what you claim."

"What about you, Graeme Campbell? Do you believe I am what I claim?"

Blair didn't need to hear his answer — the purple aura emanating from him spoke louder than words. Purple was the color of doubt and confusion. He feared her and was confused about his own feelings concerning their marriage.

Their relationship was doomed even before it began.

Chapter Three

"Would you like to eat before you bathe?" Graeme asked when the silence between them lengthened. "Your trunks haven't arrived yet, but they should be here soon."

"Aye," Blair answered. "I will bathe when I have clean clothing to change into."

Stuart chose that moment to return with another man in tow.

"This is Jamie," Graeme said, "Stonehaven's steward. You can depend on him and his wife Maeve for whatever you need."

Blair prepared herself for another rejection by Graeme's kinsmen and was pleasantly surprised when Jamie offered her a warm smile of welcome.

"So our laird has finally taken himself a wife," the elderly man chuckled. " 'Tis about time. Welcome, my lady. I will help ye acquaint yerself with Stonehaven."

"Thank you, Jamie," Blair said. She sent a sidelong glance at Graeme. "I fear I shall need all the help I can get."

"Yer chamber is prepared," Jamie said. "Ye must be exhausted. I'll have Maeve fix ye a tray so ye can eat in yer room, if ye'd like."

"That would be wonderful, Jamie. Food, a bath and a good night's sleep are all I shall require tonight."

"I'll show you the way," Graeme said, guiding Blair from the hall toward a steep flight of stairs.

A lump formed in Blair's throat. Did Graeme expect to consummate their wedding vows tonight? She sincerely hoped not. What he had begun last night had proven how easily she would succumb to him, how fast he could bring her body to the point where she actually craved him.

"Your bedchamber is part of the master's chamber," Graeme said. "I thought of putting you elsewhere, but decided it wouldna look right for the laird's wife to sleep away from her husband."

Relief spread through Blair. "You dinna intend to . . . to . . ."

"Consummate our marriage? Your father is dead. I see no reason to do something you obviously find abhorrent."

"But I thought 'twas necessary." God's nightgown, she sounded as if she were begging!

Graeme shrugged. "Only if you want it. 'Twas your decision to keep our marriage free of intimacy, not mine."

He paused before an open door and ushered

her inside. "You should be comfortable here."

More than comfortable, Blair thought as she surveyed her surroundings. The chamber, softened by candlelight, had obviously been intended for a lady. Feminine colors decorated the bed hangings and two long windows, and the walls were hung with colorful tapestries, keeping drafts at bay. Besides an intricately carved bed that rested on a dais, there were a dainty writing desk, dressing table, wardrobe, rocking chair, and several benches placed before the hearth.

"The chamber is lovely," Blair commented. "I shall be quite content here."

"If there is anything you desire, just ask Jamie."

"Is there a stillroom where I can dry my herbs and mix my salves and simples?"

"Aye, beyond the kitchen garden." He sent her a probing look. "I meant what I said, Blair. There will be no casting of spells at Stonehaven."

She whirled away from him and walked to the window. "Do you fear me, Graeme Campbell?"

"I fear no woman, lass, witch or nay." He reached her in three long strides and turned her to face him. Raising her chin with one long finger, he stared into the turbulent depths of her violet eyes. "Say the word and I will make you my wife in more than name. Right here, right now."

She lowered her lids, unable to look at him without feeling guilt over her decision. "I thought you understood why I canna give my body to you."

"Perhaps I would understand if you explained it to me again."

"The Prophecy says the Faery Woman who loves in vain will lose her powers."

"I have heard the Prophecy. It says the Faery Woman must undergo ordeals of fire, water and stone, but it says naught about refusing her husband his marital rights."

"I am afraid." The admission trembled from her lips.

"Afraid of what? That I will hurt you?"

"You could hurt me, but not in the way you think. My father did you no favor by asking you to marry me. You deserve a wife who would love you."

Graeme frowned. "Are you saying you canna love me?"

"You yourself admitted that you loved another. I could lose my powers if I were to love you and you didna return my love. You say you have heard the Prophecy, yet you dinna believe in it."

"You're right. I dinna believe in Faery Women or spirits. The Prophecy is a cruel joke one of your ancestors thought up in a moment of madness." His gaze intensified, and his hands dropped to her shoulders. "I could make you want me, Blair. You dinna have to love me. I wouldna ask that of you."

His hands curved around her narrow shoulders and he brought her against him. Heaven help her! His body was hard, and the heat emanating from him was melting her from within. Then he lowered his head and took her mouth, kissing her slowly, with rising passion. The pulse in her throat beat erratically and moisture gathered between her legs, hot and liquid, and she moaned into his mouth.

Without volition her hands slid over his back, fingers grazing tense muscles. He deepened the kiss, using his tongue to acquaint himself with her taste as her hands moved up to curl around his neck and tangle in his dark hair.

Oh, no, what was she doing? As if from a great distance she heard the sounds she made . . . soft, inarticulate cries that were somehow mixed with denial. This was not meant to be. The reality of his kisses was more intense than any of her dreams. The raw pleasure she felt was so fierce, it was as near to madness as she would ever get. And in that brief moment of madness Blair would willingly relinquish her powers in order to lie beneath Graeme Campbell.

Ravenous desire pulsed in the air around them like a living thing, hot and wild and consuming. It was heaven, it was hell . . . it was wrong. The storm of warring emotions that swelled and churned inside her escalated when Graeme swept her off her feet.

"You willna be sorry," Graeme said as he placed her on the bed and followed her down. "I want you, lass. I want to be inside you."

His hands skimmed up her legs, tangled in the moist curls at the apex of her thighs. "You were made for love, Blair."

Love. The word brought the euphoria crashing down around her. She must truly be insane to sacrifice her powers for a few moments of mindless pleasure. Nevertheless, her body refused to obey her mind, and she began returning Graeme's kisses.

"That's it, lass," Graeme encouraged against her lips. "Let yourself go. Dinna think of anything but what's going on in this bed."

He had worked her skirts up to her thighs when the door opened, letting in a draft.

"I hope there's something on this tray to tempt yer appetite, lass," Alyce said as she bustled into the chamber. "I helped fix yer dinner myself, so . . ." Her words ended abruptly when she saw Blair and Graeme intimately entwined on the bed. "Oh, I didna know . . ." She started to back away. "I'll just leave the tray and ye can help yerselves when ye're ready."

Her cheeks flaming, Blair scooted from beneath Graeme, pushing him off the bed in her haste. "Nay, dinna go, Alyce. Graeme was just leaving."

Picking himself up off the floor, Graeme sent Blair a wry look as he strode toward the door. "We'll finish this later, lass," he said in a voice too low for Alyce to hear.

"Nay, we willna," Blair returned.

"What was that all about?" Alyce asked once they were alone.

"Dinna ask."

"I thought mayhap ye'd gotten some sense and decided to enjoy the marriage bed. Ye're fortunate to have a braw young mon like the Campbell laird in yer bed."

"I havena changed my mind, Alyce."

Alyce gave a hoot of laughter. "Ye could have fooled me."

"Forget what you saw. 'Twas a mistake." She walked over to the tray and lifted the cover. "What have you brought me?"

"A slice of beef pie, cheese, poached fish and fresh bread and butter. Maeve keeps a well-stocked larder. I ate some of the beef pie myself and it was good. We willna starve here, that's for sure."

Blair tasted the pie and had to agree. In fact, everything on the tray tasted wonderful. She ate with gusto, then sat back and sighed. "When my things arrive, have my box of herbs taken to the stillroom. I'll take care of it tomorrow."

"Stonehaven has no bathing room," Alyce

informed her, "but there's water heating for yer bath in the kitchen. Yer trunks should arrive soon."

"Thank you, Alyce. I dinna know what I would do without you."

"Thank the good Lord ye dinna have to," Alyce said as she carried the empty tray from the chamber.

While Blair waited for her trunks, she explored her chamber and discovered a small door she hadn't noticed before. She worried her bottom lip with her teeth, wondering if the door led to Graeme's bedchamber. There was only one way to find out.

Gingerly approaching the door, she grasped the latch and eased it open . . . and found herself looking into a masculine version of her own chamber. Not only was she staring into Graeme's chamber, she was staring at Graeme!

He stood poised beside the washstand, his bare back to her, water dripping from his head as if he had just doused it in the washbowl. She watched in awe as his corded muscles flexed and relaxed with movement. Her fists clenched against the urge to run her hands over his smooth flesh, to feel his muscles tense beneath her touch.

"Is there something you want, Blair?"

Blair started violently. Did he have eyes in the back of his head? Drying his dripping head with a towel, he turned to face her.

"How did you know?" Blair asked.

"Training. I've learned to sense when someone is sneaking up behind me. It's saved my life a time or two."

Blair's shoulders stiffened. "I wasna sneaking up on you. I merely wanted to see where the door led."

"I told you your chamber was part of the master's chambers. "It's customary for the laird and his lady to share sleeping arrangements."

"But we're not . . . I mean, we agreed . . ."

"We must keep up appearances, Blair. Should your brother learn you're still virginal, he'll declare our marriage invalid and force you to wed another. Is that what you want?"

"Nay."

"Then let me do what I think best where you're concerned. I admit I want you in my bed, but I willna take you unless you give me leave."

"I canna," she said, backing away. "Thank you for honoring my request."

He reached for her and brought her against him. " 'Tisna going to be easy, lass. A man needs a woman in his bed. You're my wife — I shouldna have to look elsewhere for my pleasure."

His expression was dark, his blue eyes grave as his hands tightened on her shoulders. "Forget this nonsense about being a Faery Woman and let me make you a real woman."

She wasn't expecting his kiss, so she had no time to fortify her resistance. Rising up on her toes, she melted against him, her mouth soft and pliant against his. Kissing Graeme was like nothing she had ever experienced. His taste and scent were unique. She could happily drown in his kisses. She felt him edging her toward the bed and realized that she was dangerously close to surrendering her powers for a few moments of physical pleasure.

She shoved against his chest, and his arms fell away. "You're a foolish woman, Blair Campbell. Even if you had the powers you claim, I forbid you to use them at Stonehaven. You're denying both of us for something that will be of no use to you as long as you remain my wife."

"Do you forbid me to use my knowledge of healing to help your kinsmen?"

"Nay, you know better than that. I prize your healing skills. I'm referring to those magic powers you claim. While I dinna believe in such things, my kinsmen are more gullible than I am. They'll be watching you for signs of witchcraft whether you practice it or not."

She recoiled as if struck. "I am not a witch, but I dinna deny being a Faery Woman. Believe me when I say I willna harm your kinsmen."

"Return to your chamber," Graeme ordered

67

gruffly. "It wouldna take much to forget the promise I made to you and make you my wife in every way. Heed me well, lass. Stay out of my way if you wish to remain untouched."

Blair turned and fled. She had seen the dark aura surrounding him, and an angry Graeme was more than she could presently handle. It was going to be difficult to live the rest of her life with a man she wanted but could not have.

Graeme needed a woman. If his virginal wife wouldn't give him what he needed, then he would damn well find it elsewhere. Glenda slept on the third floor with the other servants and was always willing to accommodate him. All he had to do was summon her and she would come to him. He strode to the door to fetch her, then came to an abrupt halt.

Damn Blair! His father had never broken his marriage vows during all the years of his marriage; and Graeme resented the fact that Blair was forcing him to be less honorable. Blair wasn't the woman he would have chosen to wed, but the choice had not been his to make. One conversation with a dying man had turned his life upside down and gained him a witch for a wife.

Anger robbed Graeme of his usual good humor. He should march into Blair's chamber and tell her he was going to take a mistress. Aye, he would do it. He would give her one last chance to be a wife to him before he took another woman to his bed.

He strode to the connecting door and burst through before he changed his mind. What he saw stopped him in his tracks. Blair was standing in a patch of moonlight before the open window. Her arms were outstretched, as if inviting some unseen entity. A sudden breeze fluttered the curtain, lifted her hair and pressed her skirts against her legs. Curious, he moved closer, close enough to see her face.

Her eyes were closed and her lips were moving. Graeme's eyes widened in alarm as the flames in the hearth turned yellow, then blue, then blood red. What was going on?

"Blair! What in God's name are you doing? Stop it! Stop it immediately!"

Silence followed his words. No breeze stirred, no curtain twitched. He watched warily as Blair slowly came to herself, as if emerging from a trance. She turned toward him but appeared not to see him. Her violet eyes were wide and unfocused, and Graeme felt a moment of fear. Then she blinked and brought him into focus.

"Graeme . . . what are you doing here?"

"Never mind that," Graeme all but shouted. "What did I just interrupt?"

"Naught. I was just . . . communicating."

69

Red dots of rage swam before his eyes. "With whom?"

"With nature."

"Liar! Have I not forbidden you to summon evil spirits? What are you? Who are you? Your father assured me you were not evil, and I believed him."

"I am not evil, but I canna deny my legacy. Nor can I disavow my God-given powers."

"God-given?" His brows rose. "Explain the powers of which you speak."

"I can heal wounds."

"What else?"

"Spirits speak to me. Sometimes I see things before they happen."

"So you do have the 'sight,'" he said angrily.

"Some might call it that, but 'tis more."

"Go on. Do you hear voices?"

"Aye. They speak to me in my dreams . . . and at other times."

"What do your dreams tell you?"

"Dinna press me, Graeme. You willna like it."

He was utterly merciless. "Your dreams, Blair. Tell me about them."

"*You* came to me in my dreams. I saw your face long before I knew your name."

Stunned into silence, Graeme stared at her, trying to decide if she was telling the truth. Unwavering, she returned his gaze. Graeme didn't know what to think. Blair was either a liar or a dangerous woman, or mayhap a lunatic.

"You dreamed about me?"

She nodded. "You came to me in my dreams. The spirits brought you to me."

"I canna believe what I'm hearing. We didna know one another before your father summoned me to Gairloch. I'm warning you, Blair, dinna continue this foolishness. I canna protect you if you refuse to cooperate."

"What are you doing here? I didna invite you into my chamber. How can we avoid one another if you dinna follow your own rules?"

"I came to give you one last chance to be a wife to me before I bring another woman to my bed."

Blair did her best to conceal her dismay. If Graeme took a leman, she couldn't stop him. In fact, she had encouraged him to do so. Nevertheless, she wanted to be the woman in his bed.

She wanted to be loved by him and to love him in return. That thought brought another.

"Who is the woman you love?"

"What?"

"You told me you loved another. Who is she? Why have you not wed her?"

The light in Graeme's eyes dimmed even as his expression turned grim. "Aye, I love another, but there was naught between us that wasna pure and innocent. I will always love her, though she is no longer of this world."

"She's dead?" Blair gasped.

"She was never of this world. She belonged to God." His gaze sharpened as his attention returned to Blair. "Dinna try to change the subject. We were speaking about conjuring spirits and casting spells. There will be no more such goings-on at Stonehaven. I mean it, Blair. I willna tolerate disobedience." He backed away. "I bid you good night."

He marched off without another word. It was just as well. Obviously, he feared her and did not understand her powers. In her experience, people feared things they did not understand, and Graeme was no exception.

What really hurt was the knowledge that Graeme believed she was a witch.

Blair returned to the window, trying to summon the spirits that had fled when Graeme entered her chamber, but it was no use. No matter how hard she concentrated, they would not return. She hoped they hadn't deserted her, for without them she was lost.

Graeme prowled from one end of his chamber to the other, his mind still dazed by what he had just witnessed. He had been greatly disturbed by Blair's behavior. He no longer knew what to believe.

Did he want to bed a woman who dabbled in the black arts? His body said aye while his mind said nay. Why had he taken MacArthur's word that Blair wasn't a witch?

Because you don't believe in witches.

Nevertheless, seeing Blair at the window while all those unnatural phenomena were taking place in the chamber had definitely unnerved him. Magic had been in progress. Somehow he had to prevent Blair from summoning forces that could disrupt Stonehaven and its people.

Witchcraft. Did it really exist? Common sense told him it did not, but his eyes had beheld something indisputably odd. A shudder went through him. What had he done? Whom had he wed? Why did he want a woman he neither understood nor trusted?

Graeme decided he did indeed need a woman. One who neither claimed powers nor spoke to spirits. A woman willing to ease his body without complicating his life. His body hardened at the thought of Glenda's generous curves and sweet mouth working their magic on him. He had only to climb the stairs and summon her.

He strode toward the portal. His hand was on the latch when the door connecting his chamber to Blair's flew open. He whirled at the sound, shocked by the intrusion but utterly bewitched by the angry beauty confronting him.

Her hair appeared alive and glowing, her face illuminated by an inner light that made her seem otherworldly. Her figure was perfection, softly rounded and sweetly curved. But her violet eyes held a spark that did not bode well for him.

Witch or nay, he wanted her still.

"You're like all the others. You believe I am a witch," Blair charged.

"What would you have me believe?"

"That my powers come from God."

"I once knew a woman who claimed her powers came from God, and she is dead now because of it. Is that what you want for yourself?"

"Nay, of course not. But I canna refuse to heal because I fear death. I want to help people, Graeme . . . I must."

He shook his head. "I understand none of this, Blair. I will protect you because I promised and my word is my honor." He sent her an exasperated look. "In exchange, I expect to be obeyed." He turned away. "Return to your chamber."

"Where are you going?"

"To fetch a normal woman to warm my bed."

Her cheeks flaming with anger, Blair whirled on her heel and stomped off, slamming the door so hard the windows rattled. Graeme dropped his hand from the latch and leaned against the panel, shaking his head. What was a thwarted bridegroom to do?

Blair returned to her chamber in a huff. The man was impossible. What would it take for him to believe in her powers? Nothing she said seemed to get through to him. She glanced toward the closed door. Tears formed in her eyes when she imagined him with another woman.

Why couldn't Graeme Campbell be the same uncomplicated man who had visited her in her dreams? *That* Graeme accepted her as she was. *That* Graeme never questioned her powers.

Blair's fists clenched in frustration when she recalled the countless times Graeme had invaded her dreams. Why had the spirits brought him to her if he couldn't accept her as she was?

The door to her chamber opened and Alyce bustled inside, carrying a stack of towels and soap. "Are ye ready for yer bath, lass? Yer trunks have arrived."

"Oh, aye," Blair said, dashing the tears from her eyes.

Alyce pushed the door open and a manservant rolled in a tub. Other servants followed, carrying jugs of hot and cold water. Within a short time the tub was set up behind a screen and filled. Blair thanked everyone politely and began to undress.

"I'll see to yer trunks," Alyce said.

Blair sank into the tub, the hot water soothing both her body and her temper.

His decision made, Graeme left his

chamber, lifted a torch from a wall sconce and made his way up to the third floor. It mattered not that Glenda slept in a room with others, he would fetch her anyway. He wasn't a man who indulged his needs frequently, but Blair had fired his lust. But for MacArthur's death, he would have already made love to Blair and rid himself of his annoying hunger for her.

Heath had the right of it, Graeme decided. Blair had bewitched him. Would bedding another woman purge her from his system? He did not know, but was willing to find out.

Three women slept in the small chamber at the top of the stairs. Holding the torch aloft, he spotted Glenda lying on a cot in the far corner. Uncaring whether or not the others awoke, he made his way toward her cot. She awakened at his approach and rubbed her eyes.

"Laird Graeme."

"Come," he whispered, beckoning.

Without hesitation, Glenda rose naked from the cot, donned her shift and followed close on his heels. She touched his arm when she caught up to him. "What about yer wife?"

"Let me worry about her."

He entered his chamber and waited for Glenda to follow before closing the door behind them.

Glenda, whose morals were none too strict,

preened for his benefit. "I feared ye wouldna want me in yer bed after ye wed."

"Aye, well, you thought wrong." He removed his belt and pulled off his plaid, naked now but for his boots. "Climb into bed, lass. I'll be with you as soon as I remove my boots."

Glenda whipped off her shift and climbed into bed, posing seductively for Graeme's benefit. "I'm glad ye still have need of me, laird." She held out her soft white arms.

Graeme turned and stared down at her. Red-haired and buxom, she was naught like the Faery Woman he had wed. But that was a good thing, was it not? The answer surprised him. It wasn't a good thing when the woman he really wanted lay just beyond the connecting door. His cock, rampant with need but a moment ago, abruptly deflated.

He recoiled in alarm. What had Blair done to him?

"Get up!" he barked. "Return to your bed. I dinna need you, after all."

Glenda sent him a confused look. "I thought . . . What have I done to annoy ye, laird?"

" 'Tis not you," he said, his tone softening. "The mood has left me. Another time, mayhap."

He turned away as Glenda donned her shift and sidled out of the chamber. The moment the door closed behind her, Graeme flung on a chamber robe and stormed through the connecting door.

"Laird Graeme, is aught amiss?" Alyce gasped, startled by his appearance in Blair's bedchamber.

His gaze probed the dimly lit chamber. "Where is my wife?"

Alyce's frightened gaze went immediately to the screen.

"Leave us!" he ordered Alyce. "And close the door behind you."

Alyce glanced worriedly at the screen, then scooted from the chamber. Graeme marched to the screen and flung it aside.

"What have you done to me, woman?" he roared.

Blair sank down into the water. "I did naught. Get out. I prefer to bathe in private."

His heated gaze raked over her exposed flesh. "You cast a spell on me. Take it away."

"I canna take away what I didna do. What are you talking about?"

"You stole my manhood. You took from me the ability to bed another woman."

"I . . . what?"

Reaching down, he hauled her from the tub. "You heard me. I was useless to Glenda. That has never happened to me before."

Blair laughed in the face of Graeme's anger. "You give me too much credit, Laird Graeme. I couldna do that even if I wanted to."

She knew that goading him was a mistake, but she couldn't help looking down his body. What she saw, however, made her mouth drop open. He was fully aroused, his sex jutting boldly from the folds of his robe.

Graeme must have noted the shocked look on her face, for his eyes followed the direction of her gaze. Nearly as astonished as Blair, he dropped his hands from her and backed away.

"Damn you! Just touching you arouses me. I'm cursed!" Whirling, he stormed from the chamber.

Chapter Four

Graeme had already eaten and left the hall when Blair broke her fast the following morning. A fetching red-headed serving maid sidled up to her and asked if she'd like a bowl of oats or eggs and ham. The girl's manner was blatantly disrespectful. Hand on one hip, she inspected Blair from head to toe, then quickly dismissed her with a toss of her head.

"Is something out of place?" Blair asked. "Have I forgotten to fasten my dress?"

Checking first to see if anyone was looking, the girl said, "I never saw a witch before."

Blair sighed. Would it never end? Would people never tire of thinking ill of her? "I am not a witch," she replied.

"Ye must be to have bewitched our laird."

"Who are you?"

"Glenda. I serve Laird Graeme." She grinned. "If ye catch my drift."

Blair did indeed catch Glenda's drift, and she recognized the woman's name. Glenda was the one Graeme had intended to bed after Blair had refused him. The thought of

Glenda intimately entwined with Graeme sent an immediate surge of anger through Blair.

"Henceforth you will confine your duties to the kitchen," Blair said, stressing the word *duties.*

"I will continue to do as I please until Laird Graeme commands otherwise," Glenda returned. "It's not your decision to make. Have ye decided between porridge and eggs?"

"Porridge," Blair said, vowing to deal with Glenda later.

She watched Glenda stroll off, all too aware of what Graeme saw in the flamboyant flirt. Aside from being voluptuous, she boasted a blatant sexuality that all but screamed for a man's attention.

From the corner of her eye Blair spied Alyce hurrying toward her, her face flushed from exertion. Alyce's aura had turned from the usual placid blue to a more volatile violet, and Blair knew immediately that she was upset.

"Blair, lass, ye must come quickly," Alyce panted.

Blair rose from her chair. "What is it? What's happened?"

" 'Tis yer husband, lass. He's in the still-room, rummaging through yer box of herbs," she said meaningfully, "and his mood is nae good. What happened last night?"

Blair paled. "Show me the way. I will tell

you about it later."

The stillroom was situated beyond the kitchen. They reached it by way of a vine-covered arched walkway. Blair burst through the door just as Graeme was removing four candles from a box and holding them aloft to inspect them.

"What are you doing? Why are you searching my belongings? Be careful. Those herbs are precious to me."

Graeme whirled at the sound of her voice. "After what I saw last night, I canna trust you, Blair. I am making sure there is naught in here to cause mischief."

"As you can see, I brought naught but herbs, salves and simples with me to Stone-haven."

He shoved the candles beneath her nose. "What are these used for?"

Blair shrugged. "They are just candles. Sometimes I work late and need the light. Are you satisfied?"

Graeme returned the candles to the box. "For the time being." He turned to leave.

"I met your leman this morn," Blair ventured. "I suspect you'll soon hear about it from Glenda. I've confined her duties to the kitchen."

Graeme's elegant eyebrows shot upward. "You what?"

"I'd best go unpack your trunks," Alyce said, scooting out the door. "I'm not needed here."

"Coward," Blair hissed as her friend left her alone to face Graeme's wrath.

" 'Tis just as well she left," Graeme said. "Alyce is a wise woman. Now, Blair, please explain yourself. Glenda's duties are none of your concern."

"I beg to disagree, my lord," Blair said sweetly. "Am I not your wife?"

"That's debatable," Graeme groused.

Blair chose to ignore his comment. "As your wife, I have complete authority over the servants, do I not?"

"Under normal circumstances," Graeme allowed. "But our marriage is . . . unusual, to say the least. You are not truly my wife, are you?"

"Father Lachlan would disagree."

"You're avoiding the subject, Blair. As for Glenda, she is answerable to no one but me."

Blair's eyes narrowed. "As you wish, laird."

A smile stretched the corners of Graeme's lips. "Och, lass, you're jealous."

"Jealous!" Blair huffed. "I barely know you. How can I be jealous?"

His smile widened as he extended his hand and stroked her satiny cheek. "I can remedy that, lass. I know a way we can become better acquainted verra quick."

Blair was sorely tempted. Graeme must have noted her indecision. Before she knew how it happened, she was in his arms, his lips plundering hers. Then she felt the blunt force of his tongue exploring her mouth. His hand tangled in her hair, his mouth a bruising pressure as his kiss turned fierce.

The Prophecy, an inner voice warned. *Heed the Prophecy. Dinna lose your heart.*

Of course Blair knew why she couldn't lose her heart but she was in no mood to listen to reason. Graeme's kisses were making her wild to experience the pleasure she had known in her dreams. Her dreams had never shown her the glory of completion with Graeme; they had stopped just short of that wondrous knowledge.

Lust shot through Graeme as swiftly as a sword. He broke off the kiss and lifted his head to stare at Blair. Her eyes were closed, her lips cherry red and wet, her expression dazed.

She's mine, he thought exultantly. Once he bedded her, this mad desire for her would cease. Sweeping her into his arms, he took possession of her lips in a long, slow kiss that was deliberately seductive. With Blair secure in his arms, eagerly returning his kisses, he walked toward the door, wild to be inside her.

Blair must have been aware of his movement, for she shrugged free of his kiss, her eyes wide with alarm. "Where are you taking me?"

"To bed. It's what we both want."

"Nay! Put me down."

"Why are you fighting this? We're wed. The church expects us to have children. And there is only one way for that to happen. Dinna you want children, lass?"

Her face assumed a wistful expression. "Aye, I do . . . but . . ."

She would love to have children. But first she wanted to know why Graeme was so set on having her in his bed. They scarcely knew one another, and he had been a reluctant bridegroom.

"Why do you want me, Graeme? I am not beautiful. You yourself said I am . . . strange, and I am not experienced in bed play." She counted his hesitation in heartbeats.

"You think you're not beautiful?"

"People see no beauty in me, only evil."

He set her on her feet. "I see only beauty. I must admit you're not what I was led to believe."

She smiled sadly. "Did you think I had a wart on my nose and stringy black hair, and flew about on a broomstick?"

His silence answered her question. She turned away.

"If you're convinced I've brought evil to Stonehaven, go away and leave me to my unpacking," Blair said, pushing away from him. "My herbs should be hung from the rafters and my unguents and ointments put away in cupboards."

"So you're denying us again, are you, lass? Verra well, I willna press you. 'Tis your loss, after all. I will have no trouble finding a willing lass to warm my bed."

He turned to leave, then spun around, his expression dark and riveting. "Mind what you do in here. I dinna know what magic you wove last night, but it mustna happen again. 'Tis my final warning."

The aura surrounding him turned dark blue and forbidding. Blair shuddered. Why could she not be like other women? *Because God made you what you are and you canna change it,* responded a small voice inside her. Her mission in life was to heal, and nothing could change the course of her destiny.

After Graeme left, Alyce returned and helped Blair hang bunches of herbs from the ceiling and place everything else on shelves and in cupboards. Then Blair returned to the keep, more than ready to finally break her fast. Graeme sat with his kinsmen, laughing and talking without as much as a glance in her direction. Blair tried to console herself with the knowledge that being ignored by Graeme was best for both of them.

What rankled, however, was the way Glenda fawned over Graeme and how he seemed to bask in her attention. At that moment Blair would have given anything to be like other women.

After Blair finished eating, Jamie arrived to

acquaint her with the keep. They started with the storeroom on the first floor and proceeded floor by floor to the parapet. The keep was small compared to Gairloch, but it had many endearing qualities, such as tapestries on the walls to keep the wind and cold at bay and numerous fireplaces. It was well maintained and had glass windows. The hall was spotless, as were the bedchambers and kitchen, due no doubt to Maeve's vigilance and Jamie's excellent stewardship. Even the garrison was surprisingly neat and clean.

"How many people live within the keep?" Blair asked, impressed by all she had seen.

"It varies," Jamie explained, "depending on the number of guardsmen serving Laird Graeme at any given time. The laird's cousins, Heath and Aiden, live here, as does Stuart, his uncle. And those who serve the laird occupy the third floor. Maeve and I have rooms in the rear of the keep."

Jamie unhooked a ring of keys from his belt and handed them to Blair. "These are yers now."

Blair hesitated. She didn't deserve them. She was a fraud. Though she might be Graeme's chafelaine, she was not his wife in the true sense of the word. But when Jamie pressed the keys into her hand, she accepted them readily enough.

"I'm not trained to run a keep," she admitted. "I'm a healer, and my duties have always been confined to the sick and wounded. I would appreciate it if you continue on as you have before I arrived. The keep is running so smoothly in your capable hands, I see little need to change things."

Jamie grinned. "I shall be happy to continue in my former capacity. But I will still consult with ye when yer opinion is needed. Maeve mentioned that she would like to talk with ye about changes in the menu. She wants to learn what ye like so she can prepare it for ye."

Blair was touched. It seemed that Maeve was willing to accept her, after all, and even wanted to please her.

Later that day Blair met Heath, a somewhat cynical but polite man about Graeme's age, who made no bones about his reservations concerning her marriage to his cousin.

"Graeme is a special mon," Heath told her. "His faith in God was severely tested in France. He was wounded but came back to us. His kinsmen dinna want to see him hurt."

"Graeme fought in France?" Blair gasped. She knew so little about her husband.

"Aye. Ye've heard of Joan the Maid, have ye not?"

"Of course, who hasn't?"

"Graeme went to France to join her fight against England. He was one of the Scotsmen who made up her personal guard."

Puzzled, Blair asked, "Why did Graeme leave his home to fight on foreign soil?"

"He felt strongly that defeating the English in France would diffuse the King's threat to Scotland. Unfortunately, things didna turn out the way he hoped."

Blair shuddered. She felt as if someone had walked over her grave. "Joan was burned at the stake, accused of witchcraft by her own church. I canna imagine a worse death."

"Nor can I," Heath agreed. "Graeme came home a changed mon. Joan meant everything to him."

Blair went still. "He loved her?"

Heath cleared his throat and looked away, as if realizing he had spoken too freely. "I dinna know, lass. Ye'll have to ask my cousin about that." Suddenly his expression turned hard, his gaze probing. "What I'm trying to tell ye is that Graeme needs no more witch-craft in his life. He wed ye to repay a debt to yer father, he is that honorable. But I will do all in my power to protect him against ye."

Stunned by the vehemence of Heath's warning, Blair said, "I wouldna harm Graeme even if I could. Excuse me, I must attend to my duties."

Blair hurried off, only to bump into Alyce.

"Blair, what ails ye, lass? Ye look pale."

"Naught is wrong, Alyce."

"Dinna lie, lass. I know ye better than anyone. Did Laird Graeme upset ye?"

"Did you know that Graeme fought in France? He was one of Joan the Maid's guards. She was accused of witchcraft and burned at the stake, if you recall. 'Tis no wonder Graeme holds witchcraft in such contempt."

"Worry not, lass. Ye are a Faery Woman, not a witch."

"They are one and the same to Graeme."

"But we know better, dinna we?"

Little comfort that was, Blair reflected. "Are you headed to the kitchen? I am going to confer with Maeve about the menu."

"Go along with ye, then, I am off to the stillroom to mix up a batch of burn salve to add to our dwindling supply."

After Blair conferred with Maeve, she joined Alyce in the stillroom. She found the older woman grinding herbs with a pestle. The scent of yarrow root and mallow permeated the air, reminding Blair of home and her father. She'd not had time to mourn him, and she ached from her loss. Perhaps later she would go to the chapel and pray for his immortal soul. There did not seem to be a resident priest at Stonehaven, but she needed no one to assist her in her prayers.

Blair and Alyce worked together in companionable silence until the supper hour approached.

Alyce placed her hands behind her back and stretched. "The hour grows late. Ye'd best change yer soiled gown before ye join yer husband in the hall."

"You're tired, too, Alyce. Return to the keep. I will follow in a few minutes. I want to put these jars in the cupboard before I leave."

Alyce nodded and left. Blair finished her work and was preparing to leave when a loud knock sounded on the door. Surprised, Blair hurried to answer the call, guessing that someone was in need of her healing powers.

A lass of about twelve years, with tears streaming down her cheeks, fell to her knees before Blair and grasped her hand. "Please, my lady, I heard ye were a healer. Can ye help my mother?"

Blair raised the child to her feet. "What's wrong with your mother, lassie? I have to know what ails her before I can help her."

"She is in childbed, but the bairn willna come. She's in terrible pain. I dinna know where else to turn."

Blair closed her eyes. The vision that formed behind her eyes showed a tiny girl child struggling for life inside her mother's womb.

"Where is your father?"

"Papa went to Inverness. He said he'd return before the bairn arrived, but something must have delayed him. Will ye come, lady?"

"Of course," Blair said without hesitation.

"Where do you live?"

"In the village."

"Give me a moment to gather what I need."

Moving swiftly, Blair placed several pouches of dried herbs, various jars and bottles and clean linen cloths into a basket. Briefly she considered telling Graeme where she was going but decided against it. Her first duty was to the suffering woman. Explanations could wait.

The girl, whose name was Carla, lived with her mother, Mab, and two younger brothers in a cottage in the village. Blair heard Mab's pitiful moans before they reached the rowan tree planted at the front door to ward off evil spirits. Inside, Mab wasn't alone. Several neighbor women and the local midwife were gathered around the bed, each trying to help Mab in her own way. Everyone fell silent when Blair entered the crowded bedchamber.

The air inside was fetid, nearly stifling, and the first thing Blair did was to fling open the shutters.

"Here now, what are ye doing?" a woman challenged. "I'm Gunna, the midwife, and I dinna need yer help."

"Aye, she *is* needed!" Carla insisted. "I brought her. Mama's suffering has been going on for two days."

"Two days!" Blair gasped. "Please move aside. Mab needs my help."

" 'Tis the witch," someone murmured. Others picked up the whisper, until the small chamber was abuzz with the word. The women backed away, their expressions wary, even fearful. But the midwife refused to budge.

"Who gave ye leave to interfere?"

Blair saw no help for it. In order to save Mab and her unborn child, she would be forced to exert her authority. "As your laird's wife, I need no authority save my own. Leave, all of you, except you." She pointed to an elderly woman who appeared less judgmental than the others. "What is your name?"

"Rona, mistress."

"Have you ever helped birth a bairn, Rona?"

"Oh, aye, mistress, many times. I assist the midwife."

"Good. Are you willing to help me?"

"Aye, mistress."

"Now see here," Gunna said pugnaciously. "I have birthed bairns in this village since long before ye were born."

"I am not trying to usurp your position, but you've had your chance. As you can plainly see, Mab needs more help than you can provide."

"Let the laird's wife help me, Gunna," Mab said weakly. "I dinna want to lose my bairn."

Hissing her disapproval, Gunna stormed from the chamber, taking everyone but Rona with her.

"Can I stay?" Carla asked.

"Nay, child," Blair replied kindly. "See to your young brothers. They have need of you now. Rest assured that your mother is in good hands."

Blair rolled up her sleeves and got to work. Since Mab appeared to be weakened by long hours of labor, Blair decided the poor woman needed something stronger to dull the pain than a stick to bite on. Rummaging in her basket, she retrieved a pouch of dried leaves.

"Raspberry leaves," she said, handing them to Rona. "Heat some water and brew the leaves into a strong tea. The tea will ease Mab's labor."

"Can ye help me, mistress?" Mab asked, writhing in pain as another contraction contorted her body.

Once she was alone with her patient, Blair placed her hand on Mab's heaving stomach and closed her eyes. Immediately a picture of the bairn inside Mab formed before Blair's eyes. The tiny girl was turned wrong and trying to present herself feet first. Blair felt a faint heartbeat vibrating through her arm to her own heart, and she smiled. The tiny mite was a fighter, but she was in deep trouble. The birth must be hurried along.

"Close your eyes, Mab, and try to concentrate on your bairn," Blair said in a soothing voice. "Dinna think about the pain. It will soon be gone."

Silently imploring the spirits to ease Mab's suffering, Blair relied on her powers, willingly taking Mab's pain into her own body. A jolt of pain shot up her arm, so excruciating she cried out. Then she felt Mab relax beneath her hand, and, as she knew it would, Mab's pain passed through Blair's body, leaving her drained.

"What happened?" Mab asked. "The pain is gone. Oh, lady, ye are a miracle worker."

Rona chose that moment to return, bringing a mug of steaming tea. "Is Mab . . . is she . . . Her wailing stopped, and I feared the worst."

"Mab is fine," Blair said, "but we must hurry if we are to bring a healthy bairn into this world. Help Mab drink the tea, then fetch me a basin of hot water and soap."

Rona held the mug to Mab's mouth until the cup was drained. Then she hurried off to fetch the hot water and soap.

Blair's hand was still on Mab's abdomen when Rona returned, but now Blair was frowning. She sensed the bairn's distress and worried over her survival. Turning away from Mab, she washed her hands thoroughly and sent Rona out again for a fresh basin of warm water to bathe the bairn and swaddling clothes to wrap her in. Then she set to work to deliver the child.

Blair glanced at Mab, saw that she was still relatively pain free but somewhat dazed, and decided that was a good thing. "I'm going to turn the bairn so she can be born," she told Mab. "Clear your mind and think of naught but holding your little girl in your arms." Her voice flowed slow and smooth as she stared deep into Mab's eyes. "You will feel naught, Mab. I have taken away your pain. Relax until I tell you to push."

"Aye, my lady," Mab said, her glazed eyes never leaving Blair's face.

Blair set to work. Slowly, with an expertise gained from knowledge passed down through generations of Faery Women, she turned the bairn.

"Push, Mab."

The child was delivered into Blair's capable hands moments later, but Blair saw that the babe was in dire straits.

"You have a daughter, Mab," Blair said as she tied off the cord. To Rona, who had just returned with the basin of warm water, she said, "Deliver the afterbirth and see to Mab. The bairn needs my attention."

"The babe isna crying," Rona said, worry coloring her words.

"Is my bairn dead?" Mab cried.

Blair ignored their questions. She was now fighting against time and had much to do if the bairn was to live. The babe's lips were blue and her skin was ash gray, and Blair could scarcely detect a heartbeat in the tiny chest. Lowering the babe into the basin of warm water, Blair washed her and cleared mucus from her mouth. The babe did not respond. Blair closed her eyes, invoked God's grace and began to massage the thin chest above her struggling heart.

Within minutes she felt vibrations. Then the babe gasped and let out a lusty cry. Immediately her lips turned a healthy pink and her skin lost its pallor.

"She lives! I heard her cry!" Mab called from the bed.

Blair wrapped the tiny bairn in swaddling clothes and brought her to Mab, laying her gently in her mother's arms. When she looked up, she saw Graeme standing in the doorway. She hurried over to him and all but pushed him out the door.

"What are you doing here?"

"When you didna show up at supper I asked around, and Stuart recalled seeing you leave the keep with someone from the village. I wanted to know what mischief you were up to and followed."

"How long have you been standing there?"

"Long enough to know the bairn was stillborn. What did you do to bring it back to life?" He backed away, his expression a mixture of awe and revulsion. "Did you use magic? Can you raise the dead? Is that one of your powers?"

"The bairn wasna dead," Blair contended. "I canna raise the dead. Only God can do that."

"What about the mother? The women waiting outside for word of the birth said they thought Mab had died because her moans and screams stopped moments after you arrived. The midwife isna pleased with you. You've gone too far. You've furthered your reputation as a witch and earned an enemy."

"I helped a mother bring a child into the world tonight," Blair protested. She pushed past him. "I must leave instructions for Mab's care with Rona before I go."

Blair returned to the bedroom and gathered up her things. After leaving several pouches of herbs with instructions for their use, she left the small cottage. Graeme trailed behind her.

"May my brothers and I see my mother and new sister, my lady?" Carla asked timidly.

"Your mother is resting right now, but I'm sure she'd like to see you. Dinna stay too long."

Carla grasped Blair's hand and kissed it. "Thank ye, my lady. I dinna care what Gunna says, ye canna be a witch."

As a path opened up for her outside the

cottage, Blair decided Carla was the only one of that opinion. The fierce scowls that Gunna and her cronies directed at her did not bode well for her future at Stonehaven. The tense atmosphere crackled with a word that brought fear to her heart.

Witch.

"Go home," Graeme ordered the gaggle of women. "There is naught more you can do here. Mab and her bairn are well and in good hands."

As if to confirm his words, Rona appeared in the doorway, holding the babe in her arms. "The laird speaks the truth," she said, "and we have his lady to thank."

The smile she bestowed upon Blair told her she had made at least one friend in the village. In time, she hoped to gain the trust of those who feared her powers, and that included her husband.

"You shouldna have gone off on your own," Graeme chided. "Have you any idea how worried I was when I learned you had gone to the village alone? Scotsmen are a superstitious lot, as you well know. They dinna trust you yet. You put yourself in grave danger by venturing out alone."

"Mab's bairn was in distress and I couldna afford to delay."

Disbelief marched across Graeme's face. "How did you know that?"

"I . . . sensed it," Blair hedged. "Carla was

most insistent that I leave immediately, and so I did."

"You made a powerful enemy," Graeme said as he grasped Blair's arm and guided her along the path to the keep. A misty darkness had settled over the hills and rose up from the ground in eerie tendrils. The footing could be treacherous unless one was accustomed to traveling the path.

"Gunna is a trusted midwife. You should not have interfered. You must promise to be more circumspect in the future."

A wolf howled, and a shiver ran down Graeme's spine. 'Twas a perfect night for spirits and ghouls, if one believed in them.

"I canna make that promise," Blair demurred. "I must go where I am needed."

Graeme halted. The pressure on her arm brought Blair to a standstill beside him. "What is it, Graeme?" she asked.

"*I* need you, Blair."

A tense silence ensued. When she spoke, her words held a world of regret. " 'Tis not the same thing, Graeme. Loving you would be so easy, but . . ."

"But what?"

"Unless my love is returned, I will lose my powers."

"What you ask of me is impossible. I scarcely know you. I would like to know you better, but you willna allow it. Mayhap in time we would come to love one another."

"Until that day comes, I canna risk giving you my heart."

"Then give me your body."

She inhaled sharply and backed away.

"What's wrong, lass? I didna ask for your heart."

"Aye, you did, Graeme Campbell," she whispered. "I canna give you my body, for to do so would leave my heart vulnerable to love. I dinna want to lose my soul to you."

His hand remained on her arm, a visible reminder of his strength. "What if I said I loved you?"

"Then I would say you're a liar, Graeme Campbell."

Was he a liar? Graeme wondered. Had a Faery Woman he scarcely knew stolen his heart?

Nay, he decided. Only a madman would love a witch.

Chapter Five

During the following days, Graeme's words haunted Blair's every thought. How dare he lie to her! He couldn't possibly love her. His words had been meant to confuse her. He wanted her in his bed and would say anything to get her there. Even more shocking was the fact that she *wanted* to be in his bed. The only thing stopping her was the Prophecy.

Already a few of Graeme's braver kinsmen had sought her counsel for various ailments. She had treated minor burns with salves, used willow juice extracted from the bark and leaves of that tree to ease aches related to fever and colds, and dispensed red clover to colicky bairns. While she was careful to give no one a reason to fear her, she was still considered evil by Gunna and her cronies.

The midwife had made Blair a target for all the anger and hatred in the village. Each day Alyce reported new gossip circulating among the servants, most of it concerning witchcraft and the dark arts.

Blair saw little of Graeme during those

days. Obviously, he was avoiding her. One night, when the full moon rode high in the sky, Blair was lured to the stillroom by her inner voice. It was almost as if the spirits were calling to her, drawing her from her chamber with invisible cords. All that day a feeling of impending doom had troubled her. She could no more ignore the spirits than she could deny herself air.

Blair donned a robe over her flimsy night rail and quietly left her chamber. It was after midnight, and no one stirred within the keep as she tiptoed down the stairs, lighting the way with a candle. She arrived at the stillroom without incident, placed the candle on her worktable and quietly began her preparations.

Using a chalky stone she had brought with her from Gairloch, she drew a circle on the flagstones before the open window and sprinkled dried herbs inside. Then she placed candles at measured intervals around the circle, stepped inside and lit them with a faggot she had ignited from the candle.

When the candles burned strong and their flames began to change color, the moon suddenly appeared to grow brighter, shedding its light through the open window and arraying Blair in a silvery glow. Raising her arms, Blair reached out to embrace the light, opening her soul to the forces of nature and inviting the spirits into her mind and heart.

Then she chanted:

> "Spirits, come to me,
> Open my eyes and let me see."

A mist formed before her eyes as an errant breeze blew through the window, lifting the heavy weight of her hair and setting her skirts aflutter. Then the mist slowly cleared and she saw her brother as clearly as if he were standing before her. He was not alone. Donal MacKay was with him.

"What does it mean?" she cried out to the spirits. "What are you trying to tell me?"

A voice wafted to her on the wind, soft, low, urgent. "They will come and you will be forever changed."

"How will I change?"

The voice echoed hollowly in the small space. "You know what you must do to survive. Cleave to your husband. There will be trials. Beware of fire, water and stone."

"What about my husband? Will these trials you speak of affect him?"

"Only he can save you."

"I dinna understand. Niall and the MacKay can no longer harm me."

The voice was but a fading whisper. "To foil their plans, you must become a wife . . . a wife . . . a wife . . ." The words trailed off, leaving Blair more confused than ever.

"Wait, dinna leave! I am already a wife.

What more must I do?"

The reply was faint but still audible. "Danger stalks both you and your husband."

A gust of cold wind blew over her, leaving her flesh chilled and her heart icy with dread. Squeezing her eyes tightly shut, Blair willed the spirits to return, but they remained stubbornly silent. The images of her brother and MacKay were gone, but she felt their threat keenly. The spirits had revealed a great deal, yet little of it made sense.

Blair extinguished the candles and stepped outside the circle. She returned the candles to the cupboard, swept up the herbs and threw a straw mat over the circle. Then she left the stillroom and returned to the keep.

Graeme moved away from the window, his expression hardened by a mixture of disbelief and horror. It had been pure chance that he was still awake at midnight and had walked to the window in time to see Blair entering the stillroom. He couldn't account for his restlessness as he'd prowled his chamber. But he knew what had drawn him to the window. Dazzling light from the full moon had flooded his chamber, and his intention had been to close the shutters so he could fall asleep.

Blair had caught his attention immediately as she entered the stillroom. His first instinct had been to follow and see what she was up to. Then something strange happened. The moon seemed to grow brighter, momentarily blinding Graeme.

He was so stunned, time seemed to stand still. What was happening inside the stillroom? Was Blair practicing black magic? Was she conjuring evil spirits? Communicating with the devil? He shook his head in dismay. Nothing so dramatic, he'd wager. But he fully intended to find out what she was up to.

Before he could will his body to move, he spied Blair leaving the stillroom. He watched her return to the keep, then left his chamber.

Blair's mind was in total confusion as she made her way back to her bedchamber. The message she had received was neither comforting nor comprehensible. As she set the candle down on the nightstand, she felt prickles along her spine. She sensed that she wasn't alone. She froze and peered into the shadows beyond the ring of candlelight.

"Who's there?"

A figure emerged. A tall man blessed with broad shoulders, slim waist and massive chest. He wore a plaid held in place by a wide belt and naught else. Blair backed away from the menace inherent in his stance.

"What are you doing here?"

" 'Tis my home. I go where I please."

"Go away."

"What were you doing in the stillroom?

What kind of spell were you casting?"

"I dinna cast spells. I commune with the spirits of nature."

His brows lifted. "In the middle of the night?"

"The time doesna matter. I answer their call when they summon me."

"Stop it, Blair! Stop it right now! There are no spirits. There is only God, and He doesna speak to mere mortals. You are not making my vow to protect you easy. What if someone had seen you going to the stillroom at this hour? What if someone had misinterpreted your purpose and accused you of witchcraft? Must I lock you inside your chamber at night?"

Blair needed to make Graeme understand that danger stalked him as well as her. She had to find a way to reach him. "Listen to me, Graeme. There is something you should know."

He sent her a skeptical look. "Go on."

"Niall and Donal MacKay are planning mischief."

"What kind of mischief?" he asked. "Should I be afraid?"

"Aye, verra afraid. Alert your kinsmen and take precautions to protect yourself and your property."

Impatiently Graeme lanced his fingers through his disheveled hair. "How do you know this?"

"I . . . just know."

"Give me proof."

She shook her head. "I canna. You have to trust me."

"Your information isna substantial enough to act upon. I refuse to frighten my kinsmen for something you perceive but canna prove."

"The spirits —"

"What spirits?" Graeme challenged. "Evil spirits?"

"Nay! Dinna make me out to be something other than what I am. The spirits warned me of impending danger. Sometimes they come to me in dreams and visions."

Amusement colored his words. "What did they tell you tonight? Did those spiritual beings chide you for avoiding my bed?"

He was closer to the truth than Blair cared to admit. "I have told you what they said, but you dinna believe me. My brother isna a good man, and Donal MacKay is even worse. Together they present a real threat to us."

"We are wed, Blair. Niall can do naught to harm either of us. You are safe here at Stonehaven."

"What can I say to convince you to heed my warning? The danger to us is verra real. I know not how or when or what form it will take, but it will come."

Graeme paced forward until they were standing nose to nose. "I refuse to be frightened by vague threats. Your imagination is truly amazing, lass." His fingers curled around her shoulders. "I promised your father I would take care of you, and that includes protecting you from your own follies. Forget this nonsense about spirits and voices and concentrate on honing your healing skills. Give my kinsmen no reason to fear you."

His voice was so stern, Blair tried to edge away, but he would not allow it. His face, half hidden by shadows, was set in determined lines. "I mean what I say, Blair. Mayhap you should sleep in my bed so I can make sure you dinna wander off in the middle of the night."

She stared up at him, her eyes wide and her mouth open. Suddenly the whole world was held in his blue eyes and she could not look away. The glint in Graeme's gaze should have warned her about the temptation her lush lips posed. Without any other warning, he brought his mouth down hard on hers. Magic enveloped her and she lost herself in the sweet bliss of his kiss, in the intoxicating sensation of his strong arms holding her against him, and the liquid warmth surging through her.

But even as she enjoyed his kiss, Blair hated knowing that Graeme could make her want him so. Her strength was her pride. She was no weak creature whose life wasn't complete without a man. Vaguely she wondered if

Graeme had any idea of the effect he had upon her. God willing, he did not.

But she could not deny that his kisses excited her. Without volition, her body pressed forward to meld with his. Despite the pleasure she felt, she was both angry and humiliated at the way her nipples hardened and at the blossoming warmth between her legs. Then the words she had heard earlier in the stillroom came back to haunt her. If she had interpreted their advice correctly, the spirits wanted her to become Graeme's wife in every way. Still, she found it difficult to believe they wanted her to lie with Graeme, to take him into her body and become one with him.

That thought was so exciting, she unconsciously allowed herself to be drawn deeper into Graeme's kiss, to meet his tongue thrust for thrust, to open her mouth and taste him fully. Her mouth was seared by his branding possession, and she realized that she had never been closer to losing her powers than she was now. Then she felt his hand on her breast, burning her flesh through the material of her night rail and robe, and she knew that if she allowed him to consummate their marriage, she would be forever changed, just as the spirits had warned.

Blair was already half in love with Graeme and feared that the communion of their bodies would spell the end of her powers . . . unless he loved her in return. And that was not likely to happen.

She tried to bat his hand away, but he held it firmly against her breast. The iron clench of his jaw bespoke his determination, but she was just as determined to withhold herself from him.

"What are you doing?" she cried, breaking free of the kiss. "What do you want from me?"

"Naught but that which is my right to claim. Do you deny that my kisses move you? A man can tell when a woman is attracted to him. And a man has needs. Why should I satisfy them elsewhere when I have a wife?"

"I willna lie, Graeme. I am attracted to you, and your kisses do move me, but I canna give up my powers for physical pleasure. The day you tell me you love me is the day I give my body to you."

He drew back as if struck. "You want me to lie? I can never love anyone but —"

"You love a dead woman!" Blair charged. "Heath told me about Joan the Maid."

"Heath shouldna have regaled you with tales, but since he has, I willna lie. There will never be another Joan. I worshiped her for her integrity, her innocence, her zeal and her unwavering faith. I loved her as a mortal loves a goddess, too far above me to touch. 'Tis difficult to imagine myself in love with a woman less worthy than Joan. Since the world will never see another Joan, love has ceased to exist for me."

Blair's heart sank. How could she compete with a saint? Her situation was hopeless. No matter what the spirits had told her, Graeme would never love her, and she would never know the fulfillment of physical love.

"You should leave," Blair said. " 'Tis late, and we both need our sleep."

"Not until I impress upon you the folly you are courting. I was there for Joan's trial. I saw her die. I watched the flames lick at her frail body. People called her a witch. Think you I want the same fate for you?"

It suddenly dawned on Blair what Graeme wanted. "You want me to fall in love with you, even though you know you canna return my love."

" 'Tis far better to lose your powers than to die such a cruel death. 'Twas not a pretty sight. I am not convinced you possess magical powers, mind you, but 'tis not impossible. If you believe loving me will cause you to lose those powers, I consider that a good thing and am determined to make it happen. I intend to protect you, Blair, even from yourself. You are your own worst enemy."

"I refuse to let you into my heart, Graeme Campbell," Blair declared.

"Mayhap I am already there," he hinted, then frowned when he realized what he had said. "Love me with your body. Prove that you are immune to me."

Blair dragged in a shaky breath. "You know I am not immune to you."

"Do your powers mean so much to you?"

"They are the reason for my being."

"I canna protect you if you dinna cooperate."

Blair squared her shoulders. "I dinna ask for your protection. Unlike my father, I dinna believe marriage to you will protect me from those who wish me harm."

"I will leave you with one thought," Graeme said. "Love me or not, I will do what I must to protect you. And that means stopping you from conjuring unnatural powers and evil spirits. Heed me well, Blair. Think twice about flaunting my authority. I will ban you from the stillroom if I must." With those words, he departed from the chamber.

Exhausted and confused, Blair sought her bed. Her flesh still burned where Graeme had touched her, and her lips were on fire. Curling into a ball beneath the covers, she cleared her mind of disturbing thoughts and willed herself to sleep.

The dream started almost immediately. People were standing over her as she lay helplessly upon a bed. The dream became a nightmare when she saw her brother Niall and Donal MacKay, their expressions harsh as they forced her back against the mattress when she tried to rise. Then another figure moved into her line of vision.

Gunna the midwife!

Rough hands shoved her legs apart, and Gunna moved between them. The scream died in Blair's throat as the dream ended abruptly. She was panting and bathed in sweat. The warning in the dream was explicit.

Niall and Donal MacKay had not accepted her marriage to Graeme and intended to destroy it. The dream implied that Niall suspected she might still be virginal and intended to prove it in order to annul her marriage to Graeme.

Niall hated her for many reasons. He had always resented their kinsmen's loyalty to her and was jealous of her father's love. But more than that, he feared her. The times he had accused her of witchcraft and sought to turn their kinsmen against her were too numerous to count. Against her father's wishes, he had promised her to MacKay, who was even more evil than Niall. Once she was under his control, Blair knew MacKay would exploit her powers.

Blair could not allow that to happen. Her powers were to be used to heal and help those she cared about. Faery Women were free to choose their own life course, and she had chosen the path of goodness. She knew exactly what she had to do to foil Niall's nefarious plans for her.

Blair slid out of bed and faced the connecting door between her chamber and Graeme's. She reached for her chamber robe, then decided against it. She would go to Graeme as she was. Her knees were quaking as she reached for the candlestick and marched resolutely toward her destiny.

The door opened noiselessly beneath her fingers, and she stepped into the chamber. Her gaze went immediately to the large bed swathed in thick curtains.

If she hadn't been convinced this was necessary, she would have fled. Resolutely she crept forward, her thoughts focused on what would — nay, must — take place in the bed very soon. The breath left her in a whoosh when the bed hangings parted and Graeme burst through, a wicked-looking claymore in his hand.

"What the hell!" he roared when he saw Blair's shaking form. He dropped the claymore. "Never, ever sneak up on me like that. I could have killed you."

"I . . . I . . ." Words failed her.

Graeme was naked, poised on limbs as sturdy as twin oaks. Every muscle and tendon in his body rippled with suppressed energy. Blair's admiring gaze wandered over his massive torso and broad shoulders. When he had burst from the bed she had been frightened, but that was no longer true. She was totally, thoroughly mesmerized.

Slowly her gaze slid lower, pausing at the juncture of his thighs, where his manhood was beginning to stir to life. Blair wanted to look elsewhere but could not bear to turn her eyes away.

"Keep looking at me like that and naught will stop me from dragging you into my bed and taking my pleasure. What are you doing here? You made it clear you wanted naught to do with me."

"A woman can change her mind, can she not?"

Graeme was utterly flummoxed. If Blair had said she was flying to the moon, he could not have been more shocked. She looked very small and vulnerable standing before him in her shift, hair like spun gold tumbling about her shoulders and violet eyes huge in her pale face. She looked like an angel come to earth, but he knew better.

Clearly she was up to something.

He grabbed his plaid and wound it about his waist. "Exactly what have you changed your mind about, lass? What is so important that you would creep into my chamber in the middle of the night?"

"I . . . I . . . This is difficult, Graeme."

He reached her in three long steps and grasped her shoulders. "Just say what you came to say."

He watched intently as she swallowed hard and appeared to gather her courage. When she looked up at him, he forgot everything but the clawing hunger for his wife eating at his vitals. Nonetheless, he held himself aloof, waiting for her to tell him what she wanted from him. He prayed it was the same thing he wanted.

She closed the narrow gap between them, pressing so close, the heat of her body singed him. He groaned as if in pain when her pink tongue darted out to moisten her lips. He was so intent upon those lush lips, he had to concentrate to make sense of her words.

"I want to be a real wife to you, Graeme. Now. Tonight."

Surely he hadn't heard right. Why now? Why tonight? "You want me to make love to you? What changed your mind? Did you decide that preserving your powers was not worth denying yourself the pleasure of the marriage bed?"

Blair debated revealing her dream to Graeme but feared he would laugh at her. When future happenings were revealed to her in her dreams, she knew they would come true, but Graeme was an unbeliever. Their marriage had to be consummated if she wished to escape Niall's machinations.

"I was wrong to deny you," Blair said. "You are my husband."

Graeme pushed her away from him, his eyebrows raised in disbelief. "What happened to change your mind? Am I suddenly so attractive to you that you canna resist me?"

Consternation darkened Blair's brow. This wasn't going the way she'd thought it would. Why was Graeme being so stubborn? A sudden fear drained her face of color. Had her unwillingness to let him bed her killed his desire for her?

"Dinna you want me, Graeme?"

His harsh exhalation gave her hope. "You think I dinna want you? You know better than that." He searched her face. "I wonder . . . Aren't you afraid you'll lose your powers? What happened to change your mind after I left your chamber?"

"I decided I could never love you," Blair lied, thinking fast. "My powers will remain intact as long as love isna involved in our marriage." Refusing to look him in the eye, she added, "I dinna like the idea of another woman in your bed." That, at least, was the truth.

He stared at her so long, Blair began to tremble beneath his intent gaze. What was he thinking? Why was he hesitating?

"Tell me the truth, Blair. Why are you here?"

Blair sighed. There was no help for it. Graeme wanted the truth, and she would have to tell him if she wanted his cooperation. "I had a dream."

"A dream? Is that what this is all about?"

"Dinna scoff, Graeme. My dreams are portents of the future."

He led her to the bed and urged her to sit down. Looming over her, he said, "What part of the dream convinced you to come to my bed?" He took her hand between his; she was trembling and wondered if he could tell.

"Niall and the MacKay."

Graeme stiffened. "What about them? We are wed — they can do naught to hurt you now."

"They are coming to Stonehaven. Niall doesna believe we have a legal marriage, and he intends to give me to MacKay if he finds I am still a maiden."

"And of course you are," Graeme said. "Did your dream tell you how they will prove your state of innocence?"

Suddenly he went still, as if the answer had abruptly dawned on him. "Your stepbrother wouldna dare! Think you I would let him put his hands on you?"

"If I dreamed it, it will happen."

"So you decided 'twas time to consummate our marriage and came to my chamber to seduce me."

"I dinna like MacKay. He is a greedy man. I know not how or why, but he intends to exploit my powers."

"Am I the lesser of two evils?"

"You are my husband. You are the only man with the right to . . . my body."

"Can you make love with me without engaging your emotions?"

"I believe I can. I know now you are a man I canna love so neither my heart nor my powers are in danger."

The corners of Graeme's mouth lifted. "I dinna believe that dreams can come true, but I am perfectly willing to make love to you." Gripping her shoulders, he gazed into her eyes, his challenge palpable. "Kiss me, lass."

There were both question and demand in his blue eyes as his gaze searched hers. Blair tried to look away, fearing he would see through her lies, but could not. Risking her powers was indeed the lesser of two evils, but, oh, she had a feeling she was going to enjoy this.

Hesitating but a moment, Blair lifted her face and touched her mouth to his. The meeting of their lips was like setting fire to tinder, and Blair shuddered as her body turned to liquid fire. Graeme's mouth clamped down tight over hers, stealing her breath. His kiss was not gentle. It seemed that all his suppressed passion of the past several days had exploded into that one kiss.

The blunt force of his tongue exploring her mouth sent a jolt of desire shooting through her. The stirrings of passion she had felt when Graeme kissed her before were naught compared to the stark need clawing at her now. Mindlessly she pressed closer to him, hunger for more than his kisses blinding her to the Prophecy.

Chapter Six

Blair was vaguely aware that Graeme was moving her, pivoting her until she was lying on the bed. She gasped when he pushed up the hem of her shift, reluctant to let him remove her last shred of modesty.

She stilled his hand. "Must you?"

"Aye. You have no idea how I have been burning for you." He nudged her legs apart with the barest stroke of his thumb. "I need to see all of you, taste all of you. And when I have looked and tasted my fill, I want to feel you melt around me."

His name quivered on her lips when he stripped her of her shift and tossed it aside. She tried to hide herself from him, but he would not allow it. Then her legs suddenly went boneless as his fingers slid between them and into the moist cleft of her womanhood.

"Oh . . . You must not."

"Aye, I must."

He stroked her with an expertise that left her breathless and panting for more. Was this the way it was supposed to be between a man and a woman? Graeme seemed to know exactly what to do, alternating from a slow, rhythmic slide of his finger between the petals of her sex to a frenzied friction that had her clutching at him in frantic torment.

She moaned in frustration, unsure what lay beyond the titillation of Graeme's talented hands and fearing she would never be the same afterward. Then he kissed her, and the world fell away beneath her. Her body arched into his, her senses heightened by the scent of his arousal; she felt herself spinning out of control.

When his lips abandoned hers, she wanted to grasp his thick black hair and pull him back, but he took his loving to a higher level, bringing his mouth down to suckle her nipples. She felt her breasts swell as liquid heat rushed through her veins. Nothing in her life had prepared her for this.

She thought all she had to do was lie on her back and let Graeme have his way, but naught was going the way she had imagined. Never would she have thought her body capable of such intense feelings. Pleasure was a bonus she had not anticipated.

"Your breasts are perfect," he whispered. "Everything about you is perfect."

Abruptly he went still, as if suddenly aware of what he had said. Then he reared back and stared at her.

"What is it?" Blair asked, confused by his

sudden withdrawal.

Graeme withheld a reply as he reached for a candlestick and held it high above her. She squirmed beneath his dark, probing gaze, wondering what he was looking for.

"Turn around. I want to see your backside," Graeme ordered.

A groan of dismay trembled from her lips. She knew, oh God, she knew. Graeme was looking for a witch's mark upon her body. What must she do to convince him of her innocence? She was angry, angrier than she had ever been. How dare he doubt her! She started to draw away, but Graeme flipped her over and held her down before she realized what he intended. She protested violently when she felt his hand glide over her bottom and down her legs.

"What did you expect to find?" she asked when he flipped her over on her back. "Nay, dinna answer, I already know. You were looking for a witch's mark upon my skin."

Graeme shrugged. "I'm sorry, lass. I had to know."

"Did you find what you were looking for?"

"I found naught but smooth, unblemished skin." He lowered his head and kissed her abdomen. "You are flawless, lass." With a flick of his wrist, he removed his plaid. "I hope you find me as tempting as I find you."

Were all men as magnificently endowed as Graeme? she wondered. Somehow she doubted it. The sheer power of his sex, thrusting proudly from the thatch of dark curls at his groin, and the frightening size of him gave her second thoughts about consummating their marriage. Never would she be able to take all of him. This was a mistake. She lurched up from the bed, intending to flee.

As if aware of her thoughts, Graeme anchored her against the mattress with his hard body. The engorged length of his erection pressed against her belly, hot as fire and smooth as satin. A droplet of pearly moisture beaded from the thick, blunt head of his sex as it slid between them, warm and slick upon her skin.

"You are not going anywhere," he whispered against her ear. "You came to my bedchamber for this, did you not?"

"I . . . had no idea it would be like this. I canna surrender so much of myself to you."

His voice was a seductive purr as he began a slow exploration with his hands. "Can you not?"

The wonderment of what she felt returned, then swelled into something powerful, something demanding. She thought she would go mad with the pleasure of the moment, but it was naught compared to the jolt of raw sensation that struck her the instant he slid down her body, spread her legs and put his mouth to her intimate flesh.

His tongue touched her, warm and wet and rough against the tender pearl of sensation Graeme found there. She cried out and attempted to push him away, for the emotional impact was too much, too raw.

"Nay. Dinna try to escape the feeling," Graeme murmured. "It's all right. I willna hurt you."

How could anything so intense, so intimate, be all right? Without volition she began moving her hips in concert with Graeme's carnal kiss, propelled by an unnamed urgency. She arched and twisted beneath the persistent pressure of his mouth, fearing she would fly apart. As if aware of her dilemma, he held her hips down to keep her steady, coaxing her further into madness with tender kisses and tentative brushes of his mouth and tongue.

She buried her fingers in his hair and pulled him closer, moaning in frustration because she had no idea what it was she wanted from him.

Graeme must have known precisely what she wanted, for he shifted upward, his sex poised at the juncture of her thighs. She looked up at him and caught her breath. His body, bathed in silvery moonlight, was thick-muscled and elegant, his limbs and torso cast into fascinating relief. His features were stark with need, his eyes glazed with passion. She felt his muscles tense as he slowly melded their bodies, and she waited in stoic acceptance for him to begin his brutal assault. Was that not what all men did?

She did not realize she was holding her breath until she felt Graeme's sex prodding against her narrow opening; then she let it out in a whoosh. She closed her eyes and waited for the pain she knew would come when he tore into her.

"Relax, lass. I'll try not to hurt you too badly."

"You willna fit! This isna a good idea."

"This is a wonderful idea."

He edged forward, slowly slipping inside her. She felt herself stretching to accommodate him, felt pressure . . . a lot of pressure. Then there was a fiery tearing as he thrust his hard length all the way into her tight passage, a burning that pierced through her and left beads of perspiration on her brow.

"Stop! Take it out!"

" 'Tis done," he panted. "This is what you wanted, what you came here for."

He moved within her slowly, deliberately holding himself back. Though he tried to be careful, he was large, and almost too much for her tender passage. But as he moved deeper inside her, something happened. She began to feel pleasure despite the pain, pleasure that came from the slow, sensual friction of his shaft inside her body and the silken slide of his skin against hers.

Blair clung to him, suspended in a place somewhere between pleasure and pain as he thrust and withdrew, each deep penetration seeming to impale her to her very soul. The spirits had been right. This would change her forever.

Her thoughts skidded to a halt as she felt herself spinning away from reality, felt the pain of her breached maidenhead dissipate as spiraling ecstasy began to swell inside her. Closing her eyes, she clung to him, burying her fingers in the crisp hair on his chest and clutching at him as he rocked inside her.

The force of Graeme's passion was pushing her higher and higher, into a state of breathless rapture. "Graeme!" Her back rose up off the bed as he pumped harder, deeper, faster, burying himself to the hilt inside her. Then she was soaring, meeting his thrusts with an almost desperate urgency. She felt the earth careening, felt bliss building scant moments before a dizzying wave of release lifted her and swept her away.

Her climax was totally unexpected. She had no idea women could experience the same earth-shattering release that men felt. Distantly, she heard herself sobbing Graeme's name as she floated slowly back to earth.

" 'Tis my turn, lass," he growled, kissing her slack mouth as he renewed his assault on her quivering body.

With a wordless groan, he impaled her

again and again, shuddering with each deep thrust, his every muscle tense and strained. She felt him swelling, growing harder as he lifted her hips to meet his forceful strokes. His face contorted in ecstatic furor as a spasm began to shake him. With a shout he climaxed inside her, his sex throbbing against the walls of her passage as hot liquid spurted against her womb.

Graeme couldn't think.

Making love to Blair was more than he had expected. It was a frightening revelation. He was accustomed to the afterglow of sexual satiation, yet the depth of contentment that curled through him stole his mind and sapped his energy. What had Blair done to him? The first thought that came to mind was that he had succumbed to one of her spells.

What he had experienced with Blair was deeper than the pleasure he'd known with any other woman, more profound in intangible ways he could not express, and endlessly more compelling. If he wasn't careful, Blair could become addictive.

With great reluctance Graeme rolled off Blair onto his back, his harsh breathing and racing heart reminding him that what had just taken place between him and his wife was extraordinary and without precedence.

He turned his head to stare at Blair, wondering if she was truly a witch with magical powers. She was curled up in a ball beside him, sound asleep and looking like an earth angel. He wouldn't awaken her now, but in the morning she would have a great deal of explaining to do. He wanted to know more about her dreams and visions.

Unable to resist the lure of her ethereal beauty, he brushed a wayward tendril of bright hair from her forehead. The silken strand scorched his fingers, and he released it quickly, stunned. What kind of magic was this?

Though Graeme tried to sleep, he could not. Blair's reason for wanting to consummate their marriage did not please him. She had come to his bed because she feared her brother, not because she wanted her husband.

Blair said she could never love him. Mayhap not, but he had encountered no problem in arousing her. Her passion had stunned him. He'd had no idea she was capable of such an enthusiastic response, and he was willing to bet she was surprised as well.

Perhaps her physical response to him was the answer to their problems. If he could seduce her into loving him, she would lose her powers. Without her powers, no one could accuse her of witchcraft, and danger would no longer stalk her.

Aye, that was what he would do. Make Blair love him and at the same time enjoy the benefits of the marriage bed. While his own heart was well protected, he knew Blair's was vulnerable. If the only way to protect her from herself was to use her vulnerability, then so be it.

As for her dream about MacArthur and MacKay, he'd be a fool to disregard it. He would keep a watchful eye out for them.

Blair was still sleeping soundly when Graeme eased out of bed at first light. He washed and dressed and left his chamber to break his fast, careful not to awaken Blair. He took a seat beside Stuart and Heath, who were enjoying their oats and bannocks.

"Ye're late, lad," Stuart said. " 'Tis not like ye to oversleep. Do ye still intend to help us with the shearing?"

Stifling a yawn, Graeme nodded as he attacked the bowl of oats Glenda set in front of him.

"What ails ye this morning, lad?" Stuart asked. "Did ye have a bad night?"

Graeme grinned. "Actually, Uncle, I had an exceptionally good night."

Heath nearly choked on his bannock. "Never say ye bedded the witch! Are ye mad, Graeme?"

Graeme sent Heath a quelling look. "Blair *is* my wife. Bedding one's wife is a normal occurrence."

"Mayhap 'tis a normal occurrence when one's wife is normal," Heath groused. "I wasna worried about ye as long as I knew Blair hadna lured you into her bed, but this changes everything."

Graeme sent him a confused look. "How so?"

"After bedding her, ye are more susceptible to her spells. I didna want to tell you this, but now I have no choice. Aiden saw yer wife sneaking out to the stillroom last night. Lord only knows what evil she was hatching out there."

"Blair isna evil, nor is she a witch," Graeme protested. "What she has is a highly developed imagination that produces fear in others. I will do everything within my power to protect her from herself."

He bit off a chunk of bannock, chewed thoughtfully, then added, "By the way, Blair believes her brother and the MacKay are up to mischief and that she may be in danger. Warn the others to watch for them if they take it into their heads to come to Stonehaven."

Stuart shook his shaggy head. "I knew the lass was trouble. Ye shouldna have wed her, Graeme. And once ye did, ye shouldna have bedded her. Once the witch has her clutches in ye, she will manipulate ye to do her bidding."

"What exactly do you mean by that?" Graeme asked with a hint of amusement.

"How will Blair manipulate me?"

Stuart shrugged. "I dinna know, lad, but it canna be good. What do ye suppose she was doing in the stillroom in the middle of the night?"

"Communing with nature," Graeme said for lack of a better answer.

Heath rolled his eyes. "Can ye truthfully say ye trust the lass?"

Graeme hesitated. "No woman can measure up to Joan, but I trust Blair as much as I trust any woman who is not Joan," he said carefully.

" 'Tis time ye forgot poor wee Joan," Stuart advised. He made a careless motion toward Glenda, who was standing nearby, drawing a pitcher of ale from a barrel. " 'Tis no secret that Glenda has feelings for ye. Let her ease ye, lad. Ye'd be wise to take what she offers instead of falling under yer wife's spell."

Graeme pushed his bowl away and rose to his feet. "Enough of this nonsense. Blair isna a witch, nor is she capable of casting spells. What I do in the privacy of my bedchamber is my business. If you two are finished dispensing worthless advice, perhaps you'd like to join me in the sheep pens."

Grumbling, Stuart and Heath left the hall. Blair entered as Graeme prepared to follow them. "I must have overslept," she said, hesitating to meet her husband's gaze. Did he remember the passion he had unleashed in her?

Her uninhibited response to his lovemaking? Vivid color stained her cheeks.

Graeme seemed not to notice. "Today we begin shearing the sheep," he explained. "I expect to be in the shearing shed most of the day. Maeve usually sends the midday meal out to us, so dinna look for me before dark. What will you do to keep busy today?"

"I thought perhaps Alyce and I could go into the forest to gather herbs and willow bark. This time of year is perfect for gathering herbs."

"Dinna wander too far from the keep," Graeme warned.

Blair glanced up at him, wondering if he was worried. His expression nearly took her breath away. He was smiling at her, a tender look upon his face. Before he turned and strode away, he leaned down and brushed a kiss across her lips.

Mouth agape, Blair stared at his departing back, her fingers pressed over her mouth. She still felt the shock of his kiss. What was he up to? She hoped he did not expect her to share his bed on a regular basis. She had gone to his bed in order to protect herself from Niall, and there was no more to it than that.

Liar, her inner voice accused.

Her purpose did not matter. The important thing was that she was no longer a virgin and Niall could not contest her marriage. She was Graeme's wife in every way.

Blair wandered into the kitchen to seek her own breakfast when none was forthcoming. She found Maeve stirring something in a kettle over the hearth.

"I hope that's porridge you're stirring," Blair said.

The spoon clattered against the kettle. "Ye startled me, lass. Didna Glenda bring yer breakfast out to ye?"

"She must be busy," Blair returned. "I'll eat in here, if you dinna mind."

Maeve dished up a bowl of oats and placed it on the table along with a pitcher of milk and a plate of bannocks. "Sit down, lass. I'm glad for the company."

Blair pulled a bench up to the table and dug into the oats. She was exceptionally hungry this morning. With sudden insight, she realized the reason for her hunger and blushed. She was unaccustomed to the kind of activity she had engaged in last night.

Maeve's perceptive gaze settled on Blair. "Is something wrong, lass? Ye look a mite feverish."

Embarrassed, Blair tucked her chin down. "I am fine, Maeve. Have you seen Alyce this morning?"

"Aye, she was up early and went to speak to the alewife. She said something about providing some special herbs to make her ale more flavorful."

Blair finished her breakfast and rose. "If you see her, tell her I'll be in the stillroom. I'd like her to accompany me to the forest to gather herbs."

Blair wandered to the stillroom, but her mind wasn't on herbs. Her body still thrummed from Graeme's loving, and she couldn't think beyond the fact that her response had been a surprise to herself. He hadn't been brutal or harsh, causing her only the unavoidable pain of his entry. He had taken his time, aroused her slowly and given her unexpected pleasure. The pleasure was something she wished hadn't happened. How in God's holy name was she supposed to deny her feelings for Graeme Campbell when all her senses screamed that she was meant to love this strong, virile man?

Blair sensed a movement near the open door and whirled, expecting to see Alyce. Instead she saw a small lad standing on the stoop, his gaze darting this way and that, as if afraid that something or someone would swoop out and grab him.

"Ye're wanted in the village, lady," he said in a timid voice. Before she could question him further, he turned and scampered off.

"Wait! Who wants me? Is someone sick or hurt?"

"Gunna said to fetch ye," he threw over his shoulder.

He darted around a corner and was gone,

presenting a dilemma for Blair. How badly was she needed? Desperately, she thought, if Gunna had sent for her. The woman hated her. Should she go alone or ask Alyce to accompany her? The urgency of the summons convinced her to fetch her basket of remedies and not waste precious time finding Alyce.

An uncomfortable feeling settled in the pit of Blair's stomach as she strode to the village. Something was wrong — she could feel it in her bones. She tried to discredit her premonition by telling herself she was tired. But the warning she'd received in her dream last night played over and over in her mind. Perhaps it was lack of sleep that had her on edge. Whatever the reason, she wasn't going to let trepidation interfere with what she considered her God-given duty to help the sick and injured. When a call for help came, she couldn't ignore it.

When Blair reached the village, she had no idea where to go. The lad had given her no directions. For some strange reason, the streets were all but deserted at a time when women and children were usually out and about. A tremor of anxiety slid down her spine. Clutching her basket tightly, Blair decided to stop first at Mab's cottage, hoping the Scotswoman would know why she had been summoned.

She had taken no more than a few steps when Gunna called to her from the doorway of a small hut. "This way, lady," she urged. "Hurry."

"What is it, Gunna?" Blair asked. "Do you need help delivering a bairn?"

The contemptuous sneer on Gunna's face should have warned her that all was not as it should be. "I have no need of yer magic, lady. There are other matters that need yer attention."

She grasped Blair's arm. "Come with me."

Blair allowed herself to be pulled into the dim interior of Gunna's hut, expecting to find someone in desperate need of healing. Instead she found her worst nightmare come to life.

"You! What are you doing here?" She whirled on Gunna. "What have you done?"

"Naught but what is right, lady," Gunna sniffed. "We dinna need yer kind at Stone-haven."

Blair tried to flee, but Donal MacKay blocked the door with his hulking form. "Ye're not going anywhere, lass."

Then she saw her brother.

"Niall, tell your friend to move away from the door," Blair ordered.

Laughter rumbled from Niall's barrel chest. "Ye're good at giving orders, Blair, but I am the MacArthur laird now and ye must obey me. I'm taking ye home, and tomorrow ye'll be wed to the MacKay."

"I am already wed," Blair argued.

"I have it on good authority that yer marriage hasna been consummated. If that proves true, I have every right to demand yer return."

"I am not a maiden," Blair whispered, looking away in embarrassment. "I have lain with my husband."

"Ye're lying!" Niall declared. "I know the words of the Prophecy as well as ye, and I dinna believe ye would risk yer powers for physical pleasure. Besides, 'tis rumored that the Campbell loves another. He only wed ye because he owed Father a debt of gratitude.

"I intend to prove ye're still a maiden. I sought out the village midwife when MacKay told me she was his kinswoman. Gunna was more than eager to do my bidding."

Blair sent Gunna a quelling look. "She doesna like me."

"So I learned. Ye havena earned any friends here, Sister. I suspect Campbell's kinsmen will be happy to be rid of ye."

"Dinna fret, Blair," Donal MacKay said. "I dinna want ye to share my bed. I have women aplenty to fill that role. 'Tis yer powers I covet. They'll make me rich beyond my wildest dreams."

Blair stared at MacKay and shuddered. He was a huge man, with a wild thatch of red hair and a shaggy red beard. "My brother is wrong," Blair argued. "I can do naught to help you. I am a healer — my skills canna help you gain the power you desire."

"Niall has seen ye work yer magic."

She rounded on her brother. "Why are you so determined to give me to the MacKay?"

"MacKay wants ye for the powers ye possess, while I want naught to do with yer magic. He will let me keep yer dowry, which is more than Campbell will do, thereby strengthening the alliance between the MacKays and the MacArthurs. Father didna trust MacKay, but he is gone now and the decision is mine to make. Joining with the MacKays and aligning ourselves with King James will bring prosperity to our clans. The king needs us, and even now courts our loyalty. We will become the most powerful lairds in the Highlands."

"Get on with it, MacArthur," MacKay growled. "Let the midwife do what we're paying her for. If the lass is yet untouched, she is mine to wed."

Without warning, Niall made a lunge for Blair. Grasping her from behind, he pinned her arms to her sides and dragged her to the bed. Blair fought with every ounce of her strength, but it wasn't enough when MacKay entered the fray. Moments later she was pinned to the bed and held in place by MacKay and Niall.

"Begin the examination, Gunna," Niall ordered. "And ye'd best tell us what we want to hear."

His words and Gunna's mirthless grin gave Blair little hope that the midwife would truthfully report her lack of a maidenhead. She would tell Niall exactly what he wanted to hear. Would Graeme fight for her? Blair wondered. Most likely he would be glad to be rid of her.

Blair bucked wildly, making it difficult for the midwife to begin her examination despite the two men pressing her against the thin straw mattress. "It will take more than two men to hold me down," she warned. "But I promise to cooperate if you leave me alone with Gunna. 'Tisn't right that men should witness this travesty."

Niall's eyes narrowed. "I dinna trust ye."

Desperation forced Blair to resort to tactics she would normally disdain. "If you both dinna leave the room, I swear I will cast a spell that will shrivel your man parts until they resemble small worms."

She fixed Niall with a fierce glare and began an incantation guaranteed to send even the bravest of men fleeing. Loss of one's manhood was an appalling prospect, and both men took Blair's threat to heart.

"Witch!" Niall shouted, backing away.

"Nay!" MacKay cried, protecting his manhood with one hand while retreating like the coward he was.

"Verra well, ye win," Niall said. "But dinna try to escape. Ye promised ye would co-

140

operate, and ye damn well better if ye know what's good for ye. We will be waiting outside the door while the midwife examines ye."

Once alone with Gunna, Blair planned her escape. There was no way she would let the midwife touch her with her filthy hands. Closing her eyes and clearing her mind of all thought, she sent a mental plea through time and space to Graeme, directing him to Gunna's cottage in the village.

"This willna take long," Gunna cackled. "Yer brother wants to know if yer husband's rutted with ye, and I intend to give him the answer he is seeking. Ye dinna belong with our laird."

"You'd lie?"

"We dinna need the likes of ye at Stonehaven."

That was all Blair needed to hear. If Graeme didn't arrive in time, Niall would take her away, and the combined MacArthur and MacKay forces would make it impossible for Graeme to rescue her, if he were of a mind to.

Gunna moved between Blair's legs and pushed them apart.

"Wait! Wash your hands first. They're filthy."

Gunna looked at her grubby hands and shrugged. "No one has complained of my dirty hands before. Ye're too persnickety, lady."

"I mean it, Gunna. If you dinna wash your hands, I will cast a particularly nasty spell on you."

Gunna stared at her with unfettered hatred and a good deal of fear, then spun around and marched to the washstand. Using Gunna's distraction to her own advantage, Blair seized a heavy candlestick from a nearby table and brought it down on the midwife's head. Then she climbed out a back window, lifted her skirts and ran.

Chapter Seven

Graeme cocked his head and listened. He heard someone calling to him. He glanced at Heath, who was working beside him. "Did you speak to me?"

Heath sent him a quizzical glance. "Nay."

"Are you sure? I clearly heard someone calling to me."

Graeme glanced about. No one else seemed to have heard what he had. "I must be hearing things."

Heath sent him a concerned look. Then, very distinctly, Graeme heard it again . . . a plea for help. Blair? He rushed from the shearing pen, convinced that Blair needed him. Was he losing his mind? Then he heard the voice again.

The village, the voice whispered inside his head. *Come to the village. Help me, I need you.*

Blair was in trouble! Graeme took off at a run, fear pounding though his veins, his heart pumping furiously. If someone had hurt Blair, he would tear him or her apart with his bare hands.

Fortunately, the shearing pens were no

great distance from the village. He reached the outskirts and nearly collapsed with relief when he saw Blair, skirts raised to her knees, sprinting toward him. He caught her up in his arms and held her close.

"Are you hurt? Who tried to harm you?"

Gasping for breath, Blair pointed behind her, alerting Graeme to approaching danger. Glancing over Blair's shoulder, Graeme saw Niall MacArthur and Donal MacKay in hot pursuit of his wife. He shoved Blair behind him, cursing his lack of a weapon.

"What do you want?" Graeme growled when the men skidded to a halt before him. "You are trespassing on Campbell lands."

"I but wanted to speak with my sister," Niall said.

"He lies!" Blair charged. "He came looking for grounds to annul our marriage. He and MacKay lured me to the village so Gunna could examine me. They hoped to prove I was still a maiden." She shuddered. "I couldna bear her hands on me, so I bashed her with a candlestick when she turned her back."

"I heard you calling me," Graeme said, his voice pitched low. "We'll talk about that later." He turned to Niall. "How dare you insult Blair in such a vile manner? If you wished to speak with her, you should have come to the keep."

"I have a proposition for ye, Campbell,"

MacKay said. "Will ye listen to what I have to say?"

Graeme's first inclination was to order the two off his land. But he decided to hear them out before setting them straight about the state of his marriage and banishing them from Campbell lands.

"I will listen," Graeme said grudgingly. "But only if you accompany me to the keep. A public road is no place to air family matters."

"Do ye guarantee our safety?" MacKay asked.

Graeme stiffened. "Are you questioning my honor?"

"Of course not," MacKay hedged. "But a mon canna be too careful."

"At the conclusion of our conversation, you'll both be free to leave. All I shall require is your promise to leave my wife alone in the future."

"I suggest ye listen to MacKay's proposal before demanding promises from us," Niall said. "What he has to say should be of great interest to ye."

Graeme sincerely doubted he'd be interested in anything either of these two scoundrels had to say. The thought of their hands on his wife left him outraged. Placing an arm around Blair and holding her hard against his side, he strode toward the keep. He cared not if Blair's brother and MacKay followed, for his thoughts were consumed with the indignity Blair had suffered at their hands.

As they started down the path, Heath, Stuart and Aiden joined them. When Graeme had run from the shearing pen without a word of explanation, they'd become worried and decided to follow. Knowing Graeme as they did, they knew he wouldn't have rushed off without good reason.

"What are *they* doing here?" Stuart asked, jerking his head toward MacArthur and MacKay.

"I'll tell you later."

"What made ye run off like that?" Heath wanted to know.

Graeme gave Blair a squeeze. "A premonition."

"We thought ye could use help and followed," Aiden explained. "But I see ye have everything under control."

"Thanks to my resourceful wife," Graeme said grimly. "What they had planned for her wasna pretty."

When they reached the keep, Graeme gave Blair's shoulders a squeeze and said, "I would speak to your brother and MacKay alone."

Blair gave him a mutinous glare. "Why? What they have to say involves me."

"You've been through enough today. Obey me in this, Blair. Things could get ugly." She continued to stare at him. "Please," he added.

His heartfelt plea convinced her, though she liked it not. "Verra well, but I'll expect a full report after they leave."

Graeme sent her a cocky grin. "Ask your spirits, sweeting. They seem to know things before I do."

Blair sent him a sizzling look, then flounced off.

"Sending her away was wise," Niall said when he joined Graeme. "Our proposal is for yer ears alone. Where can we talk in private?"

"Follow me," Graeme said, leading them to a small anteroom off the hall where he often consulted with his steward and housekeeper. He seated himself behind a desk and tented his fingers. "I would offer a wee drop of uisge breatha but you willna be here long enough to finish it. State your business so you can be on your way. I canna forget what you tried to do to Blair, and my temper is dangling by a slim thread."

Unapologetic, Niall shrugged. " 'Twas the only way to prove no real marriage exists between you and my sister."

"You could have asked *me* about the state of our marriage," Graeme charged. "What you intended for Blair was despicable."

" 'Twas necessary," Niall maintained. "There was a prior betrothal. If yer marriage wasna consummated, I intended to give Blair to MacKay."

"I know of no prior betrothal," Graeme said evenly. "Douglas MacArthur gave Blair to me while he was alive to make the decision. Father Lachlan waived the banns and performed the ceremony in Douglas's bedchamber. According to law and the Holy Church, Blair and I are husband and wife."

"Douglas wasna in his right mind," Niall charged. "I acted in his stead when I betrothed Blair to the MacKay."

Graeme's lips tightened to a bloodless line. "Douglas MacArthur's mind was clear when he asked me to wed Blair. Our marriage is legal and binding."

"Not if the marriage wasna consummated," MacKay persisted.

An air of menace was inherent in Graeme's words as he responded. "What makes you think our marriage wasna consummated?"

"The servants at Gairloch Castle, for one thing," Niall replied. "They gossip, ye know. I heard them whispering about the lack of virgin's blood on the sheets after ye left Gairloch."

"You call that proof?" Graeme scoffed.

"There's more," Niall said with a smugness that set Graeme's teeth on edge. "Blair fancies herself a Faery Woman and sets great store in her powers."

"Do *you* believe in her powers?"

"My beliefs are my own," Niall said evasively. " 'Tis Blair's beliefs we are talking about. And what of the rumors about yerself? 'Tis said ye returned from France a changed mon, that ye fell in love with someone unattainable. 'Tis likely Blair heard the gossip. The MacArthur Prophecy says a Faery Woman will lose her powers if she loves in vain, so it stands to reason she would withhold herself from ye rather than risk losing her heart as well as her powers. I also believe ye wouldna press her since ye love another."

"You're wrong, MacArthur," Graeme charged. "We left Gairloch rather abruptly, but our marriage was consummated at Stonehaven."

"Prove it!" MacKay barked.

Graeme shot to his feet. "My word is all the proof you require. I will say it one more time: Blair is my wife in every way."

"Maybe so, but that doesna stop us from striking a deal," MacKay ventured.

"What kind of a deal did you have in mind?" Graeme demanded harshly.

"Let me be blunt," Niall began. "Can ye be happy with a witch for a bride? We all know ye wed Blair to repay a debt to Father." He held up his hand when Graeme started to protest. "Dinna deny it. Everyone knows why ye wed my sister." He leaned closer. "MacKay and I are offering ye a chance to rid yerself of the witch."

Outrage darkened Graeme's face. "Get out of here and dinna return!"

"Hear me out," MacKay said. "If ye swear yer marriage wasna consummated, my clansmen will never steal from ye again."

"I'll not lie," Graeme said from between clenched teeth.

"Ye'll be sorry," Niall spat. "Blair is more trouble than she's worth. Once she starts casting spells, ye'll wish ye had accepted MacKay's offer. I've lived with her all my life and I know what she's capable of."

"Aye, let me take her off yer hands, Campbell," MacKay urged. "I swear she'll come to no harm."

Graeme's probing gaze searched deep into MacKay's hard, cold eyes, and he liked not what he saw. "If Blair is so much trouble, why do you want her?"

" 'Tis none of yer concern," MacKay said with deliberate vagueness. " 'Tis enough that I am willing to deal with her."

"You intend to exploit her powers," Graeme charged. "For your information, Blair has no powers."

"Ye're a fool if ye believe that," Niall hissed.

"Aye, a fool," MacKay agreed. "Blair can give me something I want verra much. Furthermore, with Blair's ability to 'see' things, Niall and I can become invaluable to King James. Blair can use her powers to tell us who supports James and who does not. We can become the most powerful men in Scotland. The king already trusts us and looks to us for support."

"Get out!" Graeme shouted. "You will be driven off my land if you attempt to return."

"Dinna be too quick to refuse us," MacKay warned. "We can make ye verra sorry ye did."

"Get out!" Graeme repeated. "I assure you I am more than capable of defending myself and those I care about against the pair of you."

"The witch isna worth yer life," Niall blasted as he edged toward the door.

"Let me be the judge of that. Out, both of you. And dinna darken my doorstep again."

He strode to the door and held it open. He was not surprised to see Heath and Aiden waiting on the other side.

"Do ye need help?" Heath asked.

"Nay. MacArthur and MacKay are leaving."

Suddenly Blair came skidding around the corner. "What did they want? I hope you didna let them talk you into anything."

Graeme grinned. No one could say his wife wasn't impetuous. Her pugnacious stance, hands on hips, chin raised, was almost comical.

"I thought I sent you to your chamber."

"Ye dinna know how to handle the lass," Niall sneered. "Ye should have let MacKay take her off yer hands."

Blair's gaze collided with Graeme's. Then she rounded on MacKay, her eyes blazing with fury. "You're despicable. Do you recall that spell I spoke of earlier?"

MacKay stared at her, his hand flying downward to cover his groin. "If ye value yer life, witch, dinna try to work yer evil spells on me." He backed away, his face contorted with fear.

"Ye shouldna be allowed to live among God-fearing people," Niall charged, waving his fist in Blair's face. "Ye're dangerous, Blair. Dinna come to us for help when Campbell turns ye out. Ye deserve whatever fate brings ye."

"Shall I escort them back to Gairloch?" Aiden asked.

"Just to the front door," Graeme said. "I am sure they can find their own way back home without an escort." His gaze found Blair. "What spell did you threaten them with?"

Blair sent him a saucy look. "I told them I'd shrivel their man parts."

Heath made a gurgling sound in his throat while Graeme threw back his head and laughed. "Could you do that?" he asked, wiping away mirthful tears.

Blair shrugged. "I doubt it." Then she turned and flounced off, her skirts swishing about her curvy hips.

"That wasna funny," Heath charged. "Heed

me, Cousin, ye should have given her to MacKay. Any woman who threatens to shrivel a man's cock must be a witch." He brushed his hand over his groin as if to make sure his own manhood was still intact. Apparently satisfied with what he found, he stomped off.

Graeme stared after him, a thoughtful expression on his face. Was he the only one who refused to believe that Blair was a witch? He had seen firsthand what happened to witches, and he couldn't bear the thought of Blair suffering the same fate. He might not love Blair, but he didn't want to see her hurt. Not just because Douglas MacArthur had charged him with her safety, but because he wouldn't wish Joan's fate on anyone. It was a horrible way to die. Until he had solid proof, he refused to believe Blair capable of evil.

Blair entered her chamber and slammed the door. Anger simmered beneath the surface of her calm. If Graeme had not heard her silent plea, her body would have been violated in a most disgusting way. Furthermore, she knew she had powerful enemies in her brother and MacKay.

Blair didn't need to consult spirits to know those two wished her harm. The aura surrounding them was black, a dangerous color. She felt their animosity to the marrow of her bones. Niall had always feared her powers and been jealous of their father's love. She couldn't count the times Niall had tried to turn her father against her. Even more frightening, she feared their hostility extended to Graeme. It would serve them right if she actually did try to shrivel their man parts.

The door opened and Graeme stepped inside. Husband and wife stared at each other, separated by more than the width of the room. Between them stood the Prophecy and all it represented. She knew intuitively what Graeme was thinking, and she recoiled inwardly.

"Nay, dinna even think it," she said. "I am not a witch."

He strode toward her. "How do you know what I am thinking?"

Her gaze slid down the length of his body. He was wearing trews today. The material clung to his muscular thighs like a second skin, and she recalled with vivid clarity how those hard thighs had clasped her hips as he thrust inside her. A shudder passed through her, and she shook her head to clear it as she considered Graeme's question.

"Your aura suggests what you are thinking, and it isna good."

"My aura? What in the devil are you talking about?"

"Colors. I can read people's moods and sometimes tell what they are thinking by the color surrounding them. Right now your aura is purple, the color of doubt and accusation."

"Nonsense," Graeme snorted. "That kind of talk can get you into trouble. Let's hear no more about auras and reading people's minds."

"I canna change what I am, Graeme. Faery Women throughout the ages are born with powers few understand. I am not ashamed of my powers, for they come from God."

His mouth thinned. "Can you cast spells?"

She nibbled her bottom lip as she considered Graeme's question. How much should she tell him?

"Some might call them spells, but I do not."

"What *do* you call them?" Graeme pressed.

"Graeme, must we continue this conversation? I would never do anything to harm another human being."

"Niall and MacKay seemed convinced you could shrivel their cocks."

She shrugged. "Let them believe what they will. 'Tis not important. I fear we have both earned their animosity. Niall and MacKay were at Inverness recently, meeting with the king. They have his ear, and I fear they will convince James to act against you in some way."

"I dinna think that's possible," Graeme scoffed. "I have done naught to offend the king."

"What about his plan to unify the Highlands? Most of the Highland lairds are against it, and I assume you are too."

"Aye, unification isna welcome in the Highlands. We prefer our own laws and our own lairds. That, however, doesna make me the king's enemy."

"Mayhap not, but dinna discount Niall's influence with the king, or his deceitful ways."

"Let me worry about that, Blair. Neither your brother nor MacKay will bother you again. They are banned from Campbell lands."

Somehow Blair doubted that her brother would accept defeat. Niall's pride had been damaged, and she knew he would retaliate in some way or other.

Blair rubbed her forehead as the beginning of a headache throbbed behind her eyes. She had been under a lot of stress today and it was beginning to catch up with her. Using her powers was draining, and she had called upon them this morning to summon Graeme to the village.

Graeme's concern was immediate. "You're not well."

"I'm fine."

"No, you're not." He swept her up into his arms, carried her to a chair and sat down, settling her in his lap. He didn't speak for a long time. Then he said, "Tell me how you were able to summon me to the village. I distinctly heard you calling to me. Was I the only one who could hear you?"

"Aye. I used mental telepathy to summon you."

"What? I dinna understand."

"I dinna expect you to. I sent my thoughts to you across time and space."

"Can you do that with anyone?"

"Only with someone I am connected to in a special way."

"You mean because we are husband and wife?" Graeme probed.

Blair considered their connection and decided it went much deeper than that. Just how deep, she wasn't yet ready to explore. Because she still possessed her powers, she couldn't possibly love Graeme.

"I am not sure," she reluctantly acknowledged.

"I think you know but are afraid to admit the truth. Do you love me, Blair."

She drew back in alarm. "Nay! I canna love you."

He raised her chin with his fingertip and brushed his lips against hers. "Tell me you feel naught when I kiss you."

She shook her head. "Think you I am made of wood? You are an attractive man, Graeme. But responding to you doesna mean I love you. No woman alive could resist you."

"I want you to love me, Blair. More than

that, 'tis imperative that you do."

Blair went very still. "You want me to lose my powers."

"I want my wife to be normal. I dinna like people looking at you with fear in their eyes, sweeting. I know there isna an evil bone in your body, but others dinna share my belief."

" 'Tis my duty to fulfill the Prophecy. Difficult as it will be, I canna allow myself to love you."

His grin said otherwise. "Then it shall become my mission in life to change your mind. I am a hard man to resist when I am at my most charming."

"You dinna play fair."

"You consider it unfair for a wife to love her husband?"

"Nay, not if a husband returns his wife's love."

He reddened beneath her probing gaze. "If I could love, I wouldna withhold it from you, lass. But my heart is empty."

She placed her hand over his heart; the pulse of its steady beat echoed her own. "Unless your heart beats for me, we remain at an impasse, my lord. I realized I didna love you when you heard my mental plea for help. If I loved you, my powers would have failed me."

Graeme's heart nearly jumped out of his chest. His reaction to Blair's touch shocked him. He felt blood rush to the place where her hand rested, then drain downward to his loins. The result was an instant erection that probed insistently against her bottom. She shifted away, and he knew she had felt his arousal.

"I . . . have things to do," she demurred.

"So do I, but they can wait. Are you too sore to take me, sweeting?"

She nodded her head at the same time as her mouth formed a negative reply.

"Which is it, aye or nay? I want to make love to you."

Her eyes widened. " 'Tis the middle of the day."

"I am aware of that, and it matters not."

"I dinna think we should." She leapt from his lap. Graeme reached for her, but Blair was saved when Alyce burst into the chamber without knocking.

"I just heard, lass. Did Niall hurt ye? How did he lure you to the village?"

"Aye," Graeme said with sudden interest. "Tell us, Blair. I would like the answer to that one myself."

"Niall sent a lad to fetch me. He said Gunna needed my help." Her voice trembled over the next words. "Niall and MacKay enlisted Gunna's help to . . . to examine me. They didna believe my marriage to Graeme had been consummated. Niall claimed there had been a prior betrothal between me and MacKay, which we both know is false."

"Think you Gunna would have lied about your lack of maidenhead?" Graeme wondered.

"Aye. 'Tis no secret she doesna like me. She would have told Niall and MacKay what they wanted to hear."

Alyce looked from Graeme to Blair, apparently coming to the correct conclusion. A grin stretched her lips. "I'm pleased ye followed my advice, lass."

"What advice was that?" Graeme asked.

"Dinna you dare," Blair warned when Alyce opened her mouth to reply.

A chuckle rumbled from Graeme's chest. "Never mind, I can guess. Gunna may have lied, but it wouldna have changed the fact that Blair isna a maiden." He rose. "I suppose I should make sure our visitors found their way home." His expression hardened. "And mayhap I will pay a visit to Gunna."

"Dinna send her away, Graeme," Blair said. "The villagers need her skills."

"Are you sure 'tis what you want?"

"Aye."

"Nevertheless, I intend to have words with her. I want to make damn certain nothing like this happens again. Dinna wander far from the keep for the next few days, lass," he said in parting.

"Ye shouldna have gone to the village without me," Alyce chided.

"I considered looking for you but didna

want to delay. If there had been real trouble, wasted minutes could have meant the difference between life and death. I fetched my basket and left immediately."

Alyce searched Blair's face. "Did Niall hurt ye?"

"Nay. They waited outside while Gunna prepared to examine me." Her chin rose defiantly. "I wasna about to let that filthy old crone put her hands on me. Once her back was turned, I bashed her with a candlestick and fled out the back door. Graeme met me before Niall and MacKay caught up with me."

"How did Graeme know ye were in trouble?"

"I sent him a mental plea for help. I didna know if he would hear, but I had to try."

"Graeme Campbell is yer soul mate . . . yer destiny. Ye knew him from your dreams before he came to ye in person. And now ye belong to him in every way. I am happy for ye, lass."

"Graeme doesna love me, Alyce. His heart belongs to a woman I canna compete with. My body may belong to Graeme, but I canna give him my heart. You know that as well as I."

"I know nothing of the sort," Alyce scoffed. "Listen to a wise old woman, lass. Yer husband canna help himself. He will love ye as much as ye love him."

"But I dinna —"

Alyce held up her hand. "Dinna deny it."

"The Prophecy . . . I still have my powers."

Alyce grinned. "Does that tell ye naught?"

"I am afraid to hope. Graeme said his heart was empty."

"Och! Fill it, lass, fill it."

Having imparted those words of wisdom, Alyce took her leave. Blair remained behind a few moments to gather her thoughts. Her herb-gathering expedition was out of the question now, so instead she made a mental list of what needed to be done in the keep.

Glenda breezed into the chamber with an armload of clean linens just as Blair was leaving.

"I didna hear you knock," Blair said.

Glenda tossed her mane of red hair. "I didna know anyone was in here." She sent Blair a spiteful glare. "I just stripped the bed in the laird's bedchamber and found blood on the sheets. Graeme should have had more sense than to bed a witch."

Blair's hands flew to her flaming cheeks. Did everyone in the keep know she had spent the night in Graeme's bed? Then her senses returned. So what? She and Graeme were married and need answer to no one. Graeme's kinsmen might not like her, but they couldn't deny that she was Graeme's wife and mistress of the keep.

"If you value your job, you'd be well advised to mind your tongue," Blair said as she swept out the door.

As Blair walked out into the hall, Stuart hailed her. She smiled at her husband's uncle and waited for him to join her.

"I am sorry for what happened to ye today, lass," Stuart said. "Do ye think yer brother will make mischief for Graeme? He is close to the king and can bring trouble to our clan."

"Niall is untrustworthy," Blair answered. "He and MacKay are a dangerous pair. I know not what form their retaliation will take, but I suspect it will be leveled against me personally, not your clansmen. If I thought they meant Graeme harm, I would leave Stonehaven."

"Can ye do naught to stop trouble before it arrives? Can ye place a spell on that unholy pair of conspirators before they hatch some mischief? 'Tis what witches do, is it not?"

Shock rendered Blair speechless. Had she heard right? Was Graeme's uncle asking her to use witchcraft?

"I dinna believe what I just heard," Graeme roared from behind them. "Shame on you, Uncle! You just accused my wife of being a witch. Apologize to her."

"Come now, lad," Stuart stammered. "We all know yer wife claims to possess powers. Why should she not use them to help us?

How difficult can it be for her to place a spell on our enemies?"

"I will tolerate no more of that kind of talk," Graeme snapped. He placed an arm around Blair's narrow shoulders. "Think you I amna capable of defending my wife and my kinsmen?"

"MacArthur and MacKay have the king's ear," Stuart warned. "I fear for ye, lad."

"I appreciate your concern, but I have things well in hand."

"Ah, well then, I apologize, lass," Stuart said in parting.

"Your kinsmen fear me," Blair lamented. "I have brought trouble to Stonehaven."

"Dinna even think like that," Graeme growled. "You're mine, Blair MacArthur. And what is mine, I keep."

If Blair didn't know better, she could almost believe Graeme cared for her.

Chapter Eight

Alyce was helping Blair prepare for bed that night when Graeme strolled into her bedchamber. He dismissed the tiring woman with a nod of his head and picked up the brush Alyce had discarded. Then, to Blair's dismay, he began brushing her luxurious mane of blond hair with long, sweeping strokes.

"You dinna have to do that," she said.

"I want to. Your hair is like silk, and it pleases me to do this for you."

"If you have seduction in mind, forget it," Blair said. "We did what had to be done to foil Niall, but I see no reason to share a bed now that the deed is done."

"Do you not?" Graeme replied in a teasing tone. "You are mad if you think you can deny me your body after granting me a taste of your passion."

"Intimacy is wrong unless love is involved," Blair said softly.

"The only thing wrong is your belief that love is necessary to enjoy the marriage bed. Although," he said, lowering his voice to a seductive purr, "I wouldna mind if you fell in love with me."

"Conceited oaf," Blair muttered, plucking the brush from his hand. "Are you here for a particular reason?"

"Aye, I want to make love to my wife."

A knock on the door forestalled Blair's answer. Spitting out a curse, Graeme strode to the door and flung it open. His expression was so fierce that Heath drew back in alarm.

"What is it?" Graeme growled.

"Ye werena in yer own chamber so I figured ye were with the wit . . . yer wife. There's trouble."

Immediately alert, Graeme asked, "What kind of trouble?"

"Reivers. They swooped down from the hills and drove off some of our sheep."

"Were the reivers identified?"

"Nay, 'twas too dark, but one of the lads thought they were MacKays."

Graeme loosed another curse. "I will be down directly." He turned to Blair. "I have to go," he said. "Dinna wait up for me."

"Graeme." He glanced back at her. "Be careful."

"Does that mean you care what happens to me?"

Blair looked him in the eye without flinching. "Of course. As much as I care about anyone facing a dangerous situation."

Grinning, Graeme went to her and wound

his fingers in her hair, lifted her face up to his and gave her a quick, hard kiss. Then he was gone.

Blair touched her lips, bemused and more than a little annoyed. It was obvious that Graeme was trying to seduce her, though his reason for doing so was wrongheaded. He wanted her to love him, even if he couldn't return her love.

Before retiring that night, Blair spent a long time on her knees imploring God and the spirits to protect Graeme and his kinsmen. Finally she climbed into bed. She was weary and slipped quickly into an uneasy slumber.

No sooner had sleep claimed her than she began to dream. It was a dream she had had before, but more terrifying than she remembered. She was surrounded by fire. It licked at her clothing and singed her hair. The heat was unbearable. Through the curtain of flames she saw people leering at her, their expressions rapt with unholy glee. Their voices rose loud and shrill above the sound of her screams.

"Burn, witch, burn.
Burn, witch, burn."

Graeme trudged up the stairs to his bedchamber, so tired he could scarcely move. The chase had reaped benefits, for they had found the sheep, though not the reivers. Fortunately, he had been alerted soon after the reivers struck, which made it possible for him and his kinsmen to track them down before the sheep had been driven into the hills, where they would have been forever lost.

Donal MacKay and his clan had been a thorn in his side for as long as he could recall. Since their lands adjoined, reiving had always been a problem.

Graeme was walking along the gallery when he heard Blair scream. His tiredness fell away as if it had never existed. Muscles tense, his heart pounding with fear, he raced toward her bedchamber, ready to rescue her from whomever or whatever threatened her. Grateful that he was still armed, he gripped his claymore and burst through the door. He found Blair sitting up in bed, screaming at the top of her lungs.

Stunned, he glanced around the chamber, peering into the dark shadows, seeking some hidden danger. Finding naught to provoke Blair's fear, he dropped the claymore and approached the bed. Blair was still screaming, her slim frame trembling like a leaf in the wind. He grasped her shoulders and gave her a shake.

"Blair! What is it? Did someone try to hurt you?"

Blair stared at him with vacant eyes.

He shook her again. "Look at me,

sweeting. 'Tis Graeme. I willna let anyone hurt you."

Blair began sobbing and appeared not to recognize him. When she struggled to escape his hold, he sat down on the bed and held her close.

"Fire," Blair whimpered. "I am burning."

Thinking she might be ill, he felt her forehead and found it cool to the touch. "Nay, you're not burning, sweeting. You were dreaming. Can you tell me about it?"

Blair blinked and reached for him. "I dinna want to burn, Graeme. Help me."

Graeme's heart sank. Had Blair's nightmare been a premonition of her future? The thought was too painful to contemplate, and he silently renewed his vow to protect her from those who wished her harm.

"You're not going to burn, lass. I willna let that happen."

She pressed herself into the warm haven of his body. "My dreams are predictions of the future."

"Not this one. You have my guarantee that no one will hurt you." Lowering his head, his mouth covered hers in a kiss meant to reassure and comfort.

Blair sagged against him, taking comfort in the scent that was uniquely his — a dusky masculine essence laced with accents of night air and wood smoke. His taste, sensual beyond belief, made her yearn for more. Love, unnamed, unspoken, welled up inside her, but fear of losing her powers made her break off the kiss and look up at him. The planes and angles of his face were harshly delineated, stark and feral.

His nostrils flared with the deep breath he took as she rested her hands on his chest. Something uncurled deep inside her as she touched him. Passion ignited like a flame, slowly burning away her doubts and leaving a keen yearning in its place. But still she fought her burgeoning feelings, denying her heart's desire.

Removing her hands from his chest, she tried to retreat. He moaned and with a curse pulled her back into his arms. His entire body was rigid. He pressed his thighs hard against her, and she felt his sex swell and lengthen.

"You need me tonight, Blair. Dinna deny it. Let me help you forget."

Did she dare? She glanced up at his handsome face; his visage was dark, wicked, and dangerous as sin. She did need him, but admitting it would be tantamount to surrendering her powers.

"Love me, Blair," Graeme whispered.

"I canna," Blair whispered.

Tangling one hand in her hair, he kissed her fiercely, his tongue a persuasive pressure that forced her mouth to open. Unable to resist, silently bemoaning her weakness where

Graeme was concerned, she returned his kiss, her hands moving to clutch at him. A pulse began to beat between her thighs, strong and hot, as his hands parted her legs and his fingers slid upward to touch her.

She moaned and pressed against his hand. Nay . . . this was not supposed to happen again. Where was her willpower? He broke off the kiss long enough to strip away her shift. Then he gave her a wicked grin and did something that shocked and confused her. He lifted her legs over his shoulders and held her there, his hands moving to her breasts, fingers teasing her nipples as his mouth and teeth found her hot, slick center.

"Graeme, nay!"

He looked up. "Relax, sweeting. Your spirits sent me to you, did they not?"

She could hardly deny it. "They didna tell me to love you."

"Dinna fight what is meant to be." After a heated look, he returned to his succulent feast.

As if from a great distance she heard the sounds she made, soft, sobbing cries that were full of desire. His mouth seared her as he used his tongue and teeth to tease and torment. She shuddered as the pressure inside her wound tighter and tighter, until finally there was an abrupt release that left her shaking and crying out his name. Her hips arched into the heat of his mouth as she sobbed helplessly, writhing and clutching at him.

Drifting on the tide of surging emotion, she was barely aware when Graeme moved away. Still awash in pleasure, she felt him return, covering her with his body. His clothes were gone now, his naked flesh hot against her as he positioned himself between her thighs. But he did not enter her immediately. Instead he began to arouse her again, teasing her nipples with his tongue and teeth while his hands moved with slow deliberation over every inch of her burning flesh.

She could tell by his clenched jaw and tense muscles that he was holding back, waiting for the right moment to take her. When the moment came, he was inside her with one smooth surge, his entry hard and deep, a relentless pressure that drew her body taut as a bowstring. The steady thrust and drag of his body created an exquisite friction that soon had her scaling the heights of passion. She surrendered completely to the erotic motion, deciding that resistance was futile. She wanted this as much as he did.

She was powerless to refuse him — and powerless to prevent her own response to him. Her treacherous body refused to heed the Prophecy's warning.

"Dinna think, love," Graeme gasped, as if aware of the thoughts whirling around in her head. "Kiss me."

She lifted her lips to his, losing herself in the driving rhythm of their bodies and the sweet promise of pleasure. His kisses made her forget everything but the primitive response that he demanded and the flames of passion devouring her.

Graeme ignored the need of his own body as he guided Blair expertly to her second release. She cried out, caught in its grip, spasms of pleasure raking her body, leaving her trembling and gasping for breath. Graeme held her as she came undone, a bolt of sheer male possessiveness shooting through him as her sheath tightened around him. Unable to hold back a moment longer, Graeme pumped deeper, burying his shaft to the hilt inside her as each thrust came faster, stronger.

With a wordless groan, he impaled her fully. As his first spasm began, he lifted her hips off the bed, angling her higher to meet his fierce thrusts. With a shout he spilled inside her. Stars exploded inside his head and he knew nothing but glory.

Blair's quiet sobs brought him back to reality. He touched her cheek, infinitely gentle, infinitely tender. "Dinna worry, lass, I will take care of you."

He held her until she quieted, and continued to hold her until she fell asleep. But sleep did not come easily to Graeme. A storm of warring emotions swelled and churned inside him. He needed Blair, wanted her beyond reason. Since wedding sweet, wee Blair, Joan the Maid had become a dim memory.

Could his feelings for Blair be more than physical? he wondered. Nay! He could not love Blair. Though she had not yet fully convinced him about the powers she claimed to possess, he was no longer the doubter he once had been. Were they to share a love, Blair's powers would thrive, and he could not allow that to happen. If Blair were accused of witchcraft, she could die a violent death.

Like Joan.

He began to tremble. He would not, could not love Blair, even though his heart warned that she loved him. Making her love him had been his goal from the beginning, and he should be elated at how well he was succeeding. What he felt, however, was something entirely different. If only he could figure out just what it was.

Blair awakened the following morning feeling exceptionally well. Then she recalled her dream, and beads of perspiration broke out on her forehead. Crying out, she jerked upright and clutched at her heart. Graeme awoke with a start.

"What is it? Are you ill?"

Blair's tongue stuck to the roof of her mouth when she recalled all the ways she and Graeme had made love last night. She'd been awakened in the middle of the night by Graeme's arousing caresses. Their loving had been slower and gentler than the first time, but every bit as satisfying.

"Are you ill?" Graeme repeated.

"Nay, 'tis naught."

"Did you have another nightmare?"

She shook her head. "I am fine, Graeme, truly."

Graeme searched her face, then shrugged. " 'Tis late. I have to go. The wool must be bundled up and taken to market."

"You are leaving Stonehaven? When?"

"Soon. Tomorrow. I'll take only Heath with me and leave the other men to protect my property."

His heated expression told her that he considered her his property.

"How long will you be gone?"

"Not long — a few days at most. Dinna worry, you will be taken care of in my absence."

Blair bristled. "I can take care of myself."

For the span of a heartbeat they were locked in visual combat, neither giving ground. Then he kissed her forehead and climbed out of bed. "Dinna argue, sweeting, I will feel better knowing someone is watching over you."

Blair watched him dress. He was a man in his prime, thick-shouldered and massive.

Ridges of sinew bulged and flexed with his slightest move. The blatant sexuality of his powerful physique was almost indecent, yet Blair couldn't look away. She might have gaped for eternity had Graeme not turned and caught her staring at him.

His brows rose in unspoken challenge. Embarrassed, Blair blushed and looked away. "Will you find Alyce and send her to me?" she asked. "I'd like to bathe."

He sent her a wicked leer. "Perhaps I should linger a wee bit longer in your bed."

"Nay! I mean . . . you said you had things to do to prepare for your departure tomorrow."

"Methinks the lady protests too much." He grinned, then gave a resigned sigh. "You are right. As much as I'd like to, I'd best not tarry. Until tonight, sweeting," he promised in parting.

"Tonight?" Blair whispered after Graeme had departed. Another night of heated kisses and burning caresses would seal her fate. Loving was easy when the man was Graeme, but being loved in return was not so simple.

Alyce bustled into the chamber a few minutes later. "I ordered yer bath, lass." Her eyes twinkled. "Yer husband gave me the message."

Blair knew precisely what Alyce was thinking. "Dinna make too much of this, Alyce. I am Graeme's wife. I must do my duty to my husband. If I dinna, he will take a mistress."

"And that would upset ye?"

"Nay, I . . ." It was no use. She couldn't lie to Alyce. "Aye, it would. The spirits sent Graeme to me. I canna deny him."

Alyce's eyebrows shot upward. "I am happy ye finally saw the light. The Campbell laird is yer destiny. Be happy with him, lass. 'Twas what yer dear departed father wanted."

Blair sighed. "We both know I canna love him."

Alyce snorted. "And we both know 'tis too late for those sentiments. Place yer trust in the Prophecy, lass, and all will be well."

Their conversation ended abruptly when Blair's bath arrived. Alyce helped her into the tub, then departed so Blair could bathe in private. Resting her head against the rim of the tub, she closed her eyes and recalled the pleasurable hours she had spent in Graeme's arms the night before.

While Graeme ate his breakfast, his thoughts kept returning to Blair. Something was happening to him, and he liked it not. How had she become so important to him in such a short time? What he felt went beyond his need to protect her. Joan was no more than a sweet memory, pure and holy and un-reachable.

"Are ye not hungry, Graeme? I could fix ye

something else if porridge doesna appeal to ye."

Graeme smiled up at Glenda. "Nay, lass, porridge is fine. My mind is occupied with other things this morning."

Glenda glanced about, saw they were alone and placed her hand on his shoulder. "You have been neglecting me. Have I offended ye in some way?"

"Nay, lass, you did naught to offend me. But I have a wife now."

"Yer wife is a witch, Graeme. Dinna pretend ye want her."

Graeme stifled a grin. Want her? He desired her to the point of obsession.

"You know naught about my feelings. Mayhap 'tis time I found you a husband."

Glenda threw herself at Graeme. "Nay, laird, I dinna want to wed anyone but ye. 'Tis all *her* fault. She has bewitched ye. Ye would have wed me had the MacArthur laird not begged ye to marry his evil daughter."

Graeme tried to unwind Glenda's arms from his neck, but she clung to him like a leech. "I wouldna have wed you under any circumstances, Glenda. You came to my bed willingly. If you recall, no mention was made of marriage. I am sorry if you misunderstood my intentions."

Glenda smiled slyly as her arms tightened around Graeme's neck. "Mayhap if the witch was gone ye would want me again."

"Blair is here to stay," Graeme said firmly.

"If the witch was gone, would ye take me to yer bed again?" Glenda persisted.

Glenda was becoming a pest. Unfortunately, it seemed lying was the only way to escape her clinging arms.

"Aye, lass. If Blair wasna my wife, you would be the woman in my bed."

"I knew it!" Glenda crowed.

As Blair entered the hall, her gaze flew immediately to the only two occupants of the room. Apparently she had interrupted an intimate moment between Glenda and Graeme. She had started to clear her throat to announce her presence when she heard Graeme say, "If Blair wasna my wife, you would be the woman in my bed."

Her harsh intake of breath sounded loud even to her own ears. Glenda glanced up, saw Blair and cooed, "Ye werena supposed to hear that." Her smug smile suggested otherwise.

Graeme leapt to his feet, dislodging Glenda's arms at the same time. "Fetch something to eat for my wife, lass. I wish to speak to Blair in private."

Hands on hips, Glenda swished off, tossing Blair a challenging smile over her shoulder.

"Let me explain," Graeme began.

"There is no need. 'Tisn't as if ours is a love match. If I canna satisfy you, you have every right to seek diversion elsewhere."

Her expressive violet eyes belied her words, and Graeme immediately regretted the untruth he had told Glenda. "I dinna want another woman, Blair. You are the only woman I need."

Her lips curled in disbelief. "Dinna lie, Graeme. You and your kinsmen still believe I am a witch, no matter how vehemently I deny it. Were you and Glenda betrothed before my father convinced you to wed me?"

Graeme rose and grasped her shoulders. "There is no evil in you, Blair. Pay Glenda no heed. 'Tis true I took her as my leman after I returned from France, but I promised her naught. She came to my bed willingly. I will repeat this one last time: My wife is the only woman I want in my bed."

"I brought yer breakfast," Glenda said, putting an end to the conversation. She slammed the bowl down on the table so hard, some of it spilled out.

Blair shrugged free of Graeme's grasp and seated herself at the table. "Thank you. I willna need anything further."

"Is there aught else *ye* would like, my laird?" Glenda asked, sending Graeme a look hot enough to singe the hair from his eyebrows.

"Nay, lass. You can return to your duties."

With a flirty flutter of skirts, Glenda flounced off.

Graeme returned his attention to Blair, a frown marring his handsome features. "Will you be all right?"

"Why wouldn't I be?"

"I'll be in the sheep pens most of the day. Send Stuart or Jamie should you need me for any reason."

She gave him a curt nod, then turned her attention to her breakfast. She was hungry, but porridge didn't appeal to her this morning. She rose and wandered into the kitchen, drawn there by the smell of freshly baked bread. The thought of sinking her teeth into a thick slab of fresh bread slathered with butter made her mouth water.

"Mistress, what can I do for ye?" Maeve asked, looking up from the pot she was stirring.

"Is that fresh bread I smell?"

"Aye. Would ye like a slice?"

"If it's not too much trouble."

"No trouble at all. I'll bring it out to you as soon as I fetch some fresh butter from the churn. Would ye like a glass of buttermilk to go with it?"

"That sounds wonderful. But if you dinna mind, I'd like to eat in the kitchen."

"I dinna mind at all. I'll be back directly," she said as she placed a lid on the pot and hurried off.

Blair decided to help herself to the bread while she waited for Maeve to return. She

181

cut herself two large slices and put them on a plate. When she heard a hissing sound, she realized the pot was bubbling over into the fire. Grabbing a cloth, she lifted the lid and gave it a stir.

"What are ye doing?" a shrill voice demanded.

Blair whirled, groaning when she saw Glenda glaring at her.

"Stirring the pot — what does it look like?"

"Ye're poisoning the food!" Glenda cried.

"What nonsense," Blair scoffed. "I am merely waiting for Maeve to return with butter to spread on my bread. The pot needed stirring and I stirred it. Make what you want of it."

"No one here trusts ye. Why did ye not return to yer brother when he came for ye? Ye dinna belong here."

Glenda's words clawed deep into Blair's heart. She had hoped for understanding and perhaps even respect from Graeme's kinsmen.

"Dinna ye have anything to do, Glenda?" Maeve asked from the doorway. "Ye should show more respect for the laird's wife. Her healing skills are verra much appreciated by our clansmen."

"She has bewitched our laird," Glenda charged. Her voice lowered to a whisper. "I know what goes on in the stillroom. Her spells are pure evil."

"Pull in your claws, Glenda," Maeve warned. "Laird Graeme willna stand for yer disrespectful attitude toward his wife. If ye wish to remain in the keep, cease yer jabbering."

Blair flinched beneath Glenda's spiteful glare as the woman spun on her heel and stormed off.

"Pay her no heed, lass," Maeve said. "Glenda is jealous. She hoped to wed Graeme. She didna realize the laird had no intention of wedding her. Glenda isna good enough for Graeme. While he was off fighting in France, she denied no one her favors." She patted Blair's shoulder. "Sit down and eat yer bread and butter, lass, while I fetch ye a glass of buttermilk."

Blair's appetite had left her. Was Glenda right? Did all Graeme's kinsmen fear her? She shouldn't have wed him, no matter how badly her father wanted it. Her own kinsmen did not hate her. They might be in awe of her powers but they did not fear her. Those from other clans who thought her a witch judged her from rumors spread by her brother.

"Eat up, lass," Maeve urged. "Our laird needs an heir, and it takes a healthy mother to birth a healthy bairn."

"Did Graeme tell you he wanted an heir?"

"He doesna need to. All men want an heir, and Graeme is no exception."

Blair ate in silence, contemplating Maeve's words. She could already be carrying Graeme's child, though it seemed unlikely. Wouldn't the spirits have told her if she had conceived? That thought brought another. Had the spirits abandoned her?

Nay, she thought not. Her disturbing dream last night was a vivid reminder that her powers were still very much with her.

Chapter Nine

Graeme returned late to the keep that night. Blair was already asleep. Since Graeme was reluctant to awaken her, he merely took her in his arms and held her throughout the night.

The following morning he rose before sunup, kissed Blair's brow and left the bedchamber. After a hasty breakfast, he rode off to Inverness to take the wool to market.

When Blair awoke she sensed even before opening her eyes that Graeme was gone. She rose and prepared for the day, thinking of things she could do to keep herself busy during her husband's absence.

Blair finished her breakfast and went in search of Alyce. With Graeme away and her brother far from Stonehaven, she thought it a good time to venture out to gather willow bark.

"Where are ye going, lass?" Stuart asked as she slipped through the door.

Blair hadn't seen Graeme's uncle enter the hall and spun around at the sound of his voice. "I'm going to fetch Alyce to accompany me while I collect willow bark.

Stuart frowned. "Did Graeme give ye leave to go?

"I saw no need to ask him."

"Ye canna go without a guard, lass. I will go with ye. Find Alyce while I fetch my claymore. Mind ye, dinna leave without me."

Stuart hurried off before Blair could protest the necessity of having a guard. Deciding to accept the inevitable, she left to find Alyce. She found the tiring woman with the alewife, dispensing herbs for the new batch of ale the woman was brewing.

"Have ye need of me, lass?" Alyce asked when she saw Blair.

"Aye. 'Tis a fine day. I thought we might collect willow bark."

"I will fetch a basket and yer cloak," Alyce said.

"Stuart insists on accompanying us, though I canna imagine why we would need him. Meet us in the hall."

Alyce's eyes lit up. "Stuart is a strong, braw mon. He is but thinking of yer welfare."

A short time later, Blair, Alyce and Stuart set out along a well-trod path that led to thickly wooded hills and the loch beyond.

Blair stopped to gather heather growing on the moor while Stuart kept watch. She loved heather, and filled her basket before Stuart reminded her it was willow bark, not flowers, she should be collecting.

"Follow me, lady. I know exactly where to find the willow trees ye're seeking. They grow near the loch."

Blair followed Stuart along a path that led through thick forest. Alyce trailed behind them.

"I dinna like this," Blair said to Alyce, casting a covert glance over her shoulder. "Something doesna feel right."

Alyce raised her head and listened. "Naught seems amiss, lass. Nevertheless, we will leave as soon as we gather the bark we need."

The wood was bursting with new growth, and Blair saw many herbs she would return to gather at another time. Besides fenugreek and mallow, she noted quantities of wild parsley, red clover and mint.

When they reached the loch, Stuart used his claymore to slice long slivers of bark from willow trees growing near the shore. They had scarcely filled their basket when dark clouds rolled in from the sea. The day had suddenly turned from gloriously sunny to ominously dark and threatening.

"A storm is brewing, lass," Stuart warned. "We must leave now if we wish to reach the keep afore the storm breaks." Without waiting for a reply, Stuart urged the women toward the path that would take them back to the keep.

Suddenly Blair stopped and tilted her head,

listening to the wind sloughing through the trees. The wind was speaking to her. The words were indistinct at first, but when she concentrated on the pattern and cadence, the warning was clear.

"Danger!"

"Alyce, Stuart, danger!" she cried as she lifted her skirts and prepared to run. "Flee! Back to the keep."

Gripping his sword, Stuart took a defensive stance, determined to shield the women from harm.

"There is no time for that!" Blair cried. "Run!"

The warning came too late. Five men wielding swords and battle-axes emerged from the cover of the trees, surrounding the small party.

"Who are ye and what do ye want?" Stuart bellowed. "Get out of our way."

"We've come for the witch," shouted the man who appeared to be their leader.

"Who are ye?" Stuart asked. "Be ye MacKays? Where are yer plaids? Are ye afeared to show yer colors, lads?"

"We fear naught. Move aside, old mon," the leader warned. "We want the witch."

Stuart swung his claymore, his expression grim. "Watch who ye're calling a witch, lad. If ye hurt her, ye'll answer to the Campbell laird, and ye know as well as I that Graeme will hunt ye down like the animals ye are. He is overly fond of the lass."

Two of the five men retreated, as if considering Stuart's threat, but the leader merely laughed. "Ye dinna frighten us, old mon. I repeat, move aside."

Without pausing to consider the danger to himself, Stuart courageously lunged at the leader. Immediately he was engaged with not one but five men.

Blair sucked in her breath as she watched Stuart being driven back. This couldn't be happening! If she had a sword, she would join the fray herself. Daring a glance at Alyce, Blair saw the older woman's face go white and realized it was up to her to do something.

When Blair felt the first drops of rain splash against her face, she looked up at the turbulent dark sky and prayed for a miracle. Streaks of lightning lanced through the clouds, followed by a deafening roar. Her mouth moved in silent entreaty as she sent a plea to the spirits.

Suddenly a scream rent the air. Blair cried out as Stuart fell, struck down by their assailants. Blood spilled from what appeared to be a mortal wound in his chest. Alyce flew to his side, cradling his head in her arms to protect him from further assault. Before Blair could reach Stuart, the five assailants started edging toward her, half afraid of her yet apparently determined to see their mission through.

Blair turned and ran, with the attackers in hot pursuit. Another bolt of lightning struck nearby. Blair heard a loud crack as a tree fell to the ground. Glancing behind her, she saw smoke spiraling from its shattered branches. Almost simultaneously a clap of thunder shook the earth beneath her feet, and she turned and fled deeper into the forest, her enemies hard on her heels.

As the men gained on her, she continued to pray for divine intervention. She was but a length or two ahead of her pursuers when her prayers were answered. Lightning lit up the dark sky as another jagged bolt streaked toward earth. The bolt struck a nearby tree, and her feet took wing. An ungodly scream brought her spinning around. She gasped when she saw what the destructive forces of nature had wrought.

The tree, split by lightning, had fallen on two of the men pursuing her, crushing them beneath its heavy weight. One quick glance told her the men were beyond help. The other three men were staring at her as if the accident had been her doing. Their fear was so palpable they were shaking.

"Ye did this, witch! Ye are pure evil!" one man shouted.

Blair didn't deny it. At that particular moment in time she welcomed the men's fear of her. "Stay where you are, else I'll summon the forces of evil!" she threatened.

The three remaining assailants' faces drained of all color as they glanced at their fallen comrades. Then they turned and fled. Blair nearly collapsed with relief as they disappeared amidst a tremendous roar of thunder and a white-hot flash of lightning. Somewhere in the distance she heard another tree crash to the ground but paid it no heed. She was worried about Stuart and needed to return to him as quickly as possible.

She raced back along the path, her heart pounding with dread when she saw Alyce bending over an inert Stuart. The older woman looked at Blair through stricken eyes, while tears mixed with rain streamed down her pale face "Thank God ye're safe," Alyce whispered.

Blair dropped to her knees beside Stuart, troubled by the great amount of blood pooling beneath him. "How is he?"

" 'Tis bad, lass. The wound in his chest looks to be mortal, and he has lost a great deal of blood. The blade must have sliced something vital. Can ye help him, lass? Stuart is a good mon, I dinna want him to die."

Blair's spirits plummeted as she examined Stuart's wound. It would take a miracle to save him; he seemed more dead than alive. But this seemed to be a day of miracles. "I can try," she whispered. "Meanwhile, it wouldna hurt to pray."

Painfully aware of what it would cost her, Blair knew she would do everything within her power to save Stuart. Graeme was exceptionally fond of his uncle. Tearing aside his shirt, Blair placed both her hands on his wound and silently implored God to empower her with enough strength to bring Stuart back.

Her palms began to tingle and burn as Stuart's warm blood seeped between her fingers. The sensation traveled up her arms, and her entire body began to tremble. Bone-wrenching pain traveled through her hands and into her body. The pain flayed her until she was all but consumed by it. Then her eyes rolled back in her head and she fell forward over Stuart's supine body.

As if from a great distance she heard Alyce calling to her. "Speak to me, lass."

Blair stirred as the pain slowly subsided. Lifting herself away from Stuart, she stared at her hands. They were covered in blood. She wiped them on her skirt and returned her gaze to Stuart.

"Ye did it, lass!" Alyce cried. "The bleeding has stopped. Ye healed him."

The wound had indeed stopped bleeding, but Blair was too spent to do more than nod.

"Stay here with him while I fetch help from the keep," Alyce said. "Ye need time to recuperate."

"Wait," Blair said. "I saw some wild dill growing nearby. Fetch it and sprinkle the seeds on the open wound."

Alyce cast a worried glance at Stuart. "Are ye sure? We need to get him back to the keep as soon as possible."

"Color is returning to Stuart's face even as we speak. I think he'll be fine, but infection could undo all I've done here. Dill seed will help prevent infection."

Alyce rose. "Aye, lass, I will fetch the dill seeds."

Blair sat back on her heels, nearly too exhausted to breathe. She couldn't have moved even if the assailants had come back for her. She closed her eyes and placed her hand on Stuart's chest again, needing to reassure herself that he still lived.

Suddenly he stirred, moaned and opened his eyes. " 'Tis raining."

"Aye."

"What . . . happened?"

"You were wounded. How do you feel?"

"Like . . . the . . . very devil. Am I . . . dying?"

Blair summoned a smile. "Nay. You'll live if I have anything to say about it. What would Graeme and Heath do without you?"

"Tell me . . . how . . ."

"We were ambushed by five men. You fought them when they tried to carry me off."

Stuart frowned. "All five?"

"Aye. Ye were verra brave."

"Did I kill them?"

"Nay. Two died when they were crushed beneath a tree that had been struck by lightning. At that point the other three decided to flee."

Stuart searched her face. "Did ye use yer powers to vanquish them, lass?"

Alyce's return spared Blair from replying. "I hurried as fast as I could," Alyce panted. "Here are the dill seeds ye wanted."

"What are they for?" Stuart asked.

"Glory be!" Alyce cried as she fell to her knees beside Stuart. "Ye're awake. 'Tis a miracle."

While Alyce tried to shield Stuart from the rain, Blair crushed the dill seeds in her hands and sprinkled them onto the open gash in Stuart's chest. Then she ripped the bottom half of her petticoat and made a thick pad, placing it against the wound.

"Here, lass," Alyce said, "take some of my petticoat. Ye'll need it to hold the bandage in place."

Blair tore off the hem of Alyce's petticoat and wound it about Stuart's chest. "That's all we can do until we get him back to the keep. We must cleanse the wound with comfrey as soon as possible and feed him rich beef broth to strengthen his blood."

"I can walk," Stuart said.

"Nay, ye canna," Alyce scolded.

"Dinna coddle me, woman," Stuart bellowed as he raised himself up on one elbow.

Blair watched in awe as Stuart shoved himself to his knees, wobbled a few seconds and slowly gained his feet.

"Praise God!" Alyce cried. "I've seen ye heal when all seemed lost, but this truly is amazing."

Gingerly Stuart touched the bandage over his wound. "A miracle? Was I dead, then?"

"Nay, ye werena dead," Blair said. "I canna bring people back from the world beyond. Are you sure you can walk?" she asked, quickly changing the subject.

Stuart took a tentative step, then another. "I can manage."

"The path is wet and slick," Alyce warned. "Lean on me."

Stuart must have realized he wasn't as strong as he'd thought, for he gratefully balanced his weight against Alyce as they started down the path. Blair tried to shake off her debilitating exhaustion, but without much success. Curing Stuart was the most difficult healing she had ever attempted, and it had taken a great deal out of her. With extreme difficulty, she lifted herself from the ground and started after Alyce and Stuart.

They had just emerged from the woods when a group of men on horseback approached them. Blair sagged in relief when she recognized Aiden.

"What happened?" Aiden asked when he reached them.

"We were attacked," Stuart said. "Take me up on yer horse, mon, I am about done in."

"Be careful, he's wounded," Alyce warned. "Someone take my lady. She is in need of aid, too."

Stuart was carefully lifted onto a guardsman's horse. Another man took Alyce behind him, while Aiden took Blair up with him.

"How did you know to come for us?" Blair asked as they rode toward the keep.

"When ye hadn't returned by the time the storm broke, I grew worried."

"You arrived just in time," Blair said. Stuart might consider himself healed, but Blair knew better. He needed her care. There was still much to be done to ensure him a long, healthy life.

Later, when Blair departed Stuart's bedchamber after tending to his wound and giving him valerian to help him sleep, she found Aiden waiting for her.

"I saw Stuart's wound," Aiden said. "He should be a dead man. How did ye heal him?"

Blair went still. She knew what she had done might be called witchcraft by her enemies.

"I . . . have healing skills."

"No earthly healing skills could have saved Stuart."

"Are you accusing me of something, Aiden?"

He searched her face. "Nay, 'tis not my place to accuse. However ye did it, 'tis a miracle, and I thank ye. Stuart would be sorely missed had he died."

Despite Aiden's gratitude, Blair could tell by his expression that he suspected her of using magic. Something in his eyes revealed his fear, but there was also respect, and for that she was grateful.

"I'm taking a search party out to look for the men who attacked ye. Can ye tell me anything that would help us? Did ye or Stuart recognize the men?"

"I never saw them before, and I doubt Stuart had either. They're probably long gone by now."

"What frightened them? It seems strange that they would leave without accomplishing what they had come for. 'Twas ye they wanted, was it not?"

Blair fidgeted nervously. She did not want to say anything that would make Aiden suspicious of her.

"The storm frightened them. Two of the assailants were crushed beneath a tree that had been struck by lightning. The others fled; they probably feared the same fate awaited them."

Aiden accepted her answer, though his expression remained doubtful. "If ye say so, lady. I'll let ye know what we find when we return. Take good care of Stuart."

"Stuart left his claymore behind, and I forgot a basket filled with willow bark. Would you retrieve them for us?"

"Aye, lady," Aiden said as he took his leave.

Since Maeve was sitting with Stuart, Blair returned to her bedchamber to rest. She was utterly spent and needed to recuperate. Healing Stuart had required extraordinary strength and skill. One time she had healed a wound her father had sustained, but it hadn't been as serious as Stuart's. God and the spirits had surely been with her this day.

Alyce was waiting for her in her chamber. "Ye look done in, lass. Let me help ye remove yer bloody clothes. I've already ordered a bath. Afterward, ye can sleep as long as ye like."

Blair was grateful for Alyce's help. When the bath arrived, she soaked until the water grew cold. Then she climbed into bed and closed her eyes. Before sleep claimed her, she let her thoughts wander to Graeme and her feelings for him. Obviously, she didn't love Graeme, for her powers were still strong enough to heal a man near death. And she didn't for one minute believe she'd retained her powers because Graeme loved her. Nay, she wouldn't fool herself into imagining such an outrageous thing.

What did she feel for Graeme if it wasn't love? she wondered. That puzzling question bounced around in her head until sleep claimed her.

Blair slept the rest of the day and night and awoke ravenous. She dressed, washed her face and hands, cleaned her teeth and went immediately to check on Stuart. Alyce was sitting with him, patiently feeding him beef broth. His color was good, and his wound appeared to be free of infection. Leaving Alyce to her task, Blair went down to the hall to break her fast. Aiden was waiting for her.

"Good morrow," Blair greeted.

"Good morrow, lady. I hope ye are well this morn."

"I am fine, and so is Stuart."

"I know. I already checked on him."

"Did you learn the identity of our attackers?"

"We found the place where Stuart had been lying after he was wounded." He sent her an inscrutable look. "There was blood everywhere. Not even the rain had succeeded in washing it away." He shook his head. "His recovery is truly amazing. We found yer willow bark and Stuart's claymore and returned them to the keep."

"Thank you. Did you find the men beneath the fallen tree?

"Aye. All five men are dead. We found the three men ye thought had fled further up the path, crushed beneath another tree that had been felled by lightning. There was naught to link them to a particular clan, so we buried them. Mayhap they were mercenaries hired to kidnap ye."

"Who would do such a thing?"

"I was going to ask ye the same question, lady. Graeme isna going to like this. 'Tis best ye remain inside the walls until the laird returns."

Blair accepted Aiden's edict with little argument. Until she learned who was behind the kidnapping attempt, she wouldn't put the lives of any of Graeme's kinsmen at risk.

Blair spent the next four days dividing her time between Stuart's bedchamber and the stillroom. Stuart's wound was healing without complications. He was still pale from loss of blood but was quickly regaining his strength on a diet of herbal teas and rich beef broth.

The fourth night, Blair looked in on Stuart, saw he was sleeping and continued on to her own bedchamber. Alyce helped her undress, then left. Blair crawled into bed, letting her thoughts wander to her husband. Did he miss her? Did she care? Though she and Graeme were husband and wife, they shared no strong feelings.

Well, there was lust, she admitted ruefully.

Just thinking about his hands and mouth on her made her tremble. Despite the attraction that raged between them, Blair vowed to guard her heart. With that thought in mind, she drifted off to sleep.

Hours later, Blair woke up screaming. She was burning; flames licked at her clothing and hair and singed her skin. Fire raged all around her; there was no escape. The dream had been nearly identical to the one she'd had before Graeme left. But this time there was no Graeme to offer comfort.

Unable to sleep, she turned up the lamp and listened to the rain pounding against the windows, painfully aware that she would soon encounter the ordeal by fire . . . just as the Prophecy predicted.

Fire, water, stone.

Would she fail the test?

Drenching rain kept Graeme and Heath inside the inn. They had been at Inverness four days and were celebrating the profitable sale of their wool. Graeme planned to spend another night at the inn, then stop at Gairloch before returning home.

Naught had been done concerning Blair's dowry, and it was past time for a settlement. Graeme should already be receiving rents and taxes from Blair's lands on the Isle of Skye, but none had been forthcoming. Graeme knew that the lands produced a good income, and he suspected that Niall was reluctant to part with them. But they belonged to Blair, and Graeme could use the income.

As Graeme sipped his ale, he felt a sensation of dread in the pit of his stomach. He was overwhelmed by the feeling that he was needed at Stonehaven. The only thing that kept him from racing home was the knowledge that Stuart would have sent word if there were trouble. But the longer he sat nursing his mug of ale, the more troubled he became.

"What ails ye, Cousin?" Heath asked. "Ye look distraught. It canna be the wool, for the price we got was verra good."

"Something *is* bothering me, Heath, but I dinna know what. I've tried to ignore the burning in my gut, but it willna be denied. I am needed at home."

"I thought ye had some pressing business with MacArthur."

"My business can wait," Graeme said decisively. "I learned long ago to obey my instincts. They kept me alive in France."

"When do ye want to leave?"

"Tonight if it wasna raining so hard. Unfortunately, travel would be too difficult at night in this wretched weather. We'll leave early tomorrow, rain or no. I want to reach home before nightfall."

Blair rose at dawn to begin her day. It had

been a long night. Most of it she'd spent sitting up, staring into the shadows. She was already out of bed and dressed when Alyce bustled into her bedchamber. "Ye're up early this morn, lass."

Alyce opened the shutters to let in the light, her smile fading when she saw Blair's face. "Ye're pale. Are ye ill?"

"Nay, 'tis naught. I dinna sleep well last night."

"Was it the dream?"

"Aye."

"Och, dinna fash yerself, lass, 'tis only a dream. Yer husband willna let anything happen to ye."

"No one can escape his or her fate," Blair whispered. "If I am to perish by fire, then so be it."

"Dinna talk like that," Alyce scolded. "Come downstairs, I'll fix ye yer favorite breakfast of fresh eggs and ham."

Blair acquiesced, though she had little appetite. What she truly craved was Graeme, and the comfort he offered against the demons plaguing her. She needed to see him one last time before the flames devoured her.

Despite her worries, Blair managed to keep busy. She helped Jamie count bed linens, checked pots and pans for possible repair or replacement when the tinker came through next, and supervised the laundress. After an early dinner, she went to the stillroom to work with her herbs. There was much to be done there. She still hadn't extracted all the willow juice from the bark they had collected and intended to finish the task today.

She worked steadily until her eyes began to droop. Because she hadn't slept much the previous night, she decided to sit down and rest her eyes while the juice was draining from the willow bark. Within minutes she was asleep.

Blair knew not how long she slept, but she was awakened by frantic voices screaming inside her head. Dense smoke filled the still-room as fire licked at the wooden frame of the little building. Flames blocked the door — there was no escape there. Heat seared her; smoke choked her. She looked toward the only window in the room, and her heart sank. It was too high for her to reach.

She backed up against the rear wall as the flames crept closer, devouring everything in their path. Then the thatched roof caught fire and Blair realized she was doomed. She was living her worst nightmare. Her breath came out in quick little gasps as she tried to draw air into her seared lungs.

Suddenly her fighting spirit took over, and her gaze returned to the window. Spurred by desperation, she rolled a barrel beneath the window, then prayed to the spirits to protect those she cared about. As for herself, the one person who could save her was too far away to hear her plea. She hoped Graeme's kinsmen had noticed the fire and were fighting to keep it from spreading to the kitchens. For herself, she feared it was too late.

The window was small, but it was her only hope. Climbing atop the barrel, she grasped the frame, pushed open the shutter and pulled herself up. Unfortunately, she lacked the strength to lift herself up and out to safety, but she was grateful for the breath of fresh air when none was to be had in the burning building. Flames licked at her skirt and singed her legs. Pain seared through her as she opened her mouth and screamed.

Graeme pushed his mount ruthlessly. It was nearly dark and he was anxious to reach home. The pain in his gut had intensified, reinforcing the premonition of danger at Stonehaven. It wasn't like him to ride his horse so hard, but he could almost hear Blair's voice begging him to make haste.

Relief flooded through him when he saw Stonehaven's towers rising in the distance against a darkening sky. "We're nearly home!" Graeme called to Heath. "I'm going to ride ahead." Since his steed was more powerful than Heath's, he quickly outpaced his cousin.

Then he saw something that made his heart leap into his throat. A thin spiral of smoke rose into the air above the keep. Fire was a hazard everyone feared. It could devour a man's home, his possessions, and the lives of innocent people.

Graeme's courageous steed gave his all to his master. The beast was covered in foam and blowing hard when Graeme entered the unguarded gate and reined in before the keep. He dismounted and flew up the stairs, not surprised to find the hall deserted. Everyone would be at the site of the fire.

He called Blair's name as he raced to the kitchen, the most likely place for a fire to break out. Maeve rushed forth to meet him. Her face was smeared with tears and ashes as she fell into Graeme's arms.

"Where is the fire?" Graeme demanded.

"The stillroom," Maeve said between sobs. "Oh, laird, 'tis bad. Verra, verra bad."

"Blair! Where is my wife?"

Maeve's wails grew louder. "Gone. No one could survive that inferno."

"Where are my guardsmen?"

"Throwing water on the fire, for all the good it will do."

Graeme rushed out through the kitchen door and skidded to a halt when he saw flames shooting up through the thatched roof of the stillroom. The building was an inferno. Despite the great amount of water being handed man to man from the well to the stillroom, it seemed unlikely anyone inside could survive.

Graeme could not let Blair go like this. He had to save her. Taking a deep breath, he ran toward the door. Aiden grasped his arm, stopping him in midstride.

"Ye canna go inside, mon. 'Tis certain death."

Chills ran up Graeme's spine when he recognized the truth of Aiden's words. A mass of flames filled the place where the door had once stood, and the thatched roof looked ready to fall in. But he couldn't stand there and do nothing while Blair was being consumed alive by flames. Then he remembered the window at the rear of the building. While everyone was busy throwing water on the fire, Graeme raced around to the rear, praying for a miracle.

A miracle was what Graeme found. Blair's face, grayed by soot and contorted by pain, was visible in the window. Desperately he called her name, but she appeared too dazed to reply.

"Can you climb out, lass?" Graeme asked.

This time his voice must have gotten through to her, for she focused on him and shook her head. Cursing, Graeme glanced around for something to stand on.

"Here! This might help," Heath said, dragging an old hay wagon behind him.

Graeme didn't question how Heath had known what he needed; he merely nodded his gratitude and set about rescuing Blair.

Climbing atop the wagon, he grasped Blair's arms and pulled her through the window. Fire had eaten away the bottom half of her gown, and he used his hands to beat out the flames. Then he leaped to the ground with Blair in his arms and rolled out of harm's way moments before the roof caved in.

Chapter Ten

Blair lay in bed while Alyce spread alkanet salve on her legs. Fortunately, Maeve kept the salve in the medicine chest she stored in the kitchen for emergencies. The burns weren't serious and were unlikely to leave scars, but Alyce insisted on treating the reddened flesh. When Graeme had carried Blair into the keep, Alyce had set to work, immediately, stripping off her charred clothing and washing away the thick layer of soot and ashes coating her skin.

"Do ye hurt, lass?" Alyce asked.

"The burns on my legs sting but not unbearably. The salve is soothing. Thank you." She dragged in a ragged sigh. "Losing my herbs and remedies in the fire is a terrible blow. 'Twill be difficult to replace them."

"Be glad ye have yer life," Alyce scolded. "Do ye know how the fire started? Could one of yer candles have done it?"

"Nay. I wasna using candles. 'Twas light enough to see without them. Where is Graeme?" she asked, suddenly aware of her husband's absence.

"Maeve is bandaging his hands."

"Graeme was injured?"

"Aye, his hands were blistered beating out the flames on your clothing. I suspect he will be here as soon as Maeve finishes with him."

Blair started to rise. "I must go to him. I want to know how badly he's hurt."

Alyce gently eased her back against the pillow. "Nay, lass, 'tis best ye rest now. Ye had a harrowing experience. Ye nearly died. If not for Graeme, ye would have perished in the fire. As it was, everyone thought ye were lost to us."

"How is she?" Graeme asked from the doorway.

"She's going to be fine, thanks to ye," Alyce said. "Come in, laird, I was just leaving."

Graeme stepped into the bedchamber and approached the bed. Alyce brushed past him and out the door, closing it softly behind her.

"Your poor hands!" Blair cried, horrified by the thick bandages covering his fingers.

"They will heal," Graeme assured her. "A few blisters and a scar or two willna bother me overmuch."

"But you were hurt saving me," Blair whispered. "How did you know I needed you?"

Graeme's blue eyes darkened with emotion. " 'Twas strange how it happened. Something told me I was needed at Stonehaven. Did you summon me?"

"I did need you, Graeme, but I didna think you could arrive in time." She shuddered. "Without you I couldna have survived the first trial."

Graeme sat on the edge of the bed. "Trial? What are you talking about?"

"The Prophecy says a Faery Woman will face trials by fire, water and stone. It has been thus throughout the ages. Thanks to you, I survived the fire."

"I thought the only way you would lose your powers was if you loved someone who doesna return your love."

"Nay, there are also trials to endure. Fire was the first one; there are still water and stone."

When he raised his hand to protest, Blair let out a cry and grasped both his hands in hers. " 'Tis my fault. You were hurt because of me."

"Dinna make too much of it, Blair. They will heal. How bad are the burns on your legs?"

"Not bad at all. My skirts took the worst of it. The skin from my ankles to my knees is scorched and reddened, but Alyce said there will be no scarring."

" 'Tis a miracle you survived. Someone was looking after you. It appears we have a fire-starter at Stonehaven, but fear not, I intend to unearth the culprit."

"What are you going to do?"

"Sift through the ashes for clues, for one thing. Think you the fire could have been started by a candle?"

"I lit no candles, and I let the fire in the hearth go out after I boiled the willow bark. I fell asleep while waiting for the juices to drain. I awakened to an inferno."

Graeme tried to pull his hands from hers. "I'd best be on my way if I'm to find the criminal in our midst."

Blair refused to release them. "Wait. Dinna go yet. Let me do this for you."

Graeme slanted her a puzzled look. "Do what?"

"I can heal your hands."

Graeme stared at her. "Like you healed Stuart? Aiden told me about the attack. Stuart suffered a near fatal wound but was miraculously cured. These powers of yours frighten me, Blair. I dinna want you practicing black arts. 'Tis dangerous. Did the fire teach you naught?"

"There is naught of evil in my healing," Blair argued. "My powers come from God. Would you rather I had allowed Stuart to die?"

A flash of pain passed over Graeme's features. "Nay, I wouldna. I dinna know what to think or how to handle these 'gifts' of yours. I wouldna want you to die because of them."

"I canna stop healing, Graeme. I would be worse than dead if I did. Close your eyes."

"Why?"

"Just do as I say and dinna try to pull your hands from mine no matter what happens. Your hands are important to you. They will be badly scarred if you dinna let me help you."

"I dinna believe in witchcraft."

Blair ignored him. "Close your eyes and think pleasant thoughts. Your aura isna right for healing. You must believe in me, Graeme. Believe that I can help you. Believe in the power of healing."

Blair looked down on Graeme's bandaged hands, which now rested in her palms. Much to her relief, Graeme's aura changed from gray to light blue, though she doubted he was thinking pleasant thoughts. Exhaustion etched lines in his face, and as he relaxed beneath her soothing touch, the lines smoothed.

Blair began her incantation beneath her breath, so that Graeme couldn't hear what she was saying. Her hands began to tingle and grow warm, and pain shot up her arms, until her whole body trembled with it. She felt Graeme try to pull his hands away, but she wouldn't allow it, gripping his bandaged fingers with all her strength. Just when the pain became unbearable, she cried out and fell back, releasing Graeme's hands at the same time.

"Och, Blair, what have you done?" Graeme cried. "Are you all right, lass? Speak to me. What happened just now?"

Speech slowly returned to Blair. When her vision cleared, she reached for Graeme's right hand.

Graeme pulled it away. "What are you about? What happened just now? You appeared to be in some kind of trance." His eyes widened. " 'Twas a spell! I willna have it, Blair. You willna work your magic on me. Is that clear?"

"Please, Graeme, give me your hand," Blair said calmly. "I merely want to undo your bandage."

"Am I supposed to believe you've healed me?" Graeme demanded.

"Indulge me," Blair whispered, "just this once."

"Verra well, have it your way. Maeve willna be pleased to see her work undone, but I will do as you say if only to disprove the powers you claim."

Blair began to unwind the bandage covering Graeme's right hand. When the hand was fully exposed, the incredulous look on Graeme's face told its own story. Mayhap now he would believe in her healing powers.

Graeme gazed at his hand in stunned disbelief. Not an hour past he had watched Maeve spread salve on his burns. Now there was not so much as redness on his palm. The pain was gone, and the skin was smooth but for the calluses that had existed before. Grim-faced, he tore away the bandage on his left hand, flexed his fingers and held it up to the light to make sure he wasn't imagining things. How could this be?

"You *are* a witch," he said in a voice full of frustration and no little amount of fear.

"Nay! How can you say such a thing?"

He held up his unblemished hands. "How do you explain this? No healer, no matter how skilled, could do what you just did."

"I am a Faery Woman. My powers extend beyond simple healing."

He shoved to his feet. "Stop it!"

"Stop what?"

"Whatever it is you just did. Rumors are already spreading about Stuart's miraculous recovery." He thrust his hands before her face. "What do you suppose will happen when word gets out about this? More attempts will be made on your life. Do you value your life so little that you would openly court danger?"

Hurt dimmed Blair's violet eyes. "I am what I am, Graeme. Aye, I have powers, but I use them to help others. After you saved my life, I wanted to help you."

"At what cost?" Graeme charged. "You suffered, did you not? I felt your body stiffen, heard you cry out and knew that what you were doing hurt you in some way. How long can you continue to summon powerful forces without damaging your health?"

Blair lowered her gaze. "I canna think beyond the present. What will be will be."

"Nay!" Graeme bellowed. "I willna accept that. If I am to protect you, you must promise to confine your healing to dispensing herbs and mixing salves. No more 'miraculous' cures."

"I canna do that, Graeme. As long as I have powers, I will continue to use them." She peered up at him through lowered lids. "The day I stop healing people is the day you place me in my grave."

Graeme shuddered, his expression grim. "The stillroom is destroyed and it willna be rebuilt. Think you I want your death?"

The determined glint in Blair's eyes softened. "Nay, I never thought such a thing. But you canna change me, Graeme. Father tried and failed."

"Why can you not love me? 'Twould save us both a lot of anguish."

"You *want* me to lose my powers. That has ever been your goal where I am concerned. You know you dinna love me and never will."

"I canna love you, not if I wish to protect you."

Blair said naught, her expression sad as she blinked back tears.

Graeme groaned as he felt one of the walls protecting his heart crack. Hurting Blair was the last thing he wanted to do, but she didn't seem to realize the danger she faced. Someone had to keep a level head, and it appeared he was the only one who cared enough to keep Blair safe.

He sat down beside her and raised her chin. "Blair, look at me. Do you want to live, lass?"

"Aye."

"Do you want children?"

Her eyes lit up. "Aye, if God wills."

"Then you must do as I say. Mix your herbal remedies, but dinna ever do what you did for Stuart and me again."

She looked so forlorn, so utterly defeated, that Graeme could not help himself. Lowering his head, he kissed her sweet lips, never intending for his conciliatory gesture to go any farther. But the moment their mouths touched, an aching need welled up inside him. The possibility of losing Blair horrified him. He could not bear the thought of life without Blair. His fingers curled around her narrow shoulders as he deepened the kiss, his tongue thrusting deep to taste her sweet essence.

He felt himself grow thick and harden and would have taken her then and there had he not felt her go limp against him. It was not her surrender he sensed, but her weariness. Only a beast would want to couple with a woman who had just escaped death and was still reeling from exhaustion. Furthermore, it was obvious that healing his burns had taken a great deal out of her.

Reluctantly he released her and broke off the kiss. "I'd best find my own bed. 'Tis late and there's much to be done tomorrow. I willna rest until I find the fire-starter in our midst. You can be verra sure he or she will be severely punished. Stay in bed until your legs are healed and Alyce says 'tis safe for you to move around."

He walked to the door, stopped abruptly and turned, raising his hands and flexing his fingers. " 'Tis truly a miracle. Thank you. And thank you for saving Stuart."

Then he opened the door and strode through, leaving Blair with mixed emotions. He had demanded that she stop healing, then thanked her for helping him and Stuart. There was no understanding the man.

Graeme said he had known that she needed him. How could he know if there wasn't a strong connection between them? Was God playing tricks on her? Twice now Graeme had saved her from dire circumstances, and both times he claimed he had answered her summons. Did Graeme love her?

Blair's weary mind went blank as her spent body relaxed into sleep. God willing, no dreams would torment her this night.

To Graeme's dismay, he found no clues to the fire-starter's identity after he concluded his investigation. No strangers had been noted in or around the keep that day. There were no secret passages, and the postern gate had been sealed long ago. The conclusion Graeme reached was not comforting. Someone inside the keep had set the fire. Who would benefit from Blair's death? Who feared her enough to kill her?

Graeme didn't want to believe that one of his kinsmen would incinerate an innocent woman. He would not allow Blair to suffer. Nay, he would not! He would prevent her from using her magic powers no matter what it took.

He would make her love him, even if he couldn't return her love.

Bending, he continued to sift through the ashes, unaware that Glenda was headed in his direction.

"What are ye looking for?" Glenda asked.

Graeme glanced up at Glenda. "What are you doing here?"

"I was in the kitchen garden gathering vegetables when I saw ye poking around in the ashes. Did ye find what ye're looking for?"

"Nay. I hoped to find a clue to the identity of the man or woman who set the fire."

Glenda's eyes widened. "Ye think someone deliberately set the fire?"

"Aye, I do. Someone who wished Blair harm."

"Bah! I am more apt to believe that a spark from the hearth ignited some of those dry weeds yer wife enjoys collecting. Or mayhap a candle toppled over."

"I would like to believe that, Glenda, but I think there is a more sinister explanation. I shall keep searching until I find answers that make sense."

Glenda's gaze descended to Graeme's hands. Her eyes widened, and she sucked in a startled breath. "Yer hands! How did they heal so quickly? I helped Maeve bandage them and saw the blisters."

Graeme hid his hands in the folds of his plaid. Explaining his miraculous healing was not going to be easy. "The burns were not as bad as we thought."

Glenda grasped his hand and peered closely at it. "Yer palm isna even red. What did Blair do, Graeme? Did she use witchcraft to heal ye?"

Graeme pulled his hand away. "Dinna you have something to do?"

"Ah, well, have it yer way. Just remember, I am here should you have need of me." She turned and ambled off, flicking her skirts to reveal a shapely ankle and calf.

When Graeme returned to the hall for the noon meal, Blair was nowhere to be seen.

"Blair is still too weak to leave her bed," Alyce explained as she approached Graeme with a basin of water, soap and towel.

"Are the burns on her legs healing?" Graeme asked as he dashed his hands into the water and worked up a lather.

"She wasna burned nearly as bad as ye were."

Graeme washed and dried his hands and face and returned the towel to Alyce. "Why does she not heal herself?" he asked curiously.

"Her power doesna work that way. She recives visions about future happenings and can heal others, but she canna heal herself."

"How do you know this?"

"I was there when Blair was born. I watched over her as her powers grew and strengthened. Neither Blair's mother nor grandmother was a Faery Woman, but she recognized her powers at an early age and was guided by the spirits."

Graeme shook his head. "I dinna understand. The dark ages are long gone. How can she be a witch?"

Alyce clucked her tongue. "For shame, laird. Blair could have used her powers for evil, but she chose to follow the path of light and goodness. She isna a witch; she is a healer."

Graeme studied his unblemished hands. "Aye, a healer, but what she does extends far beyond the bounds of healing. If she continues to use magic, 'twill be difficult to protect her from those who wish her harm."

Alyce shrugged, but her eyes held a wealth of sadness. "Blair's father had the same fears, but Blair could no more stop helping people than she could stop breathing."

Graeme ate his food without tasting it. When Stuart joined him, he welcomed his uncle with a smile.

"Ye seem lost in thought, Nephew," Stuart said.

Graeme's grin widened. " 'Tis good to see you up and about, Uncle. Dinna tire yourself. Take your time recuperating."

"Och, a mon can only stay in bed so long."

"Sit down, then, and tell me about the attack. Aiden told me as much as he knew, but I still have questions. Do you have any idea who attacked you?"

"Never saw them before," Stuart groused. "They came out of nowhere and tried to carry Blair off. I dinna remember much after that." He shook his head. " 'Tis most perplexing. Clearly, someone wants yer wife dead."

"Aye, I am aware of that. I just dinna know who or why."

"Do ye not, lad?" His gaze settled on Graeme's hands. "Everyone knows Blair used magic to heal my wound and cure yer burns. I should be a dead mon, but I am verra much alive. Not that I amna grateful. But Blair's healing powers have raised questions and doubts. The king has imposed harsh penalties on those who practice witchcraft. I wouldna want anything bad to happen to yer wee lass. I worried about yer marriage at first but have since changed my mind. The lass isna capable of evil."

"Naught will happen to Blair as long as I live and breathe," Graeme vowed. "I wish all our kinsmen felt as you do about her, Uncle. Yet someone feared her enough to set fire to the stillroom with her in it."

"Ye think the fire was deliberately set?"

"Aye, I do, though I canna prove it."

Graeme finished his meal and pushed his plate away. He was rising from the table when Heath came rushing into the hall.

"Visitors are at the gate. They request entrance."

"Who are they?"

"Niall MacArthur, accompanied by a dozen men at arms. He heard about the fire and wants to see his sister. The priest is with him."

"Word travels fast," Graeme mused. He was curious, however, to hear what Niall had to say. "Let them in."

A short time later, MacArthur and his men entered the hall. Graeme ordered ale for everyone and invited Niall and Father Lachlan to join him at the high table.

"What brings you to Stonehaven?" Graeme asked. "Were you not warned to stay away?"

Niall made a careless gesture toward the priest. "I brought the priest with me to prove I plan no mischief. I am concerned about my sister. I was told there was trouble involving Blair at Stonehaven. I would like to view the body."

Graeme shuddered. "What makes you think Blair is dead?"

" 'Tis of no importance. I know you have no priest at Stonehaven, so I brought Father Lachlan to say words over my sister's body."

"Is it true?" Father Lachlan asked. "Och, the poor blessed lass. Life isna fair."

"Blessed!" Niall blasted. "The girl was possessed by the devil. I would like to take her body home to bury in the family plot. 'Tis what our father would have wanted."

"Niall, what are you doing here?"

All three men looked up at the sound of Blair's voice. One of them grinned, one crossed himself, and the other cursed beneath his breath. Graeme rose and pulled out a chair for Blair. She flashed him a smile and allowed him to seat her.

"Thank God ye're alive," the priest offered in humble thanksgiving. "I feared the rumors were true."

"As you can see, Father, I am well," Blair said. She glared at her brother. "Were you hoping to pay your final respects?"

"I heard ye died in a terrible fire."

"You heard wrong. There was a fire, but I survived."

"I am glad," Niall said sourly. He rose. "I must leave. I am needed at Gairloch."

"Mayhap I will stay on a few days," Father Lachlan ventured, "if Laird Graeme has no objections."

"You're welcome to stay at Stonehaven as long as you wish," Graeme offered. "It has been a long time since my kinsmen have attended Mass." A flash of pain darkened his eyes. "Stonehaven's priest perished in France."

Niall prepared to leave, but Graeme stopped him. "Nay, dinna leave yet. There is something I have been meaning to speak to you about."

Blair rose. "Come with me, Father. You can tell me all about what has happened at Gairloch during my absence." They left the hall together.

"What is it you wish to discuss?" Niall asked Graeme with a marked lack of interest. "I shouldna tarry."

"The terms of Blair's nuptial agreement havena been met," Graeme said.

"I took no part in the arrangements," Niall argued. "Blair was supposed to wed the MacKay. Arrangements for the disposal of Blair's dowry were made with him."

"You acted without authority," Graeme charged. "Douglas MacArthur was alive when he asked me to wed Blair. His arrangements preceded yours."

"My father was sick and old and not in his right mind. I acted in his stead."

"There are those who will swear he was lucid up to the moment of his death. My marriage to Blair was legal, but I have yet to receive income from her lands on the Isle of Skye."

Niall shot to his feet. "Those lands and their income should be mine. Had Blair wed MacKay, he would have let me keep her dowry."

Graeme stood, towering over Niall by half a head. "But Blair didna wed MacKay, she wed me."

"Ye will never have her dowry," Niall snarled.

"I will petition the courts," Graeme threatened. "You are not above the law."

"Blair's dowry reverts back to me should Blair die without issue." He sent Graeme a look of pure malice. "A witch's life is precarious at best. I wouldna count on Blair living long enough to bear a child, even if ye *are* brave enough to dip yer rod in her witch's cauldron."

"Are you threatening my wife?" Graeme roared.

"I didna say that. I know there's been trouble involving Blair at Stonehaven, even if ye dinna want to admit it. I am no fool. The odor of burning wood still lingers in the air. What happened? Does one of yer kinsmen want her dead?"

" 'Twas an accident," Graeme replied. "As

you can see, all is well at Stonehaven."

"Then I willna bother ye any longer with my concern for my sister." Niall gestured to his men, and they rose as one to follow him out the door.

"You havena heard the last of this," Graeme promised. "I will ready my petition to present to the courts. I am sure Douglas didna want you to claim any part of Blair's dowry. The land is hers. One of our children will inherit it."

Niall stormed off in a huff. Graeme watched him leave, jarringly aware that Niall was hoping for an early death for Blair. Did he want her dowry badly enough to kill her for it?

"How are things at Gairloch?" Blair asked as she and Father Lachlan seated themselves before the hearth in the solar.

"Naught is the same since yer father died," Lachlan lamented. "Niall isna loved by his kinsmen. 'Tis true he has the king's ear, but he doesna use his position for the good of our clan. He thinks only of himself and the power the king's friendship will bring him. He will use the king as he uses everyone else."

Blair sighed. "Do our people suffer because of his greed?"

"Not yet. The MacArthur clan isna poor, but that could change in time. Our kinsmen do suffer, however, for lack of yer healing skills. The Campbells are fortunate to have ye."

Blair gave a bitter laugh. "I wish they felt as you do."

Lachlan stared at her, his brows raised in question. "What is it, lass? Was Niall right? Are ye in trouble? Does Campbell nae treat ye well?"

"'Tis not Graeme," Blair confided. "Attempts have been made upon my life on two occasions."

"Holy Mother! What happened, lass?"

"Alyce, Graeme's uncle and I were attacked while gathering herbs in the forest. Stuart was gravely wounded, but I used my powers to stop the bleeding, and he is making a full recovery. A few days later, the stillroom was set afire and I nearly perished in the blaze. Had Graeme not arrived when he did, I would not be here talking to you."

"Do ye know who is behind those foul deeds?"

"Nay. All five of our attackers were found dead. As for the fire, I suspect Graeme has found naught to incriminate anyone."

"Surely God is protecting ye, lass," Lachlan said. "Ye still have yer healing powers, then?"

"Aye."

Lachlan smiled. "Then Graeme Campbell returns yer love. The Prophecy has been fulfilled. I am pleased."

Blair frowned. "What makes you think I love Graeme? Mayhap I still retain my powers because I willna allow myself to love him. Graeme loves another; there is no love between us."

"I know ye, lass. Yer eyes tell me what ye canna admit. Ye love the man ye married. If yer powers still exist, it's because Graeme returns yer love."

Blair wished it were true, but nothing Graeme had said suggested that he loved her. She had known Graeme long before she made his physical acquaintance. He was her dream lover. In life, he had become her salvation, her protector. But Graeme had known her such a short time, he couldn't possibly love her. It made more sense to believe she had been successful in withholding her own heart.

Chapter Eleven

Blair's legs were healing remarkably well. Only a dull redness and slight stinging remained. During the following days she was glad of Father Lachlan's company, for Graeme's obsession with finding the fire-starter kept him away from the keep for long periods of time. For some reason he had begun to sleep in his own bed, and Blair wondered if he feared her powers.

After a week of saying Masses and hearing confessions, Father Lachlan announced his intention to return to Gairloch. His reason for leaving was his fear that Niall might be behind the attacks on Blair's life; he wanted to keep an eye on him. Blair bade him a teary good-bye and waved him off.

The night that Lachlan departed, Graeme entered Blair's bedchamber and watched absently as she brushed her hair. He had a defeated look about him that Blair had never seen before.

"What is wrong?" she asked, giving him her full attention. Obviously, something was on his mind, and she waited patiently for him to tell her what was bothering him.

"I have no idea who set the fire and no information about the men who attacked you in the forest. Did Father Lachlan tell you anything helpful? We all seem to agree that either Niall or MacKay was behind the attacks upon your life. What puzzles me is how they or their men got inside the keep without being challenged. A MacArthur or MacKay would have been recognized as a stranger. However, no strangers were sighted that day."

"I dinna like to think it, Graeme, but mayhap one of your kinsmen set the fire."

" 'Tis deplorable," Graeme said, "but not impossible."

He rose, took the brush from her hand and began drawing it through her hair. "It pains me to think one of my own people wishes you harm."

"I canna change how people feel, Graeme, but those who know me are aware that I would do naught to harm them."

"Aye. 'Tis why I dinna believe any of my kinsmen would deliberately hurt you. They have come to know you and depend upon your healing skills. Even Stuart has changed his mind about you, though 'twas not an easy thing for him to admit."

He set the brush down and caressed her cheek with the back of his hand. Then he tipped her face up, lowered his head and kissed her.

"Sweet, so sweet," he murmured against her lips. "I want to make love to you, Blair. 'Tis been a long time."

I want the same thing. Fear of something unnamed kept her from voicing her need. "Do you think that's wise?"

"What does wisdom have to do with wanting one another? What are you afraid of? Are you still feeling pain?"

"Nay."

"Then let me make love to you."

Blair could not deny him, nor did she want to. Since she still had her powers she supposed she was safe in believing she could guard her heart, so why should she deny herself the comfort of Graeme's body? There was no shame in making love with one's husband, or so she had been taught.

She rose and turned into his arms, lifting her lips to his in blatant invitation. Graeme groaned as he dragged her against him, taking her mouth with a hunger startling in its intensity. She felt his sex stirring between them and deliberately rubbed her softness against it, creating a volatile friction that brought a flood of moisture to her aching center.

With sudden impatience, he released her and dragged his boots off. Then he reached for her and pulled her with him toward the bed. They didn't make it. Hastily he lowered her to the woven rug before the hearth, his face a study in desperate need and dark desire. He was about to remove his shirt and plaid when Blair caught his hand and pulled him on top of her.

"Later," she whispered, her haste in direct proportion to her great need.

He went down willingly, catching her in his arms, kissing her thoroughly as he raised her skirt. Sweeping aside his plaid, he plunged inside her. Then he went absolutely still, luxuriating in blissful pleasure as Blair's tight sheath drew him in. But it wasn't enough. He wanted her naked, wanted to touch her dewy skin, needed to feel the heat of her flesh against his hands.

Still connected to her in the most intimate way, Graeme worked Blair's gown over her head and off. Her shift followed. Moaning in pleasure, he molded her magnificent breasts in his hands, then buried his face between them, rubbing back and forth, exulting in their creamy smoothness.

He couldn't seem to get enough of her. His lips closed over one coral tip. Blair shuddered, her hips rocking against him. When he moved to tease the other nipple, her nails bit into his back, then slid under his plaid to dig into his buttocks.

Nothing in his past had prepared him for this heightened degree of passion, for no woman could compare with his wee Faery Woman. Patience deserted him as he caught both of her hands in one of his, pinning her wrists to the floor above her head so that her breasts lifted, giving him unlimited access to her nipples.

His mouth clamped down hard on one sweet bud as he began to move inside her. Crying out, she squirmed against him, yanking free of his grip and pulling at his clothing in wordless demand. But Graeme would not be hurried. His blue eyes were dark and feral, his teeth bared as he thrust and withdrew, reaching deep to give her the most pleasure.

"Your clothes!" Blair pleaded, tearing at the edges of his shirt.

"Later," he gasped, grinding his hips against her. "We have the whole night ahead of us, lass."

She gave a low moan of distress when he withdrew nearly all the way, then she clutched his hips and groaned when he thrust in and upward, going deep inside her. He nearly spilled when convulsions ripped though her and he felt her tighten around him in hard, rapid spasms.

He surged into her again and again, bucking wildly until he finally reached the ultimate peak and pleasure splintered through him. Panting, he rested his damp forehead against hers, waiting for his world to stop spinning.

"I canna love you," Blair whispered.

Her words tore through his contentment,

exposing the darkness that stood between them.

"So you've said before."

He rose up on his knees, scooped her into his arms and carried her to the bed, his gaze dark and inflexible as he removed his clothing. But instead of joining her, he poured water from a pitcher into a bowl and cleansed them both of his spent seed. When he returned to her, his sex was stirring again.

Blair stared at his groin, then lifted her gaze to his. "Did I not satisfy you?"

"Aye, but you left me wanting more."

"Already? Is that possible? So soon, I mean."

"More than possible."

He leaned over, parted her legs and kissed the fragile skin on the inside of her thigh. Her sighs spurred him on as he spread his hand over her belly and kneaded the gentle curve, then drew the heel down over the slight rise of her woman's mound. She moaned deep in her throat and began grinding her pelvis into his palm. The sweet scent of female arousal joined with the scent of his own rising ardor to produce the keenest aphrodisiac known to man.

He slid his fingers through the dainty blond curls and probed her intimately, grinning when he felt her wetness. Pushing her thighs apart, he gazed at her moist, pink center; the petal-like folds of her body were swollen, and the bud at their center glistened with pearly dew. She made a choking sound when he covered the sensitive bud with his mouth and suckled.

Murmuring his name, she thrust her hips upward, into the hot cave of his mouth. He continued his passionate torment until the convulsions raking her body subsided.

Throbbing and ready, he crawled upward and entered her clutching warmth, again and again, driving them both to a bone-wrenching climax.

Light-headed, utterly sated, he collapsed against her, wondering if he would ever move again. Blair's quiet sobbing brought him abruptly back to reality. Raising himself up on his elbows, he looked questioningly into her eyes.

"Did I hurt you, sweetheart? I didna mean to."

"You didna hurt me," Blair hiccuped.

"Then why are you crying?"

"I am a wanton. What must you think of me? I dinna believe what we did is within the bounds of what the church allows."

" 'Tis my belief the church has no say over what takes place in the marriage bed. I love having a responsive wife. Passion between husband and wife is what keeps a husband from straying; it keeps the marriage vital." He grinned at her. "Rest assured, I will never stray. You are the only woman I need in my bed."

Warmed by his words, Blair curled into his arms and buried her head against his shoulder. He smelled of sex and sin and dark desire. How could a woman not love such a man?

Graeme was gone when Blair awoke the next morning. A blush stained her cheeks when she recalled their loving the night before. She couldn't believe her boldness. She had responded with wanton abandon to Graeme, but he did not seem to mind. She flexed her muscles, finding aches in unmentionable places. Swinging her feet to the ground, she attempted to stand. Suddenly light-headed, she plopped back down on the bed until the feeling passed.

When the giddiness eased, she rose and began the simple tasks of washing and dressing. Feeling much better, she went downstairs to break her fast. Graeme must have seen her enter the hall, for he soon joined her.

"I hoped you would sleep longer," he said, pulling out a chair for her. "How do you feel?"

Blair sent him a covert glance from beneath lowered lids. "I feel fine. Why should I not?"

Graeme grinned. "I am glad to hear it. I too feel fine. Invigorated, in fact." He leaned forward to whisper against her ear. "You bewitch me."

Blair recoiled in alarm. "I canna bewitch people."

Graeme straightened, aware that his kinsmen were watching. "I dinna believe it. Everyone can see I am clearly besotted."

Blair's eyes widened. "You are?" Somehow that was hard to credit. Was Graeme teasing her?

He placed a chaste kiss on her brow and backed away. "I was just about to leave when you arrived."

"Where are you going?"

"To the MacKay stronghold. I need answers about the men who attacked you and Stuart."

"Think you Donal MacKay sent them?"

He touched the dirk sheathed at his waist. "I'd wager my *skean dhu* that he did. Stay close to the keep until I return."

"There is something I've been meaning to ask you."

His brow furrowed. "What is it?"

"Is there a chamber within the keep that I might use to prepare my herbal remedies after I replenish what I lost in the fire?"

A vein pulsed in Graeme temple. "Did you learn naught, woman? 'Tis best you direct your energy in another direction."

"You know I canna," she said softly. "Please, Graeme, dinna make me defy you. Let me do what I was born to do. When winter comes, your clansmen will seek cures for fevers, chills and sniffles. My salves can heal their burns, and teas brewed from certain herbs can cure minor ills and aid women giving birth."

Graeme appeared torn. "If I allow it, will you promise that no magic will be involved?"

"I but intend to gather herbs, mix salves and prepare soothing teas."

"No herb-gathering excursions without at least six of my guardsmen protecting you. Do you understand?"

"Aye. Do you have a chamber in mind?"

"There is an unused chamber on the first floor, next to the armory. It has a window and a small hearth and should serve your purpose. I may be mad for allowing it, but I canna argue with the fact that your remedies help my kinsmen."

"Thank you, Graeme," Blair said sincerely.

He gave her a hard stare, bent and kissed her lips, then strode off.

"Be careful," she called to his rapidly departing back. A nod and a wave acknowledged her warning.

Graeme crossed the boundary between Campbell and MacKay lands and rode with an escort of a dozen men toward the MacKay stronghold. As he passed through the village, he noted the run-down condition of the dilapidated huts, comparing them with the neat cottages in his own village. He had more respect for his kinsmen than to let them live in poverty. His own people were well fed and reasonably prosperous.

There was no mistaking the hostile glares directed at him by MacKay clansmen. His distinctive Campbell plaid was eyed with distrust. There had been bad feeling between the Campbells and MacKays since Graeme's great-grandfather had stolen Marta MacKay and made her his wife. Unfortunately, the lass died in childbirth and the child with her. The ensuing years hadn't softened the animosity between the clans.

Reiving was not uncommon, and many a Campbell sheep now grazed on MacKay lands. Still, Graeme had done everything in his power to keep communications open between the two clans. Blood feuds were destructive and counterproductive.

Graeme reined in before a nondescript grog shop and ordered his men to wait outside as he entered the dim interior.

"To what do we owe this pleasure?" the surly barkeep asked. " 'Tisna often we get a visit from the Campbell laird."

"I developed a thirst on my way to visit the MacKay." He slapped a coin down on the scarred counter. "Ale."

Graeme took his ale to a table and sat down. Three men seated at a nearby table eyed him warily, but when it appeared that Graeme was merely interested in quenching his thirst, they lost interest. Not so the bar-maid, who ambled over to Graeme and indicated the empty chair.

"Mind if I sit down?"

Since Graeme was after information, he invited the overblown woman to sit down.

"My name is Nell. Ye look lonely. I'm not busy right now, and my room is above stairs."

Graeme stifled a smile. There was nothing subtle about Nell. "Your invitation is tempting, but I canna linger."

Nell's eyes narrowed. "What business do ye have with our laird? I heard ye wed the witch woman the MacKay wanted." She leaned close, affording Graeme a glimpse of large, pillowy breasts. "What is it like bedding a witch? Our kinsmen were relieved the MacKay didna bring her here."

Graeme stiffened. "Blair isna a witch. She is a Faery Woman and a healer. But my business concerns your kinsmen. Have any men from the village gone missing recently?"

Alarm widened Nell's brown eyes. "How did ye know? My own brother and four of his friends have disappeared. Do ye ken what happened to them?"

Graeme decided that half-truths would have to suffice. "Aye, mayhap. We found five bodies in the forest after the summer storm that ravaged the area several days ago. They didna wear MacKay plaids, so we had no idea who they were."

"Did ye find them on MacKay lands?"

"Nay, we found them on Campbell lands. Their deaths were acts of God, not man. They were crushed beneath trees felled by lightning."

Tears filled Nell's eyes. "I am sorry to hear my brother is dead. It sore grieves me."

Graeme finished his ale and rose. His visit to the village had been enlightening. There was no way that MacKay could lie about sending the men to kidnap Blair when the truth had been so easily obtained. He withdrew a coin from his sporran and flipped it to Nell.

"I am sorry for your loss," he said as he made his way out of the grog shop.

"Did ye learn anything?" Heath asked when Graeme reappeared.

"Aye, a great deal. Five men have disappeared from the village. I see Donal MacKay's hand in this. He will stop at naught to get what he wants."

"I dinna ken why he wants Blair," Heath mused.

"He believes she can use witchcraft to bring him riches and power. You saw the state of the village. I am willing to bet his keep is in sad repair and his coffers are empty. He needs gold to support the king and gain his favor. Both MacKay and Niall MacArthur are power hungry. The king does naught without a reason, and those he befriends must pay for the privilege."

"Aye," Heath acknowledged. " 'Tis said the king's treasury is depleted, and that he hasna paid the ransom England demanded for his freedom. Not even the heavy taxes he has levied are enough to fill his empty coffers and repay his debt."

He scratched his head. "Even if Blair were a witch, I dinna ken how she could make MacKay rich. The man is a fool. Niall has filled his head with lies about Blair and what she is capable of."

When they reached the front gates of MacKay's stronghold, Graeme gave his name and asked permission to enter. A message was carried to MacKay. A short time later he appeared at the gate, his chest puffed up like a peacock.

"Ha!" MacKay snorted. "I knew ye would change yer mind. I will be happy to take the witch off yer hands." He searched the ranks of Graeme's men and frowned. "Where is she? Did ye nae bring the lass with ye?"

Graeme's hands fisted at his sides. "I have no intention of parting with Blair. I am here on business of another sort. Are you afraid to let me inside the gate?"

MacKay's heavy features hardened. "I fear no mon, Campbell or otherwise." He motioned for the gatekeeper to crank open the gate and stood aside as Graeme and his party rode through. They reached the keep, dismounted and followed MacKay inside.

The ale MacKay served was sour and not at all to Graeme's liking, and after one sip he pushed it aside.

"State yer business, Campbell," MacKay said. "I am a busy mon."

"The five men you sent to abduct Blair are dead," Graeme said without preamble.

MacKay's expression became guarded. "I dinna ken what ye're talking about."

"Save your denial for someone who will believe it."

"What makes ye think the men were MacKays? Did they wear MacKay plaids?"

"Nay. I was told by one of your kinsmen that five men left the village and failed to return."

"That proves naught," MacKay scoffed. "Five men left the village. So what? It happens all the time. If that's all ye've come to say, I bid ye farewell."

Graeme rose, his face set in harsh lines. "Heed me well, MacKay. Dinna try anything like that again or I will retaliate."

"Ye wouldna be so smug if ye knew the king's plan for those like ye who supported the Duke of Albany and his son Murdoc during his captivity. James intends to vanquish all those who sought to seize control of Scotland while he was held hostage in England. Albany met his just end, but Murdoc still conspires against James, and the Highland lairds are lending their support. But the traitors will be punished."

Graeme went still. What was MacKay talking about? "My father was cleared of conspiracy charges long ago, thanks in part to Douglas MacArthur. As for myself, I have no interest in politics. I care only for my clansmen and their well-being. Good day to you, MacKay."

MacKay's words did not sit easy with Graeme. His vague warning held elements of truth that could bring trouble to Clan Campbell. Should he believe MacKay? It wasn't implausible that the king would seek revenge on those who'd tried to seize the throne while he had been held captive in England. And many of the Highland lairds *did* support Albany and his family.

Graeme didn't have time to worry about the king. He meant what he had said. He wasn't political. As long as James proved a good king, he had no intention of conspiring against him.

Blair was pleased she'd been able to convince Aiden to send six men with her and Alyce while they gathered herbs in the forest. The herbs were at their peak and just right for picking.

Blair found a treasure trove of puffballs, an edible fungus that helped bloody wounds clot because of the tiny spores it contained. She also found lichen, which was used for stanching wounds, dill weed, parsley and other herbs.

When they returned to the keep, Blair was surprised to find that Graeme was back and in a rage. He awaited her in the solar. She handed her basket to Alyce and hurried up to the solar to learn the cause of her husband's anger.

"I thought I told you to remain close to the keep!" he shouted the moment she walked through the door. "When will you learn to listen to me?"

Blair stifled a smile at the realization that Graeme cared about her so much. "I was in no danger, Graeme. Six armed men accompanied Alyce and me. We didna linger overlong."

He caressed her cheek, then hastily pulled his hand away, as if embarrassed by his concern. "Nevertheless, I shall leave orders that you are not to stray far from the keep when I am not here."

"Verra well. I dinna want you to worry about me. What happened with MacKay? Did you see him?"

"Aye, and after our conversation, I trust him even less than I did before. The men who attacked you were his clansmen, though MacKay denied it."

"How can you be sure?"

"I stopped at the village grog shop and spoke with a barmaid. She told me that five men had disappeared from the village."

One delicate brow arched upward. "Barmaid? You spoke with a woman?"

"Aye. She was most helpful."

"Humph! I suspect she was."

One corner of Graeme's mouth tilted upward. "Jealous, lass?"

"Not in the least. I am glad she proved helpful."

"We will speak further about your jealousy tonight." Then he nodded and took his leave.

Blair sank onto a bench and tried to explain the jolt of anger that had shot through her when she learned that Graeme had obtained information from a woman. Had he used his charm to gain the information he sought? What else had the woman given him?

"God's holy blood! What is wrong with me?" she said impatiently.

"Blair . . . Heed me . . ."

Blair went still, her gaze searching the empty chamber. A breeze fluttered the drapery at the window and lifted the hem of her skirt. She felt it brush against her cheek, a coolness both startling and comforting. Blair knew immediately the spirits were trying to communicate with her. Her brow furrowed in concentration.

"What is it?" she whispered. "What are you trying to tell me?"

The words came to her on the sigh of the wind. "Beware . . . Danger stalks him . . ."

"Graeme? Graeme is in danger?"

The voice grew agitated. "If you let him leave, he will not return. Death awaits him at his destination."

A chill settled in Blair's heart. "What can I do?"

A strong gust of wind blew through the chamber, knocking over small objects and stirring the heavy bed hangings.

"You know what you must do," the voice said. "You have the power to keep the one you love safe."

"I canna love Graeme, you know that."

"Heed me well," the voice continued. "The man you love is in grave danger." The voice began to fade, the parting words barely discernible.

The spirit was gone, but the chilling message still echoed in her head. Blair shivered, cold to her very marrow. Something unexpected and potentially disastrous was going to happen to Graeme if she didn't prevent it.

She closed her eyes, striving to bring the spirit back. As she did so, a vision formed behind her lids. She saw Graeme, his lifeless body covered with blood and missing his head. She screamed and screamed, then dropped to the floor in a faint. When Alyce found and revived her a short time later, she refused to reveal the terrifying vision.

The next day Graeme received a missive from the king. All the Highland lairds were ordered to attend James at Inverness. The meeting was to take place the first day of the following month at the Court of Sessions James had instigated after he had been released from captivity.

When Blair heard about the message, she knew what her vision had meant. Somehow she had to prevent Graeme from leaving Stonehaven. His very life depended upon it.

"Must you go?" Blair asked.

"Aye. You know I canna ignore a summons from the king."

"Dinna go, Graeme," she pleaded, desperate to make him understand. "I have a bad feeling about this. I see danger awaiting you at Inverness."

"Dabbling in magic again, are you?" he asked, fixing her with a censuring glare. "Dinna do this, lass. You know I must go."

"Please, Graeme, dinna make light of my fears. You mustna leave Stonehaven."

His fingers curled around her narrow shoulders. "Stop it, lass. Naught you say will keep me from obeying the king. Your fears have no basis. Trust me to take care of myself. We will discuss this later, after I consult with Heath. Accommodations will be scarce with such a large gathering converging on the city. Perhaps I shall send Heath ahead to secure rooms for us."

"Please, Graeme, dinna go."

"There is naught more to discuss, sweeting. Go to bed, I will join you after I speak with Heath."

Closing her eyes, Blair made a solemn vow. She would save Graeme's life, even if he hated her for it afterward.

Chapter Twelve

Graeme began preparations for his journey to Inverness immediately, though he wouldn't leave for several days yet. Heath had already been sent ahead to secure accommodations. Graeme planned to take only three men, leaving the rest behind to protect Stonehaven. He had no idea why the king had called a meeting of Highland lairds but was looking forward to meeting clansmen and allies he hadn't seen in a long time.

One day when Graeme went below to check his weapons, he paused before the chamber that now served Blair as a stillroom. He was puzzled by her insistence that he not go to Inverness and wanted to discuss her strange behavior.

A smile curved his lips. He never tired of making love to Blair. He hated leaving her behind while he went to Inverness, but it could not be helped. Right now, however, he needed to know why Blair was so adamantly opposed to his leaving.

He pushed open the door and peered inside. Blair was seated at a bench, bending over a table piled high with . . . puffballs, of all things. He cleared his throat.

Blair looked up and smiled. Graeme had never seen a smile light up a room the way hers did. The first time he'd seen her he thought she looked like an angel, and his opinion had not changed.

"We need to talk," Graeme began.

"Aye," Blair agreed eagerly. "Have you decided not to go to Inverness?"

"Nay, I must go. Tell me why you think I should stay home. Your fear makes no sense."

Blair dragged in a calming breath and said, "You know I sometimes hear and see things. What I heard and saw was . . ." She shook her head. "I canna speak of it. Suffice it to say the warning I received was terrifying. You mustna leave Stonehaven."

"Where did the warning come from? I dinna believe in spirits, Blair. Tell me something I can believe."

Blair shook her head. "How can I save you if you dinna heed me?"

"You dinna need to save me, sweeting. I am in no danger. What harm can come to me in the company of my king, my allies and my friends?"

"I dinna know. If I did, I would tell you. I've learned to heed my visions. Please, Graeme, if you care for me at all, dinna go to Inverness."

"Thus far I have heard naught to change my mind."

"My vision . . . The spirits . . ."

He made a clucking sound with his tongue. "Voices and spirits. Say no more, lass." He had already seen one woman die for her belief in such things. He turned to leave.

As he went through the door, his aura changed from a pleasing blue to blood red. A startled cry left her lips and tears welled in her eyes. She couldn't let him die. With sinking heart she realized that nothing she said would change Graeme's mind. Her vision could not be proved and therefore was to be ignored. The time had come to use her powers to save Graeme's life.

Alyce pushed the door open and peered inside. "There ye be, lass. Do ye need help?"

"Shut the door and latch it," Blair said. "I am going to do something that Graeme has forbidden."

"What is it, lass? Ye look frightened. Does it have anything to do with yer fainting dead away yesterday?"

"Aye. The spirits sent me a warning. Graeme is in grave danger. He mustna go to Inverness, but he refuses to listen to me when I repeat the warning."

"What will ye do?"

"Did you replace the candles that were lost in the fire?"

"Aye."

"Get them while I gather the herbs I need."

"Are ye going to summon the spirits?"

"Aye. The candles, Alyce."

Alyce retrieved candles from a cupboard and placed them in a circle. Blair stepped inside the circle and sprinkled dried herbs around her feet. Alyce lit the candles and melted back into the shadows to watch and wait.

Blair flung her arms wide and began to chant a silent entreaty. The candle flames flickered and elongated, taking on rainbow hues. Blair's face was pale and her lips were drained of all color as she turned in a circle, lifted her arms high and called upon the spirits of nature to attend her.

> "Spirits of nature, heed me.
> Earth, moon, sun and sea,
> Send torrents of rain from the sky.
> Make the loch run high."

A sudden flash of lightning streaked across the sky, followed by a thunderous roar. Dark clouds blotted out the sun, and the wind rose to howling intensity. The warm spring day that had begun with such promise turned dark and ominous. Wind rushed through the window, snuffing out the candles. Then it began to rain, fierce, pounding rain that hammered the earth. Blair lowered her arms and sank to the floor, utterly spent.

"Lass, are ye all right?"

"Aye. Help me to a bench. I need a moment to rest."

"What did ye hope to gain by making it rain?"

"If Loch Torridon floods and washes out the bridges, Graeme canna get to Inverness in time for the meeting."

Alyce helped Blair to her feet and guided her to a bench. "Are ye sure the laird is in danger?"

"Aye, verra, verra sure."

"I dinna want to be in yer shoes when yer husband finds out what ye did."

Dread shivered down Blair's spine. "I did what I had to do to save Graeme's life."

Blair suddenly became aware that someone was pounding on the door.

"Blair! Why is the door locked? Let me in."

Alyce looked at Blair, then hurried over to unlock the door. Graeme burst inside as Alyce hurriedly gathered up the candles.

"What in God's name is going on in here?" His harsh words echoed through the chamber and bounced off the walls.

"What makes you think anything is going on?" Blair asked softly, too exhausted to raise her voice.

Graeme looked pointedly at the candles cradled against Alyce's ample bosom. "Were you casting a spell?"

"Blair did naught wrong," Alyce attempted to explain.

"Be gone, woman!" Graeme roared. "I wish to speak to my wife in private."

Alyce scooted out the door, closing it softly behind her. Graeme returned his gaze to Blair. "Tell me I am wrong. Tell me you werena using magic."

Clamping her lips tightly shut, Blair stared at Graeme. She didn't want to lie.

"Tell me, Blair, and please make it the truth."

"I canna. Just believe I would never harm you or anyone."

Graeme stared at her for the space of a heartbeat, then turned away, directing his gaze at the rain beating against the window. " 'Tis odd," he mused. "The day began with such promise. I hope this blasted rain stops before I leave. Travel is difficult during un-settled weather."

"Forget the rain. There is naught anyone can do about it. Shall we return to the hall? 'Tis nearly time for the evening meal."

Graeme turned away from the window and directed his glittering gaze at Blair. "Is there aught you want to tell me, lass?"

Blair knew that lying to Graeme would likely put an end to their relationship, but she had to save his life, even if it cost her Graeme's respect. Sighing despondently, she followed Graeme to the hall and took her place beside him at the high table.

The ferocious storm that had come out of nowhere seemed to be the topic of conversation among all those present.

" 'Tis eerie, I tell ye," Stuart ventured. He sent a furtive look at Blair before continuing. "And passing strange the way the storm came so suddenly. I hope the hail hasna damaged the crops."

"Aye. If the rain doesna stop soon, it will flood the valley and threaten our sheep," Aiden warned.

"The rain will likely end tonight," Graeme maintained. "Storms this fierce rarely last more than a few hours."

Blair lowered her eyes, unable to meet Graeme's probing gaze. She knew he was suspicious of her and was withholding judgment until he had some kind of proof. Little did he know that proof existed in the downpour that was even now raising the level of the loch. She prayed he would never know.

That night Graeme slept in his own chamber. Blair heard his footsteps pause before her door before moving on. It seemed he was as restless and sleepless as she.

Graeme couldn't escape the feeling that Blair was involved in something he would not approve of. Had she been using magic, against his express wishes? He had deliberately kept himself from her bed in order to think without being distracted, but it hadn't been easy. This morning he ached like the very devil for his willful wife. He was leaving Stonehaven soon, and God only knew when he would return. It all depended upon the king and his reason for bringing the Highland lairds together in one place.

Graeme glanced out the window, his brow furrowing when he saw that the storm was as fierce as it had been yesterday. The courtyard was flooding, the water already ankle deep. When was it going to end?

Graeme went to the hall to break his fast, not surprised by the large number of men with naught to do but talk, dice and drink ale. No one wanted to venture outdoors.

Graeme ate his porridge and joined Heath and Stuart, who were warming their backsides by the hearth.

" 'Tis wicked outside," Stuart commented. " 'Tis as if God Himself has sent a deluge to punish us for our sins."

"Or else a witch brought this upon us," Aiden muttered.

"What did you say?"

A racket at the door forestalled Aiden's reply.

"I wonder who is out and about in this wretched weather," Graeme muttered.

Four villagers, three men and a woman, staggered into the hall.

"Warm yourselves by the fire," Graeme directed. "What brings you to the keep?"

" 'Tis the witch," the first man spat. "If ye dinna stop her, the village will be flooded and our crops ruined."

"Are you referring to my wife?" Graeme asked coolly.

"Aye. No one, not even our elders, has seen anything like this before. 'Tis unnatural, I tell ye."

The woman pushed back the hood of her sodden cloak. It was Gunna, the midwife.

"I warned ye about the witch, laird. 'Tis not just the deluge she has wrought, but other things as well."

"Like what?" Graeme asked.

"Grant's goat died suddenly. And Murray's wife took sick. Then Meg's cow went dry. Now this rain. 'Tis no coincidence, I tell ye. 'Tis the witch's doing."

Graeme saw Blair enter the hall and tried to warn her, but it was too late. She had seen the small gathering and hurried over to join them.

"What's amiss?"

"There she be!" Gunna crowed, pointing a bony finger at Blair. "We dinna want her kind here."

Blair's steps faltered. Then she seemed to pull herself together. Graeme could almost see her spine stiffen.

"These good people seem to think you

259

have done something to harm them," he said.

"Why would I wish to harm your kinsmen?" Blair answered. "Have I not treated their injuries and cured their ailments?"

"Our crops are nigh ruined, Grant's goat is dead, Meg's cow went dry, and Murray's wife is sick, and her the heartiest soul alive."

"You think I am responsible?" Blair asked, clearly aghast.

Graeme placed a protective arm around her and pulled her close. "My wife had naught to do with the happenings in the village. Warm yourselves and have a bite to eat, then return to your homes and stay there. I'm sure the rain will stop soon and your crops willna suffer."

"I wouldna hurt them," Blair whispered after the delegation shuffled off. "You believe me, do you not?"

Graeme hauled her off to a private corner where they couldn't be overheard. "I believe you did naught to hurt my kinsmen, but I also know that something unnatural took place in the stillroom. I canna protect you if you dinna tell me what you did."

"You're going to have to trust me, Graeme," Blair said.

His expression turned cold. " 'Tis best you tell me now so I can head off trouble before I leave Stonehaven. Tell me you had naught to do with the dead goat, the dry cow and Murray's sick wife."

Blair made a sound of disgust deep in her throat. "Really, Graeme, think you I would stoop to such attacks against the villagers?"

"I'm beginning to think I dinna really know you. I dinna like secrets, lass."

"Do you still intend to go to Inverness?"

"You know I do. I canna disobey the king's orders."

She turned to leave, but Graeme wouldn't allow it. Too many questions remained, and he wanted answers. Grasping her waist, he kept her pinned to his side.

"Mayhap the rain will keep you at Stonehaven," she said.

He sent her an inscrutable look. "Even if I must delay my leaving by a day or two, make no mistake, I *will* leave."

"I am sorry your kinsmen fear me," Blair said. "I wouldna be surprised if MacKay and Niall are still spreading rumors about me."

"Aye, 'tis true enough," Graeme agreed. "Sit down and break your fast while I try to placate the delegation from the village. We canna afford to let this get out of hand."

"Did ye speak with her?" Gunna asked when Graeme joined them. "Did ye tell her to make the rain stop?"

Graeme might have blamed Blair for many things, but bringing down torrents of rain wasn't one of them. No mortal was capable of summoning the forces of nature.

"My wife didna bring on the rain, nor can

she stop it," Graeme insisted. "Go home and tell your families they have naught to fear from Blair."

"She should have burned in the fire," Gunna muttered.

"What did you say?" Graeme demanded.

" 'Tis true. 'Tis common knowledge someone set fire to the stillroom with yer wife inside. Give her to the MacKay if he will still have her. There was a legal betrothal between them."

"Where did you hear that?" Graeme asked. Was naught that went on in the keep private?

"Be quiet, Gunna," the leader warned. "Ye dinna want to anger the laird."

"Och, sometimes my mouth runs away with me," Gunna said.

"We'd best be getting back to our families," the leader cut in. "If the loch rises any more, we will be forced to move to higher ground."

If the loch rises any higher, it will wash out the bridge, Graeme thought. *And if the storm continues to rage unabated, not even a boat will be safe in the turbulent water; which would mean I cannot leave Stonehaven.*

Graeme cast a speculative glance at Blair. Was she or wasn't she responsible for the drenching rain that was creating such havoc? She hadn't wanted him to leave Stonehaven, had begged him to ignore the king's summons. Had she brought the rains to prevent him from leaving? Nay, he refused to accept it. If he believed such a thing, his perception of Blair would change forever.

Graeme's thoughts were interrupted when Aiden entered the hall, soaked to the skin, his trews clinging to rock-hard thighs and his hair plastered to his head. "Graeme! I just came from the valley. 'Tis bad, mon. Verra bad."

"For God's sake, spit it out!"

"The valley is flooding. The livestock must be moved to high ground right away."

Graeme spit out a curse. It would take several days to drive the livestock into the hills. His kinsmen and their livelihood came first; the king would have to understand why he had absented himself from the meeting.

Men scrambled for their rain gear after Graeme's tersely issued orders. Graeme paused a moment to speak with Blair before he followed them out into the raging storm.

"You may have your wish, after all, wife," he growled. "If I find you had a hand in this, naught will save you from my wrath."

The rain continued. Men straggled back to the keep a few at a time to rest, then went back out into the turbulent weather. Blair heard that the water hadn't yet reached the village and was glad. She hadn't intended to cause upheaval in the village or among Graeme's kinsmen.

Graeme did not return to the keep for four

days. When he staggered in, his eyes were deeply shadowed and his skin was sallow and wrinkled from constant exposure to water. His plaid was sodden and his trews were plastered to his skin. He all but collapsed onto the nearest bench, resting his head in his hands. Graeme did not wear defeat well.

Blair rushed to attend him. She took his plaid and spread it to dry before the hearth. "You must eat and rest. Why didna you return to the keep like the others?"

"No time," he growled.

She attempted to brush a strand of wet hair from his eyes, but he grasped her wrist and flung it away. "Dinna touch me! Leave me be."

"What is it?"

He looked up; his anger was so fierce that Blair flinched, retreating beneath his fury. "Dinna lie, Blair. 'Twas you! You didna want me to go to Inverness so you brought this affliction down on us. You summoned evil spirits to destroy me and all I hold dear."

"Nay! I meant no harm to you or your kinsmen."

"Did you not? Even as we speak, water is rising to the cotters' doorsteps. I told them to come to the keep if the loch rises any higher."

"I'm sorry," Blair whispered. She hadn't thought beyond saving Graeme's life.

"You got your wish," Graeme charged.

264

"There is no way I can go to Inverness now. The bridges have washed away, the boats are smashed to smithereens, and the loch is too dangerous to negotiate until the raging water subsides."

"I couldna let you go to your death," Blair whispered.

He squeezed her wrist, his expression cold, his eyes blazing with pure malice. He was so angry, Blair feared he would strike her. She flinched and tried to pull away.

"I didna want to believe it of you, Blair, but I can no longer deny the fact that you possess supernatural powers. I know now that you are capable of evil."

"I am guilty of naught but trying to keep you alive," Blair cried.

The cold, dead calm in his eyes frightened her. If he'd once had tender feelings for her, they no longer existed.

"Your heedless action brought disaster and suffering. Get out of my sight!"

She reached out to him. He pushed her away. "Dinna touch me. Go away. I dinna want you near me."

Blair nearly doubled over in pain. Nothing had ever hurt as much as Graeme's cruel dismissal. She backed away, then turned and fled down the stairs to the stillroom. She had to try to undo what she had wrought. She couldn't bear the weight of Graeme's hatred.

Graeme was literally shaking with rage.

From the beginning he had defended Blair against her enemies. Though it hadn't taken him long to realize she did indeed possess certain powers, he'd been convinced there was no evil in her. But this . . . she had all but admitted she had used witchcraft to bring the storm that had caused such havoc among his people.

Graeme recalled Blair's warning but still refused to believe his life was in danger. What could happen to him in Inverness? He'd been there many times in the past.

Graeme groaned when he saw Glenda approaching with a tray of food. He wasn't in the mood for idle talk.

"Ye should eat," Glenda said, setting a bowl of steaming cock-a-leekie soup before him.

"Thank you," Graeme muttered with as much civility as he could muster. He was hungry as well as wet and exhausted and disillusioned. Never had he been as disappointed in another human being as he was with Blair.

Glenda returned with a blanket and spread it over Graeme's shoulders. "Ye mustna catch a chill, Graeme." She hovered over him, then said, "I heard what ye said to Blair. I warned ye about her. Yer wife is a witch."

"Leave off, Glenda."

Glenda was not to be denied. "What do ye intend to do with her?"

"I dinna know. Can I please eat in peace?"

"Aye, laird. I will be waiting when ye're ready for me. Ye have but to ask."

Graeme stopped listening to Glenda long before she ceased talking. Blair's betrayal curled around his heart. How could she have done this to him? When he finished his soup, he crossed his arms on the table, lowered his head and fell instantly asleep.

Sobbing as if her heart would break, Blair entered the stillroom. To her utter horror, she felt that her powers had weakened since Graeme had rejected her. Could she be in love with Graeme? After seeing his eyes fill with contempt for her, she knew he would never return her love. According to the Prophecy, her powers would be stripped from her.

Blair gathered the candles, placed them in a circle and sprinkled herbs around the perimeter. Then she stepped inside the circle and began the ritual she knew by heart. When the candles flared into various colors, Blair lifted her arms and chanted:

> "Spirits of nature, hear me.
> Send the water back to the sea.
> Bring out the sun,
> Let the rains be done."

Suddenly a bright light formed before her eyes. It was so dazzling, it almost hurt to look at it. At the center of the light was an ethereal being. She blinked, aware that she was standing in a beam of sunshine so brilliant she could no longer look into its center. The storm clouds had rolled away, and the sun was shining once more. Her powers were still with her, though she sensed that this summoning had drained what was left of them.

The emotional drain was suddenly too much. With a soft sigh she fell into a faint. From the void came a voice.

"Do not despair. Your destinies are linked. Some things are meant to be."

Alyce found Blair lying in a circle of spent candles a short time later. Unable to awaken her, she flew up the stairs to summon help. She found Graeme bent over a table deeply asleep, his head resting on his crossed arms. Reluctant to wake him, she saw Aiden enter the hall and begged his help.

"What happened to the wee lass?" Aiden asked as he hurried after Alyce.

"I dinna know. Can ye carry her up to her bedchamber? The laird was so weary, I didna want to wake him."

Aiden bent to pick up Blair. "What are these candles? Why is she lying on herbs?"

" 'Tis nae the time for questions, mon," Alyce replied. "I must see to my lady."

Blair's pale face must have convinced Aiden to make haste for he scooped her into his arms and carried her up the stairs. As they passed through the hall, Graeme stirred and opened his eyes.

"Why is my wife in your arms?" he asked as Aiden brushed past him.

"Blair is ill," Alyce answered. "I didna want to wake ye and asked Aiden to carry Blair to her bedchamber."

"Give her to me," Graeme said, rising and stretching out his arms. Aiden obeyed without argument, placing Blair's limp form into Graeme's arms.

Graeme took the stairs two at a time, silently counting the reasons why he shouldn't worry about his wife after the disaster she had created.

"Carry her to her bed, my laird," Alyce ordered. "I will take care of her."

"Does she do this often?" Graeme asked as he carefully lowered his wife to the bed.

"Nay, but she does seem to be doing it more often of late." Alyce sent Graeme a probing look. "I wonder . . ."

"What do you . . ." The breath caught in Graeme's throat, and he rushed to the window. "The sun is shining! The rain has stopped! Thank God."

"Thank Blair, more likely," Alyce muttered beneath her breath.

"Take care of her," Graeme said as he turned away from the window. "Tell her she will no longer have access to the stillroom."

"What are ye saying?"

"I know Blair cast a spell to bring the rains and I dinna trust her. I warned her many times about using magic, but she didna heed me. Right now, I canna stand the sight of her." So saying, he whirled and stomped off.

"Blair, lass, what have ye done?" Alyce lamented.

Blair opened her eyes and touched Alyce's cheek. "Dinna fret, Alyce. I knew what I was getting myself into, but I couldna let that stop me. Graeme's life means everything to me."

"Ye love him, lass," Alyce observed.

"Aye, I admit it, but loving Graeme means the loss of my powers. He hates me, Alyce. Stopping the rain required what was left of my powers. I am now like any other woman. I am no longer a Faery Woman."

"Ye dinna know that, lass."

"Aye, I do. I feel . . . different somehow. I am light-headed and my stomach is churning. I've never felt like this before." Acute distress left her pale. "What will Graeme do to me?"

"Laird Graeme is an honorable mon. He made a promise to yer da and 'tis unlikely he will forget it."

"How am I to exist? I am a pariah among Graeme's people. My own husband thinks I am a witch."

"Dinna fash yerself, lass. Things have a way of working out."

"Not this time, Alyce. I know Graeme would never hurt me, but I canna bear his animosity." Suddenly she lurched up in bed, her face turning a sickly shade of green. "Oh, my, I think I'm going to be ill."

Alyce held the basin while Blair lost the meager contents of her stomach. Afterward, she rinsed out her mouth and fell back against the pillow. She turned her face to the wall, silent tears streaming down her face. She didn't hear Alyce tiptoe from the chamber.

Graeme and his kinsmen were celebrating the return of sunshine and cloudless skies when Alyce marched up to him and demanded his attention.

None too pleased by the intrusion, Graeme grudgingly agreed to speak with her. He walked to where they couldn't be heard and turned to confront her.

"What is it? Is this about Blair? If it is, I dinna want to hear it. I am finished with her."

"Mayhap ye are finished with her, but what about the bairn she carries?"

The veins in Graeme's neck bulged. "You lie! You and Blair have cooked this up to make things easier for her."

"I know the signs," Alyce persisted.

"Dinna talk to me of signs, woman! I want naught to do with Blair or the bairn she may or may not carry. One witch in the house-

271

hold is enough. Mayhap I should send her back to Gairloch and let her brother deal with her."

"Foolish mon," Alyce chided. "If ye hurt my lass, ye will be sorry."

"Are you threatening me, Alyce?"

Alyce glared at him. "Nay, 'tis not I who will punish ye." She stormed off in an angry flurry of skirts.

Graeme stared after her, his head spinning. He didn't for one minute believe Blair was carrying his child. What he did believe was that neither Alyce nor Blair was above lying to manipulate him.

Chapter Thirteen

Blair kept to herself during the following days. She had no intimate contact with Graeme and missed him dreadfully. It was as if she didn't exist. He rarely looked at her and never spoke directly to her. She had indeed become an outcast. Everyone suspected she had caused the storm, but no one could be sure. As a result, Graeme's kinsmen walked circles around her, going out of their way to avoid her.

Work had begun on a new bridge, keeping Graeme occupied each day until darkness settled over the land. During the evening meal Graeme avoided her like the plague, preferring to sit with his kinsmen at one of the low tables. Even more disturbing was the knowledge that Glenda had grown bolder in her pursuit of Graeme. She hovered over him constantly, ready to fulfill his every need. Blair had little doubt that one of those needs was sexual.

Though Blair rarely ventured far from the keep after the floodwaters had begun to recede, she was eager to see how work was progressing on the new bridge. Since no one seemed to monitor her comings and goings, Blair felt free to do as she pleased.

One sunny day she and Alyce walked outside to enjoy the sunshine. Blair lifted her face to the welcome heat and let it soak through her. Since she had summoned the spirits of nature to help her, she felt cold all the time. She felt utterly lost, as if an important part of herself were missing. She didn't need a vision to tell her it was Graeme she was missing from her life.

"Where do ye wish to go, lass?" Alyce asked. "I wouldna advise ye to venture far abroad. Ye know how superstitious Graeme's kinsmen are about ye."

"I know, but I'd like to see how far the bridge is from completion. We can watch from further upstream, where we won't be seen."

They skirted the village and walked past rowan trees leafed out in brilliant green. Blair smiled when she heard the distant croaking of ptarmigan and clapped in delight when she counted several blue heron on a nearby cairn. Some fifteen minutes later they reached a crag overlooking Loch Torridon, an arm of the sea thrusting inland.

"The level of the loch isna back to normal," Blair observed. "I am grateful the village escaped the worst of the flood. Did the crops survive?"

"There was some loss, but several days of sunshine have done a great deal to reverse the worst of the damage. 'Tis likely the crops will survive, except in the fields that were completely flooded. There was no loss of livestock."

Blair sighed. "I didna mean to hurt anyone, I thought only of saving Graeme's life. I knew there would be consequences, but I didna let myself think of them."

"Look," Alyce said, pointing downstream. "Ye can see men at work on the bridge."

Blair easily picked Graeme out from among the group of men. All were bare from the waist up and wearing trews that had been cut off above the knee for easy movement in the water. Graeme's impressive physique stood out among the dozen or so hearty Scotsmen.

"The bridge seems to be progressing well."

"Look, there's Stuart," Alyce pointed out. "He's verra bonny for a mon his age."

Blair's attention was so intent upon Graeme, she didn't hear the sound of approaching footsteps. Neither did Alyce, who was a little hard of hearing.

"There she be!" a woman shrieked. "Did I not tell ye she was planning mischief? 'Tis fortunate I saw her whilst I was gathering herbs outside the village."

Blair whirled, unpleasantly surprised to see Gunna leading a congregation of women and men from the village. "I dinna want any trouble," Blair said. "I mean no harm."

"Ye asked for trouble when ye called upon evil spirits to bring devastation to the Campbells."

As if to reinforce Gunna's words, a crow flew over Blair's head, cawing loudly.

"Look!" Gunna cried. "She brought her familiar!"

"Nay, 'tisna true!" Blair denied.

"She lies," Glenda said, stepping from behind the stocky midwife. "I heard Laird Graeme accuse her of using witchcraft. She didna deny it. He banished her from his life."

"Mayhap she should prove herself," Gunna said, crowding Blair closer to the edge of the crag. "I've heard that witches float. Let her prove she's nae a witch. If she drowns, we'll know she is innocent."

Suddenly a woman Blair recognized pushed Gunna aside. It was Mab, the woman Blair had helped through childbirth.

" 'Tis shameful the way ye are treating our laird's wife," Mab charged. "Look at all the good she has done. You, Mary — did Lady Blair not heal yer son's wound when he cut himself playing with his da's dirk? And you, Talia — didna Blair cure yer daughter's chest congestion?"

"Dinna listen to her," Gunna screamed. "The witch must prove herself."

Unfortunately, Mab's voice of reason could not stop Gunna's vicious attack. When a mob was roused to fury, common sense fled.

As one, the voices rose to a chilling crescendo. "Aye, let her prove herself! Throw her into the loch. If she drowns, we will know she is innocent."

Blair was terrified. She couldn't swim, for she had never had the opportunity to learn, and she knew the weight of her skirts would pull her under. She prayed that the water below was shallow.

It was obvious to Blair that Gunna's animosity was virulent enough to carry the villagers along with her. Only a few reluctant souls refused to participate. Blair looked for a way to escape but found herself surrounded.

"Save yourself," Blair hissed to Alyce. "Run before they turn on you."

Alyce looked as if she wanted to protest, but ultimately she lifted her skirts and fled. Blair was grateful that no one tried to stop the older woman. Marshaling her courage, she turned a calm face to Gunna in an effort to tamp down her rage. But nothing short of Blair's death would satisfy the midwife. She stalked toward Blair.

Suddenly Grant and another man grabbed her and dragged her to the edge of the crag. She screamed, and then she was falling . . . falling until the turbulent water came up to meet her with frightening haste. She hit the water with a loud splash before she could take a deep breath.

Down, down, she went, frighteningly aware that the loch was deeper than she had thought. She hit the bottom, then thrust upward with all her might. When she broke the surface, she took a gulp of life-giving air, but her sodden skirts dragged her back down.

Panic-stricken, she began to struggle for her very life. She didn't want to die. Not now — not before Graeme had forgiven her.

Alyce ran as fast as her legs could carry her to where Graeme was working on the bridge. Her lass was in danger, and only Graeme could save her. Would he even care? Though her old legs were ready to give way, she kept running until she collapsed in Graeme's arms.

Graeme had seen Alyce running toward him and had sprinted forward to meet her. Intuition told him that something had happened to Blair, and his intuition rarely failed him. He had tried his best these past few days to pretend she didn't exist. He knew that by ignoring Blair he was reinforcing his kinsmen's fear of her, but he hadn't been able to get past his disappointment in her. Or his anger.

But Blair needed him now, and nothing else mattered. One look into Alyce's panic-stricken eyes was all it took to goad him into action.

"What is it, Alyce? Is Blair in trouble?"

Unable to catch her breath, Alyce nodded and pointed upstream. Graeme saw a group of people gathered on a crag above the loch.

Swallowing his fear, Graeme tried again. "Does Blair need me?"

"Aye," Alyce gasped. "They've thrown her in the loch."

It was all Graeme needed to hear. He passed Alyce over to Stuart, who had come running when he saw the tiring woman fall into Graeme's arms.

"Take her back to the keep," Graeme ordered as he raced to Blair's aid.

Adrenaline pumped through his body. Shouting Blair's name, he dove into the water and swam toward where he saw her head pop up. Then she sank beneath the water and didn't resurface. Stretching his arms and kicking his legs, he put all his strength into his strokes.

Blair had no breath left. She felt herself floating, drifting, her mind and body at peace. She knew she was near death and could do nothing to prevent it. Her lungs were bursting; she wanted to end the torture, but the life force inside her was too strong. Water was seeping into her lungs, but still she fought death. Blackness edged her consciousness as she reached out to the spirits, beseeching them to spare her.

Suddenly she felt herself being lifted upward, but she knew in her heart it was too late. What she had done to Graeme and his kinsmen was unforgivable, and death was to be her punishment. This was one trial she had failed.

She sank into a dark abyss, unaware that Graeme had broken the surface with her in his arms and was swimming toward shore.

Graeme could detect no breath in Blair as he dragged her onto the bank. Quickly he rolled her on her stomach and gently pressed. Once, twice, three times. She remained pale and unmoving. He tried again, and was thrilled when water gushed from her mouth. Despite his efforts, however, he observed no signs of life. Still he would not give up. He continued to press water from her lungs.

Turning her onto her back, he lifted her head, opened her mouth with thumb and forefinger and attempted to breathe life into her by giving her his own breath.

"What have you done?" he roared, looking up at the villagers crowding around him.

"They wanted to find out if she was a witch," Mab explained. " 'Twas Gunna's doing."

He glared at Gunna. "Dinna tell me you believe in that old wives' tale about witches floating. Get out of my sight! All of you! I'll deal with you later. And, Gunna," he added tersely, "you had best find a new home. You are no longer welcome in the village."

"Think ye I care?" Gunna screamed. "I am a MacKay. My late husband was a Campbell, but I kept faith with the MacKays."

"Be gone, woman! The rest of you, go home."

He returned his attention to Blair as the crowd dispersed. Only Mab remained.

"Can I help ye, my laird? Yer lady helped me birth a healthy bairn, and I am grateful to her. I had nae part in this travesty."

Graeme continued to blow air into Blair's lungs, unwilling to let her die. "Cover her with your cloak," Graeme said between breaths. "The water was cold, and she is chilled."

Mab obeyed instantly, wrapping her cloak tightly around Blair. Then she stood aside and folded her hands in silent prayer as Graeme fought to save Blair's life.

Mab wasn't the only one praying. Graeme begged God to bring Blair back to him. Wishing to leave no avenue unexplored, he implored Blair's spirits to spare her life. Witch or no, he wanted her alive.

Suddenly breath surged into Blair's lungs. She gasped and coughed and spit out more water. Rejoicing, Graeme thanked both God and the Faery Spirits.

"Blair, lass, can you hear me?"

Blair's eyes fluttered open. They were glazed, and she appeared not to recognize him. Graeme held her close to his heart until her breathing eased and became less labored. At length she appeared to recognize him, and that seemed to comfort her.

"You saved my life," she whispered. "Thank you."

He scooped her into his arms and strode toward the keep. "I'll have you home in no time, lass." To Mab he said, "I'll see that your cloak is returned, along with a token of my appreciation. Tell the others who were here today that I will speak with them soon."

"Dinna be too hard on yer kinsmen, laird, for Gunna fueled their fears and stoked them into a wild frenzy. I hope ye will find it in yer heart to forgive them."

"We'll speak of this later," Graeme said as he brushed past her.

Blair's arms tightened around his neck. "I forgive them," Blair said. "Can you forgive me?"

"Later, Blair. Save your strength. You've been through a harrowing ordeal. I nearly lost you."

"Without you I couldna have survived. God willing, I will survive the test of stone as I did fire and water."

"There will be no stone," Graeme said through clenched teeth. "We're nearly home. I wouldna be surprised if Alyce is waiting to tuck you in bed."

"Is she all right? I told her to flee. I didna want her harmed."

"She did flee — right into my arms. If not for her warning, I wouldna have reached you in time."

A shudder ran through him, and his arms tightened around her as if he never intended to let her go. He reached the keep and entered the hall, ignoring the glances of those who had not yet heard about the tragedy that had nearly taken Blair's life. He took the stairs two at a time and pushed open the door to Blair's chamber. Alyce was waiting for them.

He let Blair slide down his body and held her until she could stand on her own feet. Alyce shoved him aside.

"Thank God ye reached her in time. I never doubted it for a minute. Ye can go now. I will take care of my lass. She needs to get out of those wet clothes." She looked pointedly at Graeme's dripping trews. "Ye should change into something dry before ye catch a chill."

Though reluctant to leave, Graeme obeyed Alyce with grudging respect. "I'll be back."

"Graeme, d-d-dinna go," Blair said through chattering teeth.

That was all Graeme needed to hear. "I can manage on my own," he told Alyce, dismissing her with a wave of his hand.

"But —"

"No buts, Alyce. You heard Blair. I assure you I am perfectly capable of caring for my wife."

" 'Tis about time," Alyce muttered on her way out the door.

"Let's get you out of these wet clothes," Graeme said, quickly working the buttons and tapes on Blair's sodden gown and under-clothing. When she was stripped bare, he dried her with a towel Alyce had provided, then carried her to bed and tucked her in.

"You're still shivering."

"I'm so c-c-cold. Verra, verra cold. I havena been warm since you turned away from me."

Graeme knew what he had to do and did not hesitate. He stripped off his boots and trews, pulled back the covers and climbed in bed beside Blair. Her body was cold as ice, and he pulled her into his arms, surrounding her with his body heat. Though he had taken the same dunking as Blair, he hadn't thought the water overly cold. But Blair's chill seemed to go bone deep.

"Is that better?" Graeme asked.

She snuggled against him. "Aye. Dinna let me go."

A long silence ensued, and then Graeme asked, "Why did you not use your powers to save yourself?"

Silence.

"Blair? Answer my question."

"My powers are gone. You've got what you wanted, Graeme."

"Are you sure?"

"Reasonably sure. The spirits no longer

speak to me." She paused, her expression pensive. "I pleaded with the spirits to save me when I felt life ebbing from me, and then you arrived. I wonder . . ."

"Alyce fetched me," Graeme said, dashing her hopes that the spirits had sent him. She had been stripped of her powers because she had fallen in love with a man who did not love her. It was as simple as that.

"Rest," Graeme urged. "I willna leave you."

Blair did not feel like resting. She snuggled closer to her husband, one arm curling around his waist as they faced one another. His breath caressed her cheek, warming her face, while her hand moved up and down his smooth back.

"Can't you sleep?" Graeme asked in a voice made harsh with desire.

"Nay. I want . . . I want . . ." Words failed her; she was unable to give voice to her needs, for what she needed was Graeme.

"What do you want, love?"

Another silence ensued. Then words came tumbling out. "You, Graeme. I want you."

"I want you more," he growled against her ear. "When I thought I had lost you, I cursed myself a thousand times for treating you so abominably."

"You forgive me, then? For bringing havoc to your life?"

"Did you really use magic to bring the rains?"

"Nay, not magic. I asked the spirits of nature to help me save your life."

"Did you really believe my life was in danger?"

"I didna believe it, I knew it."

"I canna think about this now," Graeme said, brushing aside her words.

Blair knew that asking Graeme to believe in her was expecting too much.

"Your loss of powers is cause for celebration," Graeme said tersely.

Blair did not agree but wisely held her own counsel.

"I want to make love to you," Graeme whispered. "But I will wait if you need more time to recover."

"I dinna want to wait," Blair said. "I need to feel close to you again. You are my destiny. The spirits brought you to me."

"My destiny is to be inside you," Graeme said, throwing back the covers.

Blair gaped at him. His erection thrust up at her, blue-veined, softly capped, rigid and demanding. If she didn't know better, she could almost believe he hadn't been with a woman since the last time he had made love to her.

The tendons in his neck were taut; the planes and angles of his face seemed somehow harsher, stark and feral. She smiled at him, thrilled that he wanted her so fiercely. Rising to her knees, she leaned forward and pushed her hands up the steely smoothness of his abdomen, then sent her fingers higher, into the crisp mat of dark hair that covered his chest.

Graeme had always taken the initiative before, but this time she wanted to show him how much she loved him. Since she'd lost her powers, she need no longer deny her heart's desire. The very worst had already happened. When he started to rise, she pushed him back down, pressing a kiss to his stomach, then another, much lower this time; she nuzzled him and let her mouth linger against his groin.

His eyes flashed, searing and hungry, raking her with a glance so hot it nearly stole her breath.

Air rasped out of Graeme's lungs as he pushed his cock against her soft lips in a violent crash of violent emotions. The gut-wrenching desire to have her take him in her mouth and the fear she wouldn't were driving him insane. His frustration mounting, he grasped her head between his hands and moved it until he could feel her hot breath teasing his cock.

He howled like a banshee when she opened her mouth and drew him inside. When she ran her tongue down his length and over the tip, he nearly bucked her off the bed. Then he began to move, his hips flexing as she took him deep, sucking and licking until he was nearly mad. But he didn't want to come that way. He wanted to be inside her, and he wanted her to come with him.

"Enough!" he growled, lifting her off and away. "Kneel astride me."

She lifted one knee, then the other, wrapping her arms about his neck as she knelt over him. Then she tilted her head and set her lips to his, lowering herself until her stomach met the ridged wall of his abdomen.

Groaning, Graeme pulled her head down and ravaged her mouth as he guided the head of his cock into the soft folds of her swollen flesh. He entered her slowly, giving her all of him, glorying in the feel of her body closing lovingly around him. He was fully embedded now. It felt so good, he wanted to howl like an animal.

His tongue filled her mouth as he began to move, rising high and thrusting deep inside her.

Blair matched his rhythm effortlessly, using her arms to ease herself up, using her legs for leverage. Their bodies were moving in harmony; she felt his hands move over her skin, caressing, stroking, igniting a million small fires that blazed out of control. A vortex of heat swept her up and carried her away. Her lips melded with his, her mouth and body became his to do with as he pleased.

"Mine," he said fiercely as he lifted her

pelvis off the bed, angling her higher to meet his fierce thrusts.

His possessiveness created a warm, sweet pleasure inside her, and Blair wondered if he realized what he had said. A sense of peace suddenly came upon her, and she thought she heard the spirits murmuring approval. But that was not possible, for they were no longer with her.

She was losing hold of the world around her. She felt it slipping away as the friction of their joining sent her spiraling toward sweet oblivion. With a cry of abandon, she crushed Graeme's moisture-slicked body to hers. Then her climax began. Spasms spread through her in searing waves, flinging her toward the stars as pleasure exploded.

Rocking against her, Graeme shouted, his body jerking as he spent himself inside her. When it was over, they lay limp and content in each other's arms.

Graeme couldn't think.

It was a frightening realization. No matter how hard he tried to focus on what had just taken place between him and Blair, his mind remained overwhelmed.

Graeme had no idea how long he'd lain there, stretched out naked beside Blair, her body cuddled against him, their limbs entwined. Gradually, reason returned. He knew Blair was not like other women, but it no longer seemed to matter. Nearly losing her had changed his narrow way of thinking. She had given him her all, and he had greedily taken it.

Graeme was satiated in a way he had never been before, but he still clamored for more. His gaze drifted possessively over Blair as she rested in his arms, her body warm and glowing. She was just where she should be, just where he would have her . . . forever.

Graeme knew that what he felt with Blair was more than simple contentment. It was deeper, more profound, more compelling. Loving Blair was beyond anything he had ever experienced.

What in the world was he going to do with her?

His kinsmen still feared her, and mayhap with good reason. But if Blair was to be believed, she had lost her powers and was no longer a threat to anyone. That thought brought another.

Blair loved him. According to the Prophecy, she would lose her powers only if she loved someone who did not return her love. Though Graeme cared a great deal for Blair, obviously he didn't love her. If he did, she would still possess her powers.

More confused than ever, Graeme fell into a troubled sleep. He was beginning to think the Prophecy was a myth.

Graeme woke to a ruckus at the door. He sat up and eased away from Blair. That she could sleep through the awful racket was ample proof of her exhaustion. Naked, he walked to the door, opened it and peered sleepily at his steward.

"How can a man sleep with all that racket? This had best be important, Jamie."

"I wouldna bother ye otherwise. Heath has returned from Inverness with a tale ye will want to hear."

"I'll be down as soon as I dress. How long have I slept?"

" 'Tis morning."

"Morning!" Graeme gasped. "I must have been more exhausted than I thought." He glanced at Blair, who was still sleeping soundly. "Tell Alyce not to disturb Blair."

"Aye," Jamie said as Graeme softly closed the door.

Graeme returned to his own bedchamber to wash and dress so as not to awaken Blair, then went below to greet Heath. He was anxious to know how the king had reacted to his absence.

Heath was digging into a bowl of porridge when Graeme entered the hall. He looked up when Graeme joined him. "I had a devil of a time getting here."

Graeme sat down beside his cousin. "Finish your breakfast."

"What happened? I waited for ye at Inverness."

"Rains and floods," Graeme said. " 'Twas a nightmare. The bridges across the loch were lost in the raging waters, and our fields flooded. How did you get across the loch?"

"I hired a boat on the other side. I was shocked at how high the water had risen."

Someone set a bowl of porridge in front of Graeme and he began eating. "Is the king angry with me?"

"Ah, Graeme, you canna know how happy I am ye didna show up for the meeting. Terrible things happened."

Graeme's spoon stopped halfway to his mouth. Had Blair been right all along? "What kind of things?"

"I dinna know where to begin." Heath's expression turned grim. "More than forty Highland chieftains were gathered at Inverness. The king arrived in a foul mood. Since I was merely an observer, I was able to keep apart and listen."

"Go on," Graeme urged, quite certain he wasn't going to like what Heath had to say.

"To make a long story short, James accused the chieftains of treason. He said they were unpredictable and ungovernable and posed a danger to the Crown. He also charged them with supporting the House of Albany while he was held captive in England.

" 'Twas unbelievable," Heath continued.

"James berated the chieftains for opposing the unification of the Highlands. Then he ordered them taken to Edinburgh and imprisoned."

"I canna believe it."

"MacKay and MacArthur supported James's decision. They were not among the forty arrested."

"Bastards," Graeme growled.

"Aye." Heath swallowed hard, then said, "We all assumed the Highland chiefs would languish behind bars until the king had gotten over his pique."

"What is it, Heath? Something happened at Inverness."

Heath sighed. "Five chieftains were singled out and executed. You would have been one of them had you been there."

Graeme's spoon dropped from his fingers. "How do you know?"

"Yer brother-in-law told me. He was quite put out when ye didna show up."

"What about the king? Is he sending troops to arrest me?"

" 'Tis unlikely, and I will tell ye why. While in Inverness, James learned that English soldiers are amassing on the border. England is demanding the ransom James failed to pay for his release from captivity. The English king threatens to march to Sterling and hold it hostage until the ransom is paid. James left immediately to defend his borders."

"Didna he realize he needs the Highland lairds now more than ever? James has done many good things since he returned from captivity. This is not like him."

"I believe he realized his mistake, for the chieftains were released before James left Inverness."

"Little good that does the five innocent men he executed," Graeme said bitterly.

"Had ye gone to Inverness, ye would have been one of those unfortunate men," Heath muttered. "The floods couldna have come to Stonehaven at a better time."

Graeme concurred wholeheartedly.

Blair hadn't been lying. His life *had* been in jeopardy. And she had saved it.

"Where are ye going?" Heath asked when Graeme surged from his chair.

"To beg my wife's forgiveness. Call a meeting of the clan. My people need to hear what I have to say."

Chapter Fourteen

Blair awoke slowly and stretched, amazed at how contented she felt. Graeme might not love her, but he made love to her as if he did. More importantly, the coldness she had felt since Graeme had turned away from her no longer plagued her. She had no idea what it all meant, for her voices had been ominously silent of late.

Moments later, Graeme burst into the chamber. She feared something terrible had happened until she saw his face. His expression was one of wonderment and, amazingly, respect.

"What is it?" Blair cried. "Is aught amiss?"

"Nay, lass," Graeme said as he lowered himself to the edge of the bed. "Everything is well, very well indeed."

"Are you going to tell me, or must I drag it from you?"

"You saved my life. Had I gone to Inverness, I would have been accused of treason and executed along with five other Highland chieftains. The remaining chieftains were imprisoned in Edinburgh."

Blair gasped. "Treason? How can that be?"

"Evidently James uncovered a plot by Walter, Earl of Atholl, to win the throne. He accused the chieftains of conspiring with his enemies."

"Why would James suspect you of being one of the conspirators? How do you know what happened at Inverness?"

Graeme gave a snort of disgust. "Mayhap you should ask your brother, or MacKay. They are thick as thieves with the king. I wouldna be surprised if they named me one of the conspirators simply to be rid of me. I learned what happened just this morning, when Heath returned from Inverness. He hired a boat and rowed across the loch."

"I dinna ken why Niall or MacKay want your death."

"Do you not? Your brother doesna want to part with your dowry. After hearing what went on at Inverness, I no longer doubt your powers. Forgive me, my love. Next time you warn me of danger, it willna take a flood to make a believer of me."

Blair's shoulders slumped. "My powers are gone."

"How do you know?"

"There is a strange emptiness inside me. 'Tis as if I've lost an important part of myself."

He pulled her into his arms. "Is there aught I can do to help you?"

296

Love me. "Nay, I shouldna have fallen in love with a man who canna return my love."

Graeme went still. "Blair, I —"

"Nay, dinna say anything, Graeme. Forget I said that. Every word of the Prophecy is familiar to me, and I deliberately ignored the warning about loving in vain. I should have heeded you when you said you couldna love me."

Graeme appeared at a loss for words. Then his brow furrowed, as if he remembered something. "Alyce said you were carrying my bairn. Is she right?"

Blair's hands flew to her stomach. "I dinna think so. If I am, 'tis too soon to tell."

Graeme pondered her words, then nodded, apparently willing to accept her answer. "You will tell me if I'm to become a father, will you not?"

"Of course. Why would I not?"

He searched her face, then said, "Get dressed and come down to the hall with me. I want everyone to know you saved my life. I dinna want my clansmen thinking ill of you. They should know you brought the rains for a good reason."

Blair recoiled. "Graeme, nay! If you explain about the rains, they will think I am a witch. Dinna you ken how dangerous that is? Right now your clansmen can only speculate. They have no proof I did anything. But if you admit I summoned the spirits of nature, their fear of me will intensify. Whether or not I saved your life will make little difference. They will see me as evil."

"But —"

"Leave it alone, Graeme. I dinna want to give Gunna any excuse to accuse me of using witchcraft."

"I banished Gunna from the village. You have naught to fear from her."

Blair blanched. "She is an old woman. Where will she go?"

"She is a MacKay by birth. They will take her in." Graeme's expression grew thoughtful. "I told Heath to gather everyone in the hall. I have to tell them something — they'll expect it."

"Tell them anything but the truth."

"Verra well, but I still want you beside me. Hurry. I'll wait while you dress."

Blair hurried through her morning ablutions while Graeme watched, his eyes hooded and intense. Blair sensed his desire and felt her body responding. But Graeme must have realized that now was not the time to give in to lust, for he turned his back while she finished dressing.

"I am ready," Blair said as she braided her long, pale hair and wound the braid around her head.

Graeme offered his arm. "Let us not keep my clansmen waiting."

Blair had no idea what Graeme intended to

tell his people. She knew they feared her, and she wondered what Graeme could say to ease their minds. Talk ceased the moment they entered the hall. Blair wanted to cringe at the sullen looks directed at her but walked steadily beside Graeme.

Graeme signaled for silence, and when he gained the attention he sought, began to speak. He started by explaining why King James had summoned the Highland chieftains to Inverness. Cries of protest filled the hall at the king's treachery.

"If not for the floods, I would have gone to Inverness and been executed along with five other unfortunate chieftains. Heath was there. He brought word of the executions. Forty others were charged with treason. The king ordered them taken to Edinburgh and imprisoned.

"He rescinded those orders when he received word that the English army was massing at the border and threatening to take Sterling if his ransom wasn't paid. James needs the Highlanders' help to raise money for his ransom. He also needs them to fight on his behalf should the English invade."

"What about those poor bastards he executed?" Stuart asked. "Did he strip their families of their lands?"

"I believe 'twas his intention," Heath answered. "But he left Inverness with his army before he gave the order. For the time being, their families are safe."

"Thank God for the flood!" someone yelled.

A chorus of ayes followed.

Graeme signaled for silence. "Had I gone to Inverness as planned, I would have been executed. But as you well know, I committed no treason."

" 'Twas MacArthur and MacKay who accused our laird," Heath declared.

" 'Tis the witch's fault," a voice from the back of the hall charged.

"My wife is blameless!" Graeme shouted over the din. "Yesterday she was attacked by a group of irate villagers. She almost died at their hands. My lady was thrown into the loch and would have drowned, had I not been nearby.

"I am giving everyone fair warning. I will not tolerate violence of any kind against my wife. She is innocent of any wrongdoing. 'Tis her brother who wishes me ill. He doesna want to part with Blair's dowry. Anyone who tries to harm Blair will be punished. Do I make myself clear?"

"She has bewitched ye!" one of Graeme's clansmen charged.

Graeme smiled at Blair. "Aye, Robbie, but not in the way you think. One day you or yours might need Blair's healing skills, and when that day comes, you will be glad for her help."

He grasped her hand and held it against his heart. "I am wed to a Faery Woman and glad of it. Go now and spread the word. I will protect what is mine with my dying breath."

Blair couldn't believe what she was hearing. Graeme's protective words meant everything to her. No one except her parents and those MacArthurs who knew and loved her had ever spoken in her defense.

"Thank you," Blair whispered as Graeme seated her at the high table.

"You saved my life. 'Tis the least I can do." He kissed her forehead. "I have to go. There's still work to be done on the bridge."

The following days were some of the happiest Blair had ever known. During the day she worked with her herbs, and at night she lay in Graeme's arms, making love until exhaustion claimed them.

It was wonderful waking up with Graeme beside her. Sometimes they made love in the morning, and she savored those precious moments, for something told her they wouldn't last. All her life it had seemed that happiness lay just beyond her reach. Others might attain it, but not she.

One day Blair was in the stillroom when Alyce burst through the door. "Father Lachlan is here to see ye, lass. He says there's sickness at Gairloch."

"Oh, no! I must speak to him at once. Pack my herbs and medicines. If my kinsmen need my skills, I will go to them."

"Yer husband will have something to say about that," Alyce huffed. "I dinna think he will let ye go."

"We will see about that," Blair said as she rushed out the door.

Father Lachlan was waiting in the hall. His face lit up when he saw Blair.

"Ye're looking well, lass," the priest said.

"I am verra well, Father. What's amiss at Gairloch?"

"I dinna know the nature of the illness that has felled yer brother, for he allows no one inside his chamber but one or two trusted servants. I offered to hear his confession and anoint him, but I was refused entrance to the sickroom."

"Are others sick as well? What of Gavin and Cook?"

"Niall has dismissed yer father's people and replaced them with those loyal to him. No one else is sick that I know of. Niall's man told me he has been asking for you."

Blair's eyes went round with disbelief. "Niall is asking for me? 'Tis passing strange that he would do so."

"I thought the same. What prompted me to come here was fear that his sickness would spread. Niall wouldna ask for ye unless he believed he was dying. There is no skilled healer at Gairloch, and I fear a contagious disease will decimate our people. Will ye come to Gairloch with me, lass?"

Blair considered Lachlan's request. She knew the priest would neither harm her nor allow her to be harmed, but at the same time she wouldn't put trickery past Niall. Still, if there was sickness at Gairloch, her kinsmen needed her skills to prevent an epidemic. She thanked God that despite her loss of powers, she still retained her healing skills and knowledge of herbs.

"Verra well, Father. When do you wish to leave?"

"The sooner the better, lass. I will speak with yer husband first, however."

As if on cue, Graeme strode into the hall. "Father Lachlan, I heard you were here. Is something wrong?"

"There's sickness at Gairloch," Blair explained. "Niall is ill and sent Father Lachlan to fetch me."

"You want to go to Gairloch?" Graeme asked, astounded. "Nay, you canna."

"Graeme, be reasonable. My kinsmen need me. There is no healer at Gairloch. Niall wouldna have sent for me if he wasna desperate."

"I dinna trust him."

"Father Lachlan wouldna have come for me if he sensed danger."

"Ye're right, lass," Lachlan said. "I questioned Niall's men closely, and they swore Niall is near death, and that he calls for ye."

"I would feel better about this if you had seen him yourself, Father," Graeme said.

"I must go, Graeme," Blair insisted.

"Nay."

"Father Lachlan will be with me."

"I can wield a sword as well as the next mon," Lachlan said.

"If Blair goes, so will I," Graeme insisted.

"Nay, Graeme, you are needed here. No one will harm me at Gairloch. 'Tis my home."

"I like it not," Graeme complained. "I mistrust your brother. Father Lachlan canna swear that Niall is ill, for he hasna seen him."

"If sickness threatens my kinsmen and I refuse to help," Blair said, "I will never forgive myself for the deaths I could have prevented."

" 'Tis strange that no one besides Niall is ill," Graeme observed.

"Mayhap," Blair replied, "but I must go, Graeme. Dinna try to stop me."

"I will protect her with my life," Lachlan promised.

" 'Tis not good enough," Graeme said. "If Blair insists on going to Gairloch, I will send six armed guardsmen to protect her."

"I will prepare for the journey," Blair said, hurrying off.

Graeme stared after her, his expression troubled. "I dinna like it. Something isna right. You wouldna lie, would you, Father?"

"If I thought Niall was up to something, I wouldna have come. I promised the old earl I would protect his daughter, and so I shall. I came to fetch Blair because I am a mon of God and have always done what I could to prevent human suffering. I dinna know the source of Niall's illness, but I do know he hasna left his bedchamber in a sennight."

"I canna prevent Blair from ministering to her kinsmen, but I can make sure she will be safe."

"Aye," Lachlan agreed. "I trust Niall as little as ye do. I will rest here tonight while Blair prepares for the journey. We will leave tomorrow at first light."

Graeme hurried off to make arrangements. Once they were completed, he set out to find Blair. He found her in her bedchamber, packing a bag for her journey.

Blair greeted him with a smile. "Thank you for letting me return to Gairloch."

Graeme's brows arched upward. "Would I have been able to stop you?"

"Nay. I am a healer. I go where I am needed."

"*I* need you," Graeme said with feeling.

Blair went still. "You do?"

Placing his hands on her slender shoulders,

he pulled her against him. "Why do you doubt me?"

Her answer died in her throat when he lifted her face and kissed her, sweeping his tongue across her lips, then plunging it inside her mouth. She opened to him without protest; he savored her taste and sweet essence, drawing her tongue into his mouth and sucking gently.

He didn't break off the kiss until he felt her go limp against him. "How long will you be gone?" he whispered into her ear.

"I willna know until I ken the nature of Niall's disease and the number of people who have become ill. I will send word with one of your men as soon as I have answers."

"I will miss you."

Blair's eyes grew round. "Will you?"

"Aye. I want to make love to you."

"Now?"

"I canna think of a better time."

"Nor can I," Blair said, lifting her face for his kiss.

Graeme couldn't get enough of her sweet kisses, but he wanted more, much more. His hands worked swiftly, unfastening buttons and ties until she stood naked before him. He never tired of looking at her. Sweetly rounded and feminine, she enthralled him as no other woman had. He unbound her hair and ran his fingers through the silken mass, spreading it over her shoulders and breasts until only her nipples peeked through the golden strands.

Just looking at her aroused him. He could feel his cock swelling against his trews and his balls tightening. When he had looked his fill, he swept her into his arms and carried her to the bed. He would have followed her down, but Blair whispered, "I want you naked."

Groaning at the delay, he shed his clothes, carelessly tossing them aside. Then he joined her, pulling her against him, letting her feel the strength of his need. When she ground her hips against his loins, he nearly exploded.

"Not so fast, sweeting," Graeme panted. "I dinna want this to end too soon."

He wooed her with slow, tender kisses. He loved her body with his hands and mouth, leaving no part of her untouched. When he finally entered her, he was so aroused, he wanted to release the moment he slid into her tight sheath.

"Dinna move, love. Wait until I am more in control of myself."

"Please, Graeme," Blair pleaded. "I need you now."

Her words unleashed something savage inside him. Once he began to move, there was no stopping him. Grasping her bottom in his hands, he lifted her, thrusting deep, again and again, giving her all of him. When that wasn't enough, he lifted her legs over his shoulders to gain the deep penetration he sought.

Blair went wild beneath him, bucking and moaning. He felt her stiffen, knew she was near completion and let himself go, thrusting fast and deep. He felt her body spasm, felt her sex squeezing his cock and heard her scream his name. Then he emptied himself inside her, shouting his joy to the heavens.

Blair's escort was waiting in the courtyard the following morning when she, Graeme and Father Lachlan appeared. She recognized Aiden but didn't know the names of the other five men. Graeme wore a scowl that proved his unwillingness to let Blair leave Stonehaven. Alyce trailed behind, carrying a basket of herbs and medicines.

"I'm going with ye, lass," Alyce insisted.

"We went over this yesterday," Blair said. "Someone with knowledge of healing should remain at Stonehaven. With Gunna gone, there is no midwife in the village. You are needed here."

"Heed the lass," Stuart said. "Stonehaven needs ye, Alyce."

Though Alyce didn't look happy, she accepted the decision and handed the basket to Blair.

Blair stifled a grin. Stuart was acting very protective toward Alyce. Did Graeme's uncle hold tender feelings for her tiring woman?

She didn't have time to explore the subject, for Graeme was lifting her onto her mount.

"I'll fasten this to the saddle," Graeme said, taking the basket from her. "Aiden has instructions to send word back as soon as you arrive at Gairloch."

"You worry needlessly," Blair said, while secretly pleased by his concern.

He pulled her head down and kissed her, apparently unconcerned that they were being watched. Then he stepped away. Blair glanced over her shoulder as she rode off, stunned to see Glenda join Graeme. She watched until she saw Glenda press herself against Graeme before looking away, angry with herself for letting the serving girl irritate her. If Graeme wanted Glenda, he would take her, but for Blair's own peace of mind she had to believe that he would not.

The trip to Gairloch was uneventful. They reached the keep she had called home for most of her life near dusk. The gate was opened to them immediately and they rode through. Aiden helped her dismount and handed her the basket containing her medicines as a lad ran up to take their mounts. Then the Campbell men formed a tight circle around her as they escorted her inside the keep.

A man Blair didn't recognize greeted them.

"Where is Gavin?" Blair asked.

"Gone," the man said. "I am Gordon, the new steward."

"Take me to my brother," Blair ordered.

"I will go with her," Lachlan said.

"I will settle yer escort in their quarters first," Gordon said. "The laird has made arrangements for them. He knew Campbell wouldna send ye alone."

"I wish to see Niall immediately," Blair persisted. "If he is as ill as I was led to believe, I need to see him without delay."

"Ye will do as yer brother orders, lady," Gordon said. "I will return as soon as I see to yer escort."

"I find that passing strange," Lachlan remarked as Gordon greeted Aiden and offered to show his men to their quarters.

Aiden looked to Blair for direction, and when she nodded, he and the others fell in behind Gordon.

Blair and Father Lachlan were offered a cup of ale by a shy serving maid. They accepted and sat down at one of the tables to await Gordon's return.

"I recognize no one," Blair said. "Where did Niall get these people? Are they clansmen?"

"Aye," said Lachlan. "They come from fishing villages along the coast. Some are MacArthurs, some are MacMurrays, and the rest are Kincaids. All are loyal to Niall."

Gordon returned a short time later, wearing a smug look. "Yer men are taken care of," he said. "I'll take ye to yer brother now."

Lachlan rose to accompany her, but Gordon shook his head. "Nay, Father, the lass will go alone. Laird Niall doesna wish others to catch his illness."

"I promised to protect the lass," Lachlan protested.

"No harm will come to her," Gordon promised. "If ye wish to be helpful, go to the chapel and pray for our laird's recovery. If ye are ready, lady, I will take ye to yer brother now."

Clutching her basket to her chest, Blair followed Gordon. He led her up one flight of stairs, then another.

"Why does Niall not occupy the laird's chamber?" Blair asked as she paused to catch her breath.

"He thought it best to isolate himself in the tower. Until he knew the nature of his illness, he didna want it to spread. Con MacMurray and I are the only ones allowed to serve him."

"How have you managed to stay well?"

Gordon mumbled something she didn't understand. When she started to repeat the question, Gordon stopped before a closed door. Blair knew the castle well; they had reached the tower room. The door was closed. A chill slid down her spine. What awaited her behind that closed door?

"Are ye ready, lady?" Gordon asked.

Shoving aside her fear, Blair nodded. She

would do whatever was necessary to heal her brother. The knowledge that he had asked for her had prompted a slim hope that she and Niall could mend the rift between them.

Gordon opened the door and Blair stepped inside. She whirled about when she heard the door close behind her and the key turn in the lock.

"Welcome, Blair."

Blair gasped as Niall stepped out from the shadows.

"Niall, you frightened me." She stared at him. "You are not sick at all, are you?"

"I knew ye would come, Sister," Niall gloated. "Ye have a tender heart. But I'm surprised yer husband let ye come. We worried about that."

Fear struck deep in Blair's heart. "What evil plot are you and the MacKay hatching?"

"Ye belong to MacKay. I promised ye to him. Our father sought to destroy my plans by wedding ye to Campbell, but I will prevail in the end."

"I dinna understand. What are you talking about?"

He removed a coiled parchment from his sporran and carefully unrolled it. "Ye can read, lass. See for yerself."

Blair stepped closer, her heart in her mouth as she perused the document. "Oh, no!" she cried when she came to the end and recognized the king's royal seal.

"Aye," Niall said, gloating. "The king was angry when Campbell didna show up at Inverness with the other Highland lairds. It wasna difficult to persuade him to set aside yer marriage. Ye're free to wed MacKay now. One of my men has ridden out to fetch MacKay."

"Graeme sent an escort to protect me against your evil machinations."

Niall laughed harshly. "Are ye referring to the six men imprisoned in my dungeon?"

The breath froze in Blair's throat. "How could that have happened?"

"Yer escort is as gullible as ye are. Gordon led them straight to a company of armed men. They fought bravely, but the odds were against them. They were quickly disarmed and imprisoned. Once ye and MacKay are wed, I will release them."

"Were any of them hurt? I must see to their wounds."

"Forget them. I go now to prepare for yer wedding."

"You will never get me to agree to wed MacKay," Blair spat. "I am already wed, no matter what the king says. Furthermore, no man of God would force a woman to wed a man without her consent. Dinna think ye can bully Father Lachlan to do your bidding."

Niall's smirk set Blair's teeth on edge. "He came to fetch ye, did he not?"

"You tricked him."

Niall shrugged. "I dinna need Father Lachlan. MacKay is bringing his own priest. Whether ye say yea or nay doesna matter."

"Father Lachlan willna let you do this."

"The priest has joined Campbell's guardsmen in the dungeon. He never did approve of me, and I have always disliked him."

He gestured expansively. "Make yerself at home. Food will be sent up to ye, and there's a cot where ye may rest until MacKay comes for ye."

He turned to leave. "Wait!" Blair cried. "Why does MacKay want me? I still dinna understand."

"Neither do I. The mon fears yer power, yet he seems to want ye for those very same powers. He needs something from ye, but I dinna ken what. He agreed to let me keep yer dowry and lands if I gave ye to him. I dinna want to part with yer dowry. If ye remained wed to Campbell, eventually he would have claimed it for himself. I dinna ken what MacKay has in mind for ye and I dinna care. The sooner I am rid of ye, the better.

"No more questions," he said when Blair opened her mouth to speak. "There are preparations to be made." He rapped on the door, and it opened immediately.

Blair tried to rush past him but he slammed the door in her face. She pounded on the door, to no avail, then slid down to the floor, choking on the tears that clogged her throat.

How could the king do this to her? A piece of paper might revoke her marriage, but it wouldn't end the love she felt for Graeme. That would go on forever. How could she have been so foolish as to leave Stonehaven? Had she remained, there was no way Graeme would have let an annulment part them. He might not love her, but he took his vows seriously. When he'd promised her father he would let no harm come to her, he had meant it.

What would Graeme do when he learned about the annulment? Would he storm Castle MacKay? It was her understanding that the keep was impregnable. That knowledge and the king's signature on the annulment document had sealed her fate.

She was lost.

And bereft.

And powerless. The spirits were no longer with her. Tears spilled from her eyes as she sent Graeme a mental message that she feared would never reach him.

Graeme prowled his bedchamber like a caged animal. Something was wrong. A burning sensation in his gut warned him of danger. Danger to whom? Did Blair need him? He shouldn't have let her leave. The wail of the wind through the trees beckoned

315

him, and he strode to the window. He feared he was going insane when he heard Blair's voice riding the wind. Fear for his wife escalated.

How long would he have to wait before one of his men brought word of Blair's safe arrival at Gairloch? Tomorrow at the very earliest, he supposed. Heaving a frustrated sigh, he left the chamber to join his men in the hall. Though Blair had been gone but a few hours, it felt like an eternity. Perhaps a game of cards or dice would take his mind off the woman he . . .

He halted, suddenly aware of the direction his thoughts were taking.

Could it be?

Did he love Blair?

His feelings for her were nothing like the pure, innocent adoration he had felt for Joan the Maid. What he felt for Blair was neither innocent nor pure. He wanted her with a yearning that nearly unmanned him.

Nay, he couldn't let himself love Blair. The last thing he wanted was for her powers to return.

Chapter Fifteen

Blair awoke to the sound of laughter outside her tower prison. Disoriented, she was slow to recall everything that had happened the previous day. When full awareness came to her, a cry of dismay left her lips. She was her brother's prisoner. Her Campbell escort shared her captivity, as did Father Lachlan.

Shoving herself to her feet, she caught sight of the food congealing on the tray and she recalled that she had refused to eat last night when Niall's toady had brought it. She had, however, used the hot water and soap Gordon had brought with her food.

The laughter grew louder. Then the door flew open. She wasn't surprised to see her brother and MacKay standing in the opening. She raised her chin to a defiant angle.

"I hope you are shaking in your boots. My husband will retaliate when he learns of this."

"Ye no longer have a husband, lass," MacKay said. "Ye're free now to wed me. 'Tis as it should be. We will wed immediately."

Blair squared her shoulders. "You canna force me to marry you."

"Oh, aye, I can. Ye will wed me and gladly."

"Exactly how do you intend for that to happen?"

"Do ye value the lives of yer Campbell guardsmen and that worthless priest?"

Blair blanched. "You wouldna dare!"

"I dare much, lady."

"The king will punish you."

Niall's laughter joined MacKay's. "Think again, Blair. The king is grateful to us for revealing treasonous acts against him and willna punish us for killing men accused of plotting his downfall."

She sent MacKay a chilling smile. "Dinna you fear I will place a spell on you?" She pointed a finger at his privates. "Once I threatened to shrivel your manhood. I still can, you ken."

MacKay shifted uncomfortably. "Dinna threaten me, lady. If ye attempt to place a spell on me, I will slay ye first, then the Campbells."

Horrified, she blurted out, "Why do you want me?"

"Dinna flatter yerself. 'Tis not ye I want. I covet yer powers."

"I possess no powers."

"Liar!" Niall and MacKay shouted together.

"What exactly is it you want from me? How can my powers help you?"

"Once we are wed, I will tell ye. What I have in mind is not a difficult task for ye."

"I willna wed you."

"MacArthur," MacKay said, "ye can begin executing Graeme Campbell's clansmen immediately. I recommend ye start with the priest."

"Nay!" Blair pleaded. "Father Lachlan is Niall's own kinsman. Have you no heart?"

"Wed me and all will be well. No one will be hurt, and Father Lachlan can accompany the Campbells to their stronghold after the wedding."

"I will go with you to your keep, but I willna wed you. And if you touch me, I will make you verra, verra sorry."

MacKay shook his head. "Marriage is the only way I can keep ye with me to do my bidding."

"Spare my escort and Father Lachlan, and I vow to remain with you until you have what it is you want from me."

"Dinna let her trick ye," Niall warned. "I say we execute the whole lot of them and force Blair to wed ye. 'Twill make her more amenable to yer needs."

Blair pointed a finger at Niall and slowly moved it downward to his groin. Closing her eyes, she began to chant, aware that what she did was nothing more than a scare tactic.

She could no more shrivel Niall's privates than she could make the sun fall from the sky.

Niall must have thought otherwise, for he grasped his groin and let out a high-pitched squeal.

"Damn ye! Remove the spell."

Aware that she now held the upper hand, Blair said, "Release Graeme's kinsmen."

"After we are wed," MacKay repeated, forestalling Niall's answer. "I need ye to use yer powers to find something that was lost long ago."

Blair's brows shot upward. Finally MacKay had given her a reason, though it didn't satisfy her. What was he looking for? "I told you my terms. Though I willna wed you, I vow to help you locate what you lost. If I succeed, you must let me return to my husband."

"Forget MacKay! Remove the spell!" Niall pleaded in a voice fraught with fear.

Blair stifled a smile when she saw that Niall was still clutching his groin. "Release Graeme's kinsmen, and I will consider it."

"Aye, anything ye say. I dinna want to be a eunuch."

"Dinna be such a coward," MacKay scoffed. "The moment ye release Campbell's clansmen, our control over the witch is gone."

"Ye're a selfish bastard, MacKay. It wasna ye she put a spell on."

"Nevertheless, ye canna release Campbell's clansmen just yet. Ye can set them free the day following our departure. And be sure to send a copy of the official document dissolving Campbell's marriage with them."

"Remove the spell, Blair," Niall cried. "I promise to release yer escort as MacKay directed."

Blair pretended to consider Niall's proposal. At length she said, "I willna wed MacKay, and I willna remove the spell if you force me to wed him."

"Wed MacKay or not," Niall said. "Either way yer dowry remains under my control. It shouldna be difficult to find what MacKay has lost. I promise yer escort will be released unharmed the day after ye and MacKay depart."

"If you refuse to accompany me to my keep, the priest and all your men will be promptly executed," MacKay added. "I dinna really want to wed or bed ye. I have a fondness for my cock. All I ever wanted from ye are the powers ye possess."

"God's nightgown, MacKay! Think ye I dinna value *my* cock? Make her remove the spell before ye leave."

"Mayhap we should kill a Campbell or two," MacKay said slyly. Then she will remove the hex she placed on ye."

"Aye," Niall readily agreed. "I will order it immediately."

"Wait!" Blair cried. This was getting out of hand. The mind was a powerful weapon. Though she had done nothing more than chant a few garbled words, Niall had truly believed she had placed a spell on him. Now she had to make him think her powers were even stronger than he'd believed.

"If you harm even one of my men, I vow you will never perform as a man again. I offer instead a compromise. I will willingly accompany MacKay if you promise to release Graeme's clansmen the day after our departure. Only then will the spell be lifted. If you renege, you will be permanently rendered impotent. You can depend upon it."

Blair held her breath, watching Niall closely as he pondered her words. Everything depended on his belief in her magical powers.

"Verra well, I agree. Yer men will be released the day following yer departure . . . if," he stressed, "I can still perform as a man. I will bed a serving maid before their release to make sure all is well."

"You willna fail, Niall, that I promise."

"Are ye ready to travel, lass?" MacKay asked, apparently impatient now that the terms had been set.

"Aye. The sooner we reach your stronghold, the sooner I can find what you lost. I wish to return to my husband without delay."

"Dinna ye understand the king's edict?"

Niall said. "Ye're no longer wed to the Campbell. I am yer legal guardian and keeper of yer dowry. Since no other mon in his right mind will wed ye, I care not where ye go or what ye do after MacKay finishes with ye. Return to Graeme Campbell and become his whore, if it pleases ye."

Grasping her arm, MacKay forced her toward the door. "Our horses are waiting in the courtyard."

"I want to take my things with me," Blair said, gesturing toward the basket containing her medicines and the bag of clothing sitting next to it.

"Verra well. But hurry. I wish to reach my stronghold before nightfall."

Blair retrieved her belongings, then followed MacKay down two flights of stairs to the hall. Niall trailed close behind. No words were spoken as they proceeded out the door. A dozen MacKay guardsmen milled about in the courtyard. Her own horse had been saddled and stood waiting.

MacKay gave the order to mount and hoisted Blair into the saddle. Blair grasped the reins as the party rode off at a brisk pace.

"Dinna forget your promise!" Blair called over her shoulder to Niall.

"Dinna forget yers!" Niall shouted back.

Anxiety and no little amount of fear rode

Graeme. He shouldn't have let Blair leave. What had he been thinking? He ought to have received word of Blair's safe arrival by now, yet all he had heard were vague warnings that seemed to come from inside his head.

Heath clapped him on the shoulder. "Ye worry overmuch, Graeme. I am sure we will hear from Aiden today."

"If I dinna hear soon, I will ride to Gairloch. Sickness or nay, I dinna trust Niall MacArthur."

"Methinks ye have fallen in love with the wench," Heath said. "She has bewitched ye as surely as ye live and breathe. I never thought to see the day ye'd be mooning over a woman. Ye changed after ye returned from France. Joan the Maid's death affected ye greatly."

"Joan is my past, Blair is my future," Graeme said, surprised at his willingness to reveal so much to his cousin. He was struck by the realization that it was long past time to let the memory go.

" 'Tis true," Heath said, "ye love the lass, dinna ye?"

"I canna. I didna want to believe in the Prophecy, but Blair made a believer of me. She claims to love me, and according to the Prophecy, if her love is returned, her powers will grow strong and prosper. If she retains her powers, I canna stop her from using them. And if she uses them, people will continue to fear her. You can see the danger in that as well as I."

"Willing or nay, ye love her."

Graeme shook his head, refusing to acknowledge it.

"Och, ye have always been a stubborn bastard," Heath said when silence stretched between them.

"I can wait no longer," Graeme announced, abruptly changing the subject. "I ride to Gairloch to claim my wife. I want a dozen men armed and ready to accompany me within the hour."

"As ye wish," Heath replied, hurrying off to do Graeme's bidding.

Graeme whirled about, nearly colliding with Glenda. "Out of my way, lass."

"I heard what Heath said to ye," Glenda confided. "I dinna believe ye love Blair. She has bewitched ye." She sidled close, pressing her breasts against his arm. "Let me help ye break the spell. Take me to yer bedchamber now. I know how to make ye forget ye have a wife."

"Dinna waste your time, Glenda," Graeme advised. "I willna break my wedding vows. One of God's chosen taught me the meaning of faith."

"Ye're a fool," Glenda spat. "Ye should have wed me, Graeme Campbell. Everyone believed we would wed when ye returned from France."

"You were the only one who thought that, Glenda."

Pushing past her, he continued on his way.

"Ye'll be sorry, Graeme Campbell," she muttered. "Ye and the witch will be verra, verra sorry."

Armed with claymore, shield and dirk, Graeme joined his guardsmen in the courtyard. Clad in identical Campbell plaid, they wore their bonnets sporting a sprig of rowan at a cocky angle.

"We will follow where ye lead," Heath said, riding up beside Graeme. "We have been itching for a good fight."

"I hope it willna come to that," Graeme said tersely. "Mayhap my fears are for naught."

So saying, he gave the signal to mount and preceded his men through the gate. As fate would have it, Graeme came upon Blair's escort long before he reached Gairloch. His heart in his mouth, Graeme spurred his horse to meet them. His men followed.

"Where is Blair?" Graeme shouted, reining in sharply. "What happened at Gairloch?"

"Forgive me, Graeme," Aiden replied. "I should have expected a trick. Naught inside the keep seemed amiss when we arrived. When MacArthur's steward offered to show us to our quarters, we followed. We had no idea we were being led straight into a trap.

'Twas a battle we couldna have won no matter how bravely we fought. We were out-numbered, and disarmed and imprisoned in the dungeon."

"Father Lachlan deceived us," Graeme spat.

"Nay, he joined us in the dungeon. Here he is now."

"I plead for your forgiveness," the priest said. "I had no part in Niall's machinations. If I truly didna believe him near death, I wouldna have come to fetch Blair."

Graeme's expression turned grim. "Where — is — my — wife?" he demanded.

"I know only what Niall told me," Father Lachlan explained. "He said to give ye this."

He handed Graeme a rolled parchment. Graeme tore it open, fear settling deep in his gut as he perused the words.

"Damn the man to hell!" Graeme shouted when he came to the end of the document.

"What is it?" Heath asked.

"MacArthur and MacKay have convinced the king to set aside my marriage to Blair. The bastards! I'll wring their bloody necks."

"Calm down, lad," Father Lachlan advised. "Let us return to Stonehaven and think this through. No matter how Niall obtained this document, it appears legal."

"Is Blair still at Gairloch?"

"Nay, MacKay took her away."

"MacKay! Nay!" Drawing his sword,

Graeme thrust it into the air. "To the MacKay stronghold!"

"Listen to reason," Heath advised. "We will be cut down without mercy if we try to storm the keep. 'Tis near impregnable."

"Are you suggesting I give my wife to MacKay?"

"She is no longer yer wife," Heath reminded him.

Graeme turned to Father Lachlan, his expression grim. "Did Blair's brother wed her to the MacKay?"

"Not to my knowledge. I was told she went willingly with MacKay. When I questioned one of the guardsmen, he said Blair accompanied MacKay because MacArthur threatened to execute us if she refused to go with him. The fellow knew naught about a marriage."

"What does MacKay want from her?" Graeme muttered. "Why did MacArthur want our marriage set aside?"

"I can answer the last part of yer question," the priest replied. "MacArthur doesna want to part with Blair's dowry. Once her marriage was dissolved, he regained control of her wealth. As for MacKay, yer guess is as good as mine."

Graeme stood upright in the saddle, turned his face toward the MacKay stronghold and shouted, "Death to the MacKay!"

"Nay, lad, be easy," Father Lachlan urged.

"There has to be another way. Violence will gain ye naught. Only one person can give ye back what ye lost."

"The king!" Graeme spat.

"God, not the king," the priest replied.

"I refuse to sit back and wait for divine intervention," Graeme said. "God helps those who help themselves."

"The men grow anxious, Graeme," Aiden said. "Do we ride to the MacKay stronghold or return home?"

Graeme knew what he *wanted* to do but realized it wasn't the wisest choice. Blair was a resourceful lass; he had to trust her to prevent MacKay from harming her. After all, her powers couldn't help MacKay if she were injured or dead. Then again, she might not have any powers left for MacKay to exploit.

"We'll return to Stonehaven," Graeme said woodenly. "Somehow, some way, I must convince the king to reinstate my marriage to Blair."

Blair had been locked in a sparsely furnished chamber upon her arrival at MacKay's stronghold. She had no idea what MacKay wanted from her and was impatient to find out. At least she hadn't been starved or mistreated. That thought led to another. Had Niall released Graeme's clansmen as he'd promised? Did he fear her magic enough to honor her request?

If Niall had kept his word, Graeme would have been told that he no longer had a wife. Would that make him happy? She sincerely hoped not. There was nothing he could do about the king's edict. She and Graeme were no longer husband and wife and could never be so again without the king's approval. But that wouldn't stop her from returning to Stonehaven and becoming Graeme's leman, if he would have her.

Blair spent an entire day and night in confinement before MacKay called to her through the door and entered her chamber. Blair rose to greet him, her chin raised in defiance.

"What is it you want from me?" she challenged.

"Lower yer chin, lass. A wee thing like ye doesna frighten me."

"Do you not fear my magic?"

MacKay retreated a step. "Mayhap. But I warn ye, unless ye have a death wish, dinna use yer evil spells on me."

"Tell me what you want."

He strode to the window and looked out. "Many years ago, during my great-grandfather Connor's time, the castle came under siege. The keep wasna as well fortified as it is now, and my ancestor feared it would fall to the enemy."

"What has that got to do with me?" Blair asked.

"I am getting to that. During the siege, Connor hid the wealth he had accumulated through the years and told no one where he had hidden his riches. He trusted no one with the location of the hiding place, ye see. Unfortunately, Connor fell beneath his enemy's sword. The treasure has never been found, though not for lack of searching. There isna a nook or cranny in the keep and outbuildings that hasna been searched since Connor's death."

"You want me to tell you where your ancestor hid the treasure," Blair surmised.

MacKay grinned. "I knew ye were smart, lass. Locating the treasure should be an easy task for someone with yer talents. Use yer magic, lass. I care not how ye do it, just give me what I want."

Blair shook her head. "I have no powers, no magic. I am naught but a healer."

"Ye lie! I saw ye work yer magic on yer brother."

" 'Twas a farce. I lied about the spell."

A fierce scowl contorted MacKay's face. "I dinna believe ye! Find my treasure, witch! If ye fail, ye willna like the consequences."

"Will you let me leave if I find your treasure?"

"Aye, ye have my word. After I have my treasure, ye can go, and good riddance to ye. My kinsmen dinna want ye here."

Blair sighed and let his remark pass. If she

had to explain one more time that she wasn't a witch, she would go mad. "I'll need time to find your treasure. And I must be allowed to explore the castle."

"Do ye give yer word ye willna try to escape?"

"Aye, you have it."

"Verra well. Yer door will be left unlocked, and ye can take meals with my kinsmen in the great hall. Heed me well, lass. Dinna try to trick me. Find my treasure in a reasonable length of time, else I will find a way to punish those ye care about. Niall swore ye had powers — now use them."

Blair slumped down on the bed. What would MacKay do when he learned she had no powers? She had lost them when she fell in love with Graeme. The only power left to her was her intelligence. She had bought some time from MacKay and intended to use it. She would begin by searching the castle from top to bottom. If the treasure existed, she would find it.

Blair smoothed her skirts, dragged in a deep breath and left her chamber. When she reached the hall, all conversation stopped. People turned and stared at her. She felt their fear reach out and surround her. Their combined aura was dark and menacing. They did not want her here any more than she wanted to be here. She wanted to go home . . . home to Stonehaven and Graeme, even if he was no longer her husband.

Blair took a seat at one of the lower tables and helped herself to food from the tray that was being passed around. Immediately those around her rose and moved to other tables. Chagrined, Blair ignored the insult and continued eating as if nothing was wrong.

While she ate, she noticed a man with a swollen jaw. She knew immediately the poor man had an abscessed tooth and wanted to help him.

When he passed nearby, she said, "I can help you if you let me. An herb posset placed on the tooth will bring down the swelling, and a tea of the same herbs should ease the pain."

The man recoiled in fear. "Ye'll use none of yer witchcraft on me, mistress." Then he turned and hurried off.

"Silly man," Blair muttered as she finished her food. "Let him suffer."

No one spoke to her, and everyone gave her a wide berth. Then Blair took matters into her own hands and sought out the housekeeper. Her name was Hilda, and though she didn't flee, Blair could tell she was frightened.

"I willna hurt you, Hilda, nor any of your kinsmen. I am a healer, not a witch. While I am here, I would gladly treat any of your kinsmen who need my skills."

"I . . . I dinna know about that, mistress,"

Hilda stuttered. "MacKay said ye were a witch. He brought ye here to find the treasure his ancestor hid."

"Do I look like a witch?"

Hilda stared at her. "Nay, ye look like an angel."

"I canna change your mind or those of your kinsmen, but I want you to know I am not evil. The reason I sought you out is because MacKay said I could search the castle, and I would like you to show me around."

"Duncan would be the mon to ask," Hilda said. "He's the laird's steward. I will fetch him for ye." She hurried off.

Blair realized that living among the MacKays wasn't going to be easy. How could she possibly undo the years of damage that lies about her had wrought? She hoped she would find the treasure soon so she could return home . . . home to Graeme, if he would still have her. A vision of Glenda intimately entwined with Graeme appeared before her eyes.

Her hand flew to her mouth, stifling the cry that lodged in her throat. Had a tiny bit of her powers returned? Had she been allowed a look into the future, or was her vision a figment of her imagination? *Please, God,* she prayed, *let the vision be my imagination.*

Hilda returned with Duncan. As luck would have it, he was the man with the swollen jaw she had offered to help.

"The MacKay said I might search the castle. I would like to start at the top and continue down to the dungeon. I want to inspect every chamber, no matter how small or insignificant."

His face contorted with pain, Duncan gave her a sullen nod.

"Follow me, mistress."

Blair skipped to catch up with his long stride. "Are you still in pain, Duncan?"

Duncan's muffled response told Blair that he still suffered. If she had possessed her powers, she could have healed him with a touch. But herbal remedies would have to suffice, if Duncan would allow it.

"Will you let me look at your tooth?" Blair asked. "I dinna like to see a man in pain."

Duncan stopped abruptly, causing Blair to run into his back. He turned to face her. "The pain is verra, verra bad, mistress. Can ye use magic to cure me?"

"I have no magic, Duncan, but I *am* a healer. Will you allow me to ease your pain?"

Duncan backed off, fear etching his features. Blair could tell he wanted the relief she promised, but he still believed the gossip that named her a witch.

"Do you know what a Faery Woman is?" she asked.

"Aye. According to legend, Faery Women are healers and possess powers mortals dinna ken."

"I am a Faery Woman, Duncan. My life is dedicated to helping others. I work in mysterious ways, but I am not evil, nor have I ever harmed anyone."

"So ye say," Duncan snorted. "Follow me, mistress."

"Duncan."

He turned slowly. "Aye?"

Blair approached him gingerly. Reaching out, she touched his jaw, running her fingers along the swelling. She felt her fingers tingle, felt the rush of familiar heat up her arm, followed by a jolt of pain. Her eyes grew round. How could this be? She had lost her powers. Searching Duncan's face, she saw no difference in Duncan's expression. Her imagination must be working overtime. Duncan merely sent her a strange look and continued on his way.

For the next several days, Blair poked about in every chamber in the castle and continued on to the outbuildings. Nothing she saw aroused the slightest awareness in her. Her senses remained dulled. Without her powers, she had not the slightest idea where to find the treasure, though she spent days poking around unused chambers and filthy outbuildings.

Of MacKay she saw little. He came and went about his business of reiving his neighbors' livestock. A sennight after she arrived at Castle MacKay, the laird barged into her chamber and demanded answers. Of course, Blair had none and begged for more time.

"I need that treasure now," MacKay growled. "The king is demanding money from the Highland chieftains to help pay his ransom, and my coffers are empty. If James doesna get the money he needs, a war seems likely. Ye have two more days to find the treasure. Then I leave to join the king at Hawick."

Blair immediately thought of Graeme and prayed for his safety. She knew he was a seasoned warrior, but even warriors fell in battle.

"Will all the lairds answer the call for arms and money?"

MacKay snorted. "I doubt it. They are displeased with James. He went too far when he executed five of their number."

"Six, if Graeme had gone," Blair reminded him.

"Aye, six. Graeme Campbell has more luck than sense. Consider yerself warned, lass. If ye dinna find my treasure, there are those here who would like to see ye burned at the stake."

Blair paced the chamber after MacKay left, racking her brain for an answer to her dilemma. She hadn't the slightest idea where MacKay's treasure was hidden. A knock on the door brought her from her reverie. She opened it to find Duncan standing on the threshold. The cloth was gone from around his jaw and the swelling was no longer evident.

"Mistress, forgive me," Duncan said, wringing his hands.

"For what?"

"For doubting ye. Ye healed me. The swelling is gone and my tooth no longer pains me. Ye cured me with a mere touch. Ye are indeed a Faery Woman, and I am sorry for doubting ye."

"When did this healing take place?" Blair asked, confused. How could her powers have returned when the spirits would not speak to her?

"After ye touched me."

"Why did you wait so long to tell me?"

"I was afraid, lady. At first I didna want to believe yer touch healed me, but I can no longer deny it. Thank ye, lady."

Blair couldn't speak, could only nod as Duncan took his leave. What did it mean? Had her powers returned?

Blair went to bed that night with a troubled mind. Sometime during the darkest part of night she awoke to voices echoing through her head. She was confused at first, but eventually she made out the words. The spirits wanted her to go to the window.

Ignoring the chill that seeped through to her bones, she rose and padded barefoot to the window. The moon was full, illuminating the courtyard below with brilliant light.

" 'Tis there," the voice whispered.

"What? What are you trying to tell me?"

"The treasure. 'Tis there beneath the rowan tree, buried at the bottom of an abandoned well."

A wave of dizziness swept through Blair. Blackness closed in and she knew no more.

Chapter Sixteen

Graeme, Heath, Aiden and Stuart were discussing the action that should be taken against MacKay when a message arrived from the king. Graeme sent the messenger off to the kitchen for food and drink while he perused the missive.

"What does the king want now?" Stuart asked when Graeme spit out a curse and pounded the table with his fist.

"Money to pay his ransom, and men to fight the English if he fails to raise enough gold to appease his former captors. The king has ordered the Highland lairds to gather men and arms and join him at Hawick. Damn him! He wants us to empty our coffers for him."

"What are ye going to do?" Heath asked.

"After the way the king treated me, I should ignore the summons. I willna give money to the bastard who meant to execute me."

" 'Tis not wise to anger the king," Stuart warned.

Graeme grew thoughtful. "Heath, how

many men can we muster?"

"Two hundred, if we send out the call to our clansmen who live in small fishing villages along the coast. It would take at least a sennight to muster them, but they will come."

"And perhaps another sennight to reach Hawick." Graeme stroked his chin. "It could work."

"What are ye thinking, laddie?" Stuart asked.

"Two hundred men is not an inconsiderable number. Some lairds will ignore the call, for they have not forgiven him for what happened at Inverness, and I canna blame them."

"Are ye saying we will ignore the call for arms and money?" Stuart asked.

"Nay, 'tis not what I had in mind. The king is desperate for men and money. He'll be even more desperate when he learns that those very same lairds he intended to imprison will ignore his summons. He will need our two hundred men." He grinned. " 'Tis perfect. I shall give him what he wants but demand something in return."

"Ye expect the king of Scotland to deal with ye?" Heath said incredulously.

"Aye. Dinna let the messenger leave until I prepare an answer to carry back to the king. I intend to tell James that I will bring money and two hundred men if he restores my marriage to Blair."

Stuart gasped. " 'Tis a bold move, Nephew. Mayhap ye would be better off without the lass."

Alyce, who had been standing in the background, bristled indignantly. "I canna believe ye said that, Stuart. If not for Blair, ye wouldna be here. She saved yer life."

"Alyce is right," Graeme agreed. "All that aside, I promised Blair's father I would protect her."

Heath sent Graeme a probing look. " 'Tis more than that," he muttered. "Say what you want, 'tis obvious ye love the lass."

Graeme started to deny the charge but changed his mind. " 'Tis true I am uncommonly fond of Blair."

"Ha!" Heath bleated.

"I knew it!" Alyce said, grinning smugly.

"My feelings are not the issue," Graeme said. "What think you of my plan?"

"I agree that 'tis possible the lairds will send neither men nor money," Aiden mused. "I think yer plan has merit, laird."

"Aye," the others agreed.

"Alyce, fetch the messenger."

"Think ye the king will accept yer terms?" Heath asked.

"Aye, I believe so. He isna stupid. He will agree to anything if he's desperate enough. Heath, send out the call for men. Aiden, check the weapons in the armory and set the lads to repairing those that are in need of attention. Uncle, I will leave the keep once again in your capable hands. Aiden, choose a man to accompany the messenger. He can carry the king's reply back to me."

Blair lay in a pool of moonlight. Consciousness returned to her slowly, but once she was fully awake, she recalled everything. She knew where MacKay's treasure lay. Unsteadily she rose to her feet and staggered to the bed. Her thoughts ran amok. Should she tell MacKay? Did her freedom lie at the bottom of an abandoned well? Would MacKay honor his promise to let her go free once he had his treasure?

Blair couldn't think about that right now. There were more important issues at hand. The most significant was the return of her powers. If the Prophecy was to be believed, and she had no reason to doubt it, Graeme loved her. What Blair desired above all things was Graeme's love, but until the spirits had spoken to her tonight she had despaired of ever having it. Why had it taken him so long to acknowledge his feelings?"

Despite the possibility that Graeme loved her, they were no longer wed. The king had ended their union with a stroke of a pen. It mattered not, she decided. She would go to Stonehaven and offer to become Graeme's leman. No matter what transpired, she would not be parted from Graeme.

★ ★ ★

Blair stood at the window as a bleak dawn broke through the morning mist. The overcast sky promised rain, and before long a light drizzle began to fall. Within minutes the drizzle turned into a downpour that pelted the window. A dismal beginning for such a portentous day, Blair thought.

Shivering, Blair performed her morning ablutions and went below to the hall. She was walking toward one of the lower tables when MacKay motioned for her to join him.

"Well?" he asked impatiently. "Do ye have answers for me? I can wait nae longer."

Blair filled her plate with eggs and ham and proceeded to eat. She intended to appease her hunger before she dealt with MacKay. Her appetite, despite her dire situation, had not waned. During the past few weeks she had been ravenous and feared she would soon burst the seams of her gown.

"Speak to me, lass," MacKay growled.

"I canna think on an empty stomach," Blair said, needing time to consider the ramifications of revealing the location of the treasure to MacKay.

"Eat yer fill, then tell me what I want to know. What is so difficult about using yer magic to find something of mine that is missing?"

Blair raised her head and stared at MacKay. "What's in it for me?"

"Are ye daft? Does yer freedom mean naught to ye?"

"Does a fortune in gold and jewels mean naught to you?" Blair shot back.

An idea had just occurred to her. She wanted to take something of value back to Graeme, especially if he had received the same request for money and arms from the king that MacKay had.

"The treasure does indeed exist, and 'tis worth more than you imagined."

"Ahhh," MacKay sighed, leaning back in his chair. "I knew it." He drummed his fingers on the table and stared off into space, his eyes hooded, his expression smug.

"The king need never know of this. I willna share with him." He turned to Blair and grasped her shoulders, his fingers digging into her soft flesh. "Where is my treasure?"

"Unhand me! The treasure is where you will never find it without my help."

His hands dropped away. "What are ye up to, lass?"

"If I tell you where your treasure is located, 'tis only fair that I should have a portion of it."

"Ye expect me to share my treasure with ye?"

"Only a small part. I am not greedy."

"Nay."

Blair shrugged. "Then I will never reveal its location to you."

With the return of her powers, Blair had no fear of MacKay.

She rose. MacKay grasped her arm and pulled her back down. "Dinna play me for a fool, Blair MacArthur, lest ye suffer my wrath."

"Dinna think I am incapable of making you verra sorry you threatened me. I could arrange for lightning to strike you, if I wished."

"Ye wouldna."

"Would I not? I am but asking for a small share of the treasure."

"How small?"

Blair cocked her head, closed her eyes and was granted a vision of the enormous wealth hidden within the treasure chest. "I want a quarter of the treasure's worth."

"Nay, 'tis too much! A tenth! I will give you a tenth."

Blair considered. A tenth of the treasure would be sufficient. "Verra well, I agree."

"How do ye know what the treasure consists of?"

"I have 'seen' what lies within the treasure chest. You will be pleased."

"Verra well, a tenth. Now tell me where to find all this wealth."

Blair rose. "I will fetch my wrap and lead you to it."

"Be quick about it," MacKay ordered. "I canna wait to finally possess my ancestor's legendary wealth."

Blair returned a short time later, wrapped in a sturdy cloak to protect her from the chilling rain. She walked across the hall and out the door, so sure that MacKay would follow, she didn't bother looking back.

MacKay caught up with her in the bailey. "Where is it, lass? Ye wouldna play me false, would ye?"

Ignoring him, Blair proceeded directly to the rowan tree growing a short distance from the keep. She stopped abruptly and pointed to the earth beneath her feet.

"Dig here. You'll find the treasure at the bottom of an abandoned well."

MacKay gave a derisive snort. "There is no abandoned well beneath yer feet."

"Do you doubt me?"

MacKay studied her from beneath lowered lids. He looked skeptical, as if he wanted to disbelieve her but dared not. "I'll set men to digging immediately."

Spinning about, he spoke to one of the guardsmen standing nearby. A few minutes later a half dozen men carrying shovels poured from one of the outbuildings.

"Tell them where to dig," MacKay ordered.

Blair pointed to the spot beneath her feet and moved aside. She watched dispassionately as the men began digging furiously. By the time the shovels hit something solid, Blair was soaked to the skin and shivering.

When she attempted to return to the warm fire inside the keep, MacKay snagged her around the waist.

"Stay. We will see this through together."

The solid object turned out to be a wooden barrier that appeared to cover an opening of some sort.

"Damn me, but the witch is right," MacKay crowed. "Bend yer backs to it, lads."

The lid was pried up, revealing a deep, dark hole. Blair moved cautiously to the edge. A bright light only she could see appeared before her eyes. Her gaze followed the light to the very bottom of the well. She saw the treasure chest sitting exactly where it had lain for over one hundred years.

"What do ye see?" MacKay asked. " 'Tis black as pitch down there."

"Give two men torches and lower them on ropes. The well isna deep and holds no water. They will know what to do when they reach the bottom."

This time MacKay didn't stop her when she left. He was too engrossed in retrieving the treasure chest to care. Blair warmed herself before the fire while the men toiled outside in the rain.

An hour later a jubilant MacKay returned, followed by four men lugging the chest. A crowd gathered around as the chest was placed on a table, waiting for MacKay to break the rusty lock.

"Blair MacArthur!" MacKay shouted. "Come here, lass. I want ye beside me when I view the treasure for the first time. If ye have played me false, yer head will be parted from yer body afore ye can work one of yer evil spells on me."

Blair approached MacKay, aware that the contents of the chest wouldn't disappoint him.

MacKay attacked the rusty lock with the hilt of his dirk. When that failed, he used his claymore with great vigor. Finally the lock gave, falling to the floor in pieces.

The chamber reverberated with excitement as men and women pressed close for a glimpse of the treasure. MacKay's hands were shaking as he lifted the lid. The glitter of gold nearly blinded Blair. She gasped and turned away, her face suddenly gone pale. But it wasn't the sheen of gold that startled her.

It was the pitiful cries of those who had died beneath the swords of MacKay's ancestors, the men who had raided and killed for the contents of the chest. And she was aware of something she had not sensed before. There was a curse that came with the chest. The man who claimed it would not live long enough to enjoy it.

Each precious gem and gold coin spoke to Blair of brutality, betrayal and death. A shiver raced down her spine. The treasure chest held ill-gotten gains. Would MacKay heed her if she told him about the curse?

"You have what you wanted; I will gather my things and leave," she said.

"What about yer reward?" MacKay asked, looking as stunned as Blair felt after viewing the treasure and hearing the tormented voices calling out to her.

"I want no part of it. 'Tis yours."

MacKay's eyes narrowed. "What changed yer mind? We struck a bargain. Your share of the treasure is not paltry."

"I want no part of it. 'Tis cursed. Keep it, all of it. A horse is all I require."

"Fetch the lass's horse," MacKay shouted to one of his kinsmen, as if afraid she would change her mind.

"Thank you. I'll get my things," Blair said, turning her back on the treasure and all the misery it represented. She could still hear the former owners crying out for retribution, and she had to get away from those haunting voices.

Suddenly she gasped and stiffened as a stabbing pain in the middle of her back brought her to a halt. It felt as if someone had just shoved a dagger into her flesh. Glancing over her shoulder, she was stunned to see MacKay staring at her through narrowed lids. His aura was green, the color of greed, and Blair could read his thoughts as if he had spoken them aloud.

He was reconsidering his agreement to let her leave and wondering how to use her powers to further his ambitions. Deciding it was time to flee, Blair made a wild dash out the front door and into the tempest raging outside.

"Dinna let her get away!" MacKay shouted.

Blair heard men pounding behind her and veered toward the stables. Without a horse she hadn't a chance of escaping. Darting a glance over her shoulder, she saw that MacKay and his men were nearly upon her.

She stopped abruptly, aware that her powers were all that stood between her and the return to captivity. Facing her adversaries, she spread her arms wide and silently beseeched the spirits to help her. She felt a surge of energy lance through her body and knew the spirits were with her. Raising her voice above the wail of the wind, she called forth the forces of nature. MacKay had nearly reached her when a bolt of lightning streaked to earth from a bank of angry black storm clouds, striking the ground near his feet.

MacKay and his men flew in all directions, stunned and unable to move. Taking advantage of the situation, Blair darted into the stables, mounted the first horse she saw and flew past the confused men lying on the ground. Having had no time to saddle the mare, Blair clung to her mane as she sped through the gate and set a course for Stone-haven.

Feeling an overwhelming need to help Blair, Graeme was too worried and impatient to wait for the king's reply to his offer. The knowledge that Blair was MacKay's captive drove him to madness. If MacKay so much as put his hands on Blair, the man wouldn't live to brag about it.

The day after the king's messenger left Stonehaven, Graeme began to make plans. After a sleepless night, he summoned Heath.

"What is it, Cousin?" Heath asked.

"I'm going to ride to MacKay's stronghold and demand the return of my wife. I'll require as many men as can be spared to ride with me."

" 'Tis raining," Heath said. "The ride will be an uncomfortable one."

"Since when did you worry about the weather?"

Heath stared at Graeme a moment, then shrugged and hurried off to do his bidding.

Graeme knew Heath considered his efforts to rescue Blair futile, but he didn't let that stop him. An hour later, mounted on his swiftest horse, pelted by rain and hunched beneath his plaid, Graeme led his men though the gate. If God willed, he would soon have Blair back at Stonehaven where she belonged.

Graeme grew watchful when he crossed the

border onto MacKay lands. He could see little through the sheet of rain, but an uncomfortable feeling deep in his gut made him extra cautious. His horse shied as a bolt of lightning flashed across the sky and thunder rattled the ground.

Graeme feared he was seeing things when a lone rider materialized through the thick curtain of rain. He signaled for his men to remain behind as he rode ahead. The back of his neck prickled when he became aware that the rider was a woman, her skirts flying in the wind behind her. His heart pounding, he reined in sharply.

Blair's mare was disinclined to stop, and since she had no reins, all she could do was cling to the flowing mane. Graeme must have sensed her dilemma, for he plucked her off the mare as she passed him and drew her into the saddle before him.

"Away," Blair gasped. "They canna be far behind."

Jerking on the reins, Graeme turned his horse and sped back toward Stonehaven, trusting his men to follow.

Graeme felt Blair shivering against him and covered her with his plaid. "Did you bring the rain, lass?"

"N-n-not this time," she stuttered.

"What happened? Did MacKay let you leave?"

"N-n-not exactly."

"Think you he is following?"

"Mayhap, unless the lightning stunned him more than I meant it to. He was still lying on the ground when I left."

Graeme threw back his head and laughed. "You frightened him with lightning?"

"I had to do something," came her muffled answer. "He wasna going to let me leave, even though I fulfilled my part of our bargain."

"I will have the whole story when I get you back home where you belong."

Blair peeked at him through an opening in the plaid. "Dinna you know? We are no longer wed. The king has set aside our marriage."

"I will not allow it," Graeme said through gritted teeth.

His confident tone offered Blair a wee bit of hope. Snuggling against him, she savored his scent, the warmth of his big body and the strength of his arms folded protectively around her. Nothing could hurt her now. The spirits had been right. Graeme was her future. They were fated to be together.

A tiny frown gathered between her brows. She had nearly forgotten the last obstacle that stood in the path of true happiness.

Trial by stone.

Relief washed through Graeme when he finally reached Stonehaven. After ordering the gate closed to all except his clansmen,

Graeme continued through the rain to the steps of the keep, where he carefully lowered Blair to the ground. He dismounted behind her and held her against him as a lad ran up to take his horse.

Lifting her into his arms, he carried her up the stairs. Jamie opened the door, grinning from ear to ear.

"Welcome home, mistress."

The moment Graeme set Blair on her feet, she was nearly bowled over by Alyce, who flung herself at Blair. "Ye're home, lass! What did that bastard do to ye? Is it true that Niall was neither dying nor ill?"

"Let Blair catch her breath," Graeme said. "She's in need of dry clothes and a place beside the hearth."

"I'll take care of her, my laird," Alyce said. "Jamie, my lady needs a hot bath and something warm to drink."

"Aye, I'll see to it immediately," Jamie replied.

"Go help Jamie," Graeme said. "I can take care of Blair."

Graeme swore he heard Alyce chuckle as she scurried off. And even Jamie's mouth had a suspicious tilt to it.

"We are no longer wed," Blair repeated as Graeme carried her up the stairs.

"Dinna fret, lass, I hope to remedy that soon."

"How?"

"I'll explain later." He carried her into their chamber and gently set her on her feet before the hearth. "Let's get you out of these wet clothes."

Blair shivered as he stripped her gown and underclothing from her and dried her with a towel. When her skin was glowing from his brisk rubbing, he dragged a blanket from the bed and wrapped it around her. Alyce arrived moments later with a hot toddy, followed in close order by servants bearing a wooden tub and buckets of hot and cold water. Blair sipped her toddy until her bath was prepared. Then Graeme dismissed the servants with a curt nod and locked the door behind them.

"Are you ready for your bath, sweeting?"

"Get out of your wet clothes first. If you catch the ague, I will have to nurse you back to health."

Graeme grinned and began stripping. When his damp plaid lay at his feet and his trews and shirt had been carelessly tossed aside, he plucked the blanket from Blair's shoulders, swung her into his arms and placed her in the tub. Then he knelt and began washing her with the fragrant soap Alyce had provided.

Blair relaxed beneath Graeme's tender ministrations. His hands were gentle, his touch comforting. This was the man she loved, the man with whom she was fated to spend her life. And he loved her. She had to believe it;

otherwise the Prophecy that had ruled the MacArthurs for generations was false.

"Lean your head back, love, so I can wash your hair," Graeme said.

Blair obeyed without protest, surprised at Graeme's willingness to act as her maid. There were many facets to Graeme's personality she had yet to discover; she looked forward to finding every one of them.

Dipping into a bucket of clean water, Graeme rinsed the soap from Blair's hair, then sat back on his heels and stared at her. She was so beautiful to him, it nearly hurt his eyes to look at her.

Graeme rose, took a drying cloth from a bench beside the hearth and held it open for Blair to step into. He dried her hair first, then moved the cloth seductively over her body, her breasts and between her thighs, taking great care to dry all her hidden crevices. By the time he finished, Blair was glowing inside and out.

"I want to look at you," Blair said, stepping back so she could take in every inch of his magnificent body. "You're a braw, bonny man, Graeme Campbell. I missed you."

Graeme trembled slightly when she moved against him and licked his nipples. She continued down to his stomach, caressing him with her lips. He knew he was big and strong, and that the lasses seemed to like his looks well enough, but Blair was the only woman whose opinion mattered. Her words produced a heady feeling in him. He knew she loved him, and that stirred him deeply.

Graeme groaned, wanting her lips on the place that ached for her most. When she took him into her hand, he nearly jumped out of his skin.

"You are verra manly," she whispered, caressing him gently. "Silk over steel. I canna look at you there without wanting you deep inside me."

"You have me so full and aching, I dinna know how much more I can stand."

"A great deal more, I hope." Smiling with secret glee, she lowered her head and began to love him with her mouth. The heat of her mouth, the strokes of her tongue, her clever hands, nearly brought him to his knees. For as long as he could stand it, he watched her love him. Then the ability to think left him as he lost himself in the pleasure she gave him, praying he could find the will to endure for a very long time.

His climax was nearly upon him when with a low growl he lifted Blair to her feet and carried her to the bed, laying her down on her stomach. A shiver went through her as he kissed his way down her elegant spine, then kissed and nipped at her taut little backside.

"Graeme!"

Laughing, he flipped her over, sliding his hands up to her breasts. Narrow-eyed, he watched with appreciation as her nipples hardened beneath his touch and her breathing quickened. Slowly he traced his fingers down her taut belly and slid them between her legs. His heart pounded as her violet eyes watched him stroke her, becoming glazed as her passion escalated.

"Ah, love, you are entrancing when flushed with passion." He gazed raptly at the place between her legs where his fingers stroked. "And so beautiful here."

Leaning closer, he feasted on her firm little breasts until he felt her body tremble. Then he began kissing his way down her slender body. She tensed when he reached his goal and put his mouth upon the swollen petals of her sex.

Blair arched and cried out, the heat of his mouth causing her body to burst into flame.

Suddenly he reared up. "Shall I stop, love?"

"Nay. I couldna bear it."

She threaded her fingers through his hair, urging him to return to his intimate feast. The intoxicating pleasure of his tongue and mouth upon her was driving her toward completion. She arched beneath him, crying out his name as her release tore through her.

Moving up her body, Graeme thrust hard and deep inside her, relentlessly stoking her passion. The second time she peaked, Graeme came with her, roaring his pleasure aloud.

Blair's wits were slow to return. When she finally regained her senses, she found Graeme dousing the lingering heat between her thighs with a wet cloth. She smiled at him, knowing in her heart that he loved her.

"You love me," she whispered.

Graeme went still. "What did you say?"

"Admit it. You love me."

Graeme inhaled sharply. "Nay."

"Dinna lie, Graeme Campbell. My powers have returned. They left me for a short time; there was only one way they could have returned." She grinned at him. "You finally realized that you love me."

His face wore a worried expression. "God knows I tried to guard my heart."

"Our love was meant to be," Blair said. "I knew it long before we were wed, but fought it when I learned you loved another."

Graeme lay down beside her, pulled a blanket over them and took her into his arms. "I adored Joan the Maid. I mistook adoration for love, and believed I could never love another when she died."

"Joan was a saint," Blair said. "She gave her life for God and her country."

He grasped her chin and raised her face so he could look into her eyes. "Listen well, love. You must guard yourself against those who wish you ill. Joan was accused of witchcraft and burned at the stake because she believed God spoke to her, that He told her to lead an army against the English. If someone accused you of using witchcraft and brought the matter before the king, the same thing could happen to you. That's what I've been trying to avoid. You mustna give anyone cause to accuse you of evildoing."

" 'Tis true the spirits guide me and watch over me. Sometimes I use my powers to heal when other means fail, but I amna a witch. There is a world of difference between a witch and a Faery Woman."

"I know that, love, but I fear I am the only one who understands. Promise you willna give people cause to judge you harshly."

Blair sighed. "I will try, Graeme. But when the spirits speak to me, or warn me of danger, I canna ignore them." She searched his face. "You love me, Graeme. I can feel it in my heart and see it in your eyes."

"I'm afraid for you, love, verra, verra afraid. I fear something terrible will happen and you will be taken from me if I give voice to my feelings."

It wasn't precisely what Blair wanted to hear, but it was enough for now.

Chapter Seventeen

Blair awoke to a day as gray and stormy as the previous one. Not that she minded. She was feeling too happy to care about the weather. Though Graeme had not said the words she craved, she knew he loved her. Smiling, she stretched out her arm and reached for him, surprised to find his side of the bed cold.

"Were you looking for me?"

She followed the direction of his voice and saw him sitting in a chair beside the hearth. He wore his plaid this morning, affording her a glimpse of long, bare legs stretched out before him.

"How long have you been sitting there?"

"Long enough. I've been watching you sleep. You're as beautiful asleep as you are awake."

"If you'll wait, I'll dress so we can go to the hall and break our fast together."

Uncoiling himself from the chair, he walked the few steps to the bed and sat down beside her. "We need to talk, love. I want to know everything that happened." He sent her a stern look. "Leave naught out. If MacKay touched you, I shall have to kill him."

Blair sat up in bed and pulled the blanket up to her chin.

"Naught of consequence happened . . . except," she admitted sheepishly, "I did tell Niall I would shrivel his manhood and render him impotent if he didna release your men and Father Lachlan. Did they return safely?"

"Aye. They were upset for letting their guard down at Gairloch. Aiden didna suspect a trick until Niall's guardsmen confronted them. There was a short but fierce battle. Outnumbered, they were quickly disarmed and imprisoned."

"I didna see Father Lachlan. Is he at Stonehaven?"

"He's been in the chapel on his knees since he arrived. You'll see him soon enough. Tell me what happened at MacKay's stronghold."

"MacKay wanted something from me," Blair began.

Graeme spit out a curse.

" 'Twas not what you think," Blair was quick to explain. "Have you ever heard of the MacKay treasure?"

"I've heard some such tale but didna believe it. 'Twas said one of MacKay's ancestors hid a fortune in gold and jewels when the keep was under siege. As far as I know, the treasure doesna exist."

"Oh, it exists all right. MacKay didna want to wed me because he cared for me. Nay, he wanted to exploit my powers to satisfy his greed. He ordered me to find the treasure. He promised to release me once the treasure was in his possession."

Astonishment colored Graeme's words. "So there really is a treasure. I wouldna have believed it. Did you find it?"

"Oh, aye, I found it all right. "I 'saw' the chest lying at the bottom of an abandoned well in the bailey. When I told him, MacKay set men to digging immediately."

"Was MacKay disappointed with the contents?"

"Nay, the chest held a fortune in gold and jewels. When I saw what the chest held, I asked for a portion of it. We settled on an amount that satisfied MacKay."

Graeme grinned. "Did you, now? I canna imagine MacKay agreeing to give up even a small part of his newfound wealth. What happened? Did MacKay renege on his promise?"

"Something strange happened to change my mind. When MacKay opened the chest, I heard voices crying out for justice, and knew I couldna take any of those ill-gotten gains for myself. 'Twas frightening. The voices spoke of being slain in cold blood by MacKay's ancestors. They spoke of a curse on those who claimed the treasure. I told

MacKay I didna want any part of the treasure and warned him about the curse."

"He didna believe ye," Graeme guessed.

"Mayhap he did, but it didna stop him from claiming the treasure. His greed overcame whatever scruples he had left. I knew he wouldna release me as he'd promised. I was right not to trust him. The treasure wasna enough for him. He wanted more, and thought I could give him everything he desired."

"So you fled," Graeme said.

"Aye, but I knew I couldna escape with MacKay's men hard on my heels."

"So you worked your magic and called down lightning from the sky."

"Not magic. I used my powers to save myself."

"I dinna care what you used so long as you are here with me now. Why did Niall become MacKay's ally in this?"

"We both know the answer to that. Niall didna want to part with my dowry, and MacKay promised Niall he could keep it if I wed him. 'Tis the reason Niall convinced the king to set our marriage aside."

"I have a plan," Graeme said. "The king has ordered the Highland lairds to gather men and arms and join him at Hawick. He's also demanded money to pay his ransom. He still owes most of the sixty thousand marks the English demanded for his release from captivity."

"Aye, so I heard. MacKay planned on leaving soon to join James."

"What you dinna know is that few lairds feel inclined to obey James. I have promised men and money if he restores our marriage."

Excitement darkened Blair's violet eyes. "Think you he will agree?"

"I am counting on it."

Blair frowned. "But that means you will fight in a war. You could be hurt, or killed. Dinna go, Graeme, I beg you. I care not about the state of our marriage. I will gladly, nay, happily, become your leman."

"Dinna say that, Blair. I want you for my wife, not my whore."

"And I want you alive."

"I am a warrior. I know how to protect myself." He kissed her forehead and rose. "I must confer with Aiden and Heath. I'll send Alyce up to help you."

Graeme hastened down to the hall. Father Lachlan was the first to greet him.

"How is our lass?" the priest asked.

"Blair is fine," Graeme said. "She wasna harmed."

"My prayers have been answered," Lachlan said fervently.

A group of kinsmen came up to join them. "Tell us what happened," Heath said.

"I will tell you while I break my fast," Graeme said. "But first, will someone find Alyce and send her up to Blair?"

"I'll find her," Stuart said, hurrying off, "but dinna start the tale until I return."

A servant sat a plate of food before Graeme, and he ate hungrily. By the time Stuart returned, Graeme was ready to relate most of what Blair had told him. He purposely left out the parts about the lightning and the voices Blair had heard coming from within the treasure chest. His audience listened raptly, not daring to interrupt until Graeme finished speaking.

"The lass has guts, I'll give her that," Heath said. "What do we do now?"

"We wait to hear from the king. Meanwhile, send word to our clansmen that I will let them know when they are needed."

"They will be most eager to fight the English," Aiden ventured. "As you well know, the English are nae loved in the Highlands."

"Verra good," Graeme replied. "We'll begin training immediately to hone our skills."

Everyone left except Father Lachlan, who was regarding Graeme quizzically.

"What is it, Father? Is there something on your mind?"

"Aye, lad. What will ye do if the king willna deal with ye? He has the power to give Blair to anyone he chooses. Even MacKay."

Graeme's hands curled into fists. "I willna let that happen, Father."

"Ye will have no choice. I dinna mean to upset ye, but there is always the chance

James will have enough men without yer clansmen and deny yer request."

"I dinna want to think about it," Graeme said. "If James denies me, I have another plan. Blair told me something about the MacKay that the king would appreciate knowing."

"Will ye tell me?"

"Nay, not yet. You will all know if and when I am forced to use my information."

Blair entered the hall and slid into the chair beside Graeme. "Have you eaten?"

"Aye, I was about to leave, but I am sure Father Lachlan will keep you company."

"Oh, aye," Lachlan said, waving Graeme off. "I will keep the lass company."

"Will you stay at Stonehaven with us, Father?" Blair asked after Graeme had departed. "We are in desperate need of a resident priest."

"Aye, mayhap I will bide a wee time with ye, since I am no longer welcome at Gairloch."

"You will have a place with us for as long as you care to stay."

Before Lachlan could reply, Maeve bustled in from the kitchen and enfolded Blair in her arms, nearly smothering her against her pillowy bosom. "Ah, lass, 'tis happy I am to see ye. I knew our laird wouldna let MacKay have ye. Listen to me go on," she chuckled. "I'll fix ye something to eat straightaway."

"I will leave ye to yer breakfast, lass," Lachlan said. "If I'm to stay, the chapel needs the kind of attention that only I can provide. Eat hearty, lass."

Blair's appetite fled when she saw Glenda prancing into the hall with her food. She banged the plate on the table, then stepped back, hands resting on her generous hips.

"Now who's the whore?" she goaded. "Ye are nae longer wed to the laird. Ye are naught but his leman. Graeme can put ye to work in the kitchen if it pleases him. Or give ye to his men when he tires of ye."

"That would please you, wouldn't it?" Blair charged.

"Oh, aye. Now that Graeme's commitment to ye is ended, he will turn to me."

Blair waved her away. "Your prattle is giving me a headache. I wish to eat my breakfast in peace."

"Enjoy it while ye can. Soon ye will be eating in the kitchen with the rest of the servants. Or mayhap," Glenda said slyly, "Graeme will send ye back to the MacKay." She shot Blair a triumphant smile. "I shared the laird's bed while ye were gone."

After that parting barb, Glenda tossed her head and flounced off.

Blair picked at her food while she considered Glenda's warning. Graeme would never send her away, would he? Blair didn't want to believe that Glenda had shared Graeme's bed during her absence, but it could have happened. After all, she had seen just such a vision.

Blair was glad when Alyce joined her, for she knew her tiring woman wouldn't lie to her. "I'm going to ask you a question, Alyce, and I want the truth."

Alyce's brows shot upward. "When have I ever lied to ye?"

"Forgive me for doubting your loyalty. I just spoke to Glenda and —"

"Glenda," Alyce spat. "That whore! Dinna believe anything she says."

"I canna help it. Graeme and I are no longer wed. He can bed anyone he pleases now."

"Is that what Glenda told ye? She lies, lass. Yer husband was beside himself with grief. He didna even look at another woman while he planned yer rescue. 'Tis true that Glenda flitted around him like a mare in heat, but it did her nae good. The laird paid her nae heed."

Blair squeezed Alyce's hand. "Thank you. You have greatly eased my mind. I should have known better than to believe anything that comes from Glenda's mouth. I know Graeme loves me."

"Aye. Ye still have yer powers, dinna ye? There's yer proof."

Blair sighed wistfully. "Just once, I'd like to hear him say the words."

"Ye have more than most women," Alyce scolded.

"What if the king denies Graeme's request to restore our marriage?"

"What do yer spirits tell ye?"

"Naught. They havena spoken to me since I fled the MacKay stronghold."

"Mayhap ye should ask them."

Blair rose so fast, the chair behind her wobbled. "Come to the stillroom with me, Alyce."

Alyce followed Blair down the flight of stairs to the stillroom. The door opened at Blair's touch and she stepped inside, breathing in the comforting scent of dried herbs. The pungent aroma had always soothed her, and it was no different today. The tension left her body as she walked around the table where her herbs lay drying, inspecting those that were ready to be rendered into various remedies.

"Get the candles, Alyce."

Alyce set the candles in a circle and sprinkled herbs inside. Once Blair had positioned herself within the circle, Alyce lit the candles and moved away.

Facing the open window, Blair spun around three times and raised her arms. Then she began to chant, beseeching the spirits to grant her a vision. Heat suffused her body as a breeze stirred the trees outside the window and brushed her cheek.

A vision began to form behind her eyelids.

She saw herself with Graeme in a beautiful place that gave her a sense of calm and peacefulness. They were lying on the grass and gazing up at the sky. An instant later Graeme was sprawled upon the ground, lying in a pool of blood. She screamed.

"Nay!"

Voices echoed in her head. "He will die if you don't save him."

"Tell me what I must do."

"You have the power. You will know what to do. The bairn growing inside you will need his father."

Blair's hand flew to her stomach. "I suspected but wasna sure."

"Danger still stalks you."

"Who wishes me harm?"

"Soon you will be tested again. Fire, water, stone. You have yet to conquer stone. Beware of false accusations."

"Wait! You didna answer my question. Who wishes me harm?"

Suddenly the candles flared, then went out in a puff of smoke. Alyce rushed to support Blair as she stumbled from the circle. Blair was so drained of energy, she was barely able to make it to the nearest bench.

"Are ye well, lass?" Alyce asked anxiously. "What happened? I heard naught but yer voice."

Blair summoned a smile. "I am carrying Graeme's bairn."

"Ha! Tell me something I didna know."

"You knew? I was just beginning to suspect, myself."

"Did ye tell yer husband?"

"Nay. I wanted to be sure first."

"What else did the spirits tell ye?"

"I am still in danger."

"From whom?"

"I dinna know. The spirits warned me to beware of stone. 'Tis the last ordeal. I've already survived fire and water."

"Did the spirits say naught of yer marriage? Will the king let Laird Graeme remain wed to ye?"

"They said naught about it."

"Do ye feel strong enough to leave the stillroom?"

"Aye. I have much to think about. If I amna wed, my bairn will be illegitimate and in need of protection."

"Laird Graeme will claim his bairn," Alyce maintained. "Ye must tell him."

"I will, when the time is right. I dinna want to worry Graeme when he has so much on his mind."

Graeme saw her enter the hall and hailed her.

"I decided to return to the keep for the noon meal," he explained. "The men deserve rest and a hot meal after a full morning of training in the rain."

"I thought I'd take my meal in my

chamber," Blair said.

He searched her face. "You look tired, lass. Did I do that to you?"

She sent him a rueful smile. "Nay, Graeme. Dinna fret, I'll be fine after a short nap."

He lifted her chin and kissed her mouth. "Verra well. I'll check on you later."

Blair climbed the stairs to the solar. She had just reached the top landing when Glenda stepped out of the shadows. Surprise caused Blair to teeter back on her heels; she clutched the wall to keep from falling.

"I heard ye and Alyce talking," Glenda taunted. "Mayhap ye willna survive the last ordeal. Fire, water and stone," she chanted.

"Have you been spying on me? Listening at doors is a punishable offense."

"I followed ye to the stillroom," Glenda admitted. "I couldna see what was going on inside, but I heard enough to brand ye a witch and see ye burn."

"You have a vivid imagination," Blair charged. "Stand aside."

"Are these not stone stairs?" Glenda said with sly innuendo. "Ye survived fire and water; mayhap stone will be yer downfall."

Stunned, Blair stared at Glenda. "What do you know about the Prophecy?"

"Think ye I am stupid? Everyone hereabouts has heard about the MacArthur Prophecy."

Menacingly she pressed forward. Blair moved backward as far as she could without tumbling down the stairs. When she tried to sidle around Glenda, the jealous woman blocked her path.

"Dinna try it, lady," Glenda warned. "I am bigger and stronger than ye."

Blair knew she had to do something to prevent Glenda from acting upon her jealousy and hatred. Blair's lips began to move in silent entreaty, asking the spirits to save her and her child.

"What are ye doing?" Glenda screeched.

Blair smiled. "Try to harm me and you'll find out."

Glenda recoiled, a look of horror on her face. "Dinna work yer evil spells on me, witch."

"You have it wrong, Glenda. You are the evil one. If you harm me, I promise you will live to regret it."

Glenda retreated farther into the shadows. Blair added to the dramatics by pointing a finger at her and chanting garbled words, hoping to frighten her into leaving.

"Nay!" Glenda cried as she raised her skirts, pushed past Blair and fled down the stairs.

Breathing a sigh of relief, Blair hurried to her chamber and slammed the door behind her. If she were still mistress here, she would dismiss Glenda at once. Unfortunately, she was no longer Graeme's wife, and might never be if her enemies had their way.

Blair's thoughts scattered when she heard Alyce calling to her through the door. Blair opened the panel and Alyce walked past her, balancing a tray in her hands.

"I brought yer dinner," Alyce said as she set the tray on the table. "Eat it all. Ye need yer strength. Remember, ye're eating for two now."

"You havena told anyone, have you?"

"Nay, I wouldna do such a thing without yer permission. Shall I stay with ye while ye eat?"

"Nay, thank you. I'm going to eat and take a nap."

"Verra well. Nona Campbell's bairn has a cough, and I told her I'd mix something to ease it. Stuart offered to walk me to the village."

"You and Stuart seem to get along verra well," Blair said. "He is a widower, is he not? Mayhap you and he . . ."

Alyce covered her mouth with her hand and giggled like a young girl. "Go on with ye, lass. The mon barely knows I exist."

"That's not how it looks to me. Do you have a fondness for Graeme's uncle? He's a good man. Would you not like someone to spend the rest of your days with?"

"Och, I have *ye*, Blair. And soon I'll have yer bairn. What more could I want?"

"A man to love you," Blair suggested.

"What nonsense," Alyce huffed, bustling out the door. "Who wants a grizzled old mon anyway?"

Blair smiled to herself as Alyce made a hasty exit. She thought her tiring woman protested too much.

Blair finished everything on the tray and lay down fully clothed, pulling a blanket over herself. She was asleep the moment her head hit the pillow. The dream began shortly afterward.

She was in a lovely glen surrounded by rock-studded hills. Graeme was with her. The place was the same one she had seen in her previous vision. She sensed happiness — hers certainly and mayhap Graeme's. It was a beautiful day with a clear blue sky, a few fluffy clouds wafting overhead and the scent of heather in the air.

They had just made love on Graeme's plaid. Blair didn't see that clearly in the dream but she knew because she felt her body glow with the aftermath of pleasure. Then suddenly everything changed. The sun disappeared and danger filled the air. The next thing she knew, Graeme was lying in a pool of blood.

She woke up screaming.

Moments later, Graeme burst into the chamber. "Blair! Are you all right, lass?"

As soon as he took her in his arms, her

world righted itself.

"I was on my way up to check on you when I heard you scream. Are you ill?"

Blair shook her head. " 'Twas a dream."

Graeme rolled his eyes. "One of your premonitions?"

"Mayhap, but I hope not."

"Tell me about it."

"Nay, I canna."

She refused to meet his eyes. Had she seen his death? If she was with him in the dream, then he couldn't have been soldiering with King James. The danger existed right here at Stonehaven.

"Blair, speak to me. Tell me about your vision."

"Just hold me, Graeme. Hold me and never let me go."

His arms tightened around her. "I'll never let you go, love. No matter what, you'll always be mine."

"Will you send Glenda away if I ask it of you?"

Graeme stiffened. "Has she done something to frighten you?"

Blair hadn't intended to tell him about her confrontation with Glenda, but decided she had to in order to protect her baby.

"Aye, Glenda threatened me. I didna want to tell you, but I truly believe she's mad. I would feel safer if she were nowhere near me."

Fury hardened Graeme's features. "The lass will be gone tonight. I'm sorry I didna act sooner. I thought she was harmless. I hope ye dinna think I took her to my bed after we were wed."

"I prayed you would not."

"I didna, love. You are the only woman I want in my bed."

"Where will she go if you turn her out?"

"Glenda's family lives in the village. She can bide there with them. They are capable of providing for her if she canna find work."

Blair's relief was palpable.

"Are you sure you dinna remember your dream?" Graeme persisted.

Blair refused to meet his gaze. "Dinna fret. 'Twas naught. Have you heard from the king yet?"

"Nay, but I expect word soon."

"If you go to war, you will be careful, won't you?"

"You know I will. I couldna bear the thought of never seeing you again. 'Tis true what they say. I am bewitched."

She pressed her fingers against his lips. "Dinna say that. My enemies could take your words and turn them against me."

Graeme's expression turned grim. " 'Tis not what I meant and you know it."

Blair sighed. "I love you, Graeme. I have for a verra long time."

"I know," Graeme replied after a lengthy pause.

Silence stretched between them. "I know you love me, whether or not you choose to acknowledge it," Blair said. "My powers are still with me, which proves it."

"Mayhap the Prophecy is false," Graeme suggested. He had no idea why he refused to acknowledge his feelings. Perhaps he still feared the danger her powers represented.

Blair caught his face between her hands, refusing to let him look anywhere but into her eyes. "Do you love me, Graeme?"

Graeme swallowed his denial, unable to look into her eyes and lie about his feelings. "Aye, lass, I love you well, but saying it makes me apprehensive. I ken the Prophecy and am aware of what loving you means."

Blair sighed and cuddled against him. "You dinna know how long I have waited to hear those words."

"Now will you tell me about your dream?"

Blair shook her head. "I dinna remember."

Graeme knew that Blair's dreams were often glimpses into the future. What had she seen? His death? Her death?

"Verra well, I willna plague you, love. Go back to sleep."

He started to rise, but Blair reached for him. "Nay, dinna leave me. I need you, Graeme. Make love to me."

"Sweeting, you are exhausted."

She dragged him down beside her and ran her hand up his bare leg. Her hand found his manhood, and lust shot through him. As she fondled him, he felt himself harden and thicken. There was no holding back with Blair. He unwound his plaid and tossed it aside. His shirt followed.

His unfettered cock thrust upward, blue-veined, rigid and demanding. Removing her hands from his erection, he pulled away the blanket and quickly undressed her. Then he kissed his way down her neck and pressed his lips against her collarbone. His mouth trailed lower, settling over the erect tip of her breast. He felt her tremble as he circled her nipple with his tongue, then nipped and teased it with his teeth.

He moved lower. She called out his name and shifted restlessly beneath him as his tongue ringed her navel. He kissed her belly, found the soft thatch of blond curls at the juncture of her thighs . . . and kissed her there.

When he nuzzled the softness between her thighs, she moaned and begged him to come inside her. He grinned and shook his head. Sliding his hands under her bottom, he lifted her and pressed his mouth against her sweet femininity. Then he parted the folds of her sex with his tongue and delved inside her soft center.

Blair went wild beneath him. Then she

came, her body arching into his intimate caress. She was still trembling when he moved up her body and slid inside her, drawing out her climax until his own release carried them both to oblivion.

"You'll not die," Blair whispered, holding him close. "I swear I willna let you die."

Chapter Eighteen

Blair waited anxiously for the king's reply to Graeme's proposal. She had no idea what she and Graeme would do if the king refused to restore their marriage.

One glorious sunny day, Graeme asked Blair to fetch a picnic basket that Maeve had packed for them. "There's someplace special I want to show you. Sitting here waiting to hear from the king is doing neither of us any good."

"Where?" Blair asked, excitement coloring her words. "I didna ken there was a special place nearby."

Graeme's smile set her heart to racing. "You'll see. Meet me in the courtyard. And wear a cloak. The weather can be changeable this time of year."

Twenty minutes later, Blair arrived in the courtyard with a picnic basket slung over her arm. "Is the place we're going to far?" she asked Graeme.

"Nay, it's within walking distance. But if you prefer to ride, we will."

" 'Tis such a beautiful day. Let's walk."

"Are you sure?"

"Verra sure. I can use the exercise."

Graeme relieved her of the basket, wound her arm in his and ushered her through the front gate.

They walked in companionable silence through the village, nodding to those who hailed them along the way. When they reached the loch, Graeme turned downstream, following a narrow path along the cliff.

"I've never been this far from the village before," Blair said.

" 'Tis just as well," Graeme said. "I wouldna want you venturing out here alone. Look what happened when you went into the forest to gather herbs."

Blair stopped abruptly, her gaze focused on a stone tower perched precariously on a rise near the edge of the cliff. "What is that?"

Graeme grasped her hand and pulled her toward the structure. "The ruins of an ancient Viking tower. I thought you might enjoy seeing it."

"How old is it?"

"Verra old. The Vikings came to Scotland several centuries ago and built watchtowers all along the coast."

When they reached the base of the square tower, Blair stared in awe at the ancient building and started forward. "Can we go inside?"

Graeme pulled her back. "The stairs are

too dangerous to climb. Look around you," he said, pointing to several large stones littering the ground at their feet.

"These stones have fallen from the tower at one time or another, so you can see how dangerous it would be to enter the structure. I just thought you would enjoy seeing it."

"Thank you," Blair said. "I appreciate being alone with you as much as I do seeing the tower. We have too little time to ourselves."

"My thoughts exactly," Graeme murmured. "Shall we eat?"

Graeme laid out the cloth Maeve had included in the basket and Blair set out the food. Then they feasted on bread, cheese, cold pigeon pie and fresh strawberries. They also found a bottle of wine tucked into the basket.

"Wine, Graeme?" Blair asked when she saw him uncorking the bottle.

"Aye, the occasion called for wine. 'Tis the first time we've been alone together outside the keep. The first time we've made love beneath the sky."

"We're going to make love?"

"Aye. More than once, I hope."

Blair swallowed hard. She hoped so, too.

When they finished eating, Graeme helped her pack up the remnants of their feast. Blair watched in avid anticipation as he removed his sword, spread his plaid on the ground in the shadow of the tower and offered her his hand.

"Come lie with me, love."

He settled her down on the plaid, then joined her. "The loch is calm today."

" 'Tisn't difficult to picture Viking ships approaching our shores."

Blair smiled, imagining Graeme as a fierce Viking come to conquer the land.

"What are you smiling about?"

"I always smile when I'm happy." She paused. "I love you, Graeme."

"I know, lass, and I love you."

His face suddenly taut with need, he pressed her down on the plaid, covering her with his body. "I never tire of making love to you."

He lowered his head and kissed her, his mouth devouring, hungry. She tasted wine on his lips and opened her mouth to his tongue when he sought entrance. She could deny him nothing. He was her love, her life, her future. The spirits had sent him to her.

But even as Graeme's kisses grew more fervent and his hands were hot upon her, Blair sensed danger. When a buzzing began inside her head, she tried to ignore it, concentrating instead on the heat of Graeme's aroused body and his ravenous kisses. Then voices replaced the buzzing, and she could no longer ignore the warning. When Graeme started to undress her, she braced her hands against his chest and shook her head.

"What is it, lass? Are you not in the mood?" He gave her a seductive grin. "I can change that easily enough."

"Nay," Blair answered, looking about her for the source of the danger she perceived. "Something is verra wrong."

"What do you mean? Everything is perfect."

"I sense danger. My voices speak of it."

Instantly alert, Graeme reached for his sword. "What kind of danger?"

"I dinna know. Mayhap we should leave. I feel . . ."

The words stilled in Blair's throat as a strange scraping sound caught her attention. Graeme must have heard it, too, for he glanced upward at the same time Blair did.

"Sweet Mother of God!" Graeme exclaimed.

For a moment Graeme could only stare in horror at the huge stone that had broken free of the crumbling watchtower and was hurtling down upon them. Acting from pure instinct, he swept Blair out of danger's path and attempted to follow. Unfortunately, he wasn't fast enough. The huge stone struck his right leg before continuing down the slight incline and then rolling over the cliff into the loch.

Graeme heard the bones in his leg snap and felt the searing pain of torn flesh. The last thing he recalled before passing out was the image of a woman peering through one of the arrow slits near the top of the tower. Then agony speared through him and he blacked out. When he awakened, Blair was kneeling over him, tears streaming down her cheeks.

"How bad is it?" he gasped.

She stroked his forehead, trying to ease his fears. "Dinna worry, my love. All will be well."

Graeme could tell by her expression that she was lying. Most likely he would lose the leg. Marshaling what remained of his dwindling strength, he lifted himself to his elbows and stared down at his injury. What he saw brought gorge to his throat.

His leg was a bloody mass of protruding bones and lacerated flesh. He knew instinctively that it was shattered beyond repair. He also knew that only one thing would save his life, and even then it was doubtful he would survive.

Amputation.

"Do what you have to do, lass." His voice was thin and shaky, barely discernible. "Use my dirk." Those were his last words before darkness reclaimed him.

"Nay, Graeme, you'll not lose your limb," Blair said with fierce determination. "Nor will you die."

Blair heard laughter, sensed a presence behind her and spun around. "You!" she cried. "You did this!"

Glenda glanced down at Graeme without a hint of compassion. "Now neither of us will have him. I hoped the stone would kill both of ye, but now I'll have to kill ye myself."

"You're mad!"

"Mayhap," she snarled as she launched herself at Blair.

Almost too late, Blair realized that Glenda held a dirk in her hand. Glenda was strong, but so was Blair. They fell to the ground, legs thrashing, arms flailing, rolling over and over as Blair tried to keep Glenda from stabbing her with the dirk. Somehow Blair managed to wrest the dirk from Glenda's hand and toss it away. Screaming in outrage, Glenda dove after it, stopping at the edge of the cliff as the dirk bounced once, then launched itself as if by magic into the loch.

Glenda's eyes held a hint of madness as she glared menacingly at Blair. "Prepare to die, witch."

She dove for Graeme's sword, but Blair reached it first, kicking it out of the way. It skidded along the ground to the very edge of the cliff. Glenda followed. Blair watched in horror as a strong gust of wind literally lifted Glenda off her feet and swept her over the cliff. Her scream followed her all the way down, then ended in ominous silence. Shaken, Blair crawled to the edge and peered down. Glenda was gone, sucked into the deep waters of the loch.

Trembling, Blair pushed herself to her knees. Though Glenda had nearly killed Graeme and meant to kill her, Blair had not wished for her death. Then she heard Graeme moan and turned her attention to saving the life of the man she loved.

She found Graeme in the same position she had left him, sprawled on the ground, his crushed leg stretched out before him. Blair knew what she had to do, and she needed help to accomplish it. Closing her eyes, she prayed to God and the spirits to empower her. A few moments later, she felt a comforting breeze brush her cheek and knew she wasn't alone. The spirits were with her, guiding her.

Taking a deep breath, Blair opened her eyes, her expression determined as she prayed for strength to save Graeme's limb and ultimately his life.

Her hands were shaking as she held them over Graeme's broken bones and lacerated flesh. Catching her breath, she lowered her hands until they rested directly on his leg. As she prayed and chanted words ingrained into her memory, a great calmness settled over her.

Then needles of heat surged through her hands and arms. The sensation became so intense, her entire body began to tremble.

Overwhelming pain sent fire through her veins. Nausea rose in her throat. But she refused to let her own agony distract her. She would heal Graeme or die trying.

Suddenly she felt as if she were being torn apart. Her body was afire, her head ready to explode. Then she knew no more.

Graeme awoke to the sound of squawking seabirds soaring overhead. He was aware of sunshine stabbing against his eyes . . . and little else. He moved cautiously, rising up on his elbows as his wits slowly returned. Then he saw Blair lying in a boneless heap beside him, and memory came rushing back. The stone! Had it struck Blair as well as him as it plunged to earth? Dear God, was she dead?

He had shoved himself to his knees before it occurred to him that he shouldn't be able to move about so freely. Why wasn't he writhing in pain? He had seen the bloody mass of flesh and bone that had once been his leg, and knew there was no way it could have been saved. Yet here he was, supporting himself on both legs. Daring a glance at his leg, he saw what had to be a miracle. His right leg was as whole and healthy as his left.

Stunned, he fell back on his rump, his mind refusing to accept what his eyes had seen. Then his glance returned to Blair, and everything else flew from his mind. Crawling over to her, he cradled her head and shoulders in his lap.

"Blair. Sweeting, wake up. Are you hurt?"

He ran his hand over her limbs; nothing seemed broken. There were no bumps on her head, and her heartbeat was strong, though somewhat erratic. Uncertain what to do, he held her and crooned to her until she stirred and opened her eyes.

"What happened, lass?"

Blair dragged in a shuddering breath. "Are you well?"

"More than well, sweeting. How did you do it?"

"Your leg . . . is it . . ."

"It is fine, lass. I dinna know what you did or how you did it, and dinna want to know. Naught short of a miracle could have saved my leg."

"I couldna let you die, Graeme. Even if it killed me, I would have attempted to cure you."

Graeme drew back in alarm. "Killed you? What do you mean?"

Blair shook her head, her lips tightly sealed. Graeme refused to accept her silence. "Tell me. I willna relent until I have the truth."

Blair breathed a sigh of resignation. "Verra well, I'll tell you. Normally I heal by using herbs and natural remedies. But sometimes they aren't enough. When that happens, I ask

392

God and the spirits to empower me. 'Tis through them I gain my healing powers. But each time I attempt such a healing it weakens me."

Shock and disbelief ravaged Graeme's features. " 'Tis difficult to believe that your powers are strong enough to make a shattered limb whole. I saw my leg: 'twas ruined beyond repair. The best I hoped for was a successful amputation.

"Blair, you must never reveal to anyone what you did here today. Now I know why your father feared for your life. Did you heal Stuart the same way you healed me? Stuart spoke of a miracle, but I didna ken how it could be."

"Aye, I used my powers to heal Stuart. He would have died had I not sought help from the spirits."

"Are you feeling better now?"

"Aye. I'm still weak but no longer feel pain."

"Pain? Healing causes you pain?"

" 'Tis naught, Graeme. I am fine now."

"Nay, you are not fine. You're still pale and trembling. How long does this weakness last?"

"It depends upon the seriousness of the wound or injury I am healing."

He flexed his right leg, still unable to believe the miracle Blair had wrought. "Dinna ever use your healing powers in that way again," he warned. "One day you may not recover. I couldna bear to lose you." He grew thoughtful, his mind turning in another direction as he stared up at the tower. " 'Tis strange the way that stone fell."

"It was no accident," Blair said. "Someone tried to kill us."

"Who would do such a thing?" His expression turned grim. "I'll launch an investigation immediately."

Blair stirred in his arms. "There's no need. I know who did it."

His mouth thinned. "Tell me his name."

"It wasna a man." Her expression softened. She touched his arm. "I'm sorry, Graeme. 'Twas Glenda."

"Glenda! I've known her all her life. Are you sure?"

"Aye. When she realized she hadn't killed both of us, she came after me."

Graeme stiffened. "Damn her! What happened? Did she hurt you? Where is she now?"

"She had a dirk. We fought for it, and I threw it into the loch. Then she went for your sword. I kicked it out of her grasp, and it came to rest at the edge of the cliff. She dove for it and would have gotten it if a strong wind hadna sent her over the edge. She's gone, Graeme — carried out to sea with the tide."

Graeme winced. "I knew she was jealous but hoped I'd solved the problem when I banished her from the keep. Forgive me, lass. I had no idea she presented a danger to either of us."

Graeme recalled seeing a face in the arrow slit before he'd passed out. He realized it wouldn't have been difficult for Glenda to work a stone loose from the crumbling ruins and send it hurtling to the earth below.

"I'm sorry," he said again. "If you feel strong enough, we should start back to the keep."

"Aye, my strength is returning."

Graeme stood, lifted Blair into his arms, bent to pick up the basket and started walking back toward the village.

"I can walk, Graeme."

"It pleases me to carry you. It pleases me to be able to walk. But for you, I would be missing a limb, or mayhap dead from loss of blood. Now I believe I could carry you to the ends of the earth and never feel the strain. But I meant it when I said you must never again heal anyone as you did me."

"Healing is what I do."

"You know what I mean. Your magic powers are not to be used again. All it would take to bring about your death is one voice raised in accusation."

"How can I promise such a thing?"

"You must, love. For me, and for the bairns we will have together. Will you promise?"

Blair shook her head. "I canna. If you were to come to harm, I would use any means at my disposal to heal you. Put me down. We're approaching the village, and I dinna want anyone to think something is amiss."

Graeme eased Blair to her feet. "I need to tell Glenda's parents about her death, but not now. I want to get you home first."

"What will you tell them?"

"Her parents are good people. All they need to know is that she stepped too close to the edge of the cliff and fell to her death."

"I wish I could change things."

"Dinna fret, lass. Glenda was her own worst enemy. Jealousy brought about her demise."

Blair's legs were shaking by the time she reached the keep. She was drained of energy and barely able to walk under her own power. If not for Graeme's arm around her, she couldn't have negotiated the stairs.

Alyce, who had just come from the kitchen, saw Blair and rushed to her aid. "What is it, lass? Are ye ill?"

"I'm taking Blair up to bed," Graeme said. "Come with me, she's going to need you."

Scooping Blair into his arms, he carried her up the stairs and into the master's chamber, where he set her on her feet. "If you can manage without me, sweeting, I should . . . take care of a pressing matter."

Blair knew it wasn't going to be easy for

Graeme to give the news of Glenda's death to her parents and kinsmen. She wished him well as she sent him on his way.

"Dinna worry about me," she added. "I'm going to take a nap after Alyce helps me undress."

Graeme kissed her on the lips and advised her to stay in bed until she felt strong enough to rise.

"What was that all about?" Alyce asked. "Ye're weak as a kitten. Did something happen while ye were gone?"

"I'll explain while you help me undress."

"Ye healed someone," Alyce guessed as she removed Blair's dress and helped her into bed.

In a few succinct words, Blair told Alyce what had happened. "Graeme is going to tell Glenda's family that she walked too close to the edge of the cliff and the ground crumbled beneath her feet."

" 'Tis just as well," Alyce concurred. "No need for them to know that their daughter was a murderess. Tell me about the laird's injury. How serious was it?"

" 'Twas verra bad, Alyce. The bones in his right leg were broken in numerous places and his flesh was badly lacerated. At the verra least he would have lost a limb. 'Twas more likely he would have died from the amputation."

"No wonder ye're done in," Alyce said,

clucking her tongue. "Ye have a bairn growing inside you to think about. If ye can heal a mortal wound such as ye described, there is naught ye canna do, but yer health must come first."

Blair sighed. "You dinna have to worry about me using my powers again, even if I wasna carrying a bairn. Graeme has forbidden it. He fears that someone will accuse me of witchcraft and the king will act upon it. King James seems determined to stamp out witchcraft."

"But ye're no witch," Alyce reminded her.

"To superstitious Scotsmen, Faery Woman and witch are one and the same."

"Then I pray an occasion willna arise where ye are challenged to use yer powers to heal. I know ye, lass. Ye canna let a mon or woman die when 'tis within yer power to save him or her." She tucked the blanket around Blair and closed the shutters to darken the room. "Does Graeme know about his bairn?"

"Not yet. I intended to tell him today but didna have the chance. Soon," she said sleepily. "I'll tell him soon."

"Sleep, lass. Ye need to rest and restore yerself. I'll make sure ye're not disturbed."

Blair was asleep before Alyce finished her sentence. Smiling, Alyce tiptoed from the chamber, leaving Blair to slumber in peace.

Blair's sleep was not peaceful, however.

Disturbing dreams visited her. She saw herself in the midst of a controversy. Fingers were pointed at her and voices were raised in accusation. Among her chief accusers were Niall and MacKay. She knew the king was in her dream, for she felt his royal presence. Suddenly the crowd turned ugly and she was dragged off, screaming her innocence.

Where was Graeme? Why wasn't he defending her?

Then the spirits spoke to her.

"They mean you harm. You must protect yourself and your child."

"How?"

Silence.

"Please. Tell me what I must do?"

Though she tried to keep the spirits from leaving, Blair felt nothing but emptiness. The voices were silent. Then her brain shut down as she slipped into a deep sleep.

Graeme returned from the village in a strange mood. While Glenda's parents hadn't been able to understand how their daughter could have been so careless, they accepted Graeme's explanation. He hadn't wanted to lie, but he knew the truth would hurt them even more than his fabrication.

"Ye look like ye could use a wee drop of whiskey," Stuart said when Graeme crossed the hall to join him. "Yer errand couldna have been easy."

" 'Twas more difficult than you can imagine," Graeme allowed as he accepted the glass of whiskey Stuart offered. "Especially since what I told Glenda's parents was a lie."

"I knew there was more to it than ye let on. Care to share it with yer uncle?"

Graeme took a sip of whiskey while he considered his answer. Perhaps, he thought, it would be best not to tell anyone what had happened today. He did not want talk of the miracle to spread, and the best way to ensure silence was to tell no one. " 'Tis best you dinna ken what happened," he said at length.

"Mayhap," Stuart grumbled, sounding not at all convinced he shouldn't know. "Is yer lass all right? She looked a mite peaked when ye carried her in. Think ye she is increasing?"

Graeme paused with the glass to his lips, then carefully set it down. "I dinna know. Alyce hinted as much, but Blair has said naught to me."

"Ah, well, time will tell," Stuart said, toasting Graeme with his glass. "What think ye the king will do? We should be hearing from him soon."

"If there is a God, the king will restore my marriage and I will join him in Hawick with two hundred armed men. If you will excuse me, Uncle, I think I'll go up to see how my wife is faring."

Graeme climbed the stairs to the solar and

quietly entered the bedchamber. Blair was still sleeping, so he settled into a chair to watch her. He never tired of looking at her. Faery Woman or nay, her delicate beauty had mesmerized him from the very beginning. With her golden hair spread out upon the pillow and her face in repose, she could have been an angel come to earth.

That thought brought another. Blair was as close to an angel as any mortal woman could get. She was everything that was good and pure. No matter how much pain she felt when she used her powers, or how weak the healing left her, she thought not of herself but of others. That a woman like Blair could love him was a miracle in itself. 'Twas no wonder he had fallen in love with her.

He thought about Joan the Maid and his infatuation with her, aware now that he had been captivated by her goodness, her piety and her religious conviction. What he had felt for her had never been love, he realized. He recalled the horror of her death and felt a jolt of panic. He couldn't, wouldn't allow that to happen to Blair. Blair must never use her magical healing powers again.

"Graeme? What are you doing?"

Graeme shrugged off his apprehension and smiled at Blair. "Watching you sleep. You're so beautiful. I love you verra, verra much."

Blair reached for him. "Come lie beside me."

Graeme joined her on the bed; she turned into his arms. "Today didna go exactly as I planned," he said. "I wanted to make love to you on the ground beneath the sun, with heather for our pillow."

"Make love to me now," Blair whispered.

"Nay, love, you're still too weak. Dinna fret, we have a lifetime of making love ahead of us."

"If the king allows it."

"King be damned," Graeme cursed. "We *will* be together. Have you considered my request?"

"What request is that?"

"You know perfectly well what I mean. I canna lose you. You must never use magical powers again" — he grinned suggestively — "except in bed."

"Making love with you is always magical. Dinna fret, my love, you willna lose me. We are fated to be together. You came to me in my visions long before we met."

"I dinna ken how that is possible, but if you say 'tis true, then I believe you." He started to rise. "Go back to sleep. I didna mean to awaken you."

Blair sighed. "Mayhap I'll rest a bit longer. Let's dine alone in our chamber tonight. I have something to tell you."

"I'll see to everything," Graeme answered, grinning. Did Blair intend to tell him about their bairn?

He kissed her lightly on the lips and took his leave.

Blair smiled and snuggled down into the warm bed. For a brief moment she had forgotten her dream. Nothing mattered but the comforting knowledge that Graeme loved her as much as she loved him, and that she carried his child beneath her heart. With that reassuring thought, she drifted off to sleep.

Chapter Nineteen

Graeme awoke the following morning in the best of moods. He and Blair had shared an intimate meal beside the hearth in their bedchamber and made love afterward. Their lovemaking had reaffirmed their commitment to one another despite their uncertain future.

As Graeme eased out of bed to ready himself for the day, he couldn't stop smiling. Blair had told him about the baby she was carrying. His baby. His heir.

He was still smiling when he strode into the hall a short time later. He saw Stuart and Alyce sitting side by side at a table and chose not to disturb them. Instead he joined Heath.

"Good morrow," Heath greeted. "Ye look exceedingly happy this morning. Do we have Blair to thank for that?"

Graeme wanted to tell his cousin about the baby but decided against it. The state of his marriage and the fate of the child depended upon the king's goodwill.

"Blair is an amazing woman," Graeme said. "No matter what the king decides, I will never forsake her. She is mine."

Heath grinned. "Ye are a determined mon, Graeme, but I canna blame ye. My opinion of Blair has changed. She is gentle and caring; we all appreciate her healing skills."

Graeme agreed wholeheartedly as he concentrated on his porridge and bannocks, wishing himself still in bed with his fetching wife. Graeme was spooning porridge into his mouth when Aiden rushed into the hall.

"Fergus has returned from Hawick, laird."

Graeme shot from his chair as Fergus strode into the hall. "Do you bring word from the king?"

"Aye, laird." He removed a folded document from his sporran and handed it to Graeme. Graeme read the message bearing the royal seal twice before asking, "Why is the king coming to Stonehaven? How long before I can expect him?"

Fergus shifted from foot to foot, clearly uncomfortable. "He's but two days behind me. First, let me say there will be no war with the English. MacArthur and MacKay were the only Highland lairds who showed up at Hawick to support the king. James was furious. He was forced to negotiate with the English for more time to pay his ransom."

Graeme grunted. "That still doesna explain why James is coming to Stonehaven. Does he want money from me? Did he say naught about my marriage?"

"Ye havena heard the worst of it yet," Fergus said.

"Speak, man. Should I fear the king's visit?"

"Aye. MacArthur and MacKay accused yer lady of witchcraft. The king intends to investigate the charges."

"God in heaven!" Graeme exclaimed. "The king is coming to investigate my wife at the urging of MacArthur and MacKay? I will kill them."

"Who is it you are going to kill?" Blair asked as she glided into the hall. "Oh," she exclaimed when she saw Fergus. "Your messenger has returned." She placed her hand in Graeme's. "What has the king decided about our marriage?"

Graeme dismissed Fergus and guided Blair away from the others. "The news isna what either of us expected, love."

"Tell me."

Graeme led her to a chair and urged her to sit. Then he fell to one knee before her, his expression deeply troubled. "The king is coming to Stonehaven."

"Whatever for? What about the war?"

"James negotiated for more time in which to pay his ransom, so there will be no war."

"There's more to it than that," Blair said, recalling her dream. Her vision had warned of danger, and now she was about to find out what form it would take.

"This isna easy to say, love, but you have been betrayed."

Blair froze. "By whom?"

"Your brother and the MacKay. They've accused you of witchcraft. The king is coming to investigate the charges himself."

The color leeched from Blair's face. Clasping her hands together, she closed her eyes and tried to 'see' her fate, but as often happened, her fate remained a mystery to her. Was her life to be snuffed out in a blaze of fire? The spirits had told her that Graeme could save her. How?

Concern wrinkled Graeme's brow. "Are you all right, love? Dinna fear, I willna let anything happen to you. This I vow."

"Dinna promise what you canna deliver," Blair whispered. "The king will have his way." Her hands fluttered to her stomach, where her baby rested beneath her heart. Would her baby live to see the light of day?

"Our bairn will survive," Graeme said fiercely. "Neither of you will perish. Trust me."

Blair wanted to believe him, but despair was a terrible burden. While she strived to present a calm facade so as not to worry Graeme, she was dying inside.

"I know you have duties," she said. "Dinna worry about me. I will be fine."

"There are indeed things I must do to prepare for the king's visit," Graeme reluctantly admitted. "I'll get Alyce to stay with you. You're too upset to be alone."

He left her then, pausing to speak to Alyce on his way out. Blair saw Alyce turn pale before she rose and hurried over to join her.

"Ah, lass, the laird just told me what Niall and MacKay have done to ye. Ye must trust God and the spirits to save ye. They willna let ye die."

"I wish I had your faith, Alyce. I was warned of trouble but didna know what my dreams meant."

"Trust yer husband, lass. He willna fail ye."

"I do trust Graeme, but the king's word is law. If he decides I am a witch, I will die, and my bairn with me."

That day began a whirlwind of activity as the castle prepared for the king's visit. Rooms were aired and cleaned for the king's entourage, and the hall was given a thorough scrubbing. Even the tapestries were taken down and aired, and fresh rushes were placed on the floor. When the king's herald arrived two days later to announce His Majesty's imminent arrival, all was in readiness.

Except for Blair. The thought of seeing Niall and MacKay again was a chilling prospect. As for the king, Blair feared no good would come of his visit.

The king arrived with all the pomp and ceremony befitting his station. Accompanying him was a small army of personal guardsmen, as well as Niall MacArthur and Donal MacKay, her chief accusers. Graeme awaited his guests at the bottom of the stairs. Blair stood slightly behind him, her knees shaking beneath her skirts.

"Welcome, Your Grace," Graeme said, bowing.

The king returned the greeting, but his gaze was riveted upon Blair as she dropped into a curtsey. The king, though rather short and stocky, was nevertheless an imposing figure with his flowing hair and goatee beard. He had done much good since assuming the throne. He had founded the Court of Sessions, and his reign was gradually restoring respect for the monarchy. He was also known for his determination to stamp out witchcraft in Scotland.

"So that's the witch," James said.

"Your pardon, sire," Graeme replied. "Blair is not a witch. She is a skilled healer who has proven her worth to my clansmen on more than one occasion. She is also my wife."

Niall MacArthur approached from the rear of the group to voice a protest. "I beg to differ, sire. My sister is nae longer Campbell's wife. Yer Grace has seen fit to annul the marriage. Blair is now my responsibility."

Father Lachlan came up to stand beside Blair, lending her his support. "I vouch for the lass, sire. I have known Blair all of her life and she is nae a witch. She is blessed by God."

"She cast a spell to unman me," Niall charged.

"Did she now?" Lachlan challenged. "Are ye saying ye're unable to perform as a man?"

"Nay!" Niall denied. "Blair removed the spell. I am as virile as any mon here."

"Enough of this," the king said. "I will be the one to judge her guilt or innocence. But first I will eat and refresh myself. Laird Campbell, lead the way into your keep and see that my men are made welcome."

"Aye, sire," Graeme said. "Everything is in readiness for your visit."

"Good. I will question the woman on the morrow. My journey has been long and exhausting; I will seek my chamber immediately."

Jamie appeared as if on cue, bidding the king and his entourage to follow him to their chambers. Niall and MacKay remained behind. When Graeme asked Blair to give them some privacy, she glared at him and reluctantly took her leave.

"Have you prepared chambers for us?" Niall asked. "We are important witnesses."

"Your chambers have been prepared," Graeme said grudgingly, "though I'm sure you're aware that neither of you are welcome in my home. You, MacArthur, have spoken out against Blair because her death will benefit your coffers. You want Blair's dowry for yourself. And you, MacKay," Graeme charged, "exploited Blair's powers to satisfy your greed."

Jamie reentered the hall and Graeme beckoned to him. "Show Laird MacArthur to his chamber."

When MacKay started to follow, Graeme said, "Tarry a moment, MacKay. I would like a private word with you."

"What is it ye have to say to me that MacArthur canna hear?" MacKay asked.

"I assume MacArthur doesna know about the treasure. I'm going to make you an offer you canna refuse. If you dinna testify against Blair, I willna mention the treasure to the king. You know James will want his share once he learns about your sudden wealth. He might even insist that you pay the full amount of his ransom."

MacKay cursed. "She told ye!"

"Did you think she would not?"

"The witch lied to ye. The treasure held little worth."

"Blair doesna lie," Graeme retorted. " 'Tis a known fact the king's coffers are empty. I am verra certain he will investigate the possibility that a treasure exists before dismissing it out of hand," Graeme ventured. "Think very carefully before you turn down my offer. If you retract your charges against Blair, I willna tell the king of your sudden great wealth."

"MacArthur willna like it. We had a pact. He promised that Blair would be mine if I let him keep her dowry. The dowry mattered not to me, for I had far greater wealth in mind. But since I now have what I want, I no longer need the witch. I wouldna wish her on my worst enemy."

Graeme stifled a smile. Pitting MacArthur and MacKay against one another should work in Blair's favor. MacKay was still dithering when the king's page interrupted. Graeme was ordered to present himself in James's chamber.

Graeme hurried off to answer the king's summons. He bowed before his monarch but wasn't invited to sit down.

"Laird Graeme, I was not pleased with your communication. No one, neither man nor woman, dictates terms to the King of Scotland."

"Forgive me, sire, but I was desperate. You had ended my marriage to the woman I love, and I but sought a way to reverse your edict."

"You know why I annulled your marriage, do you not?"

"Aye. Because I didna attend you at Inverness, MacArthur and MacKay suggested that you punish me by ending my marriage to Blair. If you recall, sire, 'twas your intention to execute me along with the five High-landers you suspected of treason. Had a flood not prevented my departure, I would be a dead mon now."

James frowned. " 'Twas a mistake. I sent the other lairds home."

"Too late to save the five that died. And for what reason? I know naught of intrigues. I played no part in plans to seize the Crown from you. I was falsely accused."

James held up his hand. "I am not here to revisit past decisions, be they right or wrong. I am here to interrogate and pass judgment on a woman accused of witchcraft."

"Blair is innocent."

"I was told you would deny the charges. MacArthur warned me you would lie to keep the wench's dowry."

"Dowry be damned!" Graeme blasted. "I want it not."

"Nevertheless, the law states that a woman's dowry belongs to her husband upon marriage."

"I will renounce it. Let MacArthur keep it." He paused, then blurted out, "Blair carries my bairn."

James stroked his beard. "A bairn. That complicates matters. You have given me much to ponder. You may go now," he said dismissively. "Good night, Laird Campbell."

Graeme bowed and took his leave. He didn't return to the hall but went directly to the master's chamber. He found Blair sitting on a bench before the hearth, staring forlornly into the dancing flames. She didn't bother to look up when he entered.

He perched on the bench beside her and took her cold hands in his. "I just came from the king."

She looked up at him, her eyes filled with sadness. " 'Tis the end," she whispered.

"Nay!" Graeme denied. " 'Tis the beginning."

He rose, bringing her up with him, holding her close, kissing her, desperately needing to prove that he would let no one harm her. He wanted to smooth the worry lines from her forehead, to make her forget the reason behind the king's visit, if only for the time it took to love her.

Blair wrapped a hand around his neck, kissing him with a fervor that left little doubt that she wanted the same thing as he.

"Make me forget, Graeme," she whispered against his lips. "This might be the last time we will be together."

"Nay, lass, we will always be together. Never doubt it."

Lifting her into his arms, he carried her to the bed and followed her down. He undressed her slowly, adoring her with his eyes and then his hands and mouth as he bared her body. Tenderly he kissed her stomach, where his baby grew, then returned to her mouth, ravaging it with his lips and tongue.

Blair felt her troubles dissolve as Graeme loved her. At that moment in time her whole world lay beside her in the bed. Pleasure replaced fear. Tomorrow didn't exist. There was just today, this man and their love for one another.

Blair shuddered as he weighed her lush breasts in his hands, then brought them to his mouth and suckled her nipples, first one and then the other.

"Your clothes," she murmured. "I want your naked flesh against mine, warming me with your heat and vitality. I've never felt so cold in my life."

He whispered intimate endearments as he flung off his plaid and shirt and boots, returning to her in mere seconds. "I love you, Blair," he whispered in her ear.

He teased her moist center with his thumb, rubbing the swollen bud of her femininity until she arched and cried out. Her silky curls were moist with her essence, her tender folds slick and distended, pulsing and heated with arousal.

His fingers slid between the lips of her sex. It was all he could do to keep from spilling as her sweet essence titillated his senses. He stroked her gently, laving her with the dew of her body, teasing the tiny pearl of her womanhood, feeling it tighten into a hard ball at his touch. Then he slid two fingers deep inside her, drawing out her pleasure.

"Please, Graeme, I need you inside me."

When Graeme continued his sweet torture, Blair took control. Thrusting his hands aside, she rose up on her knees and moved over him. Then slowly, sensually, she took the head of his sex inside her and gently squeezed. The hot, wet tug of her sheath drew him deep inside her.

They began to move at the same time, his hard shaft sinking deep. Her body, already heated with passion, surged into orgasm. Throwing her head back, she screamed her delight as her muscles convulsed around him.

Graeme held himself in check until she reached the crest. Then he released his restraint, pounding into her, carrying her to another orgasm at the same time as he spilled his seed into her.

Gradually his heart slowed and his breathing returned to normal. Lethargy overtook them as Blair sank down on top of him, her head resting on his chest, her trembling thighs holding him close. Gently Graeme lifted her away and brought her into his arms.

Blair sighed happily. For a few minutes she had almost believed that no one could touch her, that Graeme would keep her safe. But the fact remained that the king had traveled to Stonehaven to condemn and punish her. Even worse, she feared that Graeme's clansmen would speak out against her. Contentment fled as coldness crept into her heart.

As if sensing her thoughts, Graeme's arms tightened around her. "Naught bad will happen to you, love. You're mine, and I shall take care of you."

Since the king was supping in his chamber, Blair and Graeme took the evening meal together in the privacy of their own room. Afterward, they returned with one accord to the bed and made sweet love long into the night.

Blair's trial began the next morning. Word of the king's visit had spread, and the hall overflowed with clansmen from the village and surroundings.

The king sat in the laird's chair. Graeme was seated on one side of him and Niall MacArthur on the other. MacKay sprawled in a chair beside Niall. Blair sat before the king on a stool, looking small, vulnerable and frightened. Everyone else stood, bodies pressed close together to accommodate the crowd.

"Let us begin," the king said, waving his hand for quiet. A hush fell over the hall. "Who brings charges against the alleged witch?"

"I do," Niall said. "I lived with Blair at Gairloch and saw her cast spells with my own eyes. There is no doubt in my mind that she practices witchcraft."

"What kind of spells?" the king asked, leaning forward.

"She talks to spirits. 'Tis eerie, I tell ye. Blair uses black magic to summon evil forces. She sees things before they happen." His voice lowered to a whisper. "I've seen her magical powers at work."

The king's piercing gaze settled on Blair. "What do you have to say for yourself, Blair MacArthur? Your brother brings serious charges against you."

"I am not a witch, sire. Surely I am not the only Scotswoman with the 'sight.' I claim to be naught but a healer."

"Aye, 'tis true," a woman called out.

"Who speaks?" King James asked. "Step forward."

"I be Mab, Yer Grace," Mab said, dipping low into a curtsey. "Lady Blair used her skills to bring my bairn into the world. If not for Lady Blair, my bairn would nae have lived to see the light of day."

"I am Blair's confessor, sire," Father Lachlan spoke up. "She is sweet and good and a true child of God. She is special in His eyes."

"The woman is a witch, never doubt it!" Gunna pushed people aside until she reached the king. "Mab's bairn was born dead and the witch breathed life into her."

"Silence!" the king ordered. "Who are you?"

"I be Gunna, the midwife."

"Does anyone else wish to accuse Blair MacArthur?"

His gaze fell upon MacKay. "What about you, Donal MacKay? You were vocal enough when you and Niall MacArthur brought charges against the lass."

MacKay glanced at Graeme, then quickly looked away. Graeme returned his gaze, a warning inherent in his lowered brows and narrowed eyes.

"Mayhap I was mistaken," MacKay muttered.

"What!" Niall roared. "Are ye daft? Ye told me ye saw Blair call lightning down from the sky. Ye said it struck the ground beneath yer feet."

"It was storming something fierce," MacKay mumbled. "Mayhap I was mistaken. Mayhap the lightning came naturally with the thunderstorm."

"What say you to that, Blair MacArthur?" the king asked.

"I was trying to escape MacKay during a fierce thunderstorm. Niall tricked me into visiting Gairloch. He held me prisoner there until MacKay came for me."

"For what purpose?"

Graeme had explained to Blair that she wasn't to mention the treasure unless MacKay testified against her, so Blair told another version of the tale.

"Niall had promised me to MacKay before

419

Father died, but Father wouldna allow it. He wed me to Graeme instead. When you annulled my marriage to Graeme, MacKay sought once again to wed me. He knew I wouldna agree, so he and Niall concocted a plan to bring me to Gairloch under false pretenses. When MacKay arrived, he brought me to his keep."

"Ye left with MacKay readily enough," Niall charged.

"I had no choice. You said you would kill the escort Graeme sent with me if I didna go with MacKay."

"Is that true, Niall MacArthur?" the king asked.

"Blair misunderstood," Niall denied. "What has this to do with my sister being a witch?"

"Niall doesna wish to part with my dowry," Blair continued defiantly. "He never relinquished it to Graeme. MacKay promised Niall he could keep it if Niall gave me to him."

The king's puzzled gaze settled on MacKay. "Do you love Blair MacArthur?"

"He loves her not!" Graeme shouted. "I love her."

The king sent Graeme a quelling glance. "I am sure MacKay can speak for himself."

"Er . . . I dinna love Blair MacArthur." MacKay licked moisture onto his suddenly dry lips. "I . . . planned to exploit her powers."

"In what way?"

"I . . . er . . . I wanted her for her ability to foretell the future," he lied. "Being aware of my enemies' plans would be a great boon."

"Ah, I see. Are you rescinding your charges?"

"The charges are false," Graeme argued. "Heed me, sire. Charging Blair with witchcraft is a travesty of justice. Niall MacArthur is a troublemaker. He despises Blair because their father favored her. Douglas MacArthur left Blair a wealthy woman, and Niall covets her wealth and lands. If Blair remains wed to me, he must eventually part with her dowry. Greed lies behind his unjust charges."

"I asked MacKay a question," James said, silencing Graeme with a look. "Speak, Donal MacKay. Are you rescinding the charges?"

"Nay!" Niall screamed, leaping from his chair. "Deny the charges and deny our friendship!"

"Sit!" James ordered, pointing a finger at Niall. "I would hear what MacKay has to say."

"I . . . I may have been mistaken, sire," MacKay stammered. "I saw naught to indicate that Blair MacArthur practiced witchcraft. Niall's hatred of the lass and unfounded rumors clouded my judgment. Aye, sire. I rescind the charges."

"Traitor!" Niall charged. "I spread those rumors. I've *always* hated Blair. She was beloved by our kinsmen for her healing skills while I was scorned because they saw no good in me. But I lie not. Everything I said about spirits and magic spells is God's truth."

"Who speaks in defense of Blair MacArthur?"

Several people stepped forward.

"She healed my burns," said one.

"She saved my limb when I nearly severed it with an ax."

"She prepared soothing teas to cure my bairn's cough."

"She prepared herbs to cure my headache."

"She eased my labor when I birthed my bairn."

And so it went. Finally the king called a halt. "Enough! Who besides Niall MacArthur and Dame Gunna speaks against the accused witch?"

A profound silence fell over the hall.

"What say you in your defense, Blair MacArthur?"

Tears blurred Blair's vision. She was touched by the trust Graeme's clansmen had shown in her. She hadn't expected such an outpouring of love and respect. No one condemned her but Gunna and Niall, her own brother.

"Have you heard of the MacArthur Prophecy, sire?"

James squinted at Blair as if trying to recall

something. He shook his head. "Nay, but you must remember I spent many, many years in England. The Prophecy of which you speak is a myth, is it not?"

"Nay, sire, 'tis not a myth. I was destined at birth to become a healer and was gifted by God with certain powers. Some call me a Faery Woman; others are not so generous."

"Do you reject God, Blair MacArthur?" James asked, leaning forward.

"Nay, sire. All that I am is God's doing."

James sat back, his fingers tented beneath his chin. "What say you, Graeme Campbell?"

"You know my feelings, sire. Blair is all that is good and caring; naught about her is evil. I beg you to restore our marriage. Blair carries my bairn and my heir."

"Hmmm," James said, fingering his goatee. "Mayhap I acted precipitously. I was angry when you failed to show up at Inverness as ordered, and I let MacArthur and MacKay talk me into ending your marriage."

"I have never betrayed you, sire. If you recall, I fought against the English on French soil. I was personal guard to Joan the Maid. My clan has ever been and always will be faithful to our king."

"Why should I believe you?"

Graeme rose and dropped to his knee. "Before my clansman and God, I hereby renew the vows of fealty my father swore to yours."

James appeared impressed. Rising, he grasped Graeme's shoulders and raised him up. "Because of men's greed I planned to execute a faithful subject. Thank God for the flood that prevented you from reaching Inverness for your execution. I acted rashly, but rumors of sedition among the Highlanders caused me a great deal of anguish."

"Neither I nor my clansmen would ever betray you."

"Aye, I hold you blameless."

"And Blair? She carries my bairn. My life wouldna be complete without her."

"Come forward, Blair MacArthur."

Blair rose and approached the king on unsteady legs.

"Do you wish to remain wed to Graeme Campbell?"

Blair smiled. "Aye, with all my heart, sire. He is my life, my love."

"Do you deny all charges of witchcraft?"

"I do."

"Do you love God and promise to obey His commandments?"

"I have always done so, sire."

James motioned for his secretary. "Sir Raymond, prepare a document restoring the marriage of Blair MacArthur to Graeme Campbell. I will set my seal to it when it is done."

Blair dropped to her knees and grasped the king's hand. "Thank you, sire. I will name my son James in your honor."

"Douglas James," Graeme amended. "I would honor Blair's father for giving her to me."

"So it should be," James said, hiding a smile behind his hand.

"Sire, I protest!" Niall said. "Ye're making a big mistake."

"Return to your home, Niall MacArthur, and be glad I do not impose a punishment for attempting to keep your sister's dowry for yourself. If you do not release Lady Blair's dowry into her husband's keeping, I will call you to task.

"And you, MacKay," James continued. "You are guilty of making false accusations, even though you rescind them now. I traveled here for naught when I am needed elsewhere. Return to your keep and do not let me hear of any more trouble between the MacKays and the Campbells."

"Aye, sire, thank you, sire," MacKay said, anxious to escape the king's wrath. He owed Campbell a great deal for keeping his secret and planned no more raids on his neighbor. As for Blair, Campbell was welcome to the witch.

The king rose and waved his hand dismissively. "You may all return to your homes."

Graeme extended his hand to Blair, and she started toward him. She took but two steps when alarm bells reverberated inside her head. She spun around, searching for the source of danger. A cry caught in her throat when she saw a wild-eyed Gunna rushing toward her, a slash of sunlight glinting off the dirk she held in her hand.

Chapter Twenty

Blair's legs felt as if they were rooted to the ground. She glanced at Graeme and saw that his attention had been momentarily diverted by the king and he was leaning close to hear what James was saying. No one else was close enough to stop Gunna. The king's men-at-arms were busy ushering people from the hall, and Graeme's guardsmen were making their way to the tables piled high with food and drink.

Gunna's crazed screech did what Blair had been unable to do. It brought everyone's attention to Blair and what was happening, but Blair held scant hope that anyone could reach her in time to prevent her death.

"Die, witch!" Gunna screamed. "May the devil take yer soul."

Blair heard Graeme call her name, bringing her out of her trancelike state. Gunna was almost upon her; Blair didn't know which way to turn to escape, and Graeme was still too far away to help her.

Then something strange happened. Gunna was but steps away when she tripped over an unseen obstacle. Blair watched in morbid fascination as Gunna crashed to the floor. Graeme reached Blair a moment later, gathering her into the protective circle of his arms. She buried her face against his chest, striving to control her trembling.

Father Lachlan knelt beside Gunna and turned her over. Then he hastily crossed himself and shook his head. "Gunna is dead. God rest her soul."

Blair spun out of Graeme's arms. "How did she die?"

"She fell on her own dirk, lass," Father Lachlan explained. "The blade embedded itself in her heart. She died instantly."

"I saw her fall and still don't understand how it happened," the king said as he joined them. His probing gaze went from Blair to Gunna and back to Blair. "And I don't want to know. Take the dead woman away."

"I will take care of everything," Father Lachlan said.

Blair felt utterly drained. She couldn't believe it was finally over. Graeme's clansmen hadn't turned against her, the king had declared her innocent of witchcraft, and the spirits still protected her.

"Laird Campbell," the king called, beckoning to Graeme.

Clasping Blair to his side, Graeme approached the king.

"Aye, sire. What is your desire?"

"I intend to leave immediately for Edinburgh. I've wasted enough time here. I've already instructed my entourage to prepare for departure. I have been long gone, and my wife is most anxious for my return."

"I wish you Godspeed, sire," Graeme said. "Take whatever provisions from the kitchens you need for your journey."

King James nodded. "So I shall." He turned to Blair. "May your bairn arrive healthy and live a long life. Apprise me of the birth and I will stand godfather."

"You do us great honor, sire," Blair said, dropping into a curtsey.

" 'Tis the least I can do for what you have been put through." He searched her face, his eyes narrowed in speculation. "I still don't understand how Gunna came to such a sad end. Is there aught you wish to tell me?"

"I'm as puzzled as you are, sire," Blair replied truthfully. Had her spirits intervened to save her? She might have her suspicions, but it was not something she could share with the king.

"Well, then" — James waved airily — "I see my men are ready and so I must depart."

"Should you ever have need of the Campbells, sire, you have but to summon us. We are ever ready to defend our king and country."

Blair and Graeme stood outside on the stairs until the king and his entourage rode through the gate. Then they returned to the keep and mounted the staircase to the solar, unaware of the smiles they left in their wake.

When they reached the top landing, Graeme swept Blair into his arms and carried her to their bedchamber. She clung to him with desperate need. If her brother had had his way, she and Graeme would have been separated forever. Worse, she would have been convicted of witchcraft and burned at the stake.

"It's over, love," Graeme said as he set Blair down on the bed and settled beside her. "No one will ever hurt you again."

" 'Twas MacKay's retraction that convinced the king," Blair mused.

"Aye. I bargained with MacKay for your life. I didna tell you because I feared MacKay wouldna betray his pact with Niall."

"What kind of bargain?"

"I simply promised MacKay I wouldna tell James about the treasure if he would retract his charges against you. He knew the king would confiscate a large share of his wealth if he was made aware of its existence, and that must have decided him in our favor."

" 'Tis a shame MacKay will get to keep all the treasure for himself when the king is in desperate need of money."

Graeme grinned. "Methinks the treasure willna remain a secret long. MacKay's kinsmen know about it, and rumors will soon reach the king. Forget MacKay and your evil brother, lass. You'll never have to see them again."

Blair sent him a wary look. "You'll not stop me from using my healing skills?"

"I could no more prevent you from using your gift of healing than I could stop rain from falling. As for the voices you hear and the spirits that visit you, I canna stop that either, though I will remain watchful of those who would harm you because of them. I agree with Father Lachlan. You are blessed by God . . . and you are mine."

Blair sighed. "I have always been yours, Graeme."

"I know. You said I came to you in your dreams. Tell me how I came to you."

She snuggled against him. "You came to me naked," she confided. "Though you came to me many times, I didna see your face until the night before you arrived at Gairloch. Even then I knew not your identity."

"I came to you naked?" Graeme said, clearly intrigued.

"Aye, you were my phantom lover. I felt your body against mine, felt your heat and virility. I was told you were my future and never doubted it. But I knew I couldna love you."

"But you did."

"Oh, aye, I most certainly did . . . do." She

431

lifted her face for his kiss and he gladly obliged.

One kiss led to another and soon they were tearing off each other's clothing. Graeme bore her down onto the bed, then hesitated.

"You're tired, lass. You've been through a harrowing experience and should rest."

"I'll rest later. I need you to love me. I've never needed anything more in my life. I cringe to think how close we came to being parted forever."

His mouth claimed hers, but his kiss didn't demand. His lips settled tenderly over hers; the tip of his tongue teased as lightly as butterfly wings. Her lips opened; the sensual stroke of his tongue filled her senses. His hand moved over her breast, cupping and cradling the weight of it, massaging her distended nipple with his palm.

His weight shifted down her body. His mouth closed over her breast, his tongue stroking her nipple. She moaned as honeyed warmth spread downward. Urgency seized her, and her knees fell apart invitingly, waiting for him to come inside her. Instead he made his way down her body, parted the golden fleece at the juncture of her thighs and kissed her intimately.

She undulated sensuously beneath his tender assault, her cries filling the chamber. Overcome by turbulent emotions, she gasped out a ragged breath, her fingers tearing into the bedclothes as pleasure seared through her. Then she exploded, straining against him as anguished joy filled her senses.

"I love you, Blair," Graeme said as he shifted upward and filled her with himself.

Beyond speech, Blair let her body speak for her. Winding her legs around his waist, she raised her hips to meet his downward thrust. They moved together, her inner muscles clutching his hard flesh as his hot, slick strokes drove her toward another climax.

She screamed. His mouth caught her sobs of ecstasy. Then she felt his body wrench in a massive shudder, and she knew his pleasure matched hers in intensity. Moments later he collapsed against her, spent, his breath rasping harshly in her ear. Then, as if suddenly aware of the baby she carried, he rose up and peered down at her, his expression anxious.

"Did I hurt you, lass?" He shifted away from her and brought her into his arms.

"You would never hurt me, Graeme. The bairn and I are fine. I promise that wee Douglas James will come into this world hale and hearty."

Douglas James was born six months later, as hale and hearty as Blair had predicted. A great celebration was planned in honor of his birth. When the king was notified, he and his queen honored Graeme and his clansmen by traveling to Stonehaven for the baptism.

During the week-long celebration, Stuart and Alyce announced their intention to wed. When the king suggested that they wed before he returned to Edinburgh, an impromptu ceremony, officiated by Father Lachlan, was held.

The night following the king's departure, Graeme and Blair made love for the first time since their son's birth. Afterward, as she lay sleeping in Graeme's arms, she dreamed of the king's death . . . and woke up screaming.

Graeme held her until she was coherent enough to explain her dream.

"I saw the king's death," she whispered.

Graeme started violently. "Did he die of natural causes?"

Blair shook her head. "Nay. The king will die at the hands of conspirators who hope to win the throne."

"Who are the conspirators?"

"I dinna ken. I saw his assassination but little else. I dinna know when or where it will occur. It could happen tomorrow, next year, or years from now."

"Nevertheless, I must warn him."

Blair shook her head. "Nay, my love. 'Tis the king's fate. It's not our place to interfere." She paused. "That's not all. I also saw MacKay's death. 'Twas the curse. It wasna a pretty end."

Graeme shuddered and held her closer. "What about our future, lass?"

She smiled dreamily. "We are fated to be together always. There are more children and years of peace and prosperity in our future. We will love one another until the end of our days and beyond."

"And so we will," Graeme concurred. "Until the end of our days and beyond."

And so they did.

Author's Note

I hope you enjoyed *Laird of Stonehaven*. It's a departure from my usual historical, but I believe that changing direction from time to time keeps my writing fresh. One thing I don't want to do is bore my readers.

King James was murdered at Perth in 1437 by conspirators who hoped to win the throne for Walter, Earl of Athol. James's six-year-old son was crowned in 1437 at Holyrood Abbey, Edinburgh.

My next release, *The Last Rogue*, will return to 1815 England. Unrepentant rogue Lucas, Viscount Westmore, has no problem maintaining his reputation without his two recently wed friends, Bathurst and Braxton. But an unforeseen tragedy causes Westmore to renounce sex. And he takes his vow of celibacy so seriously that he leaves the temptations of London behind for the wilds of Cornwall.

Can a scandalous rogue change his ways? Can Luc give up sex and live like a monk? The smuggling operation he discovers brings him into contact with the kind of woman he's never met before. Can Bliss make him rediscover his lost sexuality? You'll have to read *The Last Rogue* to find out.

I enjoy hearing from readers. For a reply, bookmark and newsletter, write me at P.O. Box 3471, Holiday, FL 34690. Please enclose a long, self-addressed, stamped envelope. E-mail me at *conmason@aol.com*. To read preview chapters, view covers and find a complete listing of my books, visit my Web site at www.conniemason.com.

About the Author

Connie Mason is the bestselling author of more than thirty historical romances and novellas. Her tales of passion and adventure are set in exotic as well as American locales. Connie was named Storyteller of the Year in 1990 by *Romantic Times*, and was awarded a Career Achievement award in the Western category by *Romantic Times* in 1994. Connie makes her home in Tarpon Springs, Florida, with her husband, Jerry.

In addition to writing and traveling, Connie enjoys telling anyone who will listen about her three children and nine grandchildren, and sharing memories of her years living abroad in Europe and Asia as the wife of a career serviceman. In her spare time, Connie enjoys reading, dancing, playing bridge, and freshwater fishing with her husband.